Yellow Bird

YELLOW BIRD

Trudi Pacter, a former Fleet Street journalist, has been chronicling the lives of the rich and famous for many years. She is the highly acclaimed author of *Kiss and Tell*, *Screen Kisses*, *The Sleeping Partner* and *Living Doll*. She is married to Baronet Sir Nigel Seely.

TRUDI PACTER

Yellow Bird

HarperCollins_Publishers_

HarperCollins*Publishers*
77–85 Fulham Palace Road,
Hammersmith, London W6 8JB

This paperback edition 1994

1 3 5 7 9 8 6 4 2

First published in Great Britain by
HarperCollins*Publishers* 1993

ISBN 0 00 647630 9

Set in Linotron Sabon by
Rowland Phototypesetting Ltd
Bury St Edmunds, Suffolk

Printed in Great Britain by
HarperCollinsManufacturing Glasgow

For my husband, Nigel

Acknowledgements

For helping me to understand the ins and outs of Mauritius, I would like to thank Eddie Goldsmith, Christine Goldsmith, Ravi Misra, Nigel Watkins of the Merville Beach Hotel, Maryse and Jacques D'Espaignet, the staff of the Dodo Club, the staff of the Casino de Meurice, Air Mauritius, the Mauritian Tourist Board and Mrs Peter White.

For background on the rag trade, Shanaz Sayed was invaluable, as were Abad Dulloo and the staff of Media. My British informants, for obvious reasons, prefer to remain anonymous.

I would also like to thank John Lewis for putting me right about the hotel business and Fred Rutter for all his help and encouragement.

Mauritius, 1960

So the Indian woman was dead. Jeremy Waites watched the sun go down from the verandah of the clubhouse and wondered how he should feel about it. If he was going to be strictly honest with himself, he hadn't really known her. She had been his mistress for a moment, but that was years ago and nobody could say he'd been truly involved.

He thought about his wife and wondered if she knew anything about it. The idea was so ludicrous that he laughed out loud. Christine might have suspected that he dallied with the locals, but she didn't make a song and dance about it.

His unprompted mirth seemed to have attracted attention, for two club servants in immaculate white livery scurried over to where he was sitting.

He shouldn't have been irritated by them. They were only doing their jobs, but for some obscure reason he felt intruded upon. These people with their obsequious enquiries made him feel as if it was they who were running things and he was merely a guest over here, a rich white potentate who had to be appeased and placated and somehow separated from what was really going on.

Just to get them out of his hair, he ordered another whisky and soda. Then he thought about Neeta again.

His field workers would be building a funeral pyre for her, piling up dried cane leaves and freshly chopped branches in the middle of the holy ground they had marked out for themselves. Why did they have to drag her back to his plantation, he wondered. He'd got rid of her all that time ago, transplanting her to the opposite side of the island, but in death she had defied him, and now she was coming back to be burned at dusk on the edge of his cane fields.

A vision of her came into his mind. She was very slender, almost childlike, with tiny pre-pubescent breasts and long pliant limbs, yet there was no innocence about her at all. He hadn't felt as if he was despoiling one of the natives, though he had been, of course. His brief encounter with Neeta had totally changed her life – ruined it, some might say – and the guilt Jeremy felt threatened to overwhelm him.

There was something about the native burial ritual that filled him with terror. It was totally irrational, he knew that. The way the Hindus worshipped had nothing to do with him. Yet he felt threatened.

Jeremy knew other Europeans felt the same. The natives, the servant classes, had a strength that none of them could emulate, none of them could dispute. It was rooted in their culture. When they came here from India a century ago they brought with them all their gods and their super-stitions and their strange customs. And it was this otherness, this weirdness that glued them together and made them what they were.

The whites had tried to change all that. All the families had done their best to domesticate the Indians and neu-tralize their power. They had educated their children in Catholic schools, preaching the doctrine of Jesus and the Virgin Mary along with reading, writing and arithmetic. But it hadn't made all that much difference. The children had simply taken Jesus on board with all their other gods, lumping him together with the goddess Kali.

Jeremy sighed and took a long pull on his fresh drink. He turned round in his wicker chair and looked inwards towards the bar. The sight that met his eyes reassured him. There were white men in tropical suits standing around drinking gin and talking about cricket. If it hadn't been for the oppressive heat he could have been back in the home counties.

One of the men standing at the bar called over to him, asking him to join his group. In the normal way of things, Jeremy would have turned him down. He knew all of them and had drunk with them when he worked for the colonial office.

Tonight was different. Tonight he felt unsettled and he needed the solace of his own kind. He got up and started to make his way towards the bar, passing row upon row of glittering silver trophies.

They were all cups that had been won playing rugger, or polo, or some other comforting British sport. As he went by he ran his hand along the edge of the glass cabinet that contained them. And all at once he started to feel better.

The natives could do what they liked with Neeta as far as he was concerned. But as long as he was in here drinking with his friends, he knew he was safe.

He made a mental note to call Christine and tell her not to wait on dinner. It was going to be a very long night.

When Jeremy first ran into Neeta he hadn't been in the market for a mistress. The post had already been filled by a Chinese croupier he met in the Casino de Meurice.

He had been married for twelve years then and had had girlfriends for most of that time. They were an integral part of his life and he expected his wife to turn a blind eye to them – which she did.

When one of Christine's many friends reported seeing Jeremy out on the town with a woman, she invariably laughed it off. The truth of the matter was that the two of them didn't really fit together.

They were perfectly well suited in the face of things. They came from the same class, they'd been brought up on the same literature, they expected the same things out of life, but in private, when the bedroom door was closed,

9

things simply didn't gel. Christine failed to excite her husband.

They tried every way they knew to have a normal marriage. They even managed to produce three daughters. But their lovemaking never went beyond being a duty. In the end they stopped fooling one another and made their separate arrangements.

Christine ran into the arms of the Catholic Church, renouncing her sexuality the way an alcoholic would his drink. Jeremy took a mistress.

When Jeremy met Neeta he wasn't interested in getting involved with her. Unfortunately nobody had told Neeta this, and she pursued him as if her life depended upon it.

Jeremy first noticed her outside the store that supplied all the natives on the plantation. She was very young – fourteen or fifteen at the most. All skin and bone and long black hair. She was carrying a bag of groceries behind her and making heavy weather of it.

'Why don't you get one of your brothers to help you?' Jeremy had asked her.

Neeta had shrugged and made a face. 'This is woman's work.'

There was something insolent about her. She knew who he was, but she didn't seem to respect the fact. Another native girl would have blushed and scampered out of Jeremy's sight. But this one merely stood her ground and waited for what he would do next.

What he did surprised him; he took the groceries away from her and offered to carry them home. Neeta seemed delighted with this turn of events, giggling and leading the way to the run-down encampment.

Jeremy was reminded of a newborn kitten his eldest daughter had brought home with her. The little thing was as scraggy and needy as the girl in front of him, yet it wasn't aware of its station in life.

Neeta was exactly the same and Jeremy was fascinated.

He often found himself waiting for Neeta outside the store and round about the fourth time, she started coming on to him. It was nothing obvious. She didn't wiggle her arse or give him meaningful looks. She just made it plain that she was available if he wanted her.

Jeremy did his best not to notice. The last thing he needed was a mistress living on his doorstep, and a child at that. She's probably a virgin, he thought. I'm better off with what I've got in Curepipe.

Only Neeta wouldn't let him be. At times when he least expected it, she'd swim into his thoughts. He'd be sitting in the library after dinner when he'd remember the curve of her cheek and the way her hair billowed out around her shoulders. Once, when he was making love to his mistress, he found he was calling out Neeta's name.

She was like an itch that wouldn't go away. Finally he accepted he'd have to do something about her. He decided to pay a visit to her father.

The moment he arrived at the tumbledown village on the edge of the cane fields he wished he hadn't bothered. Plantation owners didn't get involved with their workers. His eyes took in the rows of shacks, the chicken runs, the washing hung out to dry on the roadside bushes. I must be out of my mind, he thought.

He was standing outside Neeta's house and suddenly her father came into the yard, indicating that Jeremy should follow him inside.

As he went into the house he smelt animal droppings and the stench of too many bodies in too small a space. And then he saw them. In the tiny breeze-block room, the size, he estimated, of a generous rabbit hutch, were Neeta's brothers and sisters, all seven of them sitting on the dirt floor. Their ages ranged from twelve down to toddlers. To his relief he saw the girl wasn't with them.

The old man got straight to the point. 'You want my daughter,' he said.

Jeremy wondered if he had heard right.

'I would like to spend some time with your daughter,' he said carefully. 'Away from the village.'

The Indian man looked at him out of shrewd unblinking eyes.

'You want to buy Neeta,' he offered. 'I sell her to you cheap. Three hundred rupees,' he said. 'Four maybe, if she pleases you.'

Jeremy started to move towards the door. The hot little room and the solemn staring children were starting to get to him. I shouldn't have come, he thought. I behaved like a fool.

But the old man didn't want to let him go. He clutched on to his jacket, beseeching him to reconsider.

'Two hundred rupees,' he said. 'She's a good girl. Well behaved. She'll do everything you want.'

Now he really had to go. With more force than he meant, Jeremy pushed the man away and made it out the door.

'I have things to do now,' he said. 'One of my men will be in touch with you.'

Then he fled. His polished hand-made leather shoes beat a hasty retreat down the rutted tracks and they didn't stop until they hit tarmac.

By then he was in sight of the colonnaded plantation house that had been in his wife's family for generations. Home, he thought. Home and dry.

Neeta turned up the following day outside the general store. She had timed her appearance to coincide with Jeremy's daily visit to the shop's manager. And this time she wasn't carrying a bag of groceries. She was dragging behind her everything she owned, all done up in a carrier bag.

'I belong to you now,' she said. 'My father told me.'

Jeremy fought down rising panic. The girl must have known how he felt, for she started to back away from him.

'You changed your mind,' she whispered. 'You don't want me any more.'

When he first met her he had been reminded of a kitten and the image was still with him. Only this was a stray kitten, not the pampered pet his daughter had taken in. Jeremy searched his mind for what he knew of the natives who lived on his plantation. He racked his brains. What did they do with the offspring they couldn't feed? He looked at the frightened girl cowering in front of him. I wanted her once, he thought. I planned to take her far away from here where nobody would know me. Where I could make love to her in peace and privacy.

The stupidity of what had happened started to hit him. This child-woman had wooed him and now he was lumbered with her.

He considered walking away from the situation, but knew she would probably end up begging by the roadside. Or worse, she could starve to death.

The idea horrified him and at that moment he had an idea. In the south of the island he had a friend with a plantation. If he took the girl over there and settled her with another family, then his conscience would be clear. And he would be rid of her once and for all.

He told Neeta to wait for him while he went to get his car. They were going on a journey he told her. A long journey with a happy landing at the end of it.

She started coming on to him when they passed Port Louis. They were hitting the open country now and he needed all his concentration to navigate the twisting, badly-made roads. But she wouldn't give him any peace.

It might have been safer if I'd put her in the back seat, Jeremy thought morosely. For Neeta was all over him. Her fingers twisted in his hair. Her thigh pressed against his thigh. Her whole body seemed to be in a state of continuous motion and in the end he pulled over into the kerb and had it out with her.

'Neeta,' he said, trying to keep the irritation out of his

voice, 'I can't drive and make love to you. It isn't possible.'

'Then make love to me.'

He tried to tell her no, but she was faster than he was, hurling herself into his arms, covering his face with moist, light, hungry little kisses.

Jeremy willed himself not to respond. This girl was trouble. Trouble he didn't need. But she had his number and before he could stop himself he was reaching for her, drowning in the female smell of her.

She was wearing a thin cotton dress that buttoned down the front and he found himself pulling at the fastenings. At that moment Jeremy knew he had come to the point of no return. This child had teased and flirted and played with him too long. There was only one thing he could do right now.

As gently as he could he helped her back on with her dress. Then he got out of the car and came round to her side and let her out.

They were parked by the side of an overgrown field which sloped away from the road. Once they were in among the eucalyptus and tropical grasses they would be virtually invisible. The girl seemed to know this, for she led the way, carving a tunnel through the undergrowth until they couldn't see the car any more.

Then she stopped quite suddenly and sat down. He expected her to do something. Take her dress off. Starting kissing him again. But she seemed to have run out of steam. All she could manage was a tremulous smile, a stray kitten smile. And in that moment Jeremy was vulnerable to her.

He started to stroke her hair the way he would with a highborn woman in the secrecy of her boudoir. And she responded by folding herself into the hollow between his neck and his shoulder. This time it was he who made all the moves and Neeta who followed meekly as if she were trying to impress him.

Maybe she is a virgin after all, he thought. And the

14

realization filled him with tenderness. I am her first man, he thought. Her very first experience. I have to do this properly.

This time when he unbuttoned her dress he did it slowly, marvelling at the velvety finish of her skin. She seemed to be covered in fine gossamer down and it made her sensitive to his touch. Every time his hand brushed her nipples or made tentative forays between her legs, she shuddered uncontrollably.

He started to say her name, over and over, cradling her in his arms until she was spread naked beneath him. Then he undressed himself quickly, so that she could see his swelling desire for her.

She cried out then and reached for him, but Jeremy was firmly in control. With one hand he pushed her on to her back and with the other he guided himself into her.

He had no idea how long he and Neeta made love in the field, but it must have been hours, for when it was over the sun had sunk low in the sky. He looked at his watch and got a hold on himself. It would be nightfall before they got to the plantation in the south. They'd better step on it.

He never saw Neeta again. From time to time he called Jacques Chevalier, who managed his friend's plantation. And Jacques kept tabs on her. Which is how Jeremy heard she was pregnant.

'Is there a man involved?' he asked. 'Someone who could marry her?'

Jacques replied there wasn't. 'The only reason she survives,' he said, 'is because of the money you left her.'

Jeremy was puzzled. 'Didn't you hand it over to the head of the family you settled her with?'

There was a short laugh at the other end of the line.

'I'm not a fool you know. Anyway I didn't settle her with a family. I thought she was too old for that.'

Jacques paused, considering what to say next. It was clear to him that the Indian girl was a conquest of Jeremy's. For all he knew Jeremy could be the father of the child she was carrying. He decided to go carefully.

'I managed to find her a little place of her own. There are some old houses we left empty at the back of the settlement and she took one of those.'

Jeremy made a fast calculation. When he said goodbye to Neeta it had been early spring. Now it was late summer and her pregnancy was starting to show. It could have been me, he thought. Unless she was up to something Jacques didn't know about.

'Could you do something for me?' he asked. 'Could you look in on her from time to time, after she's had the baby, keep me up to date on what's happening?'

Jacques Chevalier smiled to himself. So the girl had been Jeremy's mistress.

'It's no problem at all, old man,' he replied. 'I'll be in touch as soon as I know anything.'

Three months later Jeremy heard that Neeta had given birth to a baby boy. He had Jeremy's brown hair, Jeremy's blue eyes and Jeremy's white skin. There was no doubt whatever who he belonged to.

CHAPTER 1

Mauritius, 1962

They called her Emerald because of her eyes. Right from the moment of birth they stared out at the world, clear and limpid, the colour of jewels. None of their friends approved.

What kind of name was Emerald, they demanded. Naming your daughter after a stone was nothing short of sacrilege.

Mina Shah refused to be deflected, for she had a feeling about her youngest child. She was going to be special. She knew it in her bones.

As Emerald grew up her mother's faith in her never wavered, which was just as well, for all the other children in the village found her an oddity. She didn't look the same as them and it wasn't just her eyes that set her apart. She was taller and better made than the girls of her own age. Her bosom was fuller and she had a way of walking that made men look at her.

The logical thing would have been to marry her off as soon as they could, but Mina couldn't bring herself to do it. She dreamt her favourite daughter had a greater destiny than the drudgery of childbearing, so she taught her how to sew. For generations the Shah women had been dressmakers. It was a tradition born of necessity. None of them had had much luck with their husbands. Emerald's grandfather died in an accident before he was thirty, and it was dressmaking money that clothed and fed Mina as she grew up.

Mina needed her sewing skills for a different reason, for

she had married a lazy man. So she brought up and provided for her family single-handedly. But she vowed that Emerald would know better.

As soon as her daughter left school she made enquiries about a job for her. Mina had a large family living in Curepipe and one of her sisters came up with a seamstress's job. It entailed living with her in town, but the move was worth it for the job was for one of the top couturiers.

There were three of these high-class modistes living in Curepipe. All French, all trained in Paris, all women. They were known collectively as 'the three ladies' and between them they provided formal dresses for the landed European families who lived on the island.

To get a job with one of the ladies was something of an honour. And Miss Blanche only considered Emerald because she knew her aunt. And because, at the beginning at any rate, she wouldn't need to be paid very much.

Mina was ecstatic about her daughter's success. If she worked at this job, gave it her full attention, then she could move up in the world. Mina might have to spend the rest of her life tied to a lazy good-for-nothing, but it would be different for Emerald. The girl was destined for a brilliant future.

Emerald found herself sharing a bunk bed with two of her cousins in their breeze-block flat in town.

It didn't bother her, for she hardly spent any time with this new adopted family. Her life revolved around her job.

She made friends almost immediately among the girls in the workroom. She was naturally happy and this quality attracted people to her. Everyone was fascinated by the way she looked.

It was the green eyes that did it. When she was a little girl growing up, people thought they made her look peculiar. But now Emerald was nearly a woman, they were considered exotic.

Most of her new friends assumed that, because of the

18

colour of her eyes, her blood must be tainted. Somewhere in her family tree there had to be a foreigner. They liked her, but didn't want to get too close – or their brothers, for that matter. It was fine to be friends with a girl like Emerald, but you didn't want her marrying into the family.

At that moment in her life, marriage was the last thing on Emerald's mind. She was starting to enjoy her independence. Her salary had increased by leaps and bounds during her first year at the couturier's, as the French woman discovered she had a talent with the fine fabrics. Where the other seamstresses fumbled and made mistakes, Emerald's work was perfect. A dress or a spring suit that bore her handiwork was crisper and the clients noticed this. Emerald found herself inundated with work from Miss Blanche, and as time went on she found she was included in some of the consultations or fittings.

In her second year Emerald began to build up a clientele of her own. Miss Blanche encouraged this, knowing the girl could never leave her. She had no money to set up on her own, and no standing in the community. All she had were her astonishing looks and a God-given ability. The couturier prayed she didn't catch the eye of some rich trader who'd want to whisk her away and give her children.

Her prayers were answered. Nobody was in the least bit interested in making an honest woman of Emerald. She was fine to take out dancing, and she was inundated with young men who wanted to take her to the races or the casino, but she simply wasn't wife material.

It was her beauty that ruined her chances; at sixteen she had the look of an Italian film star. She was very curvy with a tiny waist and legs that went on forever. And her fine black hair, unlike all the other girls who wore it demurely coiled into a bun, was cut like that of an urchin. Gina Lollobrigida was popular in the movie magazines that year and Emerald did everything she could to emulate her.

Her aunt began to worry. It was clear what had to be

done. Emerald needed a husband, so she paid a visit to her sister in the south.

'We must arrange a marriage for Emerald,' she said, coming straight to the point. 'She's starting to run wild. If we don't do something soon it could be too late.'

They found her a widower called Manesh. He was quite a lot older than her, and had children that needed looking after. In an ideal world, Emerald wouldn't have looked at him. But the world wasn't ideal and Emerald didn't have a choice.

CHAPTER 2

Emerald's life changed when she was sent on an errand to fetch a bolt of silk.

It was a hot, sticky afternoon in the middle of the monsoon season, and Emerald found herself walking down the Currimjee Arcade en route to the Chinese supplier.

It was not a day to be out walking. The humidity was so intense that Emerald could feel her hair wilt and the sweat gather in the small of her back. She sent up a prayer of thanks that she was dressed for the weather.

That morning she had decided to wear the loose cotton shift she had copied out of the pages of French *Vogue*. It was by a new designer called Courrèges and left her shoulders tantalizingly bare. It also showed more of her legs than her mother would have approved of. But, she thought, the hell with it. When I marry, my husband will have me in saris round my ankles. I might as well make the most of my freedom while I've got it.

She reached Orient Textiles just before closing time and the man behind the counter seemed to be expecting her. When he heard who she was, he produced the tallest roll of silk she had ever seen. It was a delicate shade of rose pink and towered over her. Emerald felt weary just looking at it.

The assistant produced a bill of sale and Emerald scrawled her signature across the bottom in the way she had been instructed to. Then, because she was curious, she glanced at the price. The sheer magnitude of it made her tremble. She was being entrusted with ten thousand rupees' worth of fabric. An entire village could live for a year on what it cost.

Emerald gave a little sigh of resignation and lifted the fabric up in her arms. It weighed a ton, yet now she was in possession of it, there was no going back.

Once she was out in the arcade she felt better. The air was cooling down a bit and as long as she kept moving she felt she could manage. She got right round the main square without any mishap. Now all she had to do was make it across the road and she was halfway home.

She was so intent on getting to her destination that she didn't bother to look at the traffic as she stepped off the kerb. The man behind the wheel of the approaching Jaguar sports car simply didn't see her. If it hadn't been for the roll of silk, Emerald would probably have been run down, but the giant bundle she was carrying saved her life. The driver saw it just in time to slow down, but he was too late to prevent a collision.

The car hit Emerald sideways, knocking her off her feet and sending her sprawling. As she hit the rough road she felt the skin being scraped off her knees and it was in that moment of agonizing pain that she let go of the silk. It went flying out of her hands and into the gutter, but she didn't see it happen because she was beyond caring. She lay spread out in the middle of the road, and for all she knew, she was probably terribly injured. If she'd thought about it much longer she would have burst into tears but she didn't get the chance. Before she could feel sorry for herself a pair of strong arms were lifting her up.

'Thank God you're in one piece,' said the man who knocked her down. 'I was worried I might have killed you.'

Emerald looked down at herself in dismay. The white Courrèges dress was torn in several places, as were her knees and her elbows, and her shins which were starting to bleed.

Her rescuer went to work on her immediately, taking out a vast white linen hanky, which he tore into strips and fastened over her cuts.

While all this was going on, she noticed a crowd of curious onlookers were starting to gather round. Emerald suddenly remembered the silk. The precious ten-thousand-rupee bale of silk was attracting all this attention.

She edged forward and then she wished she hadn't, for the tightly rolled fabric had come undone and was billowing from the gutter right across the road. Yards and yards of the finest, palest, quality silk was lying in tatters all along the filthy rutted tarmac.

Emerald took a step towards it, but one of her injured legs gave way and she would have stumbled if the man with her hadn't grabbed hold of her waist.

'There's no point in bothering about that any more,' he told her. 'It's not worth saving.'

Suddenly tears flooded into Emerald's eyes and spilled down her cheeks. The fact that she might have been killed suddenly seemed unimportant compared to this latest tragedy. What was the point of living if she didn't have a job?

Worse, what was the point of living if she owed ten thousand rupees she couldn't afford to pay.

Very gently, Emerald's rescuer put his arm round her shoulders and led her over to the kerb, then produced yet another handkerchief and proceeded to dab her face.

'Don't get yourself in a lather,' he told her. 'It's really not the end of the world.'

'I don't suppose it is to you,' Emerald sobbed. 'Ten thousand rupees is probably tipping money where you come from.'

As she said it, she realized what kind of man this stranger was. Her first thought was that he was way out of her class. His well-cut tropical suit told her that. So did his white skin. Even to her inexperienced eyes he was a grandee. From the sound of him, a grandee from one of the landed English families.

She suddenly felt at a loss to know what to do.

He must have realized this, for he started guiding her towards the car he had left at the side of the road.

'If you jump in,' he said not unkindly, 'I'll take us to a place where we can sit down and have something to drink. Then when you've calmed down a bit, we'll talk about the silk.'

He took her to a café on a side street behind the main square. It was slightly better than most of the bars Emerald got taken to and sported checked tablecloths and a French name.

Without the Englishman saying a word, a waiter brought a whisky to their table, along with a bottle of Pepsi.

Emerald looked questioning. 'Is this for me?' she asked, picking up the drink.

The man nodded. 'It's what you wanted, isn't it?'

Just for a second Emerald felt angry. 'Actually, I don't like Pepsi very much,' she told him. 'When I'm out I like to drink a glass of wine.'

The man didn't turn a hair. 'Then have what you like,' he said. 'Do you prefer chablis or claret?'

The question threw her. She'd never had anything better than the locally bottled brew. But she wasn't going to let him know that.

'I'll have a claret,' she said grandly. 'But could you tell the waiter to make sure it's very cold.'

What she had just said seemed to amuse her companion, for a smile lit up the gaunt aristocratic bones of his face.

'Red wine suffers if you take it below room temperature, so I'll order you a glass of chablis. I suspect it's what you were after all along.'

Emerald wanted to hit him. Just because he has more money than me, she thought, he thinks he can send me up.

She remembered why she was sitting there and swung round to face him.

'Isn't it time we talked about the silk you knocked out of my hands?'

Right until this moment she hadn't thought of it that way at all. All along she had blamed herself for the accident, but her fury over being made to look a fool over a glass of wine gave her courage.

Her aggression seemed to knock her companion off balance, for he hesitated before replying.

'I never did apologize for knocking you over,' he said at last. 'You must have been terrified back there.' He went on: 'I'll pay for the silk you were carrying. It's the least I can do.'

The waiter arrived with the wine he had ordered for her and Emerald took a gulp out of the glass. The unexpected sour taste made her eyes smart, but she no longer cared about it.

Half an hour ago there was no hope for her. She had almost certainly lost her job. And was on her way to prison into the bargain. Now this Englishman had changed everything. She was saved. She was solvent and she could go back to what she was doing before everything went wrong.

'How can I ever thank you?' she said.

Jeremy Waites smiled wolfishly at the pretty little Indian girl sitting opposite him. Even with her dress all torn and covered in grime she was a dish.

'You can stay and have another glass of wine with me,' he said. 'It's not fair to ask more of you than that.'

The next day a new bolt of pale pink silk arrived at Miss Blanche's workroom. Attached to the delivery was a handwritten note addressed to Emerald.

I hope this goes towards repairing the damage I did to you yesterday, Jeremy wrote. *I'm not in the habit of knocking down attractive pedestrians and I'm truly sorry I hurt you. Next time I'm in town, perhaps I can buy you another glass of chablis?*

In the normal way Emerald would have told the other girls about the note but something stopped her. In her heart of hearts she already knew what was on this man's mind. She had known it the moment he picked her up out of the road and she realized this knowledge was best kept to herself.

Jeremy Waites turned up at the workroom a week later. It was 5.30 in the evening and he was standing in the small reception area waiting for her.

Emerald's first impulse was to turn and run. She didn't want to get involved with the Englishman. She had enough trouble with Manesh, her betrothed. All she really wanted was to be left in peace to go on with her life. But there was no ignoring Jeremy.

He stepped forward and took her arm as if they were old friends. Then before she could protest, he told her he was taking her to Port Louis for a drink.

'But that's miles away,' she said. 'My aunt expects me home for dinner.'

'Then you're going to be late,' he told her firmly.

Why Emerald went along with Jeremy she had no idea, though she suspected it was something to do with his car. She didn't know anybody who drove, and it made her feel special to sit right in front of the shiny red Jag and watch the world spinning by.

By the time they were out of Curepipe, her mood started to lighten. Her new friend was surprisingly good company. With Manesh she would have to rack her brains to think of things to say. Jeremy didn't tax her imagination at all.

He had been gambling the night before and he was full of stories about it. They were colourful, slightly scandalous stories and Emerald was a little shocked. She thought she was spending the evening with an English gentleman, but

26

the image was fading fast. So she started to ask questions.

How did he live his life, she wanted to know. Was there a wife waiting for him at home?

'Of course I'm married,' Jeremy told her openly, 'but it doesn't stop me from doing as I please.'

Then he told her what pleased him and despite herself Emerald was fascinated. Jeremy seemed to exist on many different levels. There was his home life on the sugar plantation, which was quite separate and apart from his social life playing polo at his club and his business life trading in sugar in Port Louis. Then he had another existence where he gambled and smoked opium and visited waterfront bars.

Emerald wondered where she fitted in all this. Then she looked across the front seat to where Jeremy was sitting in his thousand-dollar English suit and she knew the answer. You're dangerous, she thought. You'll gobble me up and spit me out and at the end of it you won't even remember my name.

She realized she shouldn't have come, but by then they were approaching Port Louis and it was too late for regrets. She saw they were driving into the harbour area, for the streets were meaner here, and the races more mixed. Sailors from Taiwan mingled with Arab traders in tiny red fezzes.

I hope he doesn't take me to one of his bars, Emerald thought. If anyone sees me, I'll never live it down.

She needn't have worried, for at Rivière Street, Jeremy turned the car away from the docks and headed towards the Merchant Navy Club. The premises, an old colonial-style mansion, spread the width of the entire block. As they walked in, Emerald began to feel better. Jeremy took her out on to the verandah and into the garden.

'We'll have our drinks here,' he told her. 'It's cooler.'

They found a loggia just outside in the shade of an overgrown hibiscus bush. Jeremy seemed concerned that Emerald had everything she wanted and went to considerable trouble organizing a succession of little cocktail appetizers. He even remembered she had liked chablis, and she was flattered.

Then he started to ask her about herself and out of nowhere she started to feel shy. Emerald had wanted to know about his private life, but when it came to her turn she held back and she realized it had something to do with who they were. Jeremy could be as candid as he liked and it made no difference to him. He had nothing to lose. With her it was different.

Emerald sidestepped most of his questions, then he started asking her about her job and she realized she was going to be okay. This was the one thing she could talk about freely, because she was proud of what she did. She was creating her own patterns now, which was something that previously only Miss Blanche had done. She went into considerable detail about the art of French couture.

She must have gone on for twenty minutes without stopping for the wine was halfway down the bottle by the time she was finished. She realized what she had done and pulled herself up short.

'I'm sorry,' she said, 'I must be boring you.'

Her companion shook his head. 'I would have told you if you were.' He paused for a moment. 'Have you ever thought of going into business for yourself? Someone with your talent could do very well.'

For some reason the remark rubbed Emerald up the wrong way.

'Where on earth would I get the money to do something like that?' she demanded. 'I can barely afford to pay the rent.'

Jeremy shrugged and spread his hands. 'I imagined your family could set you up, or perhaps a boyfriend.'

He was deliberately provoking her, pushing her into revealing more about herself than she wanted. And she fell right into the trap.

'I don't have a boyfriend,' Emerald said. 'Or a fancy man. I have a fiancé chosen for me by my family.'

Recently, Emerald had been ashamed of the arrangement, but now it gave her respectability and she clung to it.

Her companion wasn't impressed. He leaned back in his openwork chair and looked her up and down as if he was studying some rare form of butterfly.

'How charming,' he said. 'An old-fashioned, traditional Indian girl. You'll be telling me next you're collecting gold bangles in your bottom drawer.'

'We don't do that,' Emerald said sharply. 'The man always buys the jewellery.'

Jeremy leant forward and refilled both their glasses. Then he said, 'I suppose this husband-to-be will be setting you up as a dressmaker as well?'

Emerald thought about the village where her fiancé, Manesh, lived. It was a shanty town really, in the middle of nowhere. None of her clients would bother to come to a place like that to have their clothes made. She suddenly felt miserable.

'I don't think my fiancé has the money for a couture business,' she said. 'But I'll get by.'

There was a silence while Jeremy considered what she had told him. Then he leant forward.

'Is that what you want in your life?' he asked. 'To get by? I can't see a girl like you being happy with that.'

Emerald looked at the good-looking, expensive man sitting opposite her. She imagined he spent all his life sitting in gardens like this one.

'My happiness is of little importance,' she said bitterly. 'I have to make do with what I can get.'

Jeremy put his drink down and reached for her hand, turning it over in both of his.

'You can get better than some poor native boy,' he said softly. 'If you wanted, I could set you up in business.'

Emerald was tempted. Her hand felt very safe where it was, and just for a moment she wondered what it would be like to be cherished by a man like Jeremy.

'It would be just a business arrangement,' she said cautiously, 'wouldn't it?'

He laughed at her then. A low, rippling laugh as if she had just told a very good joke.

'Don't be a goose,' he said. 'I'm not *that* keen to go into the rag trade.'

'So you expect me to sleep with you.'

Emerald's hand was still in his and she was acutely conscious that he made no attempt to release it.

'It's not such a terrible idea,' Jeremy smiled. 'A lot of girls I know rather enjoy it.'

The way he said it, he could have been offering her another drink. Emerald felt insulted. She had no intention of going to bed with this man, but at least he could have romanced her a little.

She took her hand back. 'I think you've got the wrong idea,' she said. 'I'm not for sale.'

Jeremy raised an eyebrow. 'But you are for sale. You just told me you were marrying a man to please your family. If you came into business with me at least you'd be pleasing yourself.'

She was aware of his eyes travelling up her legs, and she knew he was imagining the way she would look undressed. For no reason at all she started to tremble all over.

'Don't be frightened,' he said softly. 'I'll look after you.'

But she was frightened. I want to go home, Emerald thought. I want to be back with my aunt and the people who know me. It's not safe for me here.

Jeremy must have sensed he had gone too far, for he drew back into himself, masking the need in his eyes with a carefully neutral expression.

'I'm not trying to rush you,' he said, 'but I think you should consider the idea. I could do a lot for you.'

He reached into a pocket in his jacket and produced a small printed card. On it was the name of a large trading company in Port Louis together with a telephone number.

'If you're interested,' he told her, 'you can reach me through this office.'

Emerald didn't want to take the card, but she knew to brush it aside would be rude. So she tucked it inside her bag. I'll throw it away later, she thought. There's no way I'm ever going to need it.

CHAPTER 3

Emerald concentrated all her attention on Manesh. Before meeting Jeremy Waites, she had brushed him aside, thinking she would figure out a way of getting rid of him. Now she knew she had been wrong. Without Manesh and the safety of marriage, she was easy prey for the likes of Jeremy Waites.

And then what would she be? A kept woman. Little more than a whore. The prospect terrified her. Any husband, she decided, even one chosen by her family, and who had been married before and already had two children in tow, even he was better than no husband at all.

Emerald's aunt noticed her new attitude and felt relieved. Manesh was a dull dog, she had to admit, but once Emerald was his wife she would learn to appreciate him. The children will distract her, she thought, then there will be her own babies. In a year or so her hands will be so full, she won't have time to feel discontented.

Then everything changed. It was Emerald's father who altered the course of her life, for he was a gambling man. He didn't frequent casinos, or anything that might be noticed by his children. His activities were stealthier than that, and centred around card games that the men played when they had nothing better to do in the afternoons.

One afternoon, he got into trouble. It happened during a poker game with a group of visiting labourers. They had somehow fixed things between them, for no matter how he played his cards, the old man simply couldn't win. He found himself being drawn into committing money he didn't have, and by the end of the day he was deeply in debt.

He tried to talk his way out of paying, but it didn't wash. Either they would have their money, they told him, or they would have his neck. He believed them. He would have to come up with the ante and he didn't want to go to his wife for it. So he did the next best thing. He went to his daughter.

Hidden underneath the bed was a small pouch containing Emerald's dowry. That night her father retrieved it, took it into town and paid it over to the men who had taken him at poker.

His family would have to be told about it in the morning. He knew that. But he didn't think that removing the dowry would make that much difference to the impending wedding. Emerald was a beautiful girl, with all the makings of a first-class mother. Her future husband would just have to understand that she couldn't bring anything else to the marriage.

But Manesh didn't understand. Worse than that, he felt he had been short-changed.

'The dowry', he said in his dry precise way, 'was part of the marriage contract. Without it we have no agreement.'

The entire family pleaded with him to change his mind. Everyone except Emerald. She wasn't exactly giddy with relief, but she was realistic about what had happened.

'This wasn't a love match,' she told her mother. 'Manesh was taking me on for what I could contribute. And without my dowry I wasn't much of a proposition.'

She was very brave about the whole thing but the rejection had hurt her badly. She had hoped against hope that Manesh had liked her for herself, that she was more to him than just a skivvy to look after his house and his children. But she was wrong.

What really depressed her was that Manesh had been her only chance. Now there was no dowry under the bed her prospects of another arranged marriage were at an end.

Emerald had no alternative now but to concentrate on her job. Even that didn't bring her any comfort. Her future, which had seemed so exciting, had suddenly turned bleak. She imagined herself ten years hence, still toiling in the workrooms of Miss Blanche. All her friends would have left to get married and there would be a whole tribe of new younger women who would exclude her.

She thought about her father and the way he had wasted her dowry. He didn't throw away my husband, she thought bitterly, he threw away my whole life. Now I have nothing, I am nothing.

Emerald's sense of hopelessness increased when Miss Blanche started pruning her staff for the hot months when business was slack. What will happen, Emerald thought, if my clients don't come back next season? Or if I fall out of favour with Miss Blanche? These thoughts had never occurred to her before. Now they were in her mind they wouldn't leave her alone.

In the wake of her doubts another phantom came to haunt her. Jeremy Waites. He could solve all her problems at a stroke. All Emerald had to do was give herself to him and she wouldn't have to worry about her job or her future. He would take care of everything. She found herself wondering what would happen if she took the option he had offered to her. She would be finished as far as her family was concerned, she knew that. Once she had crossed over to the other side of the street she was as good as dead in their eyes. But did it matter any more? Without a husband she was finished anyway.

Emerald remembered Jeremy had handed her a card with his name and a contact number and suddenly it seemed terribly important that she locate it.

It took her two days of rummaging through her things, but in the end it turned up, squashed down in the lining of her handbag, and when she saw it, she felt an enormous sense of relief.

Jeremy Waites couldn't offer her the future she had chosen for herself. He couldn't give her children or respectability, but he could help her survive. Neither her family nor her employer could guarantee that.

CHAPTER 4

Jeremy arranged to meet Emerald in the Providence, a Muslim-owned eatery in Port Louis. It wasn't a classy establishment. To get inside, Emerald had to negotiate her way past the cook, a fearsome-looking woman of vast proportions who stood in the entrance frying pimentos.

Even then she wasn't home and dry, for her path was completely blocked by a huge counter piled high with fried chicken and takeaway kebabs.

For a moment Emerald was flustered. She was standing in the centre of a mass of seething humanity. Everyone there was prepared to trample on her if it meant getting served, and she was meant to be meeting her destiny.

If I'm not careful, Emerald thought wryly, I will be meeting it, but not the one Jeremy has in mind.

Her eyes scanned the restaurant, taking in the crowded tables in each cubicle. She felt a growing sense of disbelief. Surely the character in the tailored suit and the red Jaguar would never subject himself to the indignity of sharing his space with this rabble?

Then Emerald realized Jeremy had never intended to, for right at the back of the Providence, in a cubicle all on his own, she saw him. Whether he had influence here, or he had simply paid for his privacy, she never knew, but she was impressed.

In the days when Manesh was courting her, there were no special privileges. When they went to local restaurants, they queued like everyone else until a table came free. Manesh never booked anything in advance, and never in a million years would he clear a space just to be alone with her.

Jeremy was a rogue, Emerald knew that, but at least he was a rogue who wanted her.

She walked up the short flight of steps to where he was sitting, mentally looking herself over as she did so. That day she had put on the one smart suit she owned. It was in white piqué with a short tight skirt that was popular that season. She knew the fabric made her look darker and more exotic than she was, but it didn't bother her. She wasn't ashamed of where she came from. Jeremy made no move to kiss her, or even take her hand when she sat down. He merely signalled the waiter to bring her a drink. Then he turned to her.

'So your ambition got the better of you,' he said. 'I never really saw you as a married matron.'

Emerald considered telling him about Manesh and the way he walked out on her, but some sixth sense prevented her. I need to flatter this man, she thought. He has to believe I chose him above Manesh. I can't afford to look desperate. She gave him her best smile.

'You talked me into seeing things your way,' she said. 'In the end I couldn't resist.'

Emerald expected him to flirt, or at least to soften, but Jeremy did neither. He sat up straighter, as if he were chairing a board meeting.

'We have to talk about what you expect from me,' he told her. 'There are limits to what I can do.'

Emerald felt a moment of panic. 'You don't want to help me in a business,' she said. 'You've changed your mind, after all.'

'Calm down,' Jeremy said, his voice gentler than before. 'I'm not so much of a shit. I just don't want you to think I can provide you with a setup like Miss Blanche's, because it wouldn't work.'

'Why not? I've got the clients,' Emerald countered.

Jeremy sighed. 'They won't come with you,' he told her. 'No matter how much they like your work, they'll stay exactly where they are.'

'Because I'm not French. Because I didn't train in Paris.'

Jeremy felt exasperated. Surely she knows, he thought. Then he looked at the girl in front of him, and he realized that behind the exotic green eyes and the sophisticated get-up she was really an innocent. He decided to be brutal, not because he wanted to hurt her, but because he needed to make her see sense.

'You're a very clever girl,' he said, 'and you're going to go far, but you'll never be a couturier. You're not white.'

The look on Emerald's face told him he had got through to her, so he pressed his point home.

'The clients who patronize Miss Blanche on the island don't believe an Indian girl can design for them. Whether you can or not is beside the point. You're dealing with people's prejudices here and you have to go with the market.'

Emerald was close to tears. This man was meant to be her saviour, yet he was telling her she didn't stand a hope in hell.

'So you brought me here for nothing,' she said bitterly. 'Or did you think that once you got a couple of drinks inside me you could make a pass?'

Jeremy reached out a hand to calm her. 'You're being silly,' he said. 'I didn't say you couldn't go into the sewing business. You can and you will, but you won't set up shop here as a designer.'

The truth of what he was saying started to dawn on her.

'You see me as a seamstress, don't you?' she said. 'One of those coolies who sews curtains and makes children's clothes.' She wiped her hand across her face, smearing her careful makeup. 'I'm not going to do it,' she told him. 'I haven't worked all these years to end up like my mother.'

Jeremy did his best to look patient. 'The only way you

could end up like your mother,' he said, 'is if you married someone like your father, and as that's not going to happen I don't see what you're getting worked up about. Look,' he went on, 'there are plenty of women living in Port Louis who can't afford couturiers, so they settle for dressmakers. That's how I see you. As a dressmaker, not a seamstress.'

His words seemed to mollify Emerald a little, for when the waiter arrived with the food she didn't turn it away.

After eating for a while she looked at Jeremy.

'If I'm to be a dressmaker,' she enquired, 'where will I work from?'

Jeremy realized he was making headway and he reached over and poured her some wine.

'When we've finished here,' he said, 'I'll take you to the place I have in mind.'

It took them fifteen minutes to walk to the rooming house. It was a wooden two-storey building fronting on to a leafy square. Right across from it a huge flame tree arched over the street, the redness of its blossom giving a kind of grace to the run-down neighbourhood.

Emerald considered the house in front of her a step up in the world and she wondered whether she would be living in it, or simply using the premises for work.

Jeremy didn't let on right away. He ushered her through the louvred doors of the verandah into the salon.

'You will receive your clients here,' he told her. 'There's a kitchen out at the back where you can make coffee.'

Emerald stared at the dimensions of her new workplace. All the walls were painted white, chipping in places where the plaster came loose. In the middle of the room was a kelim that had seen better days, a coffee table and a clutch of cane armchairs. Hanging over everything, casting mysterious patterns of light and shade, was an ornate Chinese lantern. Emerald stared in wonder at the shabby, run-down room, for it was more than she ever expected. A thought occurred to her.

39

'Where will I sew?' she enquired.

Jeremy hesitated for a moment and she noticed he looked uncomfortable. 'You'll sew in your bedroom,' he said stiffly. 'It's big enough to take a machine and anything else you'll need.'

Suddenly the whole scenario was clear. Emerald was to be the kept mistress, accommodating her fancy man and running her business from the same premises. So that's what I've come to, she thought.

It occurred to her to walk out while she could. She hadn't signed anything. Yet she realized the reality of her situation, for if she walked out now, where would she go? Back to her aunt where she couldn't afford to pay the rent? Back to a life where the only future was drudgery and spinsterhood?

She turned round, doing her best to be charming.

'Perhaps I should see the room,' she said.

It was a big space. Her mother, her father, her entire family could have lived here easily. Emerald began to feel grateful.

Jeremy was exploiting her, she knew that, but he was doing it with elegance.

She felt him come up behind her. 'I take it you approve,' he said.

She swivelled round to face him. 'It will do,' she answered. 'For now.'

Jeremy reached for her then and, almost as a reflex action, Emerald fought him off. She wasn't used to men grabbing at her and she struggled to free herself from the circle of his arms. Her resistance seemed to inflame him, for he lifted her up and carried her across to the bed. She started to plead with him to let her go.

'I've changed my mind,' she wept. 'I don't want to do this after all.'

Jeremy didn't take any notice. He pushed her back against the headboard and started kissing her. Emerald had been kissed before, but never like this. There was nothing gentle about him and for a second she felt she was drowning. Then he pulled away from her.

'Take your things off,' he told her. 'I'm tired of playing games.'

Emerald saw he was already half undressed. He'd taken his jacket off and his shirt was unbuttoned. In spite of herself she wanted to go on with what was happening. She had never seen this sophisticated man out of control before and the fact that she had made him this way excited her.

She took off her white piqué suit, folding it neatly on the wicker chair. Then she undid her blouse and stood in front of him in her panties. She wasn't wearing a bra and instinctively her hands came up to cover her breasts, but Jeremy was there before her, cupping her nakedness in his hands as if she were the very first woman he had touched. He kissed her again, coaxing her rather than leading her and she felt herself respond.

Emerald had no idea how she got to the bed, but suddenly she was lying there and Jeremy was sliding her panties down her legs.

'Don't,' she said, but her legs were wide apart now and his fingers probed the soft flesh between them. She felt the last fragments of shame dissolve and another feeling, a stronger feeling replaced them.

She wanted him now and her need, instead of terrifying her, elated her. For she knew that this man would please her.

She entwined herself around him, arching her back ready to receive him, and as he thrust into her she realized she had wanted him all along.

He made love to her very thoroughly as if he was indoctrinating a student or an apprentice. And in a way he was. For Emerald knew that from now on, part of her job would be to do exactly what he was showing her. Laughter started to build up in her throat.

41

'I can't believe this is what I was frightened of,' she whispered into his ear. 'I must have been crazy.'

Emerald gave in her notice the next day.

'I'm going away,' she informed her workmates. 'I've found another job.'

The other girls looked knowingly at each other. Most of them had a shrewd idea of what Emerald had found. Ever since her marriage plans had come unstuck, they suspected she'd find herself a protector. Now she was leaving, they speculated among themselves as to who it could be.

Emerald's aunt didn't bother with speculation. She came straight to the point.

'If you leave here for a man,' she said, 'don't even think of coming back. As far as your family is concerned, you're finished the minute you walk out the door.'

The girl stood stock still, her strange iridescent eyes clouding over. She had expected to hear this, yet nothing had prepared her for the pain of her aunt's rejection.

Deep down inside, though, she wasn't sorry to be leaving. Emerald didn't want to spend the rest of her days squatting on dirt floors. She didn't want to be used as a breeding machine by a man who would probably ignore her, and she didn't want to worry about money ever again.

She thought about the big room, with the mahogany wardrobe, that would be her new home. And a feeling of lightness came over her. Whatever happens to me now, she thought, it's got to be better than anything that's gone before.

She turned to her aunt, her mind made up. 'I'm sorry,' she said softly, 'for all the shame I'm going to cause you.'

CHAPTER 5

London, 1960

Tim Waites peered into the crowd arriving at Heathrow's Terminal Three, and wondered about the boy Jeremy was sending him. He was half Waites, that much his brother had assured him. The blue blood of their forefathers was flowing freely in his veins. Only it was mixed with something else.

The tall Englishman sighed. Why did his younger brother have such a thing about native girls? You would have thought Christine would have been more than enough for him. But no. Ever since the day they were married, Jeremy was off chasing every bit of skirt he could lay his hands on. And he'd got away with it, until now, when his luck had run out.

Tim thought back to the frenzied phone call Jeremy had made just a week ago.

'I'm in a spot,' Jeremy had announced. 'I've got a son. And he's nothing to do with Christine.'

To begin with Tim didn't take it very seriously. 'If one of your girlfriends has become a mother, why don't you handle it like everyone else in your position? Pay her off and wash your hands of the whole thing. As long as you look after everyone, you won't have any trouble.'

There was a silence, during which Tim realized the situation was more difficult than he'd first thought. Finally Jeremy came back on the line.

'I haven't explained it properly,' he said. 'I actually knew about the boy over twelve years ago. At the time I thought everything was taken care of. He and his mother were

43

living quite happily over on the other side of the island. There was no involvement from me except for an annual phone call to check they were okay. Then out of the blue, the girl upped and died.

'The plantation manager told me she had contracted swamp fever which finished her off. It was all very sudden and difficult because of the child. You see, there was nobody to look after him. When Neeta got pregnant her family more or less disowned her. They were prepared to bring her back and give her a decent burial. But that was all. They didn't want to know about the boy at all.'

Tim was seized with curiosity. 'Does the boy have a name?' he enquired.

His brother grunted and Tim realized Jeremy was embarrassed.

'Actually, he's called Ravi and I met him for the first time last week.'

Tim decided to keep up the pressure. 'You might tell me what this son of yours is like. I mean, does he look like a Waites? Or does he take after his mother?'

This time the silence from Jeremy was prolonged.

'He looks like me,' he said finally. 'He's a dead ringer for me at that age.'

'So what are you going to do about him?' Tim asked. 'If you let him grow up in your image, somebody on Mauritius is bound to spot the similarity. The island's too small for that sort of thing to go unnoticed.'

Jeremy sighed. 'I know, I know. Christine would kill me if she knew about Ravi. She never managed to give me a son.'

The image of Christine came into Tim's mind: large, bossy and infuriatingly overbearing. She'd kill him all right. And eat him for breakfast the next day.

'You've got to get the boy out of Mauritius,' Tim told him.

It was as if Jeremy had read his brother's mind. 'I was

44

just coming to that,' he said. 'I've decided to send Ravi to be educated in England. His Catholic school gave a good start, so the public school system shouldn't be any problem to him.'

Tim started to object, but his brother was having none of it.

'I've arranged everything,' he said. 'Ravi arrives on Air Mauritius in three days. I'm depending on you to meet him and get him into shape for the rigours of Stowe.'

So here he was standing in the arrivals hall at Heathrow, waiting for his brother's son to put in an appearance. The whole thing was so preposterous he could hardly believe he'd agreed to it.

Sending Ravi over here to be educated was one thing. But sending him to Stowe, their old school, was another matter altogether. Whatever Jeremy said, the boy had an Indian mother and had grown up on a plantation. He would look and behave accordingly. And if they weren't very careful, little Ravi would bring the entire family into disrepute.

Tim extended a wrist and checked the time on his gold Cartier tank watch. By his calculations the plane had landed half an hour ago. The Englishman had just decided to walk over to the enquiry desk when he saw the boy — or what he assumed was him. For the child making his way out of the customs hall was exactly as his brother had described. He was Jeremy down to the last chiselled feature.

Tim made an effort to hide his amusement. Good Lord, he thought, that boy really is a Waites. He's got it written all over him.

In the normal way Tim would have pushed through the crowd and introduced himself, but he decided to play for time. He wanted to study the child, get a good fix on him, before making any kind of approach. So he hung back and waited.

45

Jeremy hadn't made any efforts to smarten him up, he saw. He was dressed in a pair of dirty jeans and a tee shirt. Round his shoulders was slung a collarless jacket that had seen better days and the suitcase he lugged behind him seemed to be made of cardboard.

Now he could see him properly, Tim realized the child wasn't quite white. At a distance he had looked the perfect specimen of English manhood, but as he came up to where Tim was standing, he saw that wasn't so. His skin was a light olive colour, and that, combined with Jeremy's light blue eyes and English features, gave him an exotic look.

He'll be devastating when he grows up, Tim thought. A real heartbreaker.

He decided it was time to make his move. Stepping forward he extended his hand.

'It's Ravi, isn't it?' he said warmly. 'Your father told me to expect you.'

The boy set his case down.

'Uncle Tim,' he said, smiling. 'I've been wondering about you ever since I got on the plane.'

He didn't take the offered hand, and Tim realized the child wasn't used to this kind of greeting. Suddenly Tim did something totally instinctive. He took the boy by the shoulders and pulled him into an embrace.

'Welcome to England,' he said. 'I hope you'll be happy here.'

The boy clung to him for a long time and when he finally pulled away Tim saw there were tears in his eyes. Poor little bastard, thought Tim. Your mother's died and your father's dumped you in a strange country like a piece of lost property. You must feel you don't matter to a soul.

He took Ravi by the arm and steered him towards the glass doors leading out to the street.

'The first thing I'm going to do is get you home,' he told

46

him. 'Then I'm going to make you a hot drink and some toast. You look as though you could do with it.'

Tim lived in an exquisitely appointed mews house in London's Belgravia. It was a place designed not for wives and children, but for sophisticated adults who cared about the way things looked, yet it was comfortable. The main room, which looked out on to the cobbled mews, was furnished country-house style with brocaded sofas and deep masculine-looking armchairs. A coal fire burned out of a huge old-fashioned grate and Ravi made a beeline for it. Tim watched the boy kneel down on the rug and reach out towards the warmth.

He's starting to make himself at home, he thought. I'm going to have to be careful with him.

Tim wasn't that keen on the young. When duty called he played the kindly uncle, attending christenings and birthday parties. But he had never married and the mess and the responsibility that always came with it was anathema to him. But this was no ordinary boy. His nephew had been brought up by a servant girl on a small island.

Before Tim even got him to school, he was going to have to civilize him. Ravi had trouble coping with the bacon and eggs he had made him earlier. How was he going to fare in a hall full of snotty little Englishmen who had been brought up knowing which knife and fork to use?

He sighed, wondering why he had given in to Jeremy. It would have been far simpler to have passed the buck to his elder brother, but the boy had already known too much grief in his short life. What he needed now was guidance, gentle, patient guidance from somebody who understood his problems.

Tim caught a glimpse of himself in the looking glass above the desk where he was standing. He saw reflected back a thin man with straight blond hair and a narrow face.

On the outside he was the perfect gentleman. A strong, dependable, clever banker. A pillar of society. Except he wasn't. His sexuality put paid to that. All he was doing was living behind a façade, and he was ashamed of it. It's funny, he thought, I'm as worried about being gay as Ravi will be worried about being half-caste and illegitimate. And in that instant Tim started to understand the boy from Mauritius, for in a way they weren't so different. They were both outsiders. Maybe I can help him, Tim thought. I'm lumbered with him till the new term starts. At least there's time to give it a go.

He began by kitting Ravi out. The boy had arrived with virtually nothing. There were a couple of shirts, a denim jacket and a torn pair of shorts. And that was the sum total of it. He didn't have any underwear, except what he was wearing. It was the same with his shoes. And he didn't appear to sleep in pyjamas.

If he was going to Stowe all that would have to change. The following morning Tim took him to Harrods.

Ravi behaved in Knightsbridge's premier department store the way Columbus might have done when he discovered America. He kept wanting to touch everything. The moment they walked through the heavy doors of the main entrance, he kept picking things up from the display counters and turning them over in his hands. In the end Tim told him to contain his excitement.

'You're behaving like a suspicious character,' he told him. 'People will think you're trying to steal things.'

The boy listened to what his uncle told him. He was aware he stuck out like a sore thumb in this new world. The sooner he learnt the ropes, the easier it was going to be for him.

When they arrived at the boys' department on the third floor he stood to one side while his uncle explained to the salesman what was required. Then the man produced a tape measure, gauged his size and Ravi was shown into a cubicle. After that he had no idea what was expected of him. Quite suddenly he was presented with half a dozen pairs of trousers made of some soft grey material. Then there was a jacket like the one he had seen his father wearing, a pile of shirts that looked blindingly white and a handful of brightly coloured strips of fabric.

For a moment he stood where he was, fighting down the impulse to run out of this fearsome place. Then his uncle poked his head round the door and he started to feel better.

'Get a move on,' he urged. 'We haven't got all day.'

Ravi fought down frustration. 'What do you want me to do?'

'I should think that was perfectly obvious, old man. Get out of the rags you came in and start trying on some of this stuff.'

He did what he was told, and when he was fully dressed he marched out of the cubicle ready to be inspected. Tim did a double take. The clothes had transformed him. Half an hour previously he had walked into the store with an urchin. The boy standing in front of him was a product of the aristocracy. If he just stood there exactly as he was and never opened his mouth again he could be mistaken for a gentleman.

Over the next few weeks, Tim did everything he could to give Ravi a veneer of experience. He took him to a number of different restaurants, starting with Lyons Corner House and finishing up with his club. He made sure he saw all the usual London sights – Westminster Abbey, the Houses of Parliament, the National Gallery. It was during this tour that he learnt something about his nephew. The boy understood everything he was being shown. More than that, he actually had some idea of the history behind the sights.

'How on earth do you know all this?' Tim asked him.

Ravi looked cross. 'I went to school, you know,' he told Tim.

After that Tim treated him with more respect. The boy was foreign in many ways, but he was bright and curious and he learnt at the speed of light.

By the time the school term was due to start, Ravi had a working knowledge of how to handle himself in public. He walked with the crisp assurance of a gentleman now. He could even tie his own necktie. There was only one problem left: his name. If I let him go to school with a name like Ravi, Tim thought, he will immediately be cast as an outsider. He decided to broach the subject over supper one night.

They were dining at the Savoy Grill, the grand old establishment overlooking the Thames. Tim had been going there for years and the red plush interior, combined with the hushed impeccable service, had a calming effect on him.

The maître d'hôtel greeted him like an old friend and showed Tim to his usual table in the corner. As he did so, the banker cast a covert glance over to his nephew. He appeared to be doing well. He wasn't staring at the neighbouring party of American tourists who were oohing and ahing over the decor. He didn't even seem to notice that Laurence Olivier and his agent were sitting at the next table. Then he pulled himself up. The boy wouldn't know Laurence Olivier from a bar of soap.

He turned to Ravi: 'Why don't you order tonight? It's about time you got used to this sort of thing.'

The boy hesitated. 'I'd rather not, thank you.'

'Why, can't you cope with the menu?'

Now Ravi looked embarrassed. 'It's not that,' he said, 'it's just . . .' There was a silence while he searched for the words. Finally he said, 'Look, it would be different if they were Indians, but these are white men. Some of them are as old as the men who taught me in school. How can I ask them to wait on me?'

Tim sighed. 'These men aren't slaves, you know. They're

not being exploited. They're doing this job because they want to and because they're good at it.'

'It still doesn't give me the right to tell them what to do,' Ravi persisted.

The older man fought down the urge to box his nephew's ears. 'Listen,' he said, lowering his voice. 'You have the right to tell any man what to do, irrespective of his age or colour, just as long as you're paying him. When you grow up you'll be employing men. Some of them will be cleverer than you, but it won't stop you from directing their lives.' He stared at the boy intently now, willing him to understand.

'In this life there are two kinds of men: leaders, and those who follow after them. Your father's sending you to Stowe to learn to be a leader. Don't let him down.'

His nephew digested this new piece of information.

'So I am going to inherit,' he said slowly. 'I wondered why he'd sent me over here.'

Now Tim was on dangerous ground. Viewing the situation dispassionately, he knew there was no way his brother would take this half-caste in. He might equip him with an education, but he wasn't going to risk offending Christine by handing him the keys to the castle.

'Steady on, old boy,' he said. 'You might try asking your father about your future before you jump to conclusions. He might have other ideas.'

But nothing he could say could dampen Ravi's elation. He had a future now, a place in the world, and that gave him confidence.

He picked up the menu and signalled one of the waiters over. Then, as if he had been doing it all his life, he ordered for both of them. It was a faultless meal. Native oysters followed by pheasant with game chips. He even got the vegetables right: sprouts, braised endive and new potatoes.

Tim felt uneasy. The boy was going to do brilliantly. There was no doubt of that. He looked the part and now he was living it. But what happened when he left Stowe?

When Ravi realized his father didn't want him, he would be shattered.

Tim regarded the handsome young man sitting beside him. I won't let him be crushed, he thought. I'll find him something more interesting than running a sugar estate.

He decided to broach the subject of Ravi's name. Was it a family name, he wanted to know. Or did it have any religious significance?

Ravi shook his head. 'It's just a name,' he said. 'There's nothing special about it.'

Tim felt relieved. 'So you wouldn't mind if I suggested you changed it?'

The boy looked defensive. 'You think it makes me sound Indian?'

The older man brought the after dinner Armagnac to his lips, inhaling the perfume. 'Now you mention it, it does, but that's not the reason I want you to drop it. What concerns me most of all is that you fit in at school. Public schoolboys are a savage breed. They remind me a bit of a pack of animals. If you fit in, you make friends and you'll have a happy time there. But if there's something different about you, then you won't have any peace at all. The little monsters will hound you and make your life a misery. I know. I went through it myself.'

Ravi looked curious. 'What's different about you?' he asked.

Tim ignored the question. 'It's your future we're here to discuss,' he said crossly. 'How do you feel about taking an English name?'

The boy shrugged. In the past month or so he had acquired an English family, an English school, and a new English wardrobe. Another name wouldn't make a whole lot of difference.

'Do you have anything particular in mind?' he asked.

'I thought Richard would be appropriate.' The boy didn't react, so Tim explained his choice.

52

'Richard and Ravi aren't that far apart,' he told him. 'So it won't be difficult for you to get used to. Then there's my grandfather, he was called Richard. It's an old family name. Think of it as part of your heritage.'

He saw he had hit the right note, for his nephew was smiling now.

'Richard,' he said, trying it on for size. 'Richard Waites.' He closed his eyes and whispered the name under his breath as if imagining it in the mouth of some unseen friend. Richard ... Richard ... Richard ...

It sounded respectable. Better than respectable, it had a ring of authority. As Richard he could make a million or found an empire. As Richard he was inferior to no man on earth. He nodded his head, satisfied, then he looked at his uncle.

'I'd like to be known as Richard from now on,' he said. 'Do you think you could write and tell my father about it? You see, I don't want anyone calling me Ravi again. I've just grown out of Ravi.'

CHAPTER 6

Emerald's first client was a Eurasian woman whose husband owned a chain of supermarkets. She wasn't all that interested in fashion. When Emerald brought out her well-thumbed copy of French *Vogue*, Jenny Choo brushed it aside with the impatience of a woman used to getting her own way.

What she wanted, she told Emerald, were the same Chinese shifts she had been wearing for the past ten years but she wanted them in richer fabrics. Emerald was appalled. She didn't want to be told what to make. At Miss Blanche's the whole process of fashion was treated with a kind of mystique. Paris had reigned supreme in her hot-house establishment and the client patronized it because she valued the couturier's opinion. But Emerald wasn't a couturier any more. She was a dressmaker and dressmakers had to get used to their customers knowing best.

So Emerald swallowed her pride and put together the shifts as well as she knew how. To her surprise, a week or so later, two women friends of Jenny Choo rang up and wanted to make appointments.

Emerald began to build a reputation for her workmanship. She realized her years learning about French couture hadn't been wasted after all, and before she knew it, she found she was in demand.

It gave her confidence. She had been in business under two years and already she was a going concern. In time, she would branch out. Her bedroom in the rooming house was adequate for what she was doing, but once she expanded her operation she would need to take on assistants. When that happened she would need far more space.

She searched around town for suitable premises, and when she found what she was looking for, she came in for a short sharp shock. The rents, even on a small workroom at the back end of town, were prohibitive. If she could double her business, Emerald still couldn't come up with the right figure. She realized it was time she talked to Jeremy again.

In the time she had known him, their relationship hadn't altered. He continued to be formal and slightly patronizing with her whenever they met. Every time he took Emerald to bed, he made her feel like an apprentice being put through her paces.

Emerald didn't resent him for it. When they first got together they had made a kind of contract with each other. He would provide for all her creature comforts – the rent was taken care of, she was allowed to visit the hairdresser and the manicurist once a week, and he fed her.

In return, Emerald would be available to him whenever he wanted to visit. As that never amounted to more than once every four or five days, she'd be quite happy. Yet a small doubt nagged away at the back of her mind. She had not chosen to live like this. She had been forced into it. Somehow, because of that, it never felt right to her. The only way she was able to cope with it at all was to persuade herself that what she was doing was temporary. When she got on her feet and was making a living as a dressmaker, she would call a halt to the relationship.

Emerald didn't confess any of this, of course. There was no way she could go to Jeremy for a loan and expect to get it if he suspected that she was planning to leave him. So she hid her true feelings and set out to charm him.

She brought up the subject of her business over dinner in the Lai Min. The Chinese restaurant was a favourite with

55

Jeremy because it was virtually next door to the casino. L'Amicale, the gambling joint, handed out complimentary chips to the diners, and when Emerald started talking about the loan she wanted, Jeremy automatically pushed a pile of plastic in her direction.

She felt annoyed. It was clear to her that he hadn't been listening to a word she was saying.

'I don't want money to gamble with,' she told him crossly. 'I'm asking you for a loan so I can do better as a dressmaker.'

Jeremy looked up. He was vaguely aware that his mistress had her hands full at work, but more than that hadn't interested him. She was a convenient and beautiful woman who made no demands. As long as things went on that way he wasn't bothered what she did in her own time. Now she was making a fuss about it.

'I've got enough clients to support a bigger workroom,' she was telling him with an intent look on her face. 'The only real problem I have left is finding the money to put down on the rent. I need a lump sum and it's more than I can save up on my own.'

Alarm bells rang in Jeremy's head. Emerald had never talked like this before and it boded ill, for it meant that her business was growing out of proportion.

'I didn't know you were interested in a big-time career,' he said mildly. 'Aren't you happy as you are?'

Emerald wondered what to tell him. If she said she liked being his mistress, she knew she would get nowhere. Jeremy would just jog along visiting her now and then and she would grow old with nothing to show for her life.

So she took a chance and levelled with him. 'I work very hard as a dressmaker,' she said, 'but it doesn't pay me anything. To make any kind of a living I need to hire assistants. I can't do that without moving.'

Now Jeremy knew he was in trouble. This little girl of his wasn't interested in just making a living. What she wanted was success and independence. He shuddered at the prospect.

'You have no idea of what you're talking about,' he said patronizingly. 'You're an inexperienced girl who runs up a few dresses for your friends. There's a big difference between that and running a business.'

Emerald was furious. 'I've been in the rag trade for years now,' she told him, spitting. 'With the right backing I could run a workroom standing on my head – and turn in a profit.'

Only when the words were out of her mouth did she realize she had shown her hand. Then she saw Jeremy's face.

'When you make all this money,' he said quietly, 'don't you think it's going to change things?'

Emerald's eyes narrowed, making her look like a cornered cat. 'How could it change anything?' she asked softly. But she wasn't fooling anybody. She wasn't even convincing herself, and Jeremy latched on to her mood.

'I'll tell you how it will be,' he said. 'The minute you make enough money to support yourself, I'll be dead meat. You won't need me any more and when that happens you'll walk away.'

There was a silence while he stared across at Emerald, daring her to contradict him. She said nothing. In a minute, she thought, the waiter will come with the drinks I ordered. When that happens I'll change the subject.

But Jeremy wasn't letting the subject alone. 'Don't think I don't know how you feel about me,' he said, 'because I do. In your mind, I'm a soft touch who takes care of you and because you're a clever little girl you make a great show of pretending to care about me. Except I know you don't really give a damn. You open your legs once a week as a duty and you hate every second of it because it's not something you do of your own free will.'

Emerald felt a complete fool. All this time she imagined

57

she was handling the affair admirably and now this man had shown her he had been on to her all along.

'Now you know how things are,' she said cautiously, 'I suppose you'll want an end to it.'

Jeremy looked at her. 'Why would I want to do that?' he said. 'Your attitude doesn't make any difference to me. I don't need to be loved in order to enjoy you.'

Suddenly, the whole sordid thing came home to Emerald. In this man's eyes, she wasn't a human being at all. She was simply a receptacle he used to pleasure himself. She could have been a blow-up doll for all she mattered to him. And she knew now that she would have to leave him.

Emerald's feelings must have shown on her face, for all at once Jeremy was repentant.

'I went too far,' he said apologetically. 'I didn't mean to hurt you.'

But the damage was done. Emerald sat numbly while the drinks arrived and thought about the rest of the evening. They would go on to the casino, and then she would sleep with Jeremy. She would have to open herself to him and the idea of it filled her with dread. He made it worse by attempting to take her hand.

'Don't look so stricken,' he said gently. 'Every couple falls out from time to time, and we all say things we don't mean.'

The words went right over Emerald's head. He could have told her he was giving her the money for a bigger workroom and she wouldn't have even noticed.

Emerald liked Jeremy a little less after that evening. She wasn't furious with him any longer. She couldn't afford the luxury of temper, but she felt colder towards him and it showed.

At first he tried to placate her. I've ruffled her feathers, he thought, and all she needs is a little extra fuss. The next time he went to see her he brought with him a bottle of fine French brandy from his cellar.

Emerald smiled politely and tucked it into the mahogany dresser that stood in the salon of her rooming house. It was only afterwards he realized that Emerald didn't touch brandy.

Two weeks later he came up with a better idea. He brought her a length of silk from Paris. He had gone to considerable trouble to track it down for it wasn't just any old silk. The fabric he brought her had been dyed by a new process and was slightly iridescent. Its main distinction was that it was emerald green. Exactly the colour of her eyes.

Emerald was flattered, but not entranced. He's treating me like a child, she thought. That night, when they made love, Emerald didn't get aroused. Jeremy tried everything he knew, all the skills and tricks he'd acquired in nearly forty years of living. Yet Emerald just lay in his arms looking lost and slightly hopeless. He finally lost patience.

I'll pay her a little less attention, he thought. Once she thinks I'm cooling off, she'll get frightened and come running.

Emerald didn't. She hardly noticed Jeremy's absence for she had other things on her mind. In the intervening weeks since their discussion she had started to formulate a plan. She had decided to come up with the rent money she needed on her own. She knew the only way she could possibly do that was to increase her business, but she had to change it slightly.

High-class dressmaking was too time-consuming for her now. What she needed were bulk orders: curtains, children's clothes, hospital uniforms. All the things she had been too proud to contemplate in the beginning suddenly made economic sense. As she set her sights on this new goal, her life changed. In the days when she didn't have to worry about money, she would spend all afternoon in the beauty parlour. Now she no longer had time for that. All her hours were taken up with cutting patterns and operating her sewing machine.

Jeremy, observing this new activity, started to wonder about her. She's up to something, he thought. For the life of him he couldn't imagine what it was. He knew how much she made as a dressmaker and it was peanuts. Even if she worked round the clock, Emerald still couldn't earn more than it cost him to pay her hairdresser.

Maybe she's losing her mind, he thought. She won't be the first native girl to have done that. He started to feel gloomy. I shouldn't have taken her out of her environment, he berated himself.

Yet Jeremy didn't know quite how well Emerald was doing. She had hit upon a plan that effectively trebled her turnover, and it was based entirely on salesmanship. Emerald discovered she could bring in no end of orders if she kept her prices low and delivered fast. She had a mountain of work and no time to do it in. She solved this problem by subcontracting. Every day she would take a pile of sewing round to the local seamstresses who were only too pleased with the extra business. She charged them all a hefty commission and at the end of the day she was making money for little effort on her part.

She still wasn't making enough money, though. Then one day she was approached by a manager of a new hotel opening on the west coast. He needed uniforms for all his senior staff and had heard her prices were low.

It was the kind of order Emerald had been looking for. If she could make the top brass at Le Caprice look good, then she could set her sights on the rest of the hotel's employees: the waiters, chambermaids, kitchen staff – even the pool boys. Her head began to spin just thinking about it. By the time she had finished with Le Caprice, she would have more than enough to put down on a workroom.

CHAPTER 7

Larry Simpson watched the sun set from the comfort of the pool bar of Le Caprice. The film crew and the other actors would still be down on the beach, covered in sun lotion. The thought of the white powdery sand shimmering in the afternoon heat made Larry feel uncomfortable.

I'm too old to play at fun-in-the-sun, he thought. That was okay when I was touring in variety. A brief memory of Brighton Pier and the dank smell of the sea around England's south coast invaded his senses. I didn't like the beach then, he decided. I'm certainly not going to go a bundle on it now.

Larry was feeling sorry for himself that day. It wasn't anything anyone had said. He had walked through all his takes effortlessly, turning on the clown's charm that had made him famous in Hollywood. The trouble with all of them, he mused, is that they don't really understand what I go through to make them laugh. They think all I have to do is put on a funny voice and fall on my arse a couple of times and I've got it made. He sighed, remembering the years of grimy dressing-rooms and provincial audiences. The trouble with the film business is they're all a bunch of johnny-come-latelies who came up doing clever commercials. Not one of them, the producer, the lighting camera-man, and certainly not the director, had the foggiest idea of what he was trying to achieve. He took a large gulp of the rum concoction the barman had made for him. Sometimes, he thought, I wonder why I bother.

He noticed the bar was filling. Holiday couples in their

best boutique leisure wear were gathering round the little tables for a first drink before dinner. They were a mixed bunch. A lot of French from the prosperous towns in the north, a sprinkling of rich Chinese and one or two English families, whom he reckoned were probably locals. They all stared at him before they sat down, wondering among themselves which film they'd last seen him in.

God, how I hate them, Larry thought. They make me feel like a public monument. If there'd been a halfway decent house for hire on this godforsaken island, I would have taken it. But it was no dice. His producer, Archie, had told him that all the good houses were owned by European families who lived in them. Visitors had to make do with one of the big hotels, even if they were amazingly luxurious.

Larry's attention was momentarily distracted by a girl he hadn't seen before. She was tall and full-bosomed with the honey-coloured skin of an islander. That wasn't what drew his eye, though. What mesmerized him was her face. There was something about it that reminded him of a cat. It's her eyes, he thought. You don't find that colour in Indian girls. The eyes and the high cheekbones. If I was David Bailey or Terry Donovan, I'd sign her up for the cover of *Vogue* right now. Whoever she is, she's a natural.

Larry toyed with the thought of going across to the bar and introducing himself. Then he rejected the idea. He'd only get his fingers burnt. The last time he picked up a beautiful girl it cost him a million dollars. His wife had divorced him for a fortune and after nine months Larry realized he'd got the worst end of the bargain. For the beautiful girl hadn't loved him at all. All she wanted from him was the chance to be a big-time movie actress. And the chance to live like a lady.

Well, she hadn't made it as an actress. Despite her baby-blonde looks, she was wooden in front of the camera. Her first two films lost money and after that there were no more parts, except for the role she was good at – Larry Simpson's armpiece. That didn't last either. Her failure had somehow made her unattractive.

After her, there had been a parade of women on Larry's arm. All actresses, or aspiring actresses, and all making him uneasy.

He was jerked out of his memories by the sound of raised voices up at the bar. The girl he had spotted earlier seemed to be in some kind of trouble. At first he thought they were arguing over the price of the drink, but when he listened harder, he realized that wasn't the case. The barman wanted her to leave.

'I only serve white customers,' he told her. 'You're in the wrong place.'

The girl looked shaken, as if somebody had slapped her round the face.

'But I've come here to do some work for the manager,' she protested. 'I'm a businesswoman.'

The bartender went to a certain amount of trouble to describe what kind of business he thought she was in. Then before she could complain further, he dispatched one of his assistants to call the security guards.

Larry decided he couldn't let it go on. He got to his feet and walked over to the bar.

Close to, the woman's eyes were even more extraordinary than he'd first thought.

'Darling,' he said, taking her by the arm, 'I can't leave you alone for five minutes without you getting into an argument.'

The woman looked startled. 'I don't think I know you,' she said nervously.

Larry leant towards her, reducing his voice to a stage whisper. 'Of course you don't know me, but if you want to get out of this situation, you might pretend you do.'

She smiled then, producing large dimples in both cheeks.

63

'I was trying to be independent,' she said, speaking up, 'but obviously I did the wrong thing. I'd have been safer having a drink with you.'

At precisely that moment, two large armed guards arrived on the scene.

Before either of them could move in, Larry had his arm protectively around the Indian girl.

'What seems to be the problem?' he enquired.

The bigger of the guards regarded the actor with a certain contempt.

'The bar here is for hotel guests only.' He indicated Emerald who was clinging to Larry for dear life. 'The girl here isn't a guest.'

All conversation around the poolside bar started to die away. Larry Simpson was having some kind of trouble with the management, and there was a girl involved. The holidaymakers were all ears. This was going to be something to tell the folks back home. The screen idol didn't disappoint them.

'The young lady is with me,' he announced in a ringing theatrical baritone. 'In my book that makes her a guest.'

Both guards and the bartender went into a huddle. Natives were not allowed to mingle with the tourists. It was strict company policy.

In the end the hotel manager arrived. He recognized Emerald the minute he saw her. It was the girl he'd seen about the new uniforms. He walked over to the angry little group.

'Would somebody like to tell me what's going on?' he demanded.

The minute the words were out of his mouth, he caught sight of Larry Simpson. He groaned inwardly. God, he thought, please don't let this be happening to me.

Everyone started to speak at once, until Larry took a step towards the manager.

'There seems to have been a little misunderstanding with

your barman,' he said quietly. 'I caught him trying to throw a friend of mine out of here.'

The manager put on his best professional smile. 'Please accept my apologies,' he said smoothly. 'I had no idea that you and Emerald knew each other.'

He waved the guards away, indicated that the barman should return to his position behind the counter, then led Emerald and the actor to a quiet table away from the bar.

'I do the best I can with the staff,' he said by way of explanation, 'but I don't always get through to them. Let me make it up to you with a bottle of champagne. Compliments of the house, of course.'

Emerald rose to her feet. 'I think I should be on my way,' she said. 'There's been enough trouble here already.'

The manager was about to agree with her when he saw Larry's face.

'The trouble was the hotel's fault,' he said firmly. 'I'd take it as an honour if you'd join me for a drink.'

Larry Simpson's smile told him he'd made the right move.

CHAPTER 8

Le Caprice had been set up as an exclusive retreat for the rich. A team of interior decorators had worked for months to create just the right illusion of opulence and they had succeeded beyond the management's wildest dreams.

Everywhere you looked in the great entrance hall there were intimate little nooks and salons filled with swaying papyrus plants. There was an arcade of boutiques selling everything from postcards to diamond necklaces. And once through the entrance hall, guests had their choice of two restaurants and a bar, all of them standing beside a giant azure swimming pool.

Nothing was too much for the staff of Le Caprice. If you wanted to eat in the bar, dozens of willing hands would put together a salade niçoise, a steak sandwich, a plate of crudités worthy of a top Paris brasserie.

If your taste ran to oriental food, one of the restaurants did nothing but. Round the pool they served classic French *haute cuisine*, and if you were in the mood for fish there was an out-of-the-way little place a short walk around the beach that provided everything from oysters, to lobster, to fresh caviar.

Larry Simpson did not care for fish, but he felt an overwhelming need for privacy. He wanted to be alone with this enchantress, this damsel in distress. So when the champagne was all but finished, he suggested a light seafood supper.

Emerald hesitated before accepting. She realized she had put her foot in it by visiting the pool bar. Now she was being invited to dine in one of the hotel's fancy restaurants and she started to worry.

'If I went with you I could be in deep trouble,' she told him after the manager had left them. 'You can see the manager doesn't like natives mixing with the guests.'

So that was what all the fuss was about, Larry thought. We're allowed to admire the island from a distance, but we're not encouraged to fraternize with the locals. He was about to say something when his attention was diverted by a bright yellow tropical bird, busy demolishing a plate of cocktail biscuits. It was very beautiful and knew it, but also knew it shouldn't steal food from the tables so it kept looking around nervously. One sharp movement would be all it took to send the bird flying into the wide blue yonder. All at once Larry saw that the yellow bird and the Indian girl shared a common ground. They were natives of this island. They belonged here, yet nobody was interested in having them around for very long.

Larry felt a surge of loathing for the people who ran places like this. It seemed to him that if they had their way they would turn Mauritius into a suburb of Florida. Tidy and sanitized and boring as hell.

He turned to the girl sitting with him. 'I don't give a stuff what the manager feels about the colour of your skin,' he told her. 'It's nothing to do with him anyway. I'm the paying customer here. If I want you to have dinner in one of the restaurants with me, then he'll risk his livelihood if he objects.'

Emerald realized he was telling the truth. There was nothing anyone could do if this man wanted to take her to the 'Paul et Virginie' for lobster claws.

In her heart she knew she should still turn him down. She looked across at the actor, a refusal forming on her lips. Then she saw the admiration in his eyes. He really wanted her with him tonight and for the life of her she couldn't refuse him.

'If you don't care about the manager,' she told him, 'then I don't either.'

The 'Paul et Virginie' at Le Caprice was built with lovers in mind. It was hidden away in its own private lagoon behind the hotel, yet it was simple. The decorators had dispensed with the formal trappings of a dining-room and created instead a rustic setting of wooden tables and fairy lights under the stars.

It was just what Larry needed that night. Except for one thing: the entire film crew had decided to have dinner there.

For a moment he thought of turning tail and heading back to the hotel, but he was too late. The director spotted him walking into the bar and came hurrying over.

'Larry, my old love,' he said, 'a thousand welcomes. The lads *will* be pleased to see you.'

The screen actor went into a sulk. He'd wanted this evening to be enjoyable and now he was being sabotaged by a crowd of beer-stained oafs. The worst thing about it was there was nothing he could do. He had to work with these men at first light tomorrow morning.

With a certain amount of effort, he went into his charming actor-on-location routine. He introduced Emerald to everyone as 'a dear old friend I happened to run into over here.'

When one of the grips pressed him for details of the friendship, Emerald went cold. He's going to have to admit he picked me up in the bar an hour ago, she thought. She needn't have worried. Larry was in full theatrical flow that night.

'Emerald and I go back a long way,' he told the technician, who cast her an enquiring look. 'We met at a house party in Gstaad, darling, didn't we? I think it was Gunter's chalet. In fact I'm almost sure it was. And you were with some oilman from Texas.'

Emerald sighed at the prospect of play-acting, then

68

thought, what the hell, I'm only here for one night. I might as well go along with him.

'It was a lovely party,' she said, sipping her Perrier water. 'I remember it was so hot we all wanted to strip off and lie in the sun.'

A look of alarm spread across Larry's face. 'It wasn't that hot,' he said. 'There was still snow on the mountains. Remember, darling, we were all skiing that year.'

For a moment Emerald floundered. Then she asserted herself with more confidence than she felt.

'Of course I remember. But you really can't expect me to get all the details right,' she went on. 'Gstaad was three years ago and I have problems remembering yesterday.'

Larry shot her a look of pure admiration. This girl was a player. He'd known it from the first moment he'd run into her. She had a lot to learn of course. Her clothes were all wrong and the accent could do with work but she had all the other things that mattered. In the right hands, he thought, she could be really something.

They stayed in the restaurant by the lagoon until nearly midnight. Then Emerald looked at her watch.

'I have to get home,' she said, 'and I've missed the last bus.'

Larry considered asking her to stay with him in the penthouse. Then he thought, why push it? I've got another three or four weeks here. There's time enough for a serious seduction.

'I'll send you back in a taxi,' he told her. 'The film company will take care of the fare, so you don't have to worry.'

Emerald looked at the dark, intense man sitting beside her and wondered why he was letting her go so easily. He had been flirting with her all evening and now he couldn't wait to get rid of her.

She shrugged and got up out of her seat. The man obviously didn't live in the real world. She'd seen that already.

She walked slowly through the white marble hall of the

hotel, wondering if she would ever come there again. By now the manager would know she had stayed in all evening. He was probably already cancelling the order he had given her earlier.

She looked through the gateway that led to the outside world and saw her taxi draw up. Then she turned to Larry Simpson.

'There's one last thing I want to know,' she said. 'Where exactly is Gstaad?'

The actor smiled with genuine amusement. 'It's a village in the mountains of Switzerland. If you look at a map, you'll see it's just outside Geneva.'

He paused, considering what to say next. Finally he looked at her.

'Play your cards right, Emerald,' he said, 'and I'll take you there one day.'

CHAPTER 9

Larry rang Emerald the following day and asked if she was free for dinner. She was surprised to hear from him.

'How did you get my number?' she demanded. She heard him chuckle.

'The taxi driver,' he told her. 'He had strict instructions to find out where you lived and report back to me.'

Emerald felt flattered. The man was falling over backwards to pursue her.

'I'd love to have dinner with you,' she said, 'but would you mind if we didn't meet in your hotel?'

There was a silence. Then Larry said, 'You're not still worried about the manager, are you?'

Emerald started to feel sad. 'If you live here,' she said, 'you don't buck the system.'

Larry took her point. 'No problem,' he assured her. 'We'll go to a little French place I found in Curepipe.'

Emerald hesitated. 'That won't do either.'

The actor felt the beginnings of exasperation. 'You're not going to tell me every goddam place in the island closes its doors to locals?'

Emerald tried to make light of it. 'Of course they don't. It's the expensive restaurants that are the problem, the ones that cater for Europeans.'

She heard the actor sigh and she wished she hadn't started this.

'You're talking about the only places I'm interested in. I don't want to be stuck in some back-street dive.'

Now she knew she had lost.

'Then I'm sorry,' Emerald said, 'but we won't be having dinner tonight.'

'That's what you think,' he countered.

He came to collect her that evening in a chauffeur-driven limousine with dark-tinted windows. The minute Emerald saw him she knew they were going somewhere smart for Larry was dressed in a navy lightweight suit, a lawn shirt and an Italian silk tie. He smelt of lemony aftershave and it made him seem more sophisticated than he had been the night before.

'Where are you taking me?' Emerald asked, looking worried.

Larry patted her hand.

'Somewhere worthy of both of us,' he told her.

He's back in his dream world again, Emerald thought. Tonight he's the handsome prince and I'm Cinderella. But Cinderella won't go to the ball, because Cinderella won't be allowed through the door.

The limousine drew into the Grande Baie area on the north coast where all the rich families had their summer houses. There were one or two elegant restaurants all located on or near the beach, and the grandest of them all was La Plàge where the chef would cook the entire meal from scratch for each individual party. With a sinking heart Emerald realized La Plage was exactly where they were heading.

'We'll never get away with it,' she said under her breath. 'The other customers simply wouldn't stand for it.'

Larry Simpson turned to her and for the first time since she had met him, he looked patronizing.

'Don't underestimate me,' he said in a low, dangerous voice.

She was silent after that. Now I've got two enemies, she thought. The restaurant and my escort. It's going to be a difficult evening.

What happened next took her breath away. As the car drew up outside the restaurant the maître d'hôtel, in a morning coat and silver tie, was waiting for them outside. The moment Emerald stepped on to the kerb he was by her side.

'Good evening, madame . . . Mr Simpson,' he said. 'Let me escort you through to your table.'

Emerald was flabbergasted. The man in front of her had spent his entire life telling people like her to beat it. She had heard stories of him setting trained dogs on the poor unfortunates who happened to wander along the beach in front of La Plage.

She linked her arm through Larry's as they followed the maître into the gilded, elegant bar.

'Thank you,' she whispered in Larry's ear.

After that Larry made it a point to take her to every top restaurant on the island. They went to Mon Moulin in Port Louis where all the top businessmen in Mauritius ate. In Curepipe they had dinner in La Potinerie, which admitted only the grandest of the French families. They went gambling in the casino at the Trouée aux Biches hotel.

He even took her back to Le Caprice, though she protested when he did.

'I can't afford to be seen here,' she told him. 'The manager will cancel the work he gave me.'

But he didn't. Whenever she appeared with Larry he fell over backwards to be pleasant to her. And in the end she realized the actor must have had a word in his ear.

In the normal way of things Emerald might have fretted about what would happen after Larry left. It had been on her mind from the moment she met him, but these days she was distracted. Being with Larry had altered her vision in some subtle way, for he never ceased to tell her how lucky he was to have her on his arm.

'You're so beautiful,' he'd say. 'An old man like me doesn't deserve this kind of luck.'

73

The silly thing was Emerald found herself believing him. The combined effect of fawning restaurant owners and Larry's admiration gave her a sense of worth. As her confidence grew, she started to get careless.

She neglected her dressmaking business, abandoning her sewing machine in order to keep the actor company when he was filming. She started avoiding Jeremy. On the rare occasions when he came round to see her, she was never there.

If the planter had bothered to make enquiries about her, he might have discovered Emerald tucked up in Larry's hotel suite, for they had become lovers a week after they met.

In part, this new state of affairs explained Emerald's lack of caution. She truly believed what was happening between her and Larry was the real thing. She based this assumption on her last two years with Jeremy. Going to bed with him and going to bed with Larry were two different activities.

For a start, Larry tried to please her. Before he made love to her he would spend hours caressing her skin, standing her in front of the mirror by his bed so she could see exactly what he was doing to her. In the beginning she had been frightened to look for she wasn't familiar with her own body. Yet Larry wasn't interested in her modesty. He wanted her to enjoy what was happening and one by one he stripped her inhibitions away. After just a few days she was dressing up in the expensive underwear he bought her. Larry had a thing about basques and suspender belts and he liked to make love to her while she was wearing them. She indulged his eccentricity because by now she was seriously infatuated with him.

Then one day it all came to an end. It should have happened sooner, of course. She had known all along she couldn't waltz all over the island eating palm hearts and drinking champagne without some kind of retribution, and fate finally caught up with her on the night Larry took her to the state casino.

She had wanted to go for a long time for it was well known the Casino de Meurice was the smartest gambling joint on the island.

Larry was less impressed with its reputation than Emerald was, for he found it distinctly seedy. Legend had it the casino was originally a bridge club and it still had a slightly amateur air about it. Whoever had rigged up the tables had little faith in the punters' experience since every game was explained by a series of garish signs stuck up all over the club.

Even the bar didn't look as if it meant business, for it was situated right next door to the tables.

Larry found himself longing for the civilized comfort of the South of France. He reached over the table where they were playing blackjack and started to gather up Emerald's chips.

'Come on,' he said. 'I'll buy you a nightcap at the bar, then we'll go back to the hotel. There's an early call tomorrow, so I need to get my head down.'

Emerald looked at the lean intense lines of the actor's face and felt the beginnings of desire. He was telling lies about needing his sleep, but she let him get away with it. She knew what he needed – what they both needed – and it made her feel smug.

Over the last few weeks she had become an expert on the actor's requirements, both in and out of bed. He had taken to confiding in her and Emerald knew what made him insecure and what got on his nerves. She knew what made him happy and what made him sad. This knowledge gave her a special power over him.

No man had ever allowed her to get so close and she started to feel sorry there had been anyone before him. I wish I'd never laid eyes on Jeremy, she thought. Without him in my life everything might have been different.

It was an idle thought. The sort of regret that passes through the mind of every woman who has newly fallen in love. The last thing she expected was to come face to face with the subject of her musings.

Yet there he was. Sitting right up in front of her at the bar drinking cognac and smoking Havana cigars. Jeremy, she thought, what the hell are you doing here?

He was with two elderly gentlemen and Emerald imagined he was talking business. For a moment she felt relief. He hadn't seen her yet. If she moved fast, he wouldn't see her at all.

She leaned towards Larry and whispered she wanted to go but it was too late. In the brief moment when she was close enough to Larry to look intimate, Jeremy had glanced up and caught them.

Emerald felt the impulse to run, to put her head down and get the hell out of the place as fast as she could. But Jeremy didn't give her the chance.

Before she could move, he was on his feet and coming towards her.

'I didn't know you had such famous friends,' he said pleasantly. Too pleasantly. 'Will you introduce me?'

Emerald felt hot all over, and she was aware there were beads of sweat on her upper lip. Larry looked at her with concern.

'Is something the matter?' he asked. 'You look terrified.'

'She is terrified,' Jeremy observed. 'She didn't expect to see me tonight.'

Larry's first thought was that this new girl of his owed money. He'd known a few women who had trouble managing their businesses, and this was a funny island. If she had problems getting into restaurants, who knows what difficulties she might have getting a line of credit?

'If you have a gripe against the lady,' he told the Englishman, 'why don't you just spit it out. Then maybe I can do something about it.'

Jeremy was furious. He hadn't expected the actor to protect Emerald and anyway, this was none of his business.

'Stay out of this,' he said tersely. 'It will be easier for her if you do.'

Now Larry was thoroughly intrigued. The man accosting them was one of the ex-pat types he'd seen around the more expensive bars. He was wearing a wedding ring and he looked loaded.

Larry thought of lapsing into character. He'd played a private detective two pictures ago who would be perfect for a scene like this. Then he thought, no. Unless he had a good idea of where the script was going he could end up with egg on his face. So he stayed with what he had.

'I'll be the judge of whether or not to get involved,' he said.

There was a silence while the two men weighed one another up. Finally it was Jeremy who spoke.

'I have a feeling there's something you don't know,' he said. He took a look at Emerald who was rooted to the spot.

'This little tart,' he went on without pausing for breath, 'has been spreading her favours further than she had a right to.'

Larry didn't miss a beat. 'Who says so?' he asked softly.

'I say so,' Jeremy replied. 'I've been keeping a roof over her head for the past two years now.'

Larry put an arm around Emerald and drew her towards him.

'Is it true?' he asked.

She nodded and he noticed her face was set and frozen. Another girl in her situation would have sobbed her eyes out, but Emerald looked humble, as if she had been kicked. He'd seen that look before and he wondered where. Then he had it. He'd been going around one of the old Apache settlements in California. It was an historic site and had been preserved intact for the tourist trade. They'd even preserved the natives whom they'd dressed up in ceremonial feathers and rawhide. They weren't really men any

77

more, for all their dignity had been taken away from them. As he looked at Emerald, he saw their faces superimposed on hers.

Why do we do it, he thought. What makes us think we're so goddam superior that we can kick the shit out of people who can't defend themselves?

He felt ashamed, both for himself and for the man standing in front of him.

'Stop it,' he said quietly. 'Can't you see you've frightened her enough?'

Jeremy's voice sounded shrill. 'Why shouldn't I give her a scare? It will do her good to get in touch with reality for once.'

The actor took a step backwards. All he needed right now was for this lover of Emerald's to start getting punchy.

'I'm not impressed with this reality you're talking about,' he said. 'It sounds to me as if you keep this girl – probably for a small fee – and expect her full attention for the pleasure of it.'

'What's wrong with that?' Jeremy demanded. 'I can't see you setting her up with a home of her own.'

Larry sighed heavily. I should give her back, he thought. This stuffed shirt obviously has a thing going with Emerald.

But he couldn't do it. He liked the girl too much to hand her over like a package. So he squared up to the hysterical man standing in front of him.

'Don't tempt me,' he said. 'I could find the idea attractive.'

As the words were out of his mouth he realized he was lumbered. In a moment of anger he had stepped in and taken responsibility for this girl and now there was no getting out of it.

If Jeremy walked away now, he'd have Emerald trailing around after him. She'd be there on every location. When he went to bed her face would be on the pillow. He wouldn't even be able to take a shower in privacy.

78

He started to smile. What's wrong with that, he thought. I like having her with me.

Jeremy interpreted his smile as a sign of assent. 'I think I'd better warn you,' he said, 'this girl comes with a dress-making business attached. Whenever you want to see her, she'll be hunched over her sewing machine.'

It was an asinine thing to say and both men knew it, but it helped to concentrate Larry's mind.

He moved closer to Emerald, putting his hand under her elbow. Then he gently pushed her in the direction of the door.

'I wouldn't worry about the sewing machine,' he shouted back over his shoulder. 'Where Emerald's going she's not going to need one.'

CHAPTER 10

London, 1965

Richard shifted uncomfortably in the tiny gilt chair and wondered if he'd got the time right. His father had told him he would meet him in the Palm Court of the Ritz at 7.30. Now it was nearly eight and there was no sign of him.

He considered making a patrol of the hotel reception and the two bars in the basement, but he'd done that twice already.

He looked at the glass of beer in front of him and realized he hadn't touched it. He laughed at himself. Most of the other boys I know would have been on to their third by now. It isn't every day a man comes into his inheritance.

Jeremy had written to him at the end of his last term at school. It had been a short letter, but it contained all the information he needed. His father was coming to Paris to tie up some business and on the way back to Mauritius he was stopping over in London especially to see him.

It's time we sat down and talked about what you'll be doing after Stowe, he had written. *I know you've been accepted for a place at Oxford, but I have other things in mind for you.*

He had suggested dinner at the Ritz. When Richard arrived he even found a reservation in his father's name.

He wondered if he'd missed his flight and was still in Paris. In a moment of doubt, he wondered if his father had decided to disown him. The fact that his father might reject him was Richard's worst fear. Nothing much else frightened him. He was invincible on the rugger field and could hold his own in every subject on the curriculum. But the thought of Jeremy abandoning him kept him awake at night.

With an effort he pulled himself together, and was jolted out of his gloom by somebody clapping him on the shoulder. He looked up from his beer to see his father standing in front of him.

'Sorry I'm late,' he said, 'but the traffic was terrible on the way in from the airport. When we got to Kensington I nearly got out of the taxi and walked.'

Jeremy seemed to have changed since Richard had last seen him. It wasn't anything obvious. He hadn't lost his hair or put on weight, but he seemed less substantial than he remembered. Less of a god.

All the panic of the last half-hour faded into insignificance. This mild-mannered middle-aged man wasn't here to give him bad news. If he had he might have made an attempt to appear hostile and the reverse was true.

Jeremy couldn't seem to do enough to make Richard comfortable. He waved away the beer, which was looking rather flat, and ordered them both whisky sours. Then he demanded to know everything about his old school. And he was eager for every detail Richard could supply on the First Fifteen rugby team.

They must have talked about school for nearly an hour, for when they looked up, most of the tables round the marble fountain were empty.

Jeremy looked at his Rolex. 'You must be starving,' he said. 'It's nearly nine.' Without waiting for an answer, he signalled a waiter and told him to put the drinks on his bill. Then he rose and led his son down the steps to the dining-room.

Richard was unprepared for the grandeur of the salon overlooking Green Park.

81

His school had been imposing in a cold, classical kind of way. This room was ornate. All the treasures the hotel possessed seemed to have crowded into one space. Giant glittering chandeliers descended from a vaulted ceiling. Antique brocade curtains looped and draped around the floor-to-ceiling windows. Everywhere he walked, his feet seemed to be sinking into acres of red plush. The whole place reminded him of a giant jewel box and he resented it, for it imposed its formality on his father. When they had been sitting together in the Palm Court they had been relaxed and easy with each other. Now a starched white tablecloth separated them and distanced them from each other.

The menu, which Richard had skimmed in minutes, laid claim to Jeremy's whole attention. It put Richard slightly off balance.

His father had brought him here to talk about the future. He was going to tell him why he wasn't sending him to Oxford and what he could expect when he took him back to Mauritius, yet he didn't seem bothered about any of it. All that mattered to him was the temperature of the wine. Richard began to wonder what the hell was going on.

As subtly as he could, he steered the conversation towards his education. He talked about all the other boys in his year who were going up to university. Then he revealed his own disappointment at not being able to take his place at Oxford. He sensed he was treading on danger-ous ground, for his father looked first uncomfortable, then bad-tempered.

'I would have thought Stowe was enough for you,' he said. 'It's given you all the gloss you'll ever need to get on in the world.'

Richard took a sip of his wine, then he faced his father.

'What world are you talking about?' he asked. 'Mauritius or over here in England?'

For the umpteenth time that night, Jeremy wondered what he was going to say to his son.

If he had been a bad scholar, he thought, it might have been easier. If he hadn't been such a damn credit to him, he could have fobbed him off with a million different excuses. But the boy was top of his year, and a leader to boot. How could he even begin to accept that there was no place for him on the plantation?

He forced himself to be tough. He'd played his son along with half-truths ever since he sent him away to England. Now the time had come for reckoning.

'I'm not taking you back with me to Mauritius,' he said as gently as he could. 'I never intended to.'

Richard took it on the chin. His worst fears were all coming true, but he still wanted the whole thing spelt out.

'Because you're ashamed of me?' he asked.

Jeremy sighed. 'No, I'm not ashamed of you,' he said. 'If anything I'm ashamed of myself, but that's another story.'

But the boy wasn't going to be deflected. 'You're kicking me out, Father,' he said. 'You're not sending me to Oxford and there's no place for me in the family firm. Don't you think I have a right to know why?'

Jeremy looked at his son with a certain admiration. The expensive school had certainly left its mark, yet he wondered whether he dared level with him.

'A lot of the problem is to do with my wife, Christine,' he ventured, testing the water. 'You see, she doesn't know you exist.'

There was a brief silence while Richard digested the information. Then he looked mystified.

'I can understand your keeping me a secret when you first found me,' he said. 'But when you decided to send me to England and turn me into a gentleman I thought you'd changed your mind.'

Jeremy felt a fierce rush of love for the young man sitting in front of him. He hadn't asked to be born. He hadn't

83

asked to be sent to Stowe either, and he realized he was in too deep to abandon him now.

'If you're going to understand about my wife,' he said, 'I think I have to tell you why I came to marry her in the first place.'

He signalled the waiter to clear away the plates and bring the next course. Then he refilled his glass for the third time. If he was going to be as candid as he had to be, he needed the wine to help him on his way.

He started out by telling Richard how he had come to Mauritius.

'I had the bad luck to be born the youngest son of a landowning baronet,' he said. 'All the family money went to my brothers and I was left to earn my keep as best I could. The problem was, I wasn't trained for anything, so I had to take whatever was on offer.'

His mother had come up with the Mauritian posting, he continued. One of her lunching friends was close to the Governor out there. And the Governor needed an ADC.

'It was a menial job,' Jeremy admitted. 'Little more than glorified servant, and after a bit I started to cast around for something else.'

'So you changed tack and became a sugar planter,' Richard said brightly.

He realized he had gone too far, for the older man put down his glass and looked angry.

'Look,' he said, 'this is difficult enough to tell without you chipping in every five minutes. Either you let me get on with it, or we'll call it a night and go home.'

The boy fell silent and looked down at the tablecloth. After a moment Jeremy went on.

'I wanted to be a planter,' he said, 'because it was something I could do. There was farming on my father's estate. I was brought up knowing about the land, but it wasn't easy to get started. What I really wanted was a small place of my own but I needed money for that, and neither my family nor the banks were interested in lending me any. So I was stuck.'

He paused. 'Then I met Christine de Seneville and suddenly there seemed to be a way out of the mess I was in.'

Richard ventured a question. 'Was she terribly rich?'

Jeremy lit a cigarette. 'Rich is an understatement,' he said. 'The lady was loaded.'

He told his son about the time he had first seen Christine at a New Year's ball in Government House, the social occasion that Mauritian society looked forward to all year.

From the word go, Jeremy had felt he didn't stand a chance. Officially he was meant to be working. One of his jobs was organizing the evening, not that it protected him from any of the husband hunters. He must have danced with every daughter of every well-connected family the length and breadth of the island. It was the first New Year's Eve he had celebrated since he had arrived in Mauritius and what fascinated him was that his lack of funds didn't seem to deter any of the girls, or any of the families.

In their eyes he had achieved enough simply by being born. He was, after all, the son of a baronet.

He chose Christine because she was less available than the other women, and because of her father, the Baron de Seneville, who was something of a legend in Mauritius. Among the locals he was known as the Sugar King. Anyone who married the de Seneville girl could expect to take his pick of her father's thriving concerns, for Christine was an only child.

Jeremy kept this firmly in mind when he approached her at the New Year's ball. She was not a beauty. She wasn't particularly charming either. Yet there was a sadness about her that got to him. For in the midst of the swirling crowd, the French heiress looked almost entirely alone. He went up to her and asked if she would dance with him. At first she seemed reluctant, but he decided to pursue her.

For the next few months Jeremy took Christine everywhere and slowly, inch by inch, he managed to gain her confidence.

He considered seducing her, then he changed his mind. He wasn't after a casual fling with this girl. He wanted whatever happened between them to mean something. So he bided his time.

Christine made her intentions clear to Jeremy at a weekend party. Like everything else she did, there was a subtlety about her move, and an unexpectedness.

She had been formal with Jeremy since they arrived at the house. Most of her time had been spent gossiping to the people she knew there. Halfway through the weekend, Jeremy wondered if the heiress was getting bored with him. He needn't have worried. For that night she came to his room.

There had been hardly any intimacy between them in the months they had known each other. Even their goodnight kisses had a chaste, chilly quality. Yet when Christine climbed into his bed, she behaved as if she owned him. In all his other encounters, Jeremy had been the prime mover, but Christine clearly hadn't been reading the rule book.

She was hungry for Jeremy and she let her hunger show and it was the worst thing she could have done. In one night she lost any mystery she might have had. For she was no longer the shy girl who challenged him with her indifference. She had turned into a huntress and Jeremy lived in fear that she would devour him.

Five weeks after they started sleeping together, Christine announced she was pregnant. She communicated this fact both to Jeremy and to her father at roughly the same time. After that the marriage was inevitable.

Jeremy and Christine tied the knot in the church of Saint Therese in Curepipe when she was four months pregnant. The Baron saw to it that his daughter's marriage was the most important event on the social calendar that year.

He also saw to it that Christine's money was adequately protected.

'From the day I married,' Jeremy told his son, 'the old man made it clear that I could spend the money I made from the plantation, but that was all. The business remained in Christine's name and if I wanted to make any changes I had to consult her before I did so.

'I could see what his intention was. He didn't want me selling off his daughter's land and property and running off with the proceeds, but by overprotecting her, he'd turned me into a kept man. If my wife disapproved of anything I did, she could bring me into line by threatening me with the business.'

He looked at Richard with defeat in his eyes. 'Now can you see why I can't take you back with me?'

He was about to say more when his attention was distracted by a commotion at the entrance to the restaurant. Jeremy checked the time. It was gone eleven, too late for any of the royals. He shifted in his seat to get a better view of what was going on, and he saw Larry Simpson. The actor was in black tie, as were the other members of his entourage. They were all congregating at a big table in the centre of the restaurant and Jeremy stared as they took their seats.

He wondered what he'd done with Emerald. Girls like that must be two a penny for the likes of him, Jeremy thought. He probably dumped her the minute he got back to London.

Larry's party didn't start dinner immediately. They seemed to be waiting for someone, for the place beside the actor was empty.

The girl made her entrance five minutes later and at first Jeremy didn't recognize her. She was thinner than he remembered. She'd grown her hair, and she was wearing the sort of makeup that Bardot made famous – all black eyelashes and pale lips. On the surface she was just another

87

dolly girl, until you looked closer and saw that her eyes were like great green jewels against the tawny darkness of her skin.

So she stayed the course after all, thought Jeremy. He would have gone on staring at her if his son hadn't interrupted him.

'Who's the dish with Larry Simpson?' Richard asked. 'You look as if you know her.'

'I do,' Jeremy replied. 'She used to be a dressmaker in Port Louis.'

Richard looked at him curiously. 'She sewed for your wife?' he asked.

Jeremy was irritated. 'She did no such thing. Christine has a girl of her own on the plantation.'

'So how do you know her?'

It would have been easy to dismiss Emerald as a girl-friend of one of his managers, but she looked exceptionally lovely tonight and she was on the arm of an international movie star. It gave Jeremy a sense of importance to think he had once possessed her.

'She was a mistress of mine,' he said casually. 'I paid her keep for a year or so.'

Now it was Richard's turn to stare.

The woman was younger than he first thought, probably about nineteen, and there was something vulnerable about her. She shouldn't be wearing all that paint, he thought. Or that dress with the low neckline. It makes her look cheap.

He turned to his father. 'Why did you give her up?' he asked.

The older man laughed. 'Emerald was the one who did the walking out,' he said. 'She latched on to Larry Simpson last year when he was filming in Mauritius. After that there was nothing I could do. She upped sticks and left.'

Richard looked at the girl again, this time with a grudging respect. You might be cheap, he thought, but you've

88

got guts. There aren't many who'd do what you did.

Just for a second he thought of his mother. She too must have been very young when she got together with his father but her attitude was different. Instead of seeing Jeremy for what he was, she thought he was a god and dedicated her life to living up to him.

The girl on Larry Simpson's arm wouldn't be caught doing that. Yet Richard felt sad for her. She's too pretty to be hanging around with old men, he thought. She should have someone of her own age. He turned to his father.

'I suppose the girl over there is another secret you kept from your wife.'

He kept his voice carefully neutral, but the meaning was not lost on Jeremy.

'I think I might have given you the wrong idea,' he told Richard. 'I didn't hate Christine when I married her. She's an intelligent woman and she's made me a very good wife. But I didn't desire her all that much either.'

'So you found other playmates.'

The planter suddenly felt his age. It was too easy for Richard to pass judgement on him. He hadn't lived in the real world and he didn't know how hard it was to be a man.

'If I'd had any choice in the matter,' he said, 'I might have had a very different kind of marriage. You don't think it's easy living the way I do?'

Richard thought about his mother and the hardship they both had had to endure because of this man. You're spoilt, he thought. You were brought up to expect everything to be handed to you on a plate, and when you didn't get it, it didn't occur to you to go out and fight for it. The best you could do was to marry a rich girl and complain about her ever after.

He regarded his father and felt disappointed. I worshipped you, he berated himself. I thought you were going to come over here and transform my life, but I was wrong.

You couldn't transform anyone's life. Your wife wouldn't let you.

'How did you manage to pay for school?' Richard asked his father. 'Surely Christine knows where all the money goes.'

The older man smiled and took his time selecting a cigar from a box the waiter put in front of him.

'My wife doesn't quite own me,' he said. 'There's a small family trust. Something my father set up to give me an allowance. It's only a few thousand a year, but I didn't touch it for a long time and when I came to look at it again I saw that there was enough in it to send you to school.'

'But not to send me to Oxford.'

Jeremy nodded. 'That's right,' he said. 'I could afford to give you a start, but I couldn't make you into a scholar.'

Richard suddenly felt small. I was too hard on him, he thought. I walked into here thinking it was my right to come into everything he owned. What I didn't realize was, I've already done that. My father gave me the only money he had a long time ago. He suddenly felt sorry for him, and sat up very straight in his chair.

'I didn't want Oxford that much,' Richard said. 'Some of my friends were going, so it would have been fun, but that's all it would have been. I can survive perfectly well without it.'

'Have you got any idea what you want to do?'

Richard considered for a moment. 'Not really,' he said. 'I'd like to work for myself, that much I do know. And I think I've got a head for business, but which business I've no idea.'

Jeremy thought about the conversation he'd been having with an old friend of his before he came to dinner. The meeting was the real reason he had been late and now he didn't regret it.

'You might take a look at the fine art world,' he said. 'Someone I know who owns galleries is in the market for

90

a trainee. You'd be running around hanging pictures and making coffee in the beginning but if you show any kind of flair, you could end up in charge of your own place.'

He reached into an inside pocket and produced a card. On it was written the name of a well-known Cork Street art gallery with a telephone number scribbled underneath.

'Give Graham Hollis a ring and tell him who you are,' he said. 'He'll look after you.'

He stood up to leave and as they made their way through the mirrored restaurant, Richard noticed that his father did not take a route that led anywhere near Larry Simpson's table. Instead they skirted the room and the boy had to look back to catch his last glimpse of the film star and his party. His eyes searched for the Indian girl and he noticed she had seen Jeremy, for she was staring at him as he strode through the doors and out into the hotel corridor. It was clear she wasn't pleased to see him for her eyes were narrow slits of green and she was frowning. Richard turned back to follow his father.

I wonder what he did to her, he thought.

CHAPTER 11

Richard did follow up his father's tip on the art gallery, but somehow the whole business seemed slightly tacky. He didn't want to spend his life telling lies about paintings he didn't even like. Tim was not impressed with Richard's story, although privately he sympathized with the boy. He had never warmed to the art business and he could understand why Richard wanted none of it. But that wasn't the point.

His nephew was a school-leaver in need of employment. He had no money of his own and should have taken the prospect of a job more seriously.

He needs to find out about the real world, he thought. The world that exists outside of public school.

'You'll be leaving Stowe at the end of term,' he said to Richard. 'What plans do you have after that?'

The boy shrugged. 'I'll look in the classified columns,' he said. 'There's bound to be something there.'

The banker did his best to look stern. 'I hope there is for your sake,' he said. 'I'm not going to put up with you lying around here all day.'

So Richard got himself a job working in the cellars of a big hotel in Park Lane. The salary was tiny and he spent most of the day humping bottles around, but he went on with it because it didn't commit him to anything. He was earning enough to support himself in a small room in Soho and it gave him a breathing space. He used the time to learn about how the world worked.

On his way home every evening he called into his uncle's

flat and picked up all the financial journals from the day before. Every night he studied the *Investor's Chronicle*, the *Financial Times, Accountancy Age* and *Campaign*. It was a hard slog at first until he found the role models he was looking for. Jim Slater, John Bentley, Jimmy Goldsmith all lived lives he aspired to. He studied every facet of them, from the places they lunched to the way they conducted their businesses, and a pattern started to emerge. These men were innovators in their fields. At some point in their lives each of them had had a single bright idea that put them head and shoulders above everyone else. He filed this piece of information away for future use and went on with his life.

After a few months Richard got bored with the cellars. The sickly smell of alcohol from the floor-to-ceiling racks of bottles was starting to cling to him. There had to be another job he could do in this hotel. He asked around the staff canteen and found two vacancies. One was for a commis waiter in the main restaurant. The second one was working in the kitchens. He chose the kitchens because there was room to learn something.

After a month of washing plates, he was moved on to preparing vegetables. Everything in the vast subterranean kitchens in Park Lane had by necessity to be pre-prepared and part cooked. So when a diner wanted a serving of green beans or sauté potatoes, they could be taken out and finished in the pan.

Richard became fascinated by the mechanics of mass catering and his enthusiasm communicated itself to the head chef, who was used to surly students doing the job for pocket money in the holidays. He found he was moved around. During the space of a year he was taught how to bone meat, trim fish and pluck game. The pastry chef showed him how to create exotic desserts. He was even initiated into the mysteries of sauce making. But the most important thing he learned had nothing to do with cooking.

What was vital for any hotel kitchen, he realized, was the right economics. How many portions could you get out of a fillet of meat? What was the right price to pay for fish? Could the leftovers be used to make something else? Above everything else they had to show a profit. If they failed to deliver that one vital ingredient, then all their culinary efforts were wasted.

For the next few years he moved around the hotel, familiarizing himself with all the departments. He did a spell as a waiter when his haircut, his fingernails and his shoes were inspected every day. He worked in the bar and on the reception desk. And he found without realizing it, he was enjoying himself.

There was a camaraderie, a mateyness about hotel life. You were part of a large family whose function it was to take in travellers. Although much of the work was menial, Richard never felt servile when he was in a hotel. He was a businessman whose job it was to make a profit out of the paying customers.

By the time he was twenty-three he had made it to banqueting manager and had a full staff working under him. He was very young to have a job like this and the achievement should have satisfied him. Yet Richard still dreamt of being Jim Slater, so he wasn't happy at all.

'I'm just a cog in an efficient machine,' he complained to his uncle. 'And I can't see any way out of it.'

Tim smiled at his impatience. He suspected his nephew had unrealistic dreams, for he knew how addicted he was to his financial journals.

'Not everyone can be a tycoon,' he told him. 'Anyway, you've done very well for yourself.'

But Richard wouldn't be dismissed so easily. 'All I am right now,' he said, 'is a rat on a treadmill. I know I'll make it up a few notches more. I might even end up managing a West End hotel, but it's not what I want to do with my life. It's a dead end and you know it as well as I do.'

Tim looked at the boy with interest. The years earning his own living had hardened him. He hadn't lost the grace that his school had given him. No one could take that away from him. But there was something rough and determined about him now that Tim hadn't seen before. It was almost as if the boy had a map of his future in front of him with every move worked out.

Tim felt guilty about the way the Waites family had treated Richard. They'd done the same to his father, of course, packing him off to an island in the sun and letting him survive as best he could.

He thought about the way Jeremy's life had turned out and it made him bitter. He deserves better than he got, Tim thought, and so does his son.

He turned to Richard. 'What are you looking for?' he asked.

The boy set his face. 'I'm looking for a chance,' he said. 'I'm looking to be in the right place at the right time when the right powerful man smiles on me.'

Tim gave the Mauritian boy a very old-fashioned look.

'I get the message,' he said. 'You want me to introduce you to someone useful.'

CHAPTER 12

Rolf Weiss was the kind of man you didn't shake hands with too easily, or if you did you made quite sure you counted your fingers afterwards, for the entrepreneur gave the impression of being somewhat less than straight. It was something to do with his background. Weiss came from middle Europe and try as he might he never quite managed to be a gentleman.

He was a tall man, carrying a little too much weight to be healthy, with jet-black hair, which he dyed, but it was his accent that damned him. It was guttural and Germanic-sounding with a slight lilt that put you in mind of the worst kind of musical comedy. When he arrived in England just before the war people had automatically shied away from him.

It didn't stop him succeeding. His Polish-Jewish family had provided him with a small nest egg. They knew they probably wouldn't survive the next few years but Rolf would carry on where they left off. Rolf would see the family name didn't entirely die out.

And he proved them right. With the money they gave him he bought a chain of sandwich bars, which in the space of a few years upgraded into cafés.

By the fifties he was running restaurants and when he saw how eagerly the post-war public clamoured for the illusion of luxury, he decided to expand into the hotel business. He bought a group of run-down properties, which he transformed into caricatures of European splendour. The English had spent too much time laughing at him. Now he wanted to turn the joke against them.

The Weiss hotels worked because they had been created at exactly the right moment. People who had money wanted to spoil themselves and it was easy to do so in one of Rolf's hotels. His carpets were thicker than anyone else's, his cream cakes creamier, his drinks were stronger and the portions in his restaurants were absolutely huge.

The people who patronized a Weiss establishment would probably part with more than they intended, but they never felt ripped off. By the end of the decade, Rolf was a millionaire several times over. He had also acquired a reputation for gross vulgarity.

It didn't bother him. As he became richer he spent his money ever more lavishly, buying racehorses, boxes at the opera and grand country houses. His biggest outlay was on his women. He liked to maintain a mistress in all the cities where he did business and his empire went on growing, not because Rolf had any real ambition to increase it, but simply because he had to keep up with his girlfriends.

Every time he found a new girl on his travels he had to have an excuse to go on seeing her, so he bought a hotel group or a restaurant chain. When the affair ended, he always managed to sell his acquisitions at the top of the market.

Then he made his first and only mistake. He fell in love with a girl in Paris who had a thing about perfume. The surest way to impress Michelle was to arrive at her apartment on the rue de Rivoli with a bottle of designer perfume. Giftwrapped.

If Rolf had stuck to buying bottles, he would have been fine, but in the first throes of infatuation he wanted to lay the world at Michelle's feet. So he bought her a perfume plant. It was a family concern based in Grasse and when Rolf arrived one evening with the deeds in his briefcase, Michelle thought she had won the pools.

Actually she had done no such thing, for the factory

started losing money from the moment it operated in her name. Rolf didn't leave her to cope with the problem on her own. That would have been ungallant. Instead he absorbed his disastrous buy into the vast Weiss empire where it went on running at a loss.

Then he and Michelle quarrelled and he did what he always did: he sought to offload the business commitment he had made during the course of their relationship.

The perfume business proved impossible to ditch for the simple reason that no one wanted it. So Rolf was stuck. Here he was, a top hotelier, making vast profits all over the world, and he had one dreary little business that was draining his resources.

Anyone else in his position would have cut his losses and closed the whole thing down but Rolf was quirky. He had never owned a company that didn't make money and it irked him to admit defeat. So he kept the factory in Grasse operational and had an attack of violent indigestion every time he saw the balance sheet.

Then one day Tim Waites, his merchant banker, called him wanting a favour. He had a clever nephew who was making his mark on the hotel business. Would Rolf meet him and give him a hearing?

Normally Rolf turned down this kind of request – he was dead against nepotism – but the day Tim called, he had learnt he was losing half a million a year in Grasse, and he needed to take it out on someone. So he asked Tim more about the bright boy who wanted a leg up . . .

When Rolf arrived at Bucks Club in Clifford Street he had made his mind up to crucify Richard Waites. He had never met the boy, but after what his uncle had said about him, he didn't need to. He disliked him already.

For Richard had everything he aspired to but could never achieve. He had an aristocratic family which dated back to William the Conquerer, a public school education and he had arranged to meet him in an old-fashioned gentlemen's club.

This fact was the final nail in Richard's coffin for it defined him as a self-satisfied little snob. By bringing him to this club, with its faded Persian carpets and sporting pictures, Rolf felt the Waites boy was almost telling him he was a vulgar foreigner who had no place in his world.

As he waited for Tim in the upstairs bar he thought about all the other spoilt darlings who had been foisted on him. He had suffered their demands and their condescension because he had to, because they were the scions of the men he did business with, because favours begat favours. Richard Waites was like all the others.

He had owed Tim for a long time and now the debt was being called in. This time he didn't feel like paying it, and he had the perfect excuse not to. He went over what he had planned to do with the boy and as he did so, a glow of satisfaction came over him. He was going to offer Richard the chance to set his perfume company to rights. If he dressed it up right, he could make it sound like the opportunity of a lifetime. Though, of course, it wasn't.

Whatever anyone did, the exercise was doomed to failure, but it was a way of settling his account with Tim, and of making a fool of the boy at the same time. When he'd finished with Master Waites, the boy wouldn't be able to hold his head up for a very long time.

He was so busy contemplating the destruction of Tim's protégé that he hadn't noticed the banker had arrived, and was settling down on the banquette beside him.

'Hasn't Richard arrived yet?' Tim asked.

Rolf glanced at his heavy gold Rolex. By his reckoning this candidate for a job was already fifteen minutes late. He notched up another black mark against him.

Five minutes later, Richard made his entrance. At least

Rolf assumed it was Tim's nephew who came thundering up the curving staircase, for he wasn't what he was expecting at all.

He was dressed cheaply in a pair of grey flannels and a sports jacket that had seen better days. And although he had the same patrician features as his uncle, he looked altogether tougher.

He was out of breath as he came to the table and Tim interrupted his excuses to make the introductions, but the boy wouldn't be deflected. He was late and he needed to explain himself.

Rolf found himself listening to a description of the usual fuck-up that happened in big hotels. There had been a power failure in the kitchens and the lunch party Richard was responsible for were having to wait for their food.

As the boy described how he dealt with the disaster, Rolf was able to get a better look at him, and what he saw intrigued him. The toughness that was written all over Richard was due in part to the fact that he wasn't entirely English. His mother might have been Southern European, or maybe darker, and Rolf suppressed a smile.

So this perfect little Waites heir wasn't so perfect after all. Looking the way he did, he must have had a problem getting into this snobby gentlemen's club.

A servant in a white apron and a ridiculous little pleated cap came and told them their table was ready in the dining-room. Tim immediately put down his glass and ushered them all downstairs.

If Rolf had been more secure about himself he might have admired the grand old London house that played host to the club. It had the faded beauty of a courtesan who had known better days and was now enjoying a well-deserved retirement, but Rolf had no time for other people's history and when they were led into the wood-panelled dining-room, he made straight for the table in the corner with the reserved sign on it. The glowing oil paintings, the silver candelabras, needn't have existed as far as Rolf was concerned.

He was here to do business, to shame a privileged young man into taking on a task he couldn't possibly handle and he started to relish the prospect of seeing him come unstuck.

First, though, he had to walk before he could run. If he presented the challenge of his perfume company with too much enthusiasm one of them was bound to get suspicious. So he bided his time, letting Tim order lunch. Then, when the club claret was on the table, he leant forward and looked Richard in the eye.

'Your uncle tells me you're looking for a job.'

He expected to see a little interest come into his face, but there was no reaction.

Instead the Mauritian boy said, 'It's not a job I'm after. I've got a job. What I'm casting around for is an opportunity.'

If Rolf had written the script himself it couldn't have been a more perfect reply. Now all he had to do was bait the trap.

He did his best to look avuncular. 'Life is full of opportunities. What did you have in mind exactly?'

Richard told him he wanted to get into hotel management. He made a big speech about his experience of coming up through the ranks and despite himself the old entrepreneur was impressed. The boy had actually got his hands dirty and Rolf wondered why he had bothered. With his connections, surely Richard could have started at the top years ago?

He must have drifted off into his own thoughts for when he next paid attention to what was going on, Richard was halfway through an analysis of the Weiss Group. He had identified a problem in one of his restaurant chains which had been bugging Rolf for some time and he had an interesting suggestion about a group of motorway hotels that was rumoured to be coming on the market.

He's done his homework, Rolf thought. He's got a good mind as well. If he'd been anyone else it might have been fun to add him to my team of executives. With an effort he hardened himself against the boy. He has this coming, he thought. Who knows, it might even do him good.

He started to talk about the problem he had in Grasse. He described how the company had been foisted on him and how from day one the whole thing had been a disaster.

As he expected, Richard was totally thrown, but before he could say anything, his uncle came to his rescue.

'Perfume isn't really Richard's subject,' the banker said drily. 'He has a working knowledge of the City and he understands the hotel business inside out, but toiletries isn't a market he's familiar with.'

Rolf leant back in his chair and pushed his plate away. The club food had been as terrible as he suspected it would be, and he had made no attempt to eat it.

'I'm sorry then,' he said turning to Tim, 'because I haven't really got anything else to offer at the moment.'

There was a silence while all three of them looked at each other. Then Richard looked at Rolf's uneaten lunch and felt slightly sick.

He's got me backed right into a corner, he thought. The company in Grasse is a mess and it's clear the old crook is looking for a fall guy to blame it on. And here I come, ready and eager and desperate for a chance to prove myself. He must think I was born yesterday.

But just as a refusal was forming on his lips, a thought came into his mind. What have I got to lose? It was such an obvious notion that he wondered why it hadn't occurred to him before.

Okay, so he would have to leave his job if he took up Rolf's offer. But he was perfectly capable of finding another. And okay, if he fell on his face at Weiss, Rolf would have him out in two minutes flat. But he was willing to take that risk as well – for he knew that if he didn't he would crawl back to his safe little life and go on being a drone for ever.

He turned to Rolf. 'Tim said I don't know anything about scent,' he said, 'and it's true, I don't, but it doesn't mean I can't learn about it. Everything I need to know has already been published. It's a matter of doing the right reading.'

'How would you know what was right?'

The boy shrugged. 'How does anyone know? All anyone can do is follow their instincts and hope that whatever flair they have will come to the rescue.'

The older man looked doubtful. 'That's a bit airy-fairy, isn't it? You're asking me to put my business in your hands on the off chance you get some kind of inspiration.'

Tim interrupted them. 'Isn't inspiration what business is all about?' he demanded. 'Anyone who puts in the time can do a routine job. Companies are full of dull little wage slaves who justify their existences from nine to five, but that isn't what you're looking for, is it? You want a whizz kid to take the perfume headache off your shoulders.'

Rolf thought it all too good to be true. Both Tim and the spoilt little rich boy were practically begging for the chance to be made to look foolish. When Richard finally came unstuck over the company in Grasse, the fallout would affect Tim as well.

Rolf hugged himself for being so clever. Shaming these people would be his own personal revenge on English society for not acknowledging him. He turned to Richard.

'You're not an expert, so you'll be sticking your neck out if you take this on.'

The boy looked insufferably confident. 'How many perfume experts have you had working on this problem?'

Rolf made a swift calculation. 'Half a dozen,' he told Richard. 'That includes a chemist I brought in from America.'

The boy nodded. 'And none of them was the slightest bit of help, was he? You probably spent thousands on consultation fees in order to come up with a big zero.' He paused. 'If you take me on I won't pretend to bring any specialist knowledge to the company, but at least I'll be outside the problem, so I'll be able to look at it objectively. That could be a major plus.'

The older man started to laugh. It was a boisterous booming sound and several of the club members looked up from their vintage port and frowned, but Rolf was oblivious to their disapproval.

'This nephew of yours', he said to Tim, 'is doing his best to talk me into letting him loose on my business. Do you think I should give him the chance?'

The banker sighed and wondered why he had got involved in the first place. Rolf was a barracuda, he had been for years, and right now he was looking at his nephew as if he wanted to eat him for breakfast. Then Tim thought, I can't go on protecting the boy for ever. Who knows, the experience may do him good.

He looked at Rolf. 'I'd back the boy,' he said shortly. 'He could just do you a lot of good.'

CHAPTER 13

Two weeks later Richard was sitting in Rolf Weiss's office getting the lowdown on his company in Grasse.

From what he could see, there was nothing wrong with it. The factory made a range of classic flower scents. The lavender had the genuine smell of the country and both the rose and the violet conjured up images of a garden in full bloom.

Richard looked at the row of glass bottles on Rolf's imposing mahogany desk and felt uncomfortable. His instincts told him the hotelier was holding something back. Some vital piece of information was missing from the company report that had been sent to him a week ago.

Richard had studied it thoroughly just as he had pored over every piece of information he could lay his hands on about the toiletries market, but he still had no idea why Rolf was losing money. He was turning out a quality product that hadn't varied in twenty years, so why had it suddenly stopped selling?

He put the question to Rolf, and instead of replying the tycoon walked him to the far end of his cavernous office where there was a projector and screen set up. While Richard settled himself on a sofa, his companion started feeding slides into the machine. For the next half-hour he was witness to the entire sales profile of Weiss Perfumes.

If he had been an accountant or a mathematician he might have made some sense of it since the whole story was told in figures.

I'm being intimidated, Richard thought. No executive

could possibly be expected to understand this mumbo jumbo. He's trying to pull the wool over my eyes.

Richard decided to try a different tack. When the slide show was finished, he rounded on Rolf and asked him if he had any new information on the fragrance market.

'You must know who buys these flower scents,' he demanded. 'Has the company done any research on its customers?'

Rolf looked wary. The boy was coming to the crux of his problem, the reason he was going out of business. He wondered whether to tell him what he knew. Then he thought, why not? He's such an eager beaver he's bound to find out sooner or later.

He turned to him. 'It's interesting you should ask that question,' he said. 'The latest survey we did turned up some results we hadn't seen before.'

He walked over to the screen and for a second Richard thought he was going to be bombarded with more figures. He needn't have worried. Rolf liked to have the physical advantage when delivering a lecture, and standing at the head of the room with the light from the window acting as a spotlight gave him an added authority.

He started out by talking about the market. It was much as Richard imagined, young marrieds and girls who worked in offices. They'd been dabbing lavender behind their ears for years now, just like their mothers and their grandmothers. Then in the early sixties everything changed. It was the pill that had done it. In the old days, when a fall from grace inevitably meant pregnancy, women didn't want to be seduced. They wanted to be put on a pedestal and treated with reverence. Smelling like a flower garden reinforced this message. Don't touch me, it said, I'm an old-fashioned girl. I break easily.

Today's girls weren't pretending to be so fragile because they didn't have to. They could sleep with whomever they liked, whenever they liked, and a tiny white tablet swallowed once a day with their morning coffee liberated them from the consequences.

The first thing to alter was the way they looked. Clothes got tighter and skimpier. They plastered on more cosmetics, and right at the end of the line their aura changed.

The liberated woman of the sixties didn't want to move around in a mumsy cloud of lavender. She wanted the come-on of musk and ambergris, and the big manufacturers were quick to respond. The shops were suddenly full of My Sin and Evening in Paris, and from that moment Rolf's sales began to sag.

'There was nothing I could do about it,' he told Richard. 'I've got thousands of pounds' worth of floral scents piled high on the wholesalers' shelves and the chemists just aren't ordering.'

Richard felt as if a light had just gone on in his head. Rolf had got himself into a terrible pickle. Right now Richard couldn't see any way out of it, but at least he knew what the problem was. He had something to worry about, to get his teeth into.

He started to fire questions at the hotelier. Had he thought of changing the look of his scents? Maybe a fancy wrapper and a change of name might make people buy.

Rolf shook his head. 'I tried that route some time ago, but it didn't wash. Women aren't stupid. When they found the same old floral smell hiding under a sexy wrapper, they thought they'd been conned. If anything it turned them off the brand even faster than if we'd done nothing.'

He sighed and led Richard back through the office until he got to his desk. Once he was settled behind it, he seemed to grow in stature. It was as if the imposing polished wood desk protected him from the world, or at least from his sales figures and in that instant Richard recognized Rolf's vulnerability.

He's isolated himself, he thought. He's become so big

and successful he thinks he doesn't need to keep in contact with his salesmen or his suppliers. I bet he doesn't even visit the factory down in Grasse any more but sends his minions out instead, who are so frightened of displeasing him they simply tell him what he wants to hear.

He thought about Rolf's stock gathering dust at the wholesalers. Unless someone thought of something the bulk of it would still be there next year and the year after that.

'How much money have you got tied up in the product?' he asked.

Rolf sighed heavily. 'Over half a million.'

'Is that what you'll lose if you close the company?'

Rolf looked as if he were going to burst into tears. 'If it was I'd call it quits tomorrow, but it's gone too far now. Eighteen months ago I tied myself into a further commitment of three years. If I go down now, it will cost me close on four million.'

Richard was not overly impressed. Four million out of the coffers of the Weiss Group would not even cause a ripple. He could see that the only reason Rolf didn't wash his hands of the whole disaster was because he was too arrogant to admit defeat.

Richard decided to use Rolf's arrogance to his advantage.

'What if I could turn it round?' he asked quietly.

For a second the tycoon looked hopeful. 'You're on to something,' he said. 'You've got some smart idea that could dig me out of this corner.'

Richard got up from where he was sitting and walked over to the window. The office was right at the top of a skyscraper in the City of London and beneath him the commuters scurried along the streets like a colony of ants.

If he told Rolf the truth, that he didn't have the faintest idea how he could rescue the operation in Grasse, he knew he'd be joining the ants in their scramble through London's underground system. And he had no wish to do that. So he lied.

'I've got a plan of sorts,' he said mysteriously. 'But it needs work. If I tried to lay it out for you now, you wouldn't be able to make any sense of it.'

He could see he had the older man's attention now, for a look of pure greed passed across his pudgy face.

'How long will you need to get it together?'

Richard took a flyer. 'If you gave me a couple of months, I should have all the pieces in place, but I'll need to be paid while I'm working and I'll need some kind of incentive.'

Rolf looked suspicious. 'What do you mean, incentive? Are you pushing me for a job if this works out?'

It was then that Richard knew he was being used. This fat bully had never intended to give him a chance. There had to be a way of making this business work. Somehow out there was an answer to the puzzle. Probably in a place where he least expected it.

Richard felt so sure he would find the answer he was looking for that he put his money where his mouth was.

'I'm not all that interested in a job with Weiss,' he told Rolf. 'What intrigues me far more is some kind of financial reward. If I can save your perfume company I'd like to be counted in for a percentage of it. I don't think fifteen per cent would be unreasonable.'

Rolf was dumbstruck. Two weeks ago he had set out with the express intention of cutting this brat down to size. Now here he was demanding a slice of his business.

In a perverse way the situation appealed to him. He had started out in this country with everyone against him, yet he'd proved his enemies wrong. Now this boy was tilting at windmills just as he had. He began to admire Richard.

He looked him in the eye. 'I'll give you ten per cent and no more,' he told him.

The boy smiled. 'You haven't said anything about a salary.'

He thought the older man might explode, but he seemed to get a hold on himself for when he spoke again there was a firmness about him he hadn't seen before.

'I'll pay you whatever you're earning now for eight weeks,' he said. 'That and ten per cent of the perfume company is all you're getting out of me.'

Richard stood up and held out his hand. 'You have yourself a deal,' he said.

CHAPTER 14

It was raining in Cannes. The terrace of the Carlton had closed its parasols and folded its tables and now it reminded Rolf more of Blackpool than the Côte d'Azur.

Even the Mediterranean, which had been calm and blue an hour or so earlier, looked decidedly bad-tempered and it fitted his mood.

He had been in a filthy temper ever since he arrived in his suite at the five-star hotel, and nothing, not the complimentary bottle of champagne nor the fresh *foie gras* that arrived with it, had managed to placate him.

I should never have let Richard go off on his own like that, he thought. I should have insisted he give me some idea of his plan – some indication of what he wanted to do.

He thought of the devastation that Richard had wreaked over just five weeks. If only I'd known, he raged, I could have stopped him before it came to this.

Rolf began to realize that something was up about ten days previously. Ken Irwin, the sales director who looked after his perfume interests, had arrived unannounced in his office and gone to town about his protégé.

The boy wouldn't attend meetings. He refused to discuss any of his plans, and when asked point blank what he was doing, all he would volunteer was he was out visiting the wholesalers.

'I couldn't stop what he was doing,' said the sales chief, 'because I knew he had your blessing. So I let it go until I started hearing rumours about us in the trade.'

Rolf sensed danger. 'What rumours?' he demanded.

Ken looked uneasy. Some of the things going around made his hair stand on end. He knew he was risking an explosion if he talked but it was Rolf's company and Rolf had a right to know.

'According to the wholesalers I've talked to, we've offered to buy all our old stock back.'

Rolf was aghast. 'Why would we want to do that? It's as good as committing suicide.'

The older man thought about the last time he had seen Richard. It had been in the office where they were now. The boy had made some mysterious claim that he could save the perfume company. He realized now it was all pie in the sky. Richard didn't have a clue what he was talking about.

'I take it Richard's behind this plan to bankrupt us?'

The sales chief nodded. 'None of my lads would come up with anything like that. They worked too damned hard selling in the stuff.'

Rolf had heard enough. He called the meeting to an end, then he asked his secretary to get hold of Richard. But he was nowhere to be found – or rather he was everywhere, he just couldn't be pinned down. The wholesalers in Manchester who were expecting him for a meeting had already waved Richard goodbye when Rolf called. It was the same story in Liverpool, Glasgow, Birmingham and Solihull. It was like trying to track down the Scarlet Pimpernel, and after two days of frustration Rolf gave up.

There was no way Richard could put down money for the perfumes he had in the wholesalers without Rolf's authorization. It limited the damage he could do, but only just. In offering to buy back their range, Weiss was effectively saying it was unsaleable.

The hotelier thought about the money he had tied up in it and rage festered inside him. When he finally caught up with young Master Waites he was going to have a lot of explaining to do.

A week later Richard called him from Grasse. He was at the factory and had something he thought Rolf would be interested in.

But the tycoon's patience was at an end.

'I want you back in my office and I want you there now,' he told him. 'Nothing you can come up with is going to make any difference now.'

He thought he heard Richard laugh. 'You sound like you finally got wind of my master plan,' he said. 'Interesting, isn't it?'

There was something about him, a confidence, an insouciance that pulled Rolf up short. If the boy was in real trouble he wouldn't be sounding this way. He would be grovelling and trying to make excuses for his behaviour, and it made him think.

Richard was up to something. Of that there was no doubt. He had so far managed to reduce his sales chief to a gibbering wreck and Rolf wasn't so far behind himself. What if they were both wrong? What if this pushy boy really did know what he was doing?

If he applied logic to the situation, he would have fired Richard on the phone and cut off his expenses there and then, but Rolf wasn't a logical man. He had built his empire by following his instincts and right now they were telling him that Richard was about to come up with the goods.

'How much longer do you need to be where you are?' he asked.

'You mean you've changed your mind about hauling me back to London?'

'I might have,' said Rolf, playing for time. 'It all depends what you've got cooking in Grasse.'

Now the boy really did laugh. 'Why don't you come down here and find out?' he said. 'I'm ready to fill you in on everything I've been doing.'

113

So Rolf did what he was told and got on a plane to Nice. He had never paid the slightest attention to anyone else's demands before and the effort knocked him off balance.

By the time he arrived at the Carlton he was beginning to think he had come out on a wild goose chase. What is it about this boy, he asked himself, that gets me in such a lather? Before he had time to consider the question, his telephone rang. It was the front desk telling him that Mr Richard Waites was on his way up to see him.

Rolf sighed and opened the complimentary Moet. He needed a drink to steady his nerves.

Richard had dressed carefully for this meeting with his boss. Instead of his usual flannels and tweed jacket, he was wearing a tailored suit his uncle had had made for him in Savile Row. To complete the effect he had added his old school tie and he had had his hair cut shorter than usual. Anyone seeing him now would have to take him seriously, and that was what he needed.

The time for playing games was over. He had intrigued Rolf. Then he had challenged him. Finally he had nearly scared him to death. Now he had his full attention it was time to go in with the marketing plan.

Rolf answered the door to the suite himself, leading Richard into the drawing-room with its view of the storm-tossed Croisette. Richard noticed he was drinking champagne, but he declined to join him. He needed his wits about him this morning. Afterwards there would be plenty of time to celebrate.

He expected Rolf to raise the subject of the dead perfume stock and he wasn't disappointed. The old man was up in arms that Richard would even consider buying it back and he ranted and raved and accused Richard of trying to ruin him. When it was over, Richard put his case. The first thing he did was to tell Rolf he had no intention of buying back the perfume.

'The whole thing was a trick,' he said. 'I had to get the wholesalers to listen to me, and, believe me, with Weiss doing so badly, it was hard to get through the door.'

'So you conned them into seeing you,' Rolf muttered.

Richard wondered how to go on. Finally he said, 'I didn't con anyone actually. I offered to take back our old stock. I didn't offer to buy it back. My idea was to exchange the old floral scents that nobody wanted for something new that everybody wanted.'

Rolf was interested now.

'It's a nice idea,' he said, 'but what happens when you can't come through with this sure-fire seller?'

Richard changed his mind about a drink. He went over to the half-finished champagne and helped himself to a glass. Then he came back to where Rolf was standing.

'Who said I can't come through with a big new line? It's ready and waiting in our factory. All you have to do is give it the go-ahead.'

Words failed the tycoon. This young man had been in the business five minutes and already he was giving birth to new products.

Then he thought about the chemists and the marketing geniuses who had taken his money over the years. These men had been experts, yet what did Weiss have to show for it? A dying line of old-fashioned colognes.

He started to smile. 'Why don't you tell me about the new line?' he asked. 'The women's market is ready for something different.'

Richard tasted the champagne and as the bubbles exploded on his tongue, he thought, what the hell – I might as well be hanged for a sheep as a lamb.

'We're no longer in the women's market,' he said. 'It's overcrowded and the big boys have a stranglehold on it, so I've decided to go in a whole new direction. We're going to be making fragrances for men.'

He paused to let this new piece of information sink in.

When Rolf didn't say anything, he started to go into his pitch in earnest.

'Until now,' he said, 'the only men who used colognes were gentlemen with expensive barbers and poofs. But between them they use so little product, they're not worth looking at. Then I saw some new research. According to a study done at one of the American universities, there's a growing number of ordinary blokes who like to smell nice for their girlfriends. In the States a few companies are already testing colognes for men and they're doing well. The aftershave market has been a fact of life in the States for some time,' he told Rolf, 'but over here the public has only just woken up to it. Which is why I want to get involved. If we can get in right at the beginning of this trend, we could stand to make a lot of money.'

Richard saw he had the entrepreneur on the hook, for Rolf stopped fiddling about with his champagne glass and started to pay attention to what he was saying.

'I've seen a bit of data on men's colognes,' he said. 'I always thought it was too rarefied for us.'

Richard nodded. 'That was the case about eighteen months ago. Posh barbers supplied it to their gentlemen clients, but things have moved on since then. Now there's a whole lot of new data that shows the man in the street is getting the habit. Ordinary working guys, the sort who go down to the pub in the evening, want to smell good. It's all tied in with sex. The men who are buying colognes nowadays do it because they think women get turned on by it.'

The older man looked thoughtful. 'So you're thinking of selling to a mass market. It could be an expensive exercise.'

Now Richard knew he was getting the message through.

'If we want to grab a lead with this product we need to make an impact fast. If we wait around to test the public's reaction, other manufacturers will cotton on to what we're up to and we'll be finished before we start.'

Rolf looked at him. 'I take it you have some sort of plan as to how you're going to spend my money?'

Richard decided to plough ahead while he had the chance. 'We'll need a national advertising campaign,' he said. 'Television, posters, magazines. The message has to stop people in their tracks, so we have to go for a top creative ad agency. At the end of the day you won't see much change out of half a million, but if it works the investment will be worth every penny.'

The hotelier sighed. It all sounded very fine, but what if it didn't work? He'd have a second dud product on the wholesalers' shelves and a massive bill for promotion. He wondered if it was too late to pull back; then he remembered that the new cologne was ready and waiting for his approval and he decided the moment had passed. His only hope of survival now was to go on with the game Richard had started.

He regarded the young man standing in front of him. A couple of months ago he was firmly convinced he was a no-hoper. Now he was backing him to the tune of half a million. I need my head examining, he thought.

The Weiss Group launched its men's cologne in November of that year. The trendy advertising agency Rolf had been persuaded to hire had named it Charisma and packaged it in a distinctive blue bottle.

It was plastered all over the hoardings along with a husky-looking, half-naked man who claimed he had char-isma because he used Charisma. The notion appealed to the public. Up and down the country every one from junior executives to bricklayers lined up to buy their ration of sex appeal in a bottle.

The cologne must have had an effect, for well before Christmas all the chemists had sold out. For the first time in years, the wholesalers were getting reorders for a Weiss fragrance.

At the time they thought it was a flash in the pan, a gimmick for the Christmas season, but the orders went on coming in right through the New Year. By spring they realized they had backed a winner.

At around that time, Rolf came to the same conclusion. He gave Richard his own office at his headquarters in the City and he started to involve him in other parts of his business. It was his way of keeping an eye on the future, because he knew the Charisma boom couldn't last for ever. Sooner or later the big manufacturers were going to bring out their versions. When that happened there was no way he could compete. He was a hotelier, not a perfumer and he still wanted to off-load the company.

The perfect solution to Rolf's problems presented itself that autumn. One of the big German pharmaceutical companies approached with a takeover bid. Without telling Richard anything about it, Rolf met them in Bonn and hammered out a deal. Then he came back to London and presented his latest protégé with the facts. He was selling his perfume division for fifteen million pounds. If the boy wanted it, there was a job for him running it, but he would have to relocate to Bonn.

Richard asked for two days to think it over. Selling the business was going to make him a rich man, for he owned ten per cent of it, but did he want to be a rich man in Bonn, and did he want to make his name in the fragrance business?

He decided he didn't. The idea for a men's cologne was a lucky break, but that's all it was. To succeed in toiletries required a certain flair, a certain instinct for fashion that he simply didn't have.

Richard was a marketing man who had done his training in hotels. That's where he wanted to stay. He went to see Rolf and told him what he was going to do.

'I've decided to take the money and run,' he said.

'What's your hurry?' the older man asked. 'Don't I keep you busy enough?'

Richard looked surprised. 'I didn't think you wanted me to stay on,' he said. 'Anyway, what's the point without Charisma?'

The hotelier ignored the question. 'I'm working on opening a chain of theme restaurants in Italy,' he said. 'It will mean spending the next three months in Milan, but you could find it fun.' He paused. 'I'll give you a rise, of course. And if the Italian venture works out, there could be a promotion in it.'

CHAPTER 15

Los Angeles, 1970

The announcer's voice boomed out of the car radio intruding on her senses. 'Hi, it's coming up to the hour and Steve and I are going to bring you the latest update on the weather here in the Valley . . .'

Emerald twisted the dial on the walnut veneer dashboard and searched for a music station. She was hitting bumper-to-bumper traffic on the San Diego freeway and she calculated she would be stuck for the best part of half an hour. She fought down a feeling of mounting frustration. There was no way she could avoid being late for Shel's lunch party.

By the time I get there, she thought, they'll have eaten their way through the caviar canapés and be going over to the barbecue. She could see them all in her mind's eye now; the men in blue blazers and monogrammed shirts, women fresh out of the beauty parlour and looking somehow man-made.

In her early days here Emerald thought them wonderful, of course. She couldn't wait to run off and get her hair bleached and her eyebrows plucked. But Larry stopped her.

'You don't need help to be beautiful,' he had told her. 'You are that way already.'

So Emerald had left herself alone and now she was glad of it.

She checked herself in the driving mirror and was reassured by what she saw. Her long black hair was wound up into a chignon that day and it made her look older. I could pass for twenty-eight, she thought, and the knowledge gave her confidence.

Five years ago Emerald had felt a bit tacky living with a man so much older than she was. It was as if Larry's age turned her into a brainless gold-digger. If she had been thirty-something and divorced a couple of times, nobody would have questioned their relationship, but she was a little girl from a faraway island. She had known that everyone in the tight little clique around her lover bitched behind her back. Yet she hadn't let it get to her. Instead, with the resources that were now available to her, she set about reinventing herself. It wasn't difficult.

Los Angeles, Emerald discovered quickly, was a city without a past. There was no tradition here, so you could be what you wanted to be, and nobody would judge you for it. Emerald decided to be a lady. She knew that looking the way she did, nobody would ever take her for Grace Kelly. So she went in the other direction. She became an exotic woman with a past.

She made a point of never discussing her life before she knew Larry. She would simply hint at things. When she referred to her parents' house, she talked about it as if it were a mansion. The Emerald she presented to the world had never worked as a humble dressmaker or travelled on the bus. The new Emerald was accustomed to grander things.

Just how Emerald had acquired this grand style was something else she left discreet clues about. She never actually named the men in her past. All anyone ever knew was that Emerald's lovers had been rich.

Larry was on to her right from the start. At first he felt angry with her. What on earth did she think she was doing playing the courtesan? Then he thought, how can I lose my temper when I do exactly the same in front of the cameras every day? The only difference between us is that I get paid for living a lie. He decided to join Emerald in her game.

'If you're going to behave like a dangerous lady,' he told her, 'you might start looking like one.'

They put together her style from the hotchpotch of boutiques in Beverly Hills. Larry decided Emerald should go for the classic look. Every little bit player could follow fashion, but it took serious money to invest in Hermès and Louis Vuitton.

They started in Rodeo Drive. A lot of the goods, Emerald noticed, were flashier than those she had seen in *Vogue*. It was almost as if the designers made a special line for their Los Angeles clients, sprinkling everything with glitter and beads.

Emerald was relieved to see Larry sidestepped these items. He was interested in two colours only: black and cream.

'Your jewellery will provide all the colour you need,' he told her.

He took Emerald into Boucheron before she found the courage to start asking questions. There he bought her vast diamond studs for her ears, a gold Rolex watch and a necklace made of emeralds that matched her eyes exactly. The sheer extravagance of the gesture terrified her.

'You can't do this,' she protested, and Larry laughed at her.

'Any other girl on this kind of outing would have been demanding to go to Cartier as well. If you're going to sleep with a man as rich as me, you've got to learn how to spend my money.'

Something inside Emerald made her hesitate. What was happening didn't feel right. It wasn't that she was against accepting gifts from a man. Jeremy had kept her for a couple of years, but that had been an arrangement born of necessity. There was nothing necessary about this spending spree. She could survive without the jewellery and the designer labels. Larry must have read her thoughts, for he looked worried.

'You're not thinking of saying no to the stones?' he asked.

'Actually I was,' Emerald responded. 'It doesn't seem right to take all this for nothing.'

The actor walked her over to the corner of the shop where they couldn't be overheard.

'How long have we been together?' he asked.

This new line of questioning frightened Emerald. Was the jewellery a way of paying her off?

'It's been six months, Larry,' she said softly. 'Why?'

'Because though I'm perfectly aware of the time I've been with you, what I wanted was to hear you say it,' Larry said.

He paused, allowing time for his words to register the correct dramatic effect.

'What stuns me about you,' he said, 'is that after six months of following me around the world, you think you count for nothing. I wasn't joking when I talked about another girl in your shoes dragging me off to Cartier. I can name half a dozen who'd do that and demand a sable coat into the bargain.'

Emerald realized they were attracting an audience. The dark-suited assistants behind the counter were straining to catch every word. She needed to get out of this place, but something in her made her stand her ground.

'I'm not a hooker,' she said in a small voice. 'I'm not with you to build up a collection of trophies.'

'Then why do you stay?' Larry asked, and there was an urgency in his voice that demanded the truth. She gave it to him.

'I stay', she said, 'because I like being with you, and because I've got nowhere else to go.'

Larry ignored her last remark. 'You like being with me,' he said, 'but you don't like accepting presents from me. What kind of affection is that?'

Now the eavesdroppers were having a field day. I've got

to get him out of here, Emerald thought, before we make the six o'clock news.

'Larry,' she said, dropping her voice to a whisper, 'I love you, you know that. Now let's go, please. You're embarrassing me.'

Larry grinned from ear to ear. She'd admitted the one thing he wanted to hear. He had embarrassed her. Victory was in sight.

'If I promise to leave, will you take the jewellery?'

Emerald's head started to spin. There's no way out of this, she thought. Whatever I do, I'm compromised. Then she saw the shop starting to fill up and thought, the hell with it, I'll take his baubles. For now. In the morning I can always send them back.

Boucheron never did get to reclaim their emeralds, or the diamond studs or the gold Rolex. Over the next five years Emerald's collection expanded. There was a diamond bracelet to go with the studs, a huge diamond and sapphire clip, an assortment of rings and another watch with a face made entirely of rubies.

Emerald wore them the way she wore her clothes, with pride. The years and Larry had changed the way she felt about herself. She had a new confidence now, and, more importantly, she knew she was worth something.

Without her, Larry simply couldn't function. When he was working he needed her with him all the time and she read his lines for him. If he had a problem with a part, she sat and listened, and when he succeeded, she was there to applaud.

Yet Emerald wasn't merely a handmaiden. She had actually taken charge of Larry's life, organizing his friends, his social calendar, even the film premières he was obliged to go to.

But there was one relationship over which she had no control: the actor's close friendship with Shel Johnson.

Now, as Emerald turned off the freeway and into the

hills, she began to think about the man she was about to visit. On the surface, he was the perfect companion for a movie star. He had been an actor once and now he was a producer. An important producer. Shel Johnson's name on the credits guaranteed a movie would be a critical success.

So why do I hate him, Emerald asked herself. Why does the prospect of spending even five minutes in his company make me feel nauseous?

She was approaching Whitely Heights, the fashionable suburb where he lived. As she drove past the mellow brick wall that bordered Shel's property, a vision of him rose up before her eyes. He was very thin, gaunt almost, with a cadaverous look that put her in mind of a villain in a horror movie. He had a habit of wearing dark silk suits when everyone else was in jeans, and that was another reason why he made her feel uneasy.

Also he didn't like her. Emerald got a whiff of this attitude the very first time she was introduced to him.

'So you're the new girl,' he said, examining her as if she was a piece of antique pottery. 'I wonder how long this little romance will go on.'

Larry was out of earshot when he said it, and Emerald didn't respond. In retrospect, she wished she had, for Shel seemed to have made his mind up to undermine her at every opportunity.

Emerald sighed as she pulled into the driveway of the producer's house. He would doubtless find a way to reduce her to misery this lunchtime, and she would pretend, as she always did, that she didn't give a damn.

She got out of the car and handed her keys to Shel's houseboy, then smoothed her hair back, put on her bravest face and strode into the house.

The party was being held out at the back where there was a swimming pool and tennis courts, not that any of the guests were availing themselves of the facilities — they were too busy networking for that.

As Emerald made her way over to the sundeck she was swallowed by a group of anxious, expensively dressed studio executives.

She knew it would take her at least half an hour to get to the pool. How long it would take her to find Larry, she had no idea, for every step of the way somebody turned to greet her.

Emerald was invited to lunch parties, screenings, tête-à-têtes, and she knew, as she turned down every invitation, that none of these people wanted to be her friend. To them she was the girlfriend of a bankable star, somebody it paid to be in with. To be on the inside track with Emerald put you just one move away from Larry Simpson.

Emerald refused to let any of it rile her. This was the way Los Angeles worked. The part of it that made movies, anyway. That she was there to be used was a fact of her life and she accepted it the way she accepted Shel Johnson.

She located Larry at last in the bar. He was sitting at one of the small tables under an umbrella and he was in deep conversation with his host.

Emerald noticed the actor was wearing his tennis whites and that cheered her for it meant he wasn't talking business. Shel couldn't possibly object if she joined the two of them.

As she approached the table, she saw Larry was watching her.

'You work well in crowd scenes,' he observed. 'Maybe you should do more of them.'

There was an edge to his voice Emerald didn't like. Either he's had too much to drink, she thought, or it's something else. Without asking to be invited, she sat down in the wrought-iron chair next to Larry and blew a kiss to Shel.

'What plots are you two hatching?' she asked. 'I saw you whispering together.'

Larry cast a furtive look at Shel. 'Shall we tell her?'

The producer didn't reply. Instead he reached into his

inside pocket and brought out a phial of white powder and a tiny silver spoon.

'Larry was trying to talk me into playing a couple of sets,' he told her. 'I agreed, but on condition.'

Emerald felt cold. She didn't care one way or the other about Shel's coke habit. As far as she was concerned he could blast his way into tomorrow, but she wasn't having Larry involved. Not with his blood pressure. Not before he went out on the tennis court.

She glanced at Larry, noting the beads of perspiration on his upper lip.

'I don't think tennis is such a good idea,' she ventured.

The actor looked sulky. 'Stop acting like a nursemaid,' he said. 'Anyone would think you own me.'

They'd had this fight before. Shel would suggest a late night in the middle of filming, or a weekend in Vegas without her. The minute she objected, Larry would start behaving like a naughty schoolboy. They never fought for long because Emerald wouldn't allow it. She would find a way of placating him, usually in bed. And by the next day Larry was back to normal again.

Emerald felt depressed. She could hardly seduce the actor by the side of the swimming pool, so she was forced to go along with Shel. I just hope too much of that white powder hasn't gone up his nose already, she thought.

She watched patiently while her host spilt six neat lines across the glass table. Then he leaned forward and snuffled it up, putting her in mind of a large, none-too-hygienic dog. Then it was Larry's turn. As he went through the same ritual, Emerald fought off a feeling of dread. It was too hot to do what he was doing. It was too hot, Larry's blood pressure was too high and both men were far too old.

Emerald saw Shel get up from the table and wander off in the direction of the cabanas. He was going to get into his tennis gear and she wondered if she should have another go at stopping the game. A glance at Larry told her it was too late. He was standing up and practising his service with an invisible racquet. She sighed and followed him on to the grass tennis courts beyond the pool area.

Half an hour into the first set she started to feel a bit better. From where she was sitting, Larry appeared to be on top form. He was the better player of the two and this afternoon he was demonstrating it. He took the first three games without any effort at all. Shel's service won through in the fourth and it seemed to knock Larry's confidence.

He had to struggle to win the next game, but he pulled it off and Emerald finally relaxed. He was in better shape than she thought. She opened the magazine she had brought with her and was into a profile of Henry Ford when she heard a shout and a scuffle.

She looked up to see Larry lying full length on the grass with Shel bending over him. The producer looked up as she hurried over.

'Call an ambulance,' he barked. 'I think Larry's had a heart attack.'

She knelt down beside him, reaching out to take his hand. It was cold as ice. Panic hit her then. He's dying, she thought. The coke and the stupid tennis game has finished him off. The coke and the tennis and Shel Johnson.

Emerald wanted to shout at him, to tell the world that he had murdered her lover. Then she looked at Larry and saw how white he was. I'll deal with Shel later, she thought. Right now I've got other priorities.

CHAPTER 16

Larry stayed in intensive care for three weeks. The doctors at the Cedars Hospital were very sympathetic, and let Emerald see him every day; mostly because they didn't think he was going to make it.

'In these cases,' the duty nurse told her, 'we usually only allow family in.'

Larry's nearest and dearest seemed to have materialized as if by magic. He had a mother in her seventies, with bright blonde hair and rouged lips, who seemed to spend all day haranguing the medical staff. His ex-wife turned up with three rather resentful-looking teenagers who ignored Emerald, and there was a brother she hadn't known existed, who lived in the North of England and ran a grocery store.

Larry didn't want to see any of them, and when the doctors tried to reason with him, he became so distressed they backed off. The man had had a massive coronary, and was living on borrowed time. It was only right that he got what he wanted.

He wanted Emerald. Now he was facing his own mortality he realized the only one he ever had wanted was her. For she loved him for himself.

As he lay in his high hospital bed, Larry thought about his first wife hovering outside in the corridor. Ellen had robbed him blind over the divorce and had the temerity to show up now he looked like dying. They're all the same, he thought bitterly, my children, my brother, even Mum. None of them gives a toss about me when I'm well, but now there's something in it for them they're all over me like a rash.

He thought about the money he had earned over the years and the houses and possessions it had bought. The family expected the lot, of course. If they'd cared for him, they might have been entitled to it. But they hadn't cared for him. They hadn't even liked him. Emerald was the only one who could make him feel better.

When Larry was off the danger list, he was moved to one of the swish private rooms on the fourteenth floor. There he saw evidence of how Hollywood regarded him, for all around him were extravagant bouquets. Someone had sent him a Jeroboam of champagne and the green bottle surrounded by all the 'Get Well' cards gave the impression of a birthday celebration.

Only it wasn't Larry's birthday and he couldn't see the point of all the fuss. He was in hospital. What he wanted, he told the doctors as soon as he was able, was to go home. Once he was there he felt confident he would make a full recovery.

The medical staff had other ideas. No one who had suffered as Larry had could hope to get better on his own. There had been too much damage. His best chance now was to stay and have a bypass operation.

The actor didn't want to know. Bypass surgery was still in its infancy. There was no guarantee it would work, and he wasn't about to put himself up as a guinea pig for some ambitious heart surgeon. I nearly died once, he thought. I'm not going to risk it a second time.

In the end Larry and the hospital came to an agreement. He would stay off work for the next six months and hire a private nurse to keep a watch on him. It was a compromise and everybody knew it, but what could they do? It was Larry's heart and he was paying the bills. There was no point in arguing.

CHAPTER 17

Larry lived on an exclusive estate in the hills of Bel Air. It was rich man's country and the scenery testified to that for the developers in this neck of the woods had shown restraint.

The skyline was uncluttered by the concrete blocks that were a feature of the rest of the town and all anyone could see when they drove through the canyons was the romantic backdrop of the snow-capped Sierras.

On a clear day, Larry could spend hours watching the mountains, but when he finally got out of hospital they held no magic for him. What he needed now was the womb-like comfort of his house. And it didn't disappoint him. The double-height living-room, the walk-in closets, the custom-made bathrooms and the private cinema were just as he left them. He thanked God for the decorator who had made it all possible, and retreated into his bedroom.

Like the rest of the rooms, it had the stagey look of a film set. For everything was designed to provide the perfect backdrop for an actor.

His majestic living-room was full of antiques and country life oil paintings, hinting that Larry's English ancestry was grander than it really was. The dining-room, with its French chandelier glittering over a table big enough for four generations, created a similar illusion. But the culmination of the decorator's skill was wrought in the master bedroom.

In the beginning the actor had wanted it laid out like a seduction pad, but he was talked out of it. If he was going to be an English gentleman in the rest of his house, he could hardly revert to type in this most intimate of sanctums. So he stood aside and let the decorator have his head.

Now that he was going to be confined to his room for the next few months he felt glad he'd given in. For it wasn't like a bedroom at all. An entire wall had been converted into a library with an oak bookcase that contained first editions of plays he had appeared in. There was a leather sofa and a couple of button-backed chairs. And dominating the room on the far wall was a vast open country-style fireplace. The bed was positioned to face the fire, which burnt all year round.

Emerald thought it was strange that Larry needed the fire when the temperature outside was in the seventies but she didn't question him. It gives him reassurance, she reasoned, and there can't be anything wrong with having it.

She had learnt to surround the actor with tranquillity after a session she had with his private doctor. He had explained to her that Larry's condition had been caused by stress rather than the drugs he put up his nose. The agonies he went through every time he created a role had changed his body chemistry in some subtle way, narrowing his arteries and weakening the essential blood supply to his heart. If the actor was going to survive at all, the doctor told her, the pressure had to be turned off. Nobody could be allowed near him if they were going to make him anxious.

When she left the surgery, Emerald drove straight home and wrote out a list of all the people she was going to have to bar from the house. At the top of it were the producers of the film Larry was working on when he had his attack. The project had been temporarily shelved and the backers were running around all over town like headless chickens moaning about how much money they were losing. They're not going to kvetch to Larry for a long, long time, Emerald decided. They can complain to his agent instead. That's what he gets paid for.

Second on her list were Larry's poker-playing cronies. They were all in the business and they loved to gossip. They'll stir him up, Emerald thought. He'll want to get out of bed and back into the Hollywood game and I'm not having it. Not under any circumstances.

Her confidence deserted her when she reached Shel's name. By rights she should let him see Larry. He was his best buddy in the world. But he was also involved in the film he was making and Shel wanted him back on the set.

He had actually taken Emerald to one side and enquired when the actor would be well enough to work again. When she said it would be six months he had become very heavy.

Emerald sighed. She would allow Shel to visit, but on condition the picture was never mentioned.

The same rule applied to Larry's lawyer, and his agent. Everyone else she kept away from the house. The arrangement worked perfectly for a month. Then the cracks started to show, for without the worries over the film, Larry had nothing to occupy his mind. He realized for the first time how much of his energy went into his work.

He enjoyed playing too, but without the counterbalance of the business all his leisure activities were meaningless. The old movies he used to relish bored him stupid now. Even making love to Emerald had lost its magic for she was so careful with him. Before his heart attack there had been a glory about their sex. Larry had taught Emerald everything she knew – all the tricks, all the subtle ways of pleasing him – and in his hands she had become an expert. Now all that was a thing of the past. These days when Emerald came to bed she dressed herself from head to toe in a demure cotton nightdress, and when Larry tried to get her to take it off, she would look worried.

'I don't want to get you all stirred up,' she'd say. 'Remember what Dr Jacobson said.'

133

What the good doctor said would be engraved on Larry's mind for ever, for it amounted to a death sentence. Larry could do everything he used to do, only less so.

It was a ridiculous notion. The very thought of making love to Emerald without passion was foreign to him. It simply wasn't possible. So he abandoned the whole thing. When he was recovered, he promised himself, he'd make love to Emerald like a man again. Meanwhile, they'd just have to rub along as best they could.

It wasn't easy. The lack of physical contact made Larry irritable. He normally liked Emerald to prepare his lunch, but now he'd complain. The soup was too thin, the salad dressing too oily. It seemed Emerald could do nothing right.

She would go out and fetch him a prerelease movie and he would find fault with it. She would pretty herself up for dinner, dressing in the designer labels she knew he loved and he would make her take the whole lot off and change into jeans. She couldn't seem to please him any more, and the harder she tried, the worse it got.

She searched around for friends to listen to her troubles, and she discovered she had none. There were endless acquaintances, but her only true confidant had been Larry and he was the last person she could go to.

In the end she found herself talking to Shel. Looking back on it, she supposed she turned to him because he was there. And because he wasn't critical of her. In a way Shel Johnson was the only person who understood what she was going through, because he was going through the same agony himself.

Larry took out his frustrations on the people closest to him. His nurse, his mistress and his best friend. When the actor had a bad dream, or a morbid worry, all three of them would become his audience and his whipping boys. When he got really depressed, the only person who could laugh the actor back to normal was Shel. He had a cruel sense of humour, a wicked way of cutting everything down to size, even Larry's heart condition. And Emerald found herself starting to feel grateful to him.

At times like this, it was hard to believe that she had once hated him, for Larry's illness had changed everything in her life. The people she counted on as friends turned out to be mere acquaintances. And her arch enemy had turned overnight into an ally.

It was Shel's concern that touched her, for he was always bringing things up to the house. He knew she wasn't getting out, so he would arrive with the latest copy of *Variety* or *Vogue*. Sometimes he would bring a bottle of her favourite perfume. That would worry Emerald a little, but she didn't dwell on it.

Then one night when she was walking him to his car he asked her to have dinner with him in town and an alarm sounded in her head.

On the surface it was all very innocent. All he did was ask her very casually if she wasn't finding it lonely cooped up with Larry all day. Without thinking Emerald blurted out the truth.

'Yes,' she admitted. 'It's starting to drive me crazy.' The minute the words were out, she felt ashamed.

'Forget I said that,' she whispered. 'It was disloyal of me.'

But Shel wouldn't let it go. 'Stop being so hard on yourself,' he said. 'You've been a skivvy for Larry. A devoted skivvy and it's wearing you out.' He paused for a moment. 'Even that nurse of his doesn't do as much for him as you do,' he went on. 'And she doesn't do it twenty-four hours a day either. What you need is to get the hell out for a bit. Go and have lunch with a girlfriend. Or let me buy you dinner one night. You'll feel better afterwards, I promise you.'

Shel's limousine materialized out of the darkness, and he was sliding across the back seat and blowing a kiss through the window before a reply had formed on her lips.

Emerald stood in the drive for a long time after the car had disappeared. Did he mean it, she asked herself. Or was he just trying to protect me? The whole episode had an unreal quality to it.

When Emerald was back in the house organizing a tray for Larry, it was easy to believe it hadn't happened at all.

The next time Shel visited he made a point of talking about his parents. His father had been ill after the war and his mother had borne the brunt of it, suffering in the end more than he did. Emerald knew where the producer was heading, but she also knew Larry was no fool.

He needs a better excuse than his mother to get me out for dinner, she thought.

She stepped outside to fetch the coffee the maid was brewing, and when she came back the two men appeared to have come to some sort of agreement. It was Shel who broke the news.

'Larry thinks you should have some time off,' he said. 'I've volunteered to look after it.'

Emerald did a double take. Someone, somewhere was having her on. She took the hot drink over to Larry and regarded him closely.

'You don't really want me to go cavorting around town with Shel, do you?' she asked.

The actor looked apologetic. 'I'm a lousy patient,' he said, 'I always have been. You deserve a night out.'

'But I don't want to go out without you.'

Now Larry put on his stern look, the one he used when he was being photographed after an Oscar nomination. 'We've been getting on each other's nerves recently,' he told her. 'It's my fault, I know it is. But when I get in this kind of state I have to have space. It's the only thing that works.'

'And me going out to dinner will give you space?' she said.

Larry nodded.

Emerald suddenly felt very tired. She'd been fighting for months to keep this man afloat. More than that, she'd been fighting for his life itself. And all he wanted to do was to get rid of her.

She sighed. 'Have you two decided when the big night out is going to be,' she asked, 'or do I get a choice in it?'

It wasn't as difficult as she thought it would be. Shel took her to Chasens, which he knew she adored. And the minute they got there, he did a very good imitation of her big brother.

He announced to the maître d' and anyone else who would listen that he was looking after Emerald for his buddy Larry. And to please make sure they came up with a table worthy of her.

As the evening progressed, Emerald began to feel better about the whole thing.

They had been put right in the centre of the room. On her left Peter Sellers was having dinner with Roman Polanski and his wife. Right behind them Sean Connery was holding court. Everywhere she looked there were studio executives, most of whom found their way over to their table.

If Emerald had been with Larry the constant stream of table-hoppers would have got on her nerves but with Shel sitting by her, she welcomed the distraction.

She had no desire to get closer to him than she already was. He was her buddy and her confidant and with half the film colony paying their respects, there was no danger he would become anything else.

Halfway through the meal they started talking about Larry. He was never far from either of their thoughts and even Chasens' glitter couldn't cancel him out. Shel brought me here to cheer me up, Emerald thought ruefully, and yet here we are in the same old routine.

Yet their conversation didn't exactly echo the past, for when they were up at the house, Shel never mentioned the possibility that Larry could die.

She did her best to brush it aside. 'You're being morbid,' she told him. 'In a couple of months the three of us will be sitting here eating chilli and we'll wonder what all the fuss was about.'

The producer wasn't convinced. 'If he had agreed to the bypass, I'd go along with you,' he said, 'but he didn't. He decided to tough it out. And now I don't think there's any future for him at all.'

Shel had never spoken this way before and it chilled Emerald. It was almost as if he was convinced his best friend was on the way out and she started to wonder about his motives.

Then she wrinkled her brow. I'm being too hard on him, she thought. The guy's his best buddy.

Shel interrupted her thoughts. 'Have you ever wondered what will happen to you if Larry dies?' he asked.

The question brought Emerald up sharp. She had never considered her future, and the whole idea of Larry dying frightened her too much. She took a long gulp of her white wine.

'Do we have to talk about this?' she asked.

Shel looked at her hard. 'Of course we have to talk about it. If you don't make some kind of plan, you could be in big trouble.'

Her head started to spin. 'What kind of trouble are you talking about?'

Emerald thought she saw Shel's lip curl, but she could have been imagining it.

'Don't tell me you don't know what you're in for? When Larry goes, you'll be stony-broke. His three kids are due to get everything. Which leaves you with the clothes you stand up in.'

If the Shel she had once known had said that kind of

thing to her, Emerald would have got up and walked out. But they weren't enemies any more. This man seemed truly concerned for her and she took what he said in that spirit.

'What do you think I should do?' Emerald asked. 'I can't work in this town. I haven't even got a green card.'

The producer looked thoughtful. 'You could start looking out for another lover,' he said.

It was a crude remark, and for a moment it knocked the stuffing out of her.

'You can't be serious,' Emerald said.

But Shel was serious, for he went on talking about the future as if Larry was a lucrative job that was coming to an end.

'I don't think you realize what a lovely girl you are,' he told her. 'There'll be a queue of candidates just waiting to pick up your option.'

Emerald had a sudden depressing view of what her life could become. She would move out of Larry's house when the time came. Then without drawing breath she would climb into her car and drive along the coast to where the next protector lived.

All I have to do, she thought, is send out change of address cards, and nobody would bat an eyelid. She looked around at the women in the restaurant. They were all younger than their escorts, she noticed, and half of them weren't wearing wedding rings but they were wearing everything else. Diamonds glittered in their ears and around their throats. One babyish blonde was wearing a sapphire pin the size of a dinner plate.

From nowhere Emerald felt a deep sense of disgust. I can't live like that, she thought. I can't allow myself to be passed around a coterie of middle-aged men to keep a roof over my head. She saw Shel staring at her.

'You don't look all that interested in what I've been saying.'

Emerald was suddenly angry with him. 'I don't know

what kind of girls you go in for, but one thing's for sure: I'm nothing like them. I'd rather starve than do the Hollywood rounds.'

As she spoke, her eyes, which were normally the colour of good jade, darkened, and Shel found himself staring into deep green fire.

I've rattled her, he thought. And now she's good and frightened she might just climb off her high horse. She won't do it tomorrow, or the next day, or even the next month. But sooner or later she'll come to terms with the truth. And when she does, I'll be waiting.

CHAPTER 18

Shel made it his business to take Emerald out once a week. If it was over a weekend they'd have lunch at the Bisto Gardens or Ma Maison. Occasionally she and Larry would go over to his house in Whitely Heights. But even the short trip seemed to tire the actor and he was happy to stay home while Emerald took a break.

She often wondered if she should warn Larry that his friend was starting to monopolize her, but she decided not to. He was still too fragile to cope with a worry like that. Anyway she was a big girl, big enough to handle the likes of Shel Johnson.

Not that he was giving her any problems. By tacit agreement they never talked about the future again. Instead Shel entertained her with snippets of showbiz gossip and small talk about the latest releases. It was the sort of conversation Emerald would have with others in their set, and it relaxed her.

She realized she needed her time alone with Shel. More so as things with Larry deteriorated, for the actor couldn't come to terms with being ill.

Emerald got the worst of his frustration and it started to get to her. For the first time since Larry had been ill, she started to fight back. Their quarrels would rage for hours, each of them trying to inflict real damage.

They got to a point beyond quarrelling when words could no longer express the rage they felt towards each other. It was then that silence took over. Days would pass when they simply didn't communicate. Emerald would remove herself to another part of the house where she would watch television or sit by the pool. They ate their meals apart and at night Emerald would go to bed in another room.

Eventually, Larry would break the deadlock, contriving to make a joke of the whole thing.

'I was having one of my spasms,' he would say. 'It doesn't mean anything.'

But it did. Every time they made it up, Emerald felt something had gone out of the relationship. Larry's heart will probably survive this illness, she thought, but will we survive it? Will there be anything left by the time all this is over?

Her dates with Shel became landmarks on a battlefield. She could live through what was happening at home because she knew that for one evening or one afternoon she would be with a friend who didn't expect anything of her.

Then Shel asked her to lounge by his pool one Saturday and everything changed. The weather had turned hot that spring and the producer thought the time was right to have brunch outside. He had a big sundeck where he gave lavish parties. Because he knew Larry needed to be quiet, he suggested they kept it to just the three of them. It turned out to be just the two of them, since Larry cried off at the last moment.

Emerald wasn't sorry. For the last week Larry had been turning their lives upside down with a new obsession involving the occult and it was infuriating her.

As Emerald arrived at Shel's beach property, she felt like a refugee from a madhouse. At least with Shel, she thought, I'll be back in the real world.

He greeted her in faded blue jeans, bearing in front of him a fresh pitcher of martini. Behind him, she could see the bar had been set up with the usual appetizers and three glasses.

'I'm afraid I'm on my own today,' she told him. 'Larry was in one of his moods.'

Shel shrugged. 'It doesn't make any difference to me,' he said. 'I hadn't planned anything elaborate.'

He meant what he said. When she had a drink in her hand, they wandered through the house and out on to the sundeck. Shel must have been halfway through the Sunday papers for they were scattered in a great pile at the foot of one of the sunloungers. There was something reassuringly domestic about the mess. It's going to be an easy day, Emerald thought. I can let go for a while.

They finished the pitcher of martini sitting by the pool. Shel was in the middle of a complicated deal with one of the big studios and, while they drank, he told Emerald about it. He was very open with her, naming names and telling her exactly how much money was involved and Emerald felt flattered.

In their early days together, Larry had talked to her like this. He had taken her seriously then, listening to her opinions. Taking everything she said into account. Now he preferred the claptrap spouted by some hippie who claimed to know the mysteries of the other world.

Normally Emerald wouldn't have had any more to drink, but Shel wanted to mix up more martini and she didn't stop him.

At some stage they must have eaten lunch, though Emerald had no memory of it. Just as she had little knowledge of how she found herself inside the house sitting on Shel's bleached linen sofa. She tried to get to her feet, but the effort made her head spin.

'I think I've drunk too much,' she apologized.

The producer grinned and for some reason she thought it made him look vulnerable.

'We've both had too much,' he said. 'The only thing to do is to sleep it off.'

He helped her to her feet. 'I'll show you to the spare room.'

When Emerald woke up, she saw it was dark outside.

She struggled into a sitting position and realized she wasn't wearing anything. If her head hadn't hurt her so much, she might have worried about it. As it was, she reached over and switched on the bedside lamp. It was then that she saw she wasn't alone.

Shel was in bed beside her and she felt a sense of outrage. This was meant to be the spare room, and he didn't belong in here.

Emerald saw he was awake and grabbed the sheet to cover herself.

'What happened?' she demanded.

'We got drunk,' Shel said. 'It could have happened to anyone.'

Emerald felt foolish. 'I know we got drunk,' she retorted. 'Was there anything else?'

Shel was smiling now. 'You mean you don't remember?'

In desperation Emerald raked through the events of the afternoon. She had a dim recollection of being shown to the guest room, but how she came to be in bed without any of her clothes she had no idea.

She took a deep breath. 'Did we make love?' she asked.

Shel looked at her for a long moment, then he reached across and pulled the covers down around her waist.

'Why don't I jog your memory?' he responded.

Before Emerald could stop him, Shel had his arms round her. She tried to turn her head but he was stronger and faster than her, and there was no avoiding his kiss.

It was then she realized he had been lying. There was no way, drunk or sober, she had ever been near this man, but it was too late to protest. He was lying on top of her and his hands were everywhere.

She moaned softly and just for a moment he pulled away from her.

'You wanted this to happen,' he said. 'You wanted it for a long time.'

Emerald shook her hair out of her eyes. 'You've got it wrong,' she whispered.

But he wasn't listening. Instead he came astride her and she felt his hardness at her entrance. Then it started.

There was no preamble to Shel's lovemaking. With Larry, even with Jeremy, there had been kissing and tenderness. But this man didn't know the meaning of the word.

When it was over Emerald wasted no time getting out of bed. She wanted to get under the shower, and she wanted to stay there until every trace of Shel had been washed away. He made no move to stop her, and she felt relieved. This was a single encounter, she reasoned. A single act of possession, done after too much to drink. The moment she was back in her clothes and out of the house, she could forget it had ever happened.

Shel was waiting for her when she came out of the bathroom. He was wearing a towelling dressing-gown and he looked pleased with himself.

'That was fun,' he said pleasantly. 'We should meet every weekend.'

Emerald fought down a feeling of dread. 'You know that's not possible,' she said.

'Why not? We see each other often enough.'

Now she was really rattled. 'What about Larry?' Shel raised his eyebrows and spread his hands, and something told her he was experienced at this kind of game.

'I won't tell him, if you don't.'

Emerald was nearly dressed now and the street clothes made her feel more in control.

'I think we'd better get something clear,' she said patiently. 'What happened between us just now meant nothing at all. You must know that.'

Shel smiled, but there was no humour in it. 'I'm not all that interested in feelings,' he said. 'What turns me on is sex.'

'But you can have sex with half the actresses in Hollywood,' Emerald protested. 'Why pick on me?'

Shel looked her over, appraising the tapering legs, the long silky hair, the unusual green eyes. Finally he said, 'I want you because you're Indian, because you're exotic and because you belong to Larry. It's the forbidden fruit thing. It makes me horny as hell.'

Now Emerald felt really dirty. 'I've told you once,' she said, 'I'm not interested.'

Shel shrugged his shoulders. 'Then get interested. You don't want that boyfriend of yours finding out about today.'

Suddenly Emerald realized she'd been duped. Shel couldn't care less about her feelings, or about Larry's. The only person he wanted to please was himself, and heaven help anyone who got in his way.

'You'd tell him, wouldn't you?' she said cautiously.

Shel nodded. 'If you don't co-operate.'

Emerald considered her options but realized she was caught. She needed time to think.

Shel got up from the bed and came over to her. 'Have you decided to be sensible?' he asked.

She fought down the impulse to run. 'I'm not sure,' she told him firmly. 'I'll let you know.'

Even before she was out of the house, Emerald knew she would have to tell Larry, and the realization chilled her, for she knew that it meant the end of the road.

All the way home, she went over what she was going to say and every time she rehearsed it it sounded worse. She had gone of her own free will to Shel's house. Nobody had forced her to drink too much and when she felt like sleeping it off, she let herself be led into the spare room like a lamb to the slaughter.

There were few excuses for what she had done but she knew better than to invent any. She was going to tell it

146

straight, she decided, and when Larry told her to pack her bags, she would go quietly.

Any other girl would have felt bitter about what had happened. In one afternoon, Shel had removed both Emerald's identity and her security, yet she didn't waste time planning to get even. Her first priority now was to survive. It was something she had been doing ever since she left the shanty town in Mauritius. She knew if she was to move forward, she couldn't afford the luxury of resentment.

As she pulled into the driveway of the big house in Bel Air, she allowed herself a moment of regret, then she cleared her mind and planned the next half-hour. She was going to find Larry, she was going to tell him everything, and she was going to do it fast.

She called his name out as she came through the front door, but she didn't get any answer. He must be asleep, she thought. Then she looked at her watch. The nurse wasn't due in for another hour.

Emerald assumed Larry would be in bed, so she was surprised when she didn't find him there. Where else would he nap, she wondered. He hardly goes into the living-room or the pool area. She searched them all the same. Then she started to panic. He couldn't have gone out, she thought. He was hardly strong enough to make it to the bathroom.

That's it, she realized, quickening her step. He's in the bathroom. And in that instant, she knew something was wrong.

It took her less than five seconds to get to him. He must have been about to take a shower for he was undressed but that was as far as he had got. Whatever had happened to him had felled him before he reached the cubicle, and now he lay spreadeagled across the floor.

Emerald's reaction was instantaneous. She reached for Larry's pulse. When she found it, she knew there was hope.

*   *   *

147

According to the doctors, they had only just been able to save him. If Emerald had found Larry twenty minutes later it would have all been over but the actor had pulled through, and he was doing fine. He'd be able to go home in ten days, provided he wasn't subjected to any undue stress.

Emerald felt the first stirrings of worry, for she knew she was about to burden Larry with information that could flatten him. She tried to imagine how Larry would take the news that she'd slept with his best friend. Would he fly into a rage and call her every name in the book? Or would he tense up inside and order her off the property?

Both scenarios terrified Emerald, for she knew there was only one way they could end: Larry's heart would collapse altogether.

It's my life or his, Emerald thought bitterly. If I tell him the truth, he dies. If I go along with Shel, I die.

If only I didn't love him, she fretted, it would be so straightforward. But she did love Larry and because of that she did the only thing open to her. She called Shel.

'I'd like to come and see you,' she said. 'There are things we have to discuss.'

All Emerald's discussions with Shel took place at his house on Sunday afternoons, and Emerald came to dread Sundays.

If Shel had merely repeated what he had done the first time he had seduced her, she could have put up with it, but he didn't. Now he knew he could do whatever he liked with her, he took full advantage of the situation. It started the second time she visited him. Shel told her he was in the mood to play cinema games and at first she had no idea what he was talking about.

'What is this cinema game?' she wanted to know. Shel told her he'd show her in the bedroom.

It was a different kind of room than the one Emerald

shared with Larry. Where the actor's was overdecorated and rather cosy, Shel's bedroom was stark. There was a bed and a built-in console with a tape deck and a television set, and at the end of the room there was a desk. There was a soulless atmosphere about the place, and Emerald realized it suited Shel perfectly.

On the day of the cinema games, Shel started by telling her to get undressed, then he disappeared into his walk-in closet. When he came out he was carrying a skirt that looked like it was made of tassels and a garland of flowers.

'Put these on,' he instructed. 'Then I'll tell you what comes next.'

Emerald did as she was told, feeling slightly ridiculous.

In the past she had dressed up in suspender belts to please Larry and it hadn't bothered her. Lots of girls did that kind of thing with their lovers, but this was different. The outfit she had on now made her look like a slave girl. She turned to Shel.

'What now?' she asked. She couldn't read his expression.

'I want you to dance for me,' he told her. 'One of the native dances you learnt when you were a little girl in Mauritius.'

'I think you're getting Mauritius mixed up with some-where else,' Emerald said slowly. 'We don't do native dances where I come from.'

She saw Shel's lip curl and felt frightened.

'I don't give a shit what you did back home,' he said. 'And I don't give a shit for your excuses either. You're a darkie, aren't you? Just swing your hips and show me your tits and we'll both be happy.'

Emerald started to say no, then she saw how angry he looked. This is his fantasy, she thought. His way of getting horny. He probably pays girls to do this.

Shel pressed a button on the tape deck and the room was flooded with African music. It was loud and insistent

149

and punctuated by the throb of drums. Emerald moved to its rhythm.

Halfway through the dance the tape clicked off and Shel came up to where she stood. Then he took hold of her hands and pulled them behind her back.

'I'm going to handcuff you,' he said gently. 'It won't hurt.'

Emerald felt cold metal pinning her wrists together and she started to panic. If this crazy man wanted to murder her now, she couldn't defend herself.

'Do you have to do this,' she asked quietly. 'I'm not very happy.'

Shel ignored her. Then he walked her over to the bed where he made her lie face downwards. The first time he hit her Emerald screamed, and she went on screaming until she realized Shel was getting off on her pain. Then she clammed up. The bastard could torture her if he had a mind to, but she didn't have to help him enjoy it.

She had no recollection of how long it went on for. Her only feeling was one of relief when it stopped. When Shel started to unshackle her wrists, she asked if she could go. But he shook his head.

'I haven't finished with you yet,' he said.

The beatings became a regular prelude to Shel's love-making. Emerald would arrive at the beachhouse every weekend where she would find a different costume. Some-times he would provide her with harem pants and a filmy veil. Once she had to be a French maid. But the theme was always the same. She was the victim and Shel had the power to make her suffer.

Her only solace during this time was Larry. His last heart attack had subdued him. Before he had fought against being an invalid. Now he gave into it and it brought a tranquillity to their relationship.

Emerald went along with his new mood, but behind the smiling façade she presented every day, she was filled with fear. It was almost as if Larry seemed to know he didn't have very long to live, and she realized now what their fights had been all about. He was struggling for survival then. Fighting not her, but death itself and now he had no more strength for the battle.

Emerald felt as if she had two spectres in her life: Shel and Larry. She shuttled between the two of them as helplessly as an insect caught in a beam of light. They had taken over her life and she wondered if she would ever be free of them.

The nightmare ended six months later when Larry had his third and final attack. None of the doctors could bring him round this time and Emerald was the first to be told the news.

She took it calmly. Larry had been in rehearsal for this event for a long time now. He had given her detailed instructions of who should be contacted and where the funeral was to be held and now it had happened Emerald went through the motions.

She called his family in England and arranged for them to fly in. All his friends in Hollywood had to be told. His lawyers had to be given notice and the house had to be put on the market. There was a ski lodge in Aspen and an apartment in New York to be taken care of as well, but his executors could handle these.

On the day of the funeral she finally thought of herself. She was alone now. There was no one to look after any more. No one to worry about. No one to placate. She was overcome with relief. Nothing that happened to her could ever be as bad as the last six months.

For a moment she thought about Shel Johnson and the beatings he subjected her to. They were history now, and suddenly she made her mind up to leave town. She was finished with Shel, finished with Larry and she was all washed up with Los Angeles.

She was putting on her hat in the bedroom when she

was interrupted by the ringing of the phone. It was Larry's lawyer, Steve Brady. He wanted a meeting with her before she set off for Forest Lawns. Emerald hesitated. It didn't seem right to be talking to lawyers at a time like this, but Brady insisted and she gave in.

They agreed to meet downtown at lunchtime and she wondered what Steve wanted. Larry's entire family, led by his aggressive mother, had been camping on the lawyer's doorstep for two days now. Surely they could take care of any outstanding business. She sighed. Even in death, Larry couldn't leave her be.

Emerald arrived at Brady's practice in the black dress she was going to wear later on. She had taken her hair back in a severe chignon and all her diamonds were on show. Today would be her last public appearance and she wanted to leave looking like a winner.

The effect wasn't lost on Steve, who whistled slowly as she came into his office.

'So you're starting the way you mean to go on,' he observed.

Emerald frowned. 'I don't know what you mean.'

Now it was the lawyer's turn to look confused. 'You're kidding me,' he said. 'You have to know what Larry's intentions were.'

Emerald was worried. What new problems was her beloved Larry presenting her with?

'Suppose you tell me,' she suggested.

The attorney picked up a sheaf of papers from his desk and flicked through them. Then he turned to Emerald.

'Larry's left you everything he owned,' he told her. 'You get all three properties, the copyright on all his films and two million dollars.'

Emerald was astonished. There had to be a mistake.

'What about his family?' she asked in a whisper. 'I thought Larry was leaving everything to them.'

Brady smiled. 'He was,' he told her. 'Only he changed his mind at the last moment.'

Emerald felt uneasy. She had read about situations where a rich man changes his mind on his deathbed and rewrites his will. The family never let him get away with it, of course. They threw mud and queried the balance of his mind and she knew Larry's relations were no exception.

She thought about the three sulky-looking boys who were his sons. She thought about his mother with her dyed blonde hair and red lipstick. She thought about his sour-faced ex-wife.

'I don't stand a chance,' she said quietly. 'The Simpsons will sue me from here to eternity.'

The lawyer shuffled his papers and looked embarrassed. He had been on at Larry to leave nominal sums to his offspring from the moment he started to make a new will, but the actor would have none of it.

'They don't care about me,' he had said. 'They never did. I sent them presents and money for years without getting even a thank-you letter, and now I've had enough of it. Emerald was the one who loved me and she should be rewarded for it.'

It was a typical Hollywood way of looking at things. Even love had to be priced and labelled and properly accounted for. The attorney turned to the woman sitting in front of him and did his best to reassure her.

'Larry loved you,' he said, 'and the kids knew that. I don't think they'll interfere now he's gone.'

Emerald looked doubtful. 'How can you be so sure?'

Steve Brady looked at her with something approaching despair. Why was it that all the really beautiful girls valued themselves so little?

'He was planning to marry you,' he said tersely. 'He even made me write to the family, so it was all above board. Then he became really ill and he put all his plans on the back burner.'

Emerald's eyes filled with tears. While Larry was dreaming of making her his wife, she was being blackmailed by his best friend. We never did get it right, she thought. What a pointless waste it all was.

She reached inside her plain lizard bag, brought out a tissue and started dabbing her makeup, but it was no good. Now the tears had started in earnest there was no stopping the flow. They ran down her perfect paint job, blurring the mascara so that it made great smudges on her tawny skin.

'This is awful,' she said to no one in particular. 'I'm going to look like hell at the funeral.'

CHAPTER 19

London, 1980

The girl was very pretty in a disorganized sort of way, and she was trying her best to make an impression. Not that it was doing her any good. She had bombarded Richard Waites with every question in the book. She had used all her tricks, all her expertise, and he wasn't giving an inch.

The man didn't want to be interviewed. She had realized that the minute she walked into his office in the Weiss building, for he hadn't put himself out for her.

In the normal way of things, she wouldn't have wasted her time. Captains of industry fell over themselves to be in her column and Waites wasn't that big a deal. Except he was. Or at least he was going to be. She had a pretty shrewd instinct about that.

Caroline Fellows' instincts had made her one of the most influential city columnists of her generation. If she announced in the *London Evening Post* that a share was on the way up or a company was about to succumb to a takeover, then the world sat up and took notice.

Her Wednesday column was compulsory reading for everyone who wanted to get ahead in business. If you were lucky enough to appear in it, your future was assured.

So why was Richard Waites resisting her? She decided to forget about charming him and go for the throat.

'You took over from Rolf Weiss just over a month ago,' she said. 'Did you push him out, or did he go of his own accord?'

Richard shifted uncomfortably in his deep leather chair. He had promised Rolf that he wouldn't breathe a word about his illness but this woman had backed him into a corner.

'The day-to-day running of the conglomerate got too much for the Chairman,' he said cautiously. 'He hasn't been in the best of health recently, so he handed that side of things over to me. But it was his decision. Nobody forced his hand.'

Caroline's eyes glittered dangerously. So the young lion wasn't claiming total victory. That was unusual. Most men in Waites' position couldn't stop talking about how they fought their way to the top. The way he told it, he had become Managing Director almost by default.

She decided to give him another push. 'But all the really big strides the company made in the past ten years have been due to you. You can't deny that.'

Richard sighed. She wasn't going to let him off the hook until Rolf had been well and truly sold down the river. Well, he couldn't do that.

Sure, he might have had a few bright ideas, but without the framework the old tycoon provided, none of his innovations would have seen the light of day. The ice-cream parlours, the airport cafés, the motorway motels, would have all been pie in the sky without Rolf's canny manoeuvring. The old man was one of the best negotiators this side of the Atlantic. He hoped the years sitting at his right hand had given him half his expertise.

He turned to the girl. 'No business is a one-man band,' he said. 'I might have taken the credit for a lot of our success, but I couldn't have done it on my own.'

The girl smacked her pad down on the shiny walnut desk that separated her from the stuffed shirt sitting opposite.

'I don't seem to be getting through to you at all,' she said. 'What am I doing wrong?'

Just for a second Richard felt remorse. She's got a job to do, he thought, and all I can do is stand in her way. He allowed himself a closer study of his opponent and he liked

156

what he saw. She was a natural redhead, you could tell that from her freckles. And she had the fragile, classy look that he liked so much in women.

I can't give her the story she wants, he thought, but there must be some way I can compensate her. He looked at his watch and saw it was getting on for seven.

'Would you by any chance be free for dinner tonight?' he asked her.

Caroline pouted. 'You haven't answered my question.'

He walked out from behind the desk, picking her note-pad up as he did so.

'If you can make dinner,' he said, handing it over to her, 'there'll be time to talk about your problem some more. How's that for a deal?'

She considered resisting him. Richard Waites was beginning to make a reputation for himself in the gossip columns. He had an appetite for women. A different woman for every night of the week, if you believed everything you read. The chances were that by the end of the evening she'd be no closer to her story than she was now.

Then she thought, what the hell. She wasn't doing anything that night. Whatever happened it had to be a lot more fun than watching television with a low-fat yogurt.

He took her to Le Gavroche just behind Sloane Square and Caroline was immediately sorry she hadn't worn something better when she came to see him. The little wool suit from Jaeger had looked very smart two years ago, but in the dark restaurant, with its ankle-deep carpets and fawning waiters, she felt out of place. All the other women dining there were in dark understated little dresses and real jewellery. I look like some poor relation up from the country, she thought. It isn't fair.

She concentrated her attention on getting Richard to open up about himself. The cuttings the library had provided told her he was related to Tim Waites, the merchant banker.

He had been educated at Stowe, which accounted for his old-fashioned manners. But the most interesting thing about this man was his beginnings. He came from one of the exotic islands in the tropics and it was rumoured that his father and mother had never been married. He never talked about it, of course, at least not publicly, but he wasn't pure Waites stock. Somewhere along the line there was other blood.

Caroline felt a shiver of excitement and instantly felt ashamed. She looked at the handsome man sitting opposite her and wondered why being a little bit coloured should matter. She reminded herself that she was here on business and needed to know more about the Weiss empire.

She started to probe into his relationship with Rolf and how they had met. Richard told her the aftershave story. If he hadn't been suspicious of her, he might have gone into the fights he had had with Rolf – the times when the old man had physically to turn him out of the office when he pushed him too far. But he didn't. He stuck to the facts instead, and he sensed her impatience with him.

'You're a close one, aren't you?' Caroline said, looking at him over the rim of her glass. 'Is there anyone you trust? Or is everybody in the world a potential enemy?'

Again Richard deflected her questions. 'Beautiful women have never featured on my hit list,' he smiled.

'They do if they talk about business,' she countered.

Instead of replying, Richard signalled the waiter and started to arrange dinner.

'I can recommend the Soufflé Suisse,' he told her. 'You can't get it anywhere else. I can guarantee it's an experience.'

Caroline nodded her assent. If Richard wanted to show off his superior knowledge of the menu it was all the same to her. Her mind was made up she was going to win tonight. Whatever she had to do she would get the truth out of this man, even if she had to flatter him to death.

She started to talk about racing. Richard was a well-known figure at the track and she knew he had a passion for horses.

Now they were on neutral territory, some of the reserve went out of him. He had had a good day at the Oaks the previous weekend and as he talked about it, he became animated. Caroline joined in his enthusiasm, demanding to know what system he used with the bookies, whether he had any inside contacts with the trainers.

Her only experience of racing had been from the inside of a private box at Ascot, when she discovered that horses were a boring intrusion to an otherwise amusing party. But she didn't let on. As far as Richard was concerned, if he loved something she loved it more.

The whole evening went on like that. She would bring up a topic she knew he was fascinated with. Then she would expound on it. Her journalist's training had taught her to be an instant expert on everything. No one subject went very deep with her, but it didn't have to. Caroline's talent lay in the fact that she could listen.

She listened to Richard until nearly midnight, then she feigned tiredness.

'I have to get my beauty sleep,' she told him.

Richard prevailed on her to have one last drink, a night-cap at his apartment in Eaton Square, and she let him talk her into it. She was getting close to him now. Almost behind his guard. Out of the corner of her eye she could see the winning post.

When Richard opened the door to his flat, Caroline was impressed. She had expected a man with Richard's background to go for a vulgar new money look. She could almost visualize the Victorian oil paintings and the glass-and-gilt coffee tables. Instead, it had been decorated by David Hicks.

What was clever about it, she realized, was the way the decorator mixed together the new and the antique, until what you were left with was an international look. The person that lived here, the room in its various shades of cream told you, was rich and stylish with just a hint of grandeur.

She sat herself down on the pale silk sofa and asked for a Scotch and water. Caroline prided herself on drinking like a man.

Richard brought the decanter over to the table and poured drinks for both of them, then he took a position over by the fireplace and waited for her to make the first move. The girl wanted to be made love to, he was sure of that, but she wanted something else as well and that bothered him.

They were talking about the opera when she removed her jacket. It was a very ordinary gesture. The sort of thing any girl would do when she was relaxing over a drink. Except most girls would have bothered to put something on underneath.

All Caroline was wearing was a black lacy bra. A skimpy arrangement with padding underneath that pushed her breasts forward. The contrast between the tarty underwear and the proper little business suit she was wearing banished every suspicion from Richard's mind. He no longer cared about what she was up to. He just wanted to get his hands on her.

She made it easy for him. As he came towards her she unhooked the back of her skirt. Then she stood up and let it fall round her ankles.

She had the kind of body you saw on Victorian postcards. All handspan waist and flaring hips, but the most disturbing thing about Caroline was her skin.

It was white, almost see-through. If Richard touched her too roughly he knew he was in danger of bruising her, and it excited him. There was something about this girl that cried out to be damaged.

They kissed for a long time and he was surprised at her

hunger. He had expected something softer but she was all steel and determination. He pushed her back on to the sofa and she reached out her tapering alabaster arms and held him close. They were both naked now and almost before Richard realized it, he was inside her. It was then he knew he had been fooled. This was no fragile ingénue. Caroline knew exactly what she was doing. He couldn't hurt her even if he tried.

He spent a long time making love to her, and it was an education, for this girl was the first one who knew as much as he did. It shocked him slightly. Women weren't meant to take the initiative and while he revelled in her boldness, he knew in his heart he didn't want to repeat the experience. There was one other thing about her he didn't like. She wanted to stay up half the night talking. It was as if the lovemaking was a warm-up to a greater intimacy. She went on about her private life with no shame whatever, telling him in detail about her other lovers and what they liked to do to her. Richard knew he should have stopped the confession, but he couldn't. There was something terribly compelling about her stories.

A warning light went on in the back of his mind. Why is she doing this, he wondered. What does she want? But before he could concentrate on what was bothering him, she was sitting in his lap making love to him all over again.

They spent the whole night exploring their senses. There was nothing Richard could do to surprise Caroline and it challenged him. He wanted to claim her attention in some way. So in the end he started telling her stories of his own.

He told her about his childhood growing up in Mauritius. He talked about his mother, and his father who had abandoned both of them, and the confession made him feel better. It was as if he were unloading all the ghosts in his past. And the girl must have sensed this, for she encouraged him to go into detail.

He started remembering names he thought he had buried

years ago. Incidents, many of them shaming, flashed through his mind and came pouring out of his lips. And when he had told her the whole thing, he finally let go and fell into a deep sleep.

Caroline left him as the dawn came up, putting on her little Jaeger suit, her neat dark stockings, her patent leather court shoes. It was as if she had applied a kind of mask. The wanton creature who had shared Richard's bed all night had turned herself back into a businesswoman. Now she was every inch the city page journalist with an urgent deadline to meet.

He saw her to the door, kissing her goodbye and promising to call in a day or so. Then he summoned his butler and asked for hot black coffee and croissants. He had a heavy day ahead of him and he needed to clear his head.

Richard was in Amsterdam when he saw the story Caroline had written about him. His secretary had sent the paper to him by special courier and it arrived just before lunchtime.

The minute Richard saw it, he realized she had taken him for a fool. For it was all there. His illegitimacy, his Indian mother, his early life on a sugar plantation. Everything he had told her had been printed on the city pages of the *London Evening Post*. But it was worse than just an exposé of his background, for Caroline Fellows had added her point of view to the story.

She didn't damn him exactly – that would have been too obvious – but she patronized him. *It's praiseworthy*, she had written, *that a man like Richard Waites, with no formal qualifications, can end up heading a multinational conglomerate. It says much for his native cunning and even more for Rolf Weiss's belief in his formidable talents.*

To the casual reader it appeared that Caroline was behind him every inch of the way, but people who read city pages look behind the surface to what the writer is really saying. The fact that Caroline referred to Richard's expertise as 'native cunning' wasn't lost on him. In a few short paragraphs she had dismissed him as an ignorant savage who would have done everyone a favour by staying behind on his plantation.

Richard took out the pack of Turkish cigarettes he always smoked and lit one impatiently. Then he started to calculate the damage she had done to him.

He started with his business associates. Rolf wouldn't give a damn, of course. His own origins weren't exactly true blue and they had never held him back. But Rolf's different, he thought. He didn't pretend to be anyone other than he was.

Richard considered the face he always presented to the public: the English gentleman with the public school background. He looked the part, he dressed the part, dammit he lived the part. Now this ambitious slut of a journalist had exposed him as living a lie. Would people trust him less now they knew who he really was?

He decided to test the water. Picking up the phone he placed a call to Rolf in London. The old man came on the line the instant he announced himself. It was almost as if he expected the call.

'I saw the piece in the *Evening Post*,' he said without preamble. 'It was a wonderful puff for Weiss. I've already sent the journalist a bunch of flowers.'

Richard couldn't believe what he was hearing. 'You did what?' he said incredulously. 'After all the things she said about me?'

Rolf's laughter echoed down the line. 'I suppose you're going to tell me you're mortally insulted. Well, can it, there's a good boy. Caroline Fellows spelt your name right and she got it in the headline. That alone makes up for everything else she did.'

There was the briefest of pauses while Richard took in what had been said. 'You mean the exposé of my background isn't important?'

'Of course it's important, dear boy. You're going to feel no end of a fool the next time you visit your club. But as far as business is concerned you don't have any worries. The only issue of colour, as far as the banks are concerned, is the colour of your money, and you've got plenty of that. So has Weiss.'

The young man lit another cigarette.

'Won't the financial community think it strange that I'm not what I appear to be?'

Again the entrepreneur chuckled. 'Why should they?' he asked. 'Nobody who deals at your level wears their heart on their sleeve. You wouldn't expect them to. The important thing is track record. You've had ten years of success behind you now. You've built up businesses from nothing. You've paid back all your loans and you've turned in healthy profits. I don't see what you've got to worry about.'

Richard leant back in his chair. So she hadn't hurt him after all. His pride had been punctured, but his wallet was intact. He guessed he could live with that.

'Thanks for the pep talk,' he said to his partner. 'It was very reassuring. Though next time I take a journalist out for dinner I'll be a lot more careful.'

The business in Holland went remarkably smoothly. Richard was there to take over a small hotel group and he had expected difficulties with the owners. Instead, nobody questioned any of his proposals. They had all seen the piece in the London evening paper and it had given him a certain credibility. If Caroline Fellows considered him important enough to lead her column with, he had to be taken seriously.

On the plane back to London, Richard started to think about her again. She had behaved disgracefully, trading her body for secrets he would rather have kept hidden, yet she fascinated him. He wasn't used to women taking the initiative. All his girlfriends had been there strictly for decoration. They made the right sort of small talk at dinner parties and knew how to handle themselves at the races, but they were always under his control. Caroline was different because she had a mind of her own.

He didn't see her hanging on the end of the phone waiting for some suitor to call. He didn't suppose she'd change her plans for any man on earth. And it was this independence that made up his mind. He would definitely see her again. There would be a full-blown affair. But before it got off the ground, he wanted to be sure of one thing: the relationship would have to be on his terms. He started to figure out how he was going to take Caroline down a peg.

CHAPTER 20

Caroline was sitting in her office when her secretary, Valerie, told her Richard was on the line. She started to panic.

'Tell him I'm not here,' she whispered. Valerie did as she was told, then she looked up from the phone.

'He wants to know when you're expected in the office.'

She sighed. There was no point in avoiding Richard. If he wanted to tear her off a strip, she was going to have to face him.

'Ask him what he wants,' she said to the secretary, 'and tell him I'll get back to him in twenty minutes.'

She watched the girl as she asked the question, searching her face for clues. Usually when one of her victims had a gripe, they tried it on her secretary first but Valerie wasn't making her usual anguished frown. Instead she looked amused.

'I'll give Miss Fellows the message,' she said, replacing the receiver. Then she turned to the columnist. 'Richard Waites wanted to know if you were free to have lunch with him in Paris tomorrow. He has a reservation at the Plaza d'Athéna and if you're interested he can give you a lift in the company jet.'

Caroline looked bemused. If Richard wanted revenge for the story she stole from him, he had a funny way of going about it.

'I wonder if I should go?' she asked no one in particular.

Valerie looked at her as if she were mad.

'I'm not trying to put you down,' she said, 'but that's

the best offer you've had in all the time I've known you.'

Caroline shook herself. 'You're right,' she replied. 'Ring him back and find out what time I have to be at the airport.'

Caroline wasn't exactly short of glamorous invitations. It was one of the reasons she chose to work in the city office. While the other writers on the paper interviewed single-parent families and visited pop stars in cramped hotel rooms, Caroline floated around the West End drinking champagne and holding court. When Richard had asked her to dinner at Le Gavroche it had been one of her days for staying in the office, so she hadn't been at her best. Now he had given her proper warning, she pulled out all the stops.

When she met him in the VIP lounge at Heathrow, she was wearing a navy-and-white Chanel suit. She had had it for three years now, hauling it out for high days and holidays, and she knew she looked good in it. Her hair was pulled back into the nape of her neck and fastened with a flat grosgrain bow, and when Richard set eyes on her he knew his plan was working.

Taking her to Paris for lunch hadn't just dazzled her. It had blinded her. It must have taken hours to put herself together like this, he thought. If I'd invited her to Langan's, she probably wouldn't have bothered to turn up. He smiled inwardly. There was a lot to be said for having enough money to do whatever you liked.

He took Caroline through to a door at the back of the airport building, which led on to a private field. There, in a row, were the company jets, each with its own livery. A man in a peaked cap came up and took them over to the Weiss plane.

Caroline started to feel out of her depth. She had been in chauffeur-driven limousines, but never chauffeur-driven aeroplanes. Her ignorance really came home to her when she got inside. For instead of tiers of seats on either side of a gangway, she was confronted by what was, to all intents and purposes, a drawing-room. There was a sofa and two easy chairs grouped around a low table. On it was the latest *Vogue*, a pile of Richard's papers and a crystal vase of fresh-cut flowers.

She wondered whether Richard would offer her champagne and was disappointed when he didn't. Then she glanced at her watch. It was just gone eleven. She didn't normally start drinking till well after midday. Nobody did. I'm behaving like a tourist, she thought. She looked at Richard studying the papers that had been left on the table. This was a normal morning for him, she realized. He probably makes a trip like this two or three times a week.

For a moment she wondered what other girls he took with him on his travels. Then she stopped herself. She had no claims on this man. They'd slept together, once, in the name of business. It didn't give her the right to feel jealous.

They got to Paris just before lunch. A customs official met them at the plane and gave them the necessary clearance to enter France. Then they climbed into a long dark limousine and twenty minutes later they were standing on the pavement outside the Plaza d'Athéna.

The hotel, just off the Champs-Elysées, was in the centre of the couture district.

Right opposite, Caroline could see Christian Dior's shopfront and she wondered if their clients made a point of dropping by for a new outfit before visiting the hotel. Never in her life had she seen so many expensively dressed women. When she left London she thought she was the last word in elegance. Now, sitting in the bar of this jet-set watering hole, she merely felt out of date. She was a working journalist in a three-year-old Chanel she'd got cheap at a sale. Her handbag was the one she used every day at the office and looked it. Her shoes were cheap imitations of the designer version. And her jewellery was non-existent.

She sat up straighter in her chair and tried to look as if none of it mattered. Why is it, she wondered, that with this man, I always feel cheap.

Richard turned to her and asked what apéritif she was having. She was tempted to order Kir Royale, but she compromised and settled for dry white chablis. She didn't want him to think that she was anxious to spend all his money.

Now she wasn't grilling him for a story, Caroline was free to see her companion for who he was and she found herself warming to him. She knew he was bright, but she didn't realize how literate he was. If she hadn't known otherwise she would have imagined he had a classics degree, or at least an Oxbridge education. He was at ease with a whole range of topics none of the other financial whizz kids would have had time for.

She asked him where he got his education and he laughed.

'Back in the jungles of Mauritius,' he said lightly. 'The white settlers were very generous with the native boys.'

It was the only time he alluded to the piece she had written about him and it bothered her. Anyone else would have had it out and laid their hurt feelings right on the line. But Richard behaved as if nothing had happened. From the way he was treating her, she might have written her profile on the same lines as the Weiss publicity department's handout.

He must have liked what I did in bed, she thought. Maybe he's lining me up for a rematch. The notion of it made Caroline tingle. There was something powerful about Richard, something masculine that woke her up inside. If he had said right then, 'Let's skip lunch and go to my suite,' she wouldn't have hesitated. But he didn't. Instead he went on about the excellence of the hotel cuisine, and she felt let down. She wanted to devour this man and all he was interested in was the *plat du jour*.

When they finished their drinks, the maître d'hôtel led them through to a leafy courtyard where lunch had been set up. It was a hot June day and everyone seemed to be eating outside. There was something about the scene that reminded Caroline of a society race meeting. All the men were in formal dark suits and a number of women were wearing hats. They look as if they tried, she thought, as if lunch here were the high spot of their calendar. For some reason it excited her.

All her lunches to date had been for business. Pleasure was the sole reason for being in Paris. She gave herself up to it.

When Caroline looked at her watch again it was getting on for four. Richard saw her look of alarm and smiled.

'Are you worried about getting back?' he asked.

She took one of the flat Turkish cigarettes he offered and lit it.

'Not really,' she said. 'I told the office I'd be away all day, so they're not expecting me.'

Richard looked brisk. 'You're luckier than me,' he told her. 'I've got a meeting in half an hour at the Bourse. I was going to suggest you took my car on to the airport.'

Richard saw her look of disappointment. So she was planning on spending the day here, he thought. Probably the night as well. He wondered if he should make it hard for her and send her home straightaway. Then he thought, no I can still achieve what I set out to do, without that.

'This is another option,' he said carefully. 'We could have dinner after my meeting and make a night of it.'

Caroline looked curious. 'Where would we stay?'

Richard signalled the waiter for the bill. 'Why, here, of course,' he told her. 'I have a permanent suite on the top floor.'

Caroline spent the afternoon walking around Paris. She had visited the city briefly in the past, but then she had been on holiday. Now she wasn't interested in climbing the Eiffel Tower or walking round the Pompidou Centre. She wanted to pretend she was like all the women she had seen at lunch today. She wanted to be decadent and rich.

So she played a game of make-believe in the rue du Faubourg Saint Honoré.

She started at Louis Vuitton where she told the assistant who came to help her she wanted a set of luggage. The man brought out half a dozen cases in the famous gold-and-brown logo. Each one would have cost Caroline a month's salary, yet she was picky about them.

'Gucci have the same thing in real leather,' she said. 'I'll come back when I've compared prices.'

Now she had her confidence she sailed into boutiques she never dared go near before. In Saint Laurent she tried and discarded half a dozen tailored suits. In Maude Frizon she considered real crocodile shoes. Then she had an attack of conscience and decided she couldn't get involved in stamping out an endangered species.

Only in Chanel did she weaken. For it was there she found a bag that worked perfectly with the suit she was wearing. It was a tiny quilted number in navy leather with the famous chain shoulder strap and Caroline fell in love with it. She was badly overdrawn at the bank and there was no way she could afford it, but she bought it anyway. In her head she was already the most important woman in Richard Waites' life.

He would want me to have it, she convinced herself. If we were together on this shopping spree he might have already bought me half of Paris.

Caroline was high on a dangerous drug and she knew it. She was getting off on somebody else's money and power. A man she barely knew. A man who had every reason to resent her for what she had done to him, but her logic seemed to have deserted her. All she could focus her mind on was the fact that they were spending the night together. It fuelled her imagination and stirred her senses and for the first time in her highly successful career she let her guard down.

When she got back to the hotel she discovered that

Richard was already in the suite. The concierge escorted her into the private lift, the one that served the penthouse. Then when she was outside the door he finally left her to it.

She couldn't believe the apartment when she first saw it. If she had despised Richard a little when she first met him, all that was gone now. Any man who could keep a place like this as an occasional *pied-à-terre* had her full attention. The furniture here was real French empire, the sort of thing she had only seen in museums. Caroline spotted a Fragonard on the wall, and what she thought was a Degas. And when she asked if they were real, Richard shrugged and told her they were part of a private collection he kept for investment purposes.

Then, before she could ask any more questions, he put his arms round her and held her close. The desire she had felt for him earlier that day washed over her again.

I should be dignified about this, Caroline thought. I should walk through into the other room, take my clothes off nicely and lie down on the bed. But she couldn't do it. Instead she pulled him down with her on to the silk rug and started undoing his trousers. This time Richard was prepared for her.

With the women he had known in the past, he had always been gentle. There was something precious about their femininity. Something that required seduction. This creature didn't know the meaning of the word, so he made no attempt to be a gentleman. She was lying underneath him in her smart Chanel suit with all her red hair loose and spread out around her.

This is how I want her, he thought. Hot and hungry and dressed to the nines. He took hold of her skirt and pulled it up around her waist. She was wearing stockings and an old-fashioned suspender belt over lace panties.

He got rid of the panties. Then he parted her legs so she looked like a dirty postcard. After that his need for her was so urgent, he didn't have time for anything else. They made love exactly as they were, then shed their clothes and went on making love right through the time when most self-respecting Parisians were ordering dinner and asking for the wine list. At ten o'clock they finally released each other. All through the apartment was a trail of discarded clothes. The chic little ensemble that had seen Caroline through the day lay crumpled and ruined.

The blouse was torn and smeared with lipstick and several of the gilt buttons that decorated the jacket had come off. She looked in horror at what they had done.

'There's no way I can go out in that,' she wailed.

Richard grinned. 'Then why go out? The Plaza don't mind serving dinner up here.'

Caroline agreed to it because there was no other way, but as the food arrived, she noticed the waiter had a very good knowledge of the apartment. He found the knives and forks without being told. He knew whereabouts in the fridge the ice was kept. Even the linen cupboard where the napkins lived was no mystery to him.

Caroline watched while all this was going on and just for a moment her confidence deserted her. He's done all this before, she thought. He scoops up a girl, makes love to her like a stallion, then he orders room service as an afterthought. She started to feel vulnerable. Somehow, without realizing it, she had lost the initiative. If she had been in London she would have walked out and taken a taxi home. But she was on Richard's territory now and she couldn't do that.

She looked at her new lover prowling around his dining-room in blue jeans and a silk shirt knotted casually around his waist. He was smiling slightly and it worried her. She had seen that look before on the faces of men who had pulled off takeover deals. I wonder what's on his mind, she thought.

*　　　*　　　*

173

Seasoned travellers can always tell which city they're in by the quality of the light. In Rome the early morning sun bleaches out the pastel-coloured buildings bringing with it a promise of the heat of the day. In Cairo the light dazzles and scorches minutes after the dawn. But in Paris everything is muted. At daybreak a slight haze hangs over the city, throwing all the colours into sharper relief. The trees that line the boulevards look greener at this hour. The streets themselves have a newly minted look as if an invisible army of cleaners had been at work all night.

No other city in the world looks quite like Paris in the early morning. And when Caroline opened her eyes in the Plaza d'Athéna, she knew exactly where she was.

Instinctively she reached out an arm to find her lover of the night before but the space where Richard had been sleeping was empty.

He's probably in the shower, she thought sleepily, or on the phone to some financial centre. She sat up in bed and shook herself awake. Then she remembered it was Saturday. He won't be doing any deals today, she reasoned. Everything's closed.

Caroline got up and walked over to the window, marvelling at the beauty of the city that lay at her feet. They would walk today, she decided. Richard's driver could take them over to the Bois de Boulogne and let them loose in the landscaped gardens. A feeling of animal contentment stole over her. Nothing in the world compared to discovering Paris all over again in the arms of a new lover.

She thought back to the night before and to the things Richard had done to her. It wasn't what he had done that surprised her, it was the fact that she had allowed a man, any man, to take the lead in the bedroom. Years ago she had established a kind of pattern with her men. In every affair, Caroline set the pace. It kept whoever she was involved with on their toes. It also gave her complete control over her relationships.

Every new affair was planned out to the last detail. She behaved a little like a Second World War general orchestrating a military campaign. Before a relationship even started Caroline had assessed the strengths and weakness of her adversary, then she simply sat back and played on them.

One of her girlfriends once asked her if she ever loved any of her boyfriends and Caroline had laughed.

'Love's an indulgence,' she had replied. 'You can't win when you fall in love.' Now as she looked at the watery sun lighting up the streets below her, she wondered whether she would win with Richard.

She wandered over to the dressing-table and pulled a brush through her tangled red hair. As she did so, she made a fast inventory of her assets. It was a sexy body and she knew it. Her breasts were full and ripe and the tapering waist only made them look more so. Her bottom was a bit too big, she noted. She'd have to start doing the exercises again. And cutting down on the booze.

She turned round and checked her back view and decided it wasn't such a disaster after all. She may not be a couturier's beanpole, but men liked something to get hold of.

Richard came into her mind again and she decided she couldn't wait around for him all day. Whatever he was doing in the bathroom, he'd have to stop. She wanted him and she wanted him now.

Without bothering to dress she padded down the hall to the main bathroom.

'Richard,' she shouted. 'What are you up to?'

But there was no answer. She tried rattling the doorknob and when she got no response, she pushed her way in. Richard was nowhere to be seen. What was really strange was that the room didn't appear to have been used. All the towels were neatly folded on their racks, there wasn't a mark on the handbasins and the shower curtain was dry. Where is he, she wondered.

She went back into the hall and tried all the other rooms in the penthouse apartment.

There was no trace of Richard in the study. The dining-room where they had eaten the night before must have been tidied before dawn for now it was like a room in a museum, a priceless showpiece where nobody lived. It was the same story everywhere she looked. At some time during the early hours of the morning, Richard had simply removed himself and instructed his staff to clean up after him. She searched around to see if he had left a note for her. But there was nothing.

Caroline had been dumped in Paris in the middle of a sunny weekend without even a goodbye. Suddenly the look she had seen on Richard's face after dinner made sense to her. He'd been planning this all along, she thought. The romantic Paris routine, followed by a sharp slap in the face. He wanted to hurt me, she realized. He wanted to pay me back for the story I did about his mother.

For no good reason, her eyes filled with tears. She wiped them away angrily. What was she doing feeling sorry for herself? She was a big girl now playing a big game. If the going got rough from time to time, that was the price she paid.

She trailed back into the bathroom and turned on the tub. Then, as she was waiting for it to fill, she picked up the phone and called the concierge. She wanted a seat on the lunchtime plane to London to be charged to her American Express card.

'Which class will madame be travelling?' the man on the desk enquired.

Caroline swallowed angrily, and told him economy. Now she was picking up her own tab, she couldn't afford unnecessary luxuries.

Caroline Fellows was the daughter of a brigadier and a retired dancer from the London Palladium. Her mother had always been something of an embarrassment to her, for Caroline liked to pretend that she came from the very top drawer of society.

At her prep school in Surrey the other girls called her 'the princess' because of her airs and graces but she didn't take it to heart, for quite early on she realized that people believed only what they saw. If her friends perceived her as a princess, that was fine. All she had to do now was to make sure none of them ever came back to her home.

Her parents were concerned that she had no close friends. Caroline was an only child and they wanted her to be popular with girls of her own age. It made up for their being unable to afford the luxury of any more brothers and sisters for the Brigadier wasn't a rich man. Caroline never forgave him for that.

When she was seventeen Caroline announced that she was moving out of their semi-detached in Surrey and going to London. She had found herself a job with a stockbroking firm, making tea and running errands. The pay was derisory, but her father made her a small allowance so she could afford to share a flat in Kensington with three very debby girls who wanted to let their boxroom.

It was in London that Caroline finally came into her own, for now she really could play the princess and nobody would be any the wiser. She acquired an even smarter accent and learnt a new expression – PLU. To those in the know, PLU stood for 'People Like Us'. With the expression went a set of rules.

PLUs came from a country background and lived in south-west London. Yet everything about them boasted of their origin in the leafy shires. They wore Barbours and hacking jackets on shopping trips. Their houses and flats were decorated in old chintzes and Victorian antiques. Even if the furniture was bought in the Fulham Road, PLUs always lied through their teeth and said it had been passed down to them by a very grand ancestor.

The best thing about PLUs, Caroline discovered, was that they all knew each other. If you were a member of this exclusive, snobby little club you had certain advantages other people didn't enjoy.

To live this kind of life, of course, you had to have a certain amount of money. You couldn't go to cocktail parties in your office clothes, for instance, just as nobody would be seen dead wearing jeans out hunting. So Caroline put her mind to raising the necessary funds.

Her father was a dead loss when it came to this. On his army pension all he could do was provide her rent, so she was forced to consider a career.

Because she was a realist, she knew she couldn't go from tea-maker to stockbroker. She had never had much of a head for figures. Caroline's talent was her ability to talk herself out of a tight corner. She was a natural-born communicator and one of the boys in the finance house where she worked suggested she apply for a job in the company's public relations department. She did as she was told and discovered to her joy that the man who ran the outfit was another PLU. They recognized each other on sight and within days Caroline was installed as a junior account executive.

Now she had a decent salary, she started to enjoy life. Men had always found her attractive and she embarked on a series of affairs that did nothing for her reputation. For she was ruthless in love.

In a way she was reacting against the girls she shared with, for they all seemed to have a dreadful time with their boyfriends. Every time she walked into the flat there was always someone in tears over a date that had been cancelled or a call that never came. Caroline came to see love not as a blessing, but as a terrible disease.

If you cared for somebody, she reasoned, you were as good as inviting them to turn round and deal you a killing blow, so it concerned her not at all that she felt little affection for any of the men in her life.

Then she met Ross Llewellyn, who was so useful to her that she stopped in her tracks and concentrated her entire attention on him. Ross was a top columnist on one of the heavy Sunday papers. He was fortyish, divorced and good-looking in a slightly raffish sort of way. Normally Caroline would have had a quick fling with him and added his name to her growing list of conquests. Except for one thing: Ross thought he could make her into a journalist. The idea attracted her.

At a certain level, city journalists were privy to inside information. None of them admitted to it, of course, but she knew that Ross didn't run his elegant Mayfair department on the money his paper paid him. He had other dealings that supported a life style far grander than any of his colleagues, and Caroline wanted some of those perks for herself.

It took her six months to learn the basics and as she did, Ross watched her and felt both proud and possessive. This new woman of his was a little like a thoroughbred racehorse. She was elegant, she was nervy, and in the right hands she was absolutely lethal.

When he felt she was ready, he introduced her to Derek Johnson on the *London Evening Post*. Johnson had been running the city office for twelve years with the help of a small highly motivated team. One of that team had been head-hunted over to the rival *Evening Standard* and he needed a replacement fast.

Caroline got the job on Ross's recommendation. She didn't let him down. In her first year she proved herself useful. In her second she became necessary. It was then Ross asked her to marry him, which put her in a difficult spot.

Caroline was twenty-six, financially independent and a target for every playboy in London. Her whole life was a round of parties, race meetings and country weekends. If she settled down with Ross she knew everything would change. He would expect her to have children, and though he would provide her with every comfort, the fun would go out of her life. She would be tied down in some middle-class suburb, cooking dinner parties and playing second fiddle to a newspaper executive.

When she had met Ross, she thought he was very glam-orous, but she knew plenty of other Rosses now. She was almost one herself and the gloss had gone off him. She was fond of him the way she was fond of her cat or her parents, but that didn't mean she was going to throw herself away on him.

Caroline fobbed him off with an excuse that she had to concentrate on her career. Then when he became really insistent, she told him the truth.

'When I marry,' she said, 'it will be to somebody far richer than you could ever be.'

It was a cruel rejection and Ross took it badly, but it couldn't be helped. Caroline had her own interests to look after.

When she broke it off with Ross, she didn't waste her time with any more newspapermen. If she was going to catch the sort of husband she was looking for, she had to be more selective. There was no shortage of suitable candidates but something always seemed to go wrong with her romances. Men liked having affairs with her, but the prospect of marrying her daunted them. She was too head-strong, too independent and her reputation with men was a little too public. A man like Ross wouldn't be worried about any of those things, but a serious man, a man with money and social standing, would think twice before com-mitting himself.

Caroline was twenty-nine now, and past her sell-by date. She knew she couldn't change herself so she sought to compromise. If she couldn't land the handsome prince she deserved, then she would lower her sights. The man still had to be rich, of course – she wouldn't accept anything less — but he didn't have to come from the top drawer of society. She started cultivating the second echelon — foreigners with phoney titles and men who had made their money in the retail business.

But she couldn't take any of them seriously. Compared to the lovers she was used to, they seemed lightweight and somehow ludicrous. She couldn't see herself as a contessa or a German baroness lording it over the flotsam that made up the jet set. She had almost become resigned to her single state, when she ran into Richard. And that concentrated her mind, for he was exactly what she was looking for. A nearly gentleman. He was attainable, or at least Caroline thought he was when he took her to Paris. Then he ran out on her and she thought again. The nearly gentleman had a temper. He wasn't going to be messed around by the likes of her.

It didn't discourage her. If anything it made him even more intriguing, even more of a challenge. She would land this one, she decided.

CHAPTER 21

On her return to London Caroline called Richard at his office. His secretary told her he was in a meeting and would get back to her. Two days later she still hadn't heard from him.

Then she tried calling him at his apartment, where she managed to reach him in person, but he was offhand with her. Caroline felt like a newsdesk reporter or an insurance salesman, and she hated it. She also knew Richard was playing games. Anyone who made love to her the way he had, had to feel something.

She invited him to a drinks party in her apartment that she knew would be hard to resist. All the top men from the leading financial institutions were on her guest list. She even invited Tim Waites and Rolf Weiss. Then for good measure she asked the managing director of the merchant bank that underwrote a major block of Weiss stock. There was no way Richard couldn't turn up.

Caroline was right. Richard did come to her drinks, but with him, dangling on his arm like an accessory, was a leggy blonde who was currently on the front pages of all the glossy magazines.

The sight of the girl finally made Caroline lose her temper. She had gone to a considerable amount of trouble to attract this man's attention and all he could do was play childish games. Then she pulled herself together. There was no way she was going to seem petulant in front of all her important contacts. No, if anyone was getting out of here it would be Richard — and the Barbie Doll on his arm.

Caroline went across to where they were standing and waited for a break in the conversation. As she did she saw Richard looking at her. If she had been anyone else she might have turned tail and headed across to the other side of the room, for what she saw in his eyes wasn't polite at all. The only word for what Richard was doing was appraising her. Caroline had seen men on building sites look over girls like that and it made her feel self-conscious.

He must have realized her discomfort, for he disentangled himself from his girlfriend and moved closer to her.

'I'm sorry about Paris,' he said. 'You must have felt bloody awful waking up in the morning with nobody there.'

It took the wind out of Caroline's sails. She had been all ready to send him packing and here he was trying to make it up. She found herself smiling.

'It wasn't nice,' she said, 'particularly after everything else that had happened.'

Richard took her by the elbow and propelled her into her tiny front hall. Like the room they were in, it was knee deep in people but it didn't seem to inhibit him.

'If you tried behaving like a lady instead of a bitch,' he said, 'I might treat you like one.'

Caroline looked him in the eye. 'Is that what I have to do to make you get rid of your girlfriend?'

'She isn't my girlfriend. She's just somebody I take to parties.'

Caroline recalled the gossip column items she had seen about Richard. His name was always linked to some vacuous glamour girl.

'You think women are disposable, don't you?' she said fiercely. 'You have your girls for parties and your girls for sex and you keep us all in neat little compartments. You've probably even got a category under journalists where I fit in.'

Richard extracted two cigarettes from his thin silver case, lit one and passed it over to her. It was an intimate gesture and its flattery wasn't lost on Caroline.

'The category I've got you under,' Richard said, 'is unfinished business.'

Caroline didn't say anything because she didn't have to any more. Since Paris she'd been making all the running, now whatever happened next was up to Richard.

Out of the corner of her eye she saw Rolf Weiss approach with Richard's girl in tow.

'It's time I wasn't here any more,' she said under her breath. Then she brushed her lips across his cheek and disappeared back into the party.

Richard called Caroline the next morning before she left for the office. He wanted to know if she was free for dinner that evening and she stopped herself from saying yes too quickly. If she was too eager, too available, all she would do was end up in the same boat as all his other women.

She told him she had a hectic work schedule for the coming week and she was out of town over the weekend. He didn't protest the way she expected him to so they arranged to meet in ten days' time. Richard had tickets for Covent Garden and even though she didn't understand the opera, Caroline did her best to sound enthusiastic.

After he rang off, she made a note they were going to see *Tosca* and the minute she got to the office, she sent Valerie out to buy the entire score of Puccini's opera. By the time she met Richard, Caroline was going to be totally *au fait* with what was going on.

It paid off. Richard seemed relieved to find a companion who didn't seem bored to tears. Most of the girls he escorted usually fell asleep in the second act, then drank too much in the interval. He asked Caroline if she was interested in going to Glyndebourne with him and once more she lied through her teeth and said she couldn't think of anything she'd rather do.

That summer Caroline became expert on a number of things. She sharpened up her tennis when she discovered Richard enjoyed the game. She learned to play blackjack and chemin de fer when she found he liked casinos. And she acquired an in-depth knowledge of the hotel business.

By September the couple were seeing each other twice a week and every weekend. Richard still kept in touch with his regular girlfriends, but less so, for there was little need. Caroline supplied everything he wanted. And he became lazy.

At Christmas Richard suggested Caroline leave some of her clothes at his London apartment. When he was in town, they seemed to see each other the whole time now. There was no harm in putting things on a more permanent basis.

Caroline was so pleased by this move that Richard wondered whether things were going just a little too fast. For he wasn't in love with Caroline. He liked her, he had a passion for her in bed, but she failed to get under his skin. When he was with her he always felt there was a part of her he couldn't reach. It was almost as if she had locked away her soul. And because he couldn't get close to her, he responded by leaving his defences in place. Sometimes late at night, he wondered if what he had with Caroline was all he could expect from a relationship. She certainly gave him more than any other girl he had known. She was bright, she was funny and she was sexy as hell. I worry too much about her shallowness, he thought. I could do worse than settle for her.

CHAPTER 22

New York, 1981

The limousine pulled up outside the 21 Club and Emerald waited for the chauffeur to let her out. She wondered how long she'd be there. It was to be a literary party or so the invitation promised. That meant the airheads would be about tonight.

Her driver opened the door and waited for her to dismiss him. She hesitated. It would be tempting to ask him to come back in half an hour but she'd told David she'd be free for dinner tonight and she couldn't go back on a promise.

Emerald got out of the car and wrapped the dark mink coat more securely around her. It was bitterly cold and the short distance between the car and the plate-glass doors was enough to chill her. She shivered, wondering if she'd ever get used to the winter.

Once inside the building, she was ushered up the long red-carpeted staircase to a room humming with the familiar undercurrent of excitement that was typical of New York. In LA people went to parties as part of their business. It was a duty rather than a pleasure and they usually wound up going home well before midnight. In New York it was different. None of the people here tonight would be in bed before the early hours.

Usually Emerald enjoyed this sort of thing, she had been doing it for long enough. But tonight she was on edge and instead of joining the throng, she stood on the sidelines wondering where to start.

Her eyes wandered to a small chunky man who was

famous for walking the president's wife. She had met him at dinner three nights ago. She supposed she should go and find David. He was her lover after all.

Emerald squinted into the cigarette smoke that hung like a pall over the crowd and for a moment all she could see were dozens of ingratiating smiles on the faces of people she half knew. She had seen almost everyone in this room somewhere else. Half the women had been at the Paris couture, the other half with their escorts had been glimpsed at Longchamps or Ascot or any one of a dozen discreet gatherings in capital cities of the world.

Emerald felt that looking at this crowd was like looking at the past ten years of her life laid out in front of her. What am I doing here, she asked herself. I've got nothing to say to any of these people. Nothing I haven't said before. Then she remembered David and her promise to join him for dinner.

She spotted him standing over by the bar. He had no idea she was just yards away, for he was busy holding court to a small group who seemed to be hanging on his every word. They have to be talking about money, Emerald thought. They look too damned spellbound to be discussing anything else.

Emerald looked again at David. He was affluent, this lover of hers. His hand-made suit and his Sulka tie reeked of money and power. His complexion told the rest of the story, for his colour was just a little too high from too many whisky sours, too many gourmet meals, too many Havana cigars. He was heavy as well – too heavy to be really handsome. But there was an energy about him that more than compensated for any physical shortcoming.

When Emerald had first met him, the energy was the only thing she saw. Then she got to know him better and she discovered his gentleness. In the end it was this gentleness that had made her choose him. She could be safe with David. Safe and comfortable. If she closed her eyes, she could even pretend she no longer needed to feel passion.

A waiter passed right by her carrying a tray of champagne glasses and she took one. It was her first drink that day, yet it tasted sour in her mouth.

She realized she didn't want to stay any longer. There was no point in drinking champagne she didn't want with a man she didn't want.

She glanced across at David and realized he hadn't looked up from his conversation. That meant he hadn't seen her.

He won't miss me, she thought. He'll go on to a restaurant with people here and spend a pleasant evening making even more money.

Emerald murmured a social excuse to her companions, then she slid her way through the crowd and down the staircase. There was a large party at the bottom, pushing its way into the bar and she was forced to slow down and wait for them to pass.

As she did, she glanced at her watch. It was getting on for 7.30. The evening traffic would be at its height now and she wondered if it would be difficult to find a taxi.

She remembered how cold it was when she had got there and the thought of struggling her way down West 52nd Street lost its appeal. She decided to go to the bar and have a nightcap while the doorman got hold of her car.

Emerald found herself a table at the far end of the wood-panelled room. Then she ordered herself a martini and settled back on to the banquette. At this time of night, she knew she'd have to wait at least forty minutes, so she might as well relax.

There was a man looking at her. She noticed him when she sat down, but she didn't think too much about it. Men always stared at her. If she didn't look back, they soon lost interest.

But this man didn't take the hint. He seemed mesmerized by her and Emerald wondered if she had met him somewhere and forgotten who he was. Without seeming too obvious she checked him out. He was tall with an unmistakable look of class. There was something familiar about him and she racked her brains trying to remember where she'd seen him last.

Richard signalled the barman for another Gibson and went on studying the girl. It's definitely her, he thought. I've never seen eyes like those anywhere else. His mind went back to the dinner he had had with his father when he was leaving school. They had been at the Ritz when he had pointed the woman out on the arm of a movie star. 'She was a mistress of mine,' his father had told him. 'I paid her keep.'

At the time Richard had been shocked by the confession, but he had been a boy then. Now he was a man and he was intrigued. What held him was the fact that the woman was Indian. He had been brought up with women who looked like her. Except she didn't have the passive look of those he knew. This girl belonged to herself. She's either a model or some executive in an ad agency, he thought. Then he looked at the way she was dressed and he reconsidered.

The little Yves Saint Laurent dress she was wearing probably set someone back the best part of thirty thousand dollars. He recognized it was from the latest couture collection and he wondered how she could afford to dress that way.

Then Richard laughed at himself for being naïve. She's probably found a rich man to look after her, he thought. Maybe another movie star.

He looked at his watch and saw he had an hour to kill before dinner. It pushed him into a decision. He sauntered over to where Emerald was sitting. 'We've met somewhere before,' he said. 'Do you mind if I join you?'

Now Emerald was utterly confused. She was convinced she knew this man, only she couldn't think how.

'I'm waiting for my driver,' she told him, 'so I'm not

going to be here for much longer.' She paused for a moment. 'What did you say your name was?'

Richard thought on his feet. If he told her his name was Waites, she'd connect him to his father. If he was going to find out anything about this girl, she'd have to assume he was a stranger. He extended his hand.

'Richard Hutton,' he said. 'We met at the Cannes Film Festival a couple of years ago.'

Emerald took his hand, but there was doubt in her eyes. 'Which company were you with?'

'I wasn't,' Richard said quickly. 'I was staying with Adnan Khashoggi.'

There was a flicker of recognition. 'Then you were at the party he threw on the *Nabila*.' Emerald felt relieved. 'I knew I knew you. I never forget a face.'

Richard sat down and signalled the waiter for another drink. She'd been easier to fool than he thought. Then he thought, girls like her go to so many parties they hardly remember which country they're in, let alone who they met at the film festival.

Her name was Emerald. With eyes that colour it wasn't an easy name to forget. Yet when she introduced herself, he did his best to look surprised. Then he asked her where she came from and she backed off a little.

'I was born in Mauritius,' she said looking startled. 'Why do you ask?'

Richard was tempted to tell her he came from the same place, but caution stopped him. He sensed she was brighter than she looked. Mauritius was too big a clue to drop, so he ignored her question and went on probing.

He wasn't sure of the precise moment when he became fascinated. Maybe he had been all along and he wouldn't acknowledge it, but when Emerald began talking about Larry Simpson he felt himself being drawn towards her. There was something innocent about the way she related to the star. Other girls like her would have dropped names.

Emerald simply talked about the man himself. She had had a unique understanding with him. It was almost love, but not quite for Larry was an actor and a difficult one.

As Emerald told Richard her story, he realized he had read about her in the newspapers. Larry Simpson had left everything he owned to some woman he was living with. He hadn't read the story closely, so he didn't know it was her. He looked at Emerald with new respect. She must have something, he thought. Men like Larry Simpson don't bequeath their fortunes to any little bimbo who happens to be sharing their bed.

'Are you still based in LA?' he asked her. 'From all accounts, the house in Bel Air was quite something.'

Emerald seemed to retreat from him. It was nothing obvious, but Richard noticed a new wariness in the green eyes. When she was nervous they became almost opaque.

'What have you been reading about me?' she cautiously asked.

Now Richard was at a loss. He didn't keep up with Hollywood gossip and it was pointless trying to pretend.

'I'm based in London,' he told her, 'so I don't hear everything that goes on this side of the Atlantic.' He paused. 'Has there been some kind of problem?'

Emerald looked surprised and slightly lost. 'You mean you don't know about the court case? The endless court cases. They've even been on television.'

Richard sighed. 'I'm a businessman,' he said. 'The only thing I watch on the box is the share index. Suppose you tell me what's been going on in your life.'

There was no stopping Emerald. It was as if Richard had tapped into all her troubles with that one request, yet as she rambled on he began to be intrigued.

The fortune Larry Simpson left her hadn't really materialized. On paper she was a millionairess several times over but she couldn't get her hands on the money because of his children. Apparently the actor altered his will in Emerald's favour months before he died and the family were claiming she'd pushed him into doing it.

'There are times when I don't know where to turn,' she told him.

Richard smiled. Now he was sitting next to her he could see the jewellery she was wearing was the real thing.

'You don't look exactly destitute,' he said.

For a moment Emerald looked angry, then she said, 'Of course I'm not destitute. Larry looked after me when he was alive and the courts give me some leeway. I can live in the New York apartment and I'm allowed the income from the money that was left.'

She was telling this man too much and she knew it but she couldn't stop herself. She wanted him to like her, more than like her. She wanted him to want her and she felt ashamed.

I don't know him, she chided herself. He's probably married with a family. What on earth am I thinking of?

She swallowed the rest of her drink and looked across the bar. As if on cue, she saw her driver making his way to her table.

'My car's arrived,' she said abruptly. 'I really have to be going.'

She started to get up, but Richard put a hand on her arm.

'Don't walk out of my life,' he said softly. 'I've only just found you.'

Emerald had heard better lines, but there was an ache in Richard's voice that stopped her. It was as if he really meant what he said and she felt the beginnings of attraction.

'Maybe I'll see you around,' she told him. 'We seem to go to all the same parties.'

Richard didn't take his hand away and she sat wedged into the leather banquette, wanting to move but not daring to. She didn't mean to look at him directly, but there was no avoiding his eyes and she gave in to the inevitable. Between a man and a woman there is a silent communication that gives an instant forecast of the future. Sitting in the bar of the 21 Club, Emerald knew she had met the man who was going to be her next lover. She had spoken to him for less than half an hour, they hadn't even exchanged telephone numbers, but none of this seemed to matter. All she wanted was to go on sitting close to him, the way she was doing now. Then she saw her driver standing in front of her and she pulled herself together.

'This is getting silly,' she said. 'We're not teenagers.'

Richard let go of her then, but his eyes still challenged her.

'Meet me for lunch tomorrow,' he said. 'I'll be in the Pool room of the Four Seasons.'

Emerald heard herself agreeing to the arrangement and felt an enormous sense of relief. A decision had been taken and the situation was out of her hands now.

Richard ordered another drink after she left and looked at his watch. His dinner was still twenty minutes away and he was glad of the respite. The woman had muddled his senses and he needed a clear head for what lay in front of him.

He thought once more about David Reuben. When he had last seen him, he had been a meek little boy at Stowe, the butt of every bully in his year. From everything he'd heard, David had changed a lot since then. It would be an interesting reunion.

CHAPTER 23

Richard was surprised at how big David had grown. When they shared a dormitory, David was a butterball. Now the years had filled him out, giving him height as well as girth. Today the man who confronted him had the dimensions of a giant.

He had been at some book launch party in the upstairs restaurant and he was out of sorts because he had been stood up by a woman. In a way Richard was relieved about that. He could do without stray females at dinner tonight. The matter he had come from London to discuss needed all David's attention.

For the next half-hour they talked about school. Then when they moved to the grill in the back of the bar, they got down to business.

Richard had made contact with David in New York because he had a proposition for him. He wanted to take over part of his business.

David had gone into his family's property business the minute he had completed his education. After Stowe he had attended Harvard Business School and when he was well versed in company law, his father let him loose in his office.

It was a shrewd move. The boy had a flair for wheeling and dealing. By the late seventies the Reubens owned office blocks in New Jersey, parking lots all around Queens and Brooklyn and a string of hotels in Manhattan.

It was the hotels that interested Richard. They were small old-fashioned properties, the sort of places a maiden aunt would stay at when she was up from Houston on a shopping trip. At a first glance there was nothing much in their favour. Then you looked at their locations: 62nd Street and Park Avenue, 81st Street and Fifth, 77th and Madison. With money spent on them, these run-down guesthouses could be flagship properties, the sort of hotels Weiss was famous for.

The deal was important to Richard, not just because he was doing business with an old friend. New York was the only major capital city in which Weiss hadn't made its mark and he was anxious to rectify the omission.

It was not an easy negotiation. All the gossip he had heard about David had been right. He was no pushover.

Richard decided to take his deal slowly. He needed to renew his friendship with David and he had to make him remember that all those years ago, he was the one boy in his class that stood up for him.

They finished dinner amicably enough, making plans to meet again the day after next. Then Richard got into a taxi and went back to his suite at the Plaza. Normally after a business dinner, he slept soundly. He'd done his homework and if the thing didn't work out, then he knew enough to try something else. But tonight rest eluded him.

It was the girl, he thought, the one he had picked before dinner – he couldn't get her out of his head. He wondered if he should tell her who he was when he met her the next day. He decided he had to. If he wanted to be taken seriously he couldn't go on playing games.

He flirted with the idea of having a relationship with her. If the hotel deal came off, he would be in New York every other week. It would make sense to have a permanent girl in the city. Caroline was too involved with her own job to follow him halfway across the world.

A vision of his father floated across his mind. He had possessed Emerald once. He tried to imagine what they'd had between them and he found himself getting angry.

What had his father been doing picking on women less than half his age, for Chrissake? Just for a moment the possibility it was more than a convenient affair occurred to Richard.

He got up and went over to the fridge where he helped himself to a Scotch and water. Nursing his drink, he sat on the edge of the bed and looked out over the Manhattan skyline. Some of the tallest office buildings still had their lights on and he wondered how many driven souls there were in the city still burning the midnight oil.

His mind returned to Emerald, and he wondered whether he should keep the date he had made with her. She was trouble. He knew that already. She had a track record that took in Larry Simpson and a number of jet-set Europeans, and that was before you even got to his father. What am I doing, he asked himself. I've got to be every kind of fool to even consider her.

Richard finally slept in the early hours, but it didn't do him any good. When he woke he had a king-sized hangover and no firm decision on what he was going to do.

In the end he decided to go through with lunch. He reasoned that, once he had told Emerald who his father was she'd walk out anyway. At least like this, he would come out of a situation looking like a gentleman.

He arrived at the Four Seasons at 12.30 and made straight for his table. He saw her sitting there as he came into the room. Emerald smiled as he approached and he saw how lovely she looked. She'd coiled her hair around her head in some artful way that made her look sophisticated. Last night, Richard had dismissed Emerald as a jet-set bimbo. Now he realized how wrong he had been. Sitting before him was a woman, a lovely woman who had spent all morning putting herself together and for a moment he felt sad she had wasted her time.

Then he thought, I'll put off telling her for a while.

There's no harm in doing that. So long as I come clean by the time coffee comes, everything will be all right.

It was one of those long lunches where they ordered everything on the menu and ate very little. They both needed to know more about each other and Richard started by telling Emerald about the business he was in. She seemed to know nothing about hotels, which made it easier. He could talk about Rolf and the Weiss companies with little danger of her recognizing who he was.

Emerald seemed fascinated by what Richard had to say. For a woman she had an almost intuitive understanding of the intricacies of business and just for a moment he thought of Caroline. She knew about his world as well, but the two women couldn't have been more different. The English girl had a masculine approach in all her dealings. If she thought he was wrong about something she made no bones about it, shouting him down if she had to.

Emerald used persuasion to get her point across. She would approach a problem from a dozen different angles, nibbling away at it until she had charmed you into agreeing she was right. There was something uniquely Indian about the way she behaved. Something that reminded Richard of himself, and he began to imagine they'd be talking like this in years to come.

I'm behaving like a fool, he thought. I don't have years with this woman. I don't even have days. In an hour's time the bill will arrive and I'm going to have to level.

It suddenly became important to know more about her life. He asked her what she had been doing in the years after Larry, and Emerald held nothing back.

She had gone to New York two days after the funeral. A lot of her things were in the apartment already so it didn't take her long to make the move. For the first few months she was there, she did very little. She thought she had prepared herself for Larry's death, but now he was gone she realized how alone she really was. She also realized she was vulnerable, for she had money as well as sex appeal.

She turned down all the obvious playboys, concentrating on the women and the married couples she knew. Then just when she started to relax, Larry's family started hounding her.

'If they had come and explained themselves to me,' she said, 'I might have handed everything over. I didn't expect anything from Larry and I was quite prepared to go and find a job. But they didn't do that. They served papers on me instead. And that made me mad as hell.'

From the way she told it, she had spent years of her life fighting the Simpson children. It took up most of her time and attention. And whatever emotion she had to spare, went on having a good time.

She could cope with the reality of her life only by running away from it. She started to drift around the smart restaurant circuit. If someone was putting on a charity ball or getting up a party for the races, Emerald was invariably on the guest list. The skirmishes with Larry's family had given her a certain notoriety and people fell over themselves to include her.

One of the reasons she never settled down with anybody was the ongoing fight with her former lover's family. It took precedence over everything and Richard wondered why she still went on with it.

'Can't you come to terms with them?' he asked her. 'Surely there must be a middle way?'

Emerald sighed. 'I wish there was, but it's gone too far now. We're not quarrelling about money any more. The issue at stake is pride.' She pushed her plate away wearily. 'I won't be dismissed like a servant.'

Richard looked at Emerald with worry. If she gets this het up about what people think, what's she going to do when I tell her who my father is?

The waiter came and started to clear away their plates

and he realized time was running out for them. He reached across the table and took her hand.

'I've got something to tell you,' he said. She interrupted him before he could go on. 'I know what you're going to say. You're married and you love your wife and you don't go in for affairs.'

There was something brave about the way she said it. Brave and silly at the same time, and Richard saw that underneath the good clothes and the bright makeup Emerald was vulnerable. In that moment his heart went out to her.

'I'm not married,' he said softly, 'and you're not an affair. Whatever it is between us, goes deeper than that.'

She looked at him. 'I know,' she said. 'What are we going to do?'

It was then he should have told her the truth. The timing was perfect and there were no more reasons not to. But the words stuck in his throat. I can't do it, Richard thought. I can't bear to see her hurt. He let go of her hand and signalled the waiter for the bill.

'What we're going to do,' he said, 'is go back to my suite at the Plaza and love each other. We have no other choice.'

Emerald was like those Indian women Richard had read about in classical love poetry. He had expected a houri and she didn't disappoint him. But it wasn't her beauty that held him. It was her shyness. Richard had been used to Caroline, who wasn't afraid to ask for what she wanted. Emerald didn't behave like that.

When they got into the drawing-room of his penthouse she instantly wanted to know if she could have some tea. She was like a teenager on her first date and it mesmerized him.

This woman was my father's mistress, he thought. She lived with Larry Simpson for years, yet she's acting like a virgin. He looked at Emerald sitting nervously on the gold brocade sofa. She had pulled her short tight skirt down around her knees, and hadn't even taken her jacket off. All at once Richard wanted to rumple her a little.

He came on to the sofa and took hold of her by the shoulders. Then very deliberately he eased her jacket off and started unpinning her hair. Emerald didn't do anything to stop him. She just sat there passively, regarding him with those great green eyes, letting him do as he wanted. Her hair was thick and dark and when he'd unravelled it, it came right down to her waist.

Then Richard reached round to the back of her skirt and unhooked it. He pushed it down around her hips and on to the floor. All she was wearing was a chemise and a pair of plain white briefs, the sort a schoolgirl would have chosen.

Then he saw the outline of her breasts through the silk vest and he decided she wasn't like a child at all. There was something voluptuous about her, something soft and ripe and every part of him screamed out to touch her.

He took her in his arms, kissing her roughly so her mouth came open. She tasted warm and slightly sweet and he couldn't get enough of her, but this woman deserved better than a casual coupling on the drawing-room sofa. He helped her to her feet and without saying a word, she followed him through to the bedroom.

The hotel had provided the standard double divan covered in a chintz petticoat and while Richard undressed, Emerald pulled the cover off the bed and disappeared under the sheets. He had no idea whether she was frightened of him or whether she played this game with all the men she knew, but he felt suddenly furious with her. She was meant to be a jet-setter, not some retiring housewife.

He stripped the bed in one action, then he got rid of Emerald's chemise and the ridiculous schoolgirl briefs. Then he started to touch her. It was as if he had set off a thousand electric currents for she shuddered and moaned and begged him not to stop. Richard willed himself to be gentle, but something inside him snapped. Emerald, with her teasing and her timidity, had taken him beyond the point of no return. Now she would have to look out for herself.

He reached between her legs until he found her entrance, then he moved on top of her, easing himself into her. She came alive. It was as if she had been waiting for this moment all along, for now she showed all her hunger and all her need and in that afternoon Richard finally knew her.

Emerald slept quite peacefully afterwards, lying on her stomach with one hand thrown out in front of her. The emotion had drained her completely and he marvelled at her. Emerald had given herself more fully than any woman he had ever known. He knew now that in some subtle way she belonged to him. She would be his chattel or his wife, or whatever it was he wanted, and he felt blessed.

I don't care what she did before she met me, Richard thought. She could have slept with the entire Waites family and it wouldn't matter a damn. The only thing that really counts is now, the precious present. The fact that we found each other. He would have to explain that to her when the time was right.

He frowned slightly and felt the return of the headache he started out with that day. I wonder if she'll understand, he thought.

CHAPTER 24

Richard never found the words. He and Emerald would sit together in the morning before he went off for his endless round of takeover meetings and she would ask him what his plans were.

They were so close that it should have been simple to bring up the past. Only Richard couldn't do it. And as the days went on, he stopped wanting to.

He realized he was falling in love with Emerald. He couldn't contemplate eating dinner, watching television, taking a shower without knowing she was somewhere near. If I tell her, he thought, I'll lose her and then what will I do?

After their first night together, Emerald hadn't come back to the Plaza. She said it made her feel like a transient staying in hotel suites and Richard went along with her. At the time he was not aware he was moving into her apartment, because it all happened so naturally.

Emerald lived in the somewhat overdecorated splendour of the Ritz Tower. In a city where every spare inch was made use of, the apartment on Park Avenue was a monument to waste. There was a circular hall the size of a ballroom that served no special purpose except to display a series of antique mirrors. Off the hall were libraries and receiving rooms and closets the size of other people's bathrooms. A family could have moved in and hardly made an impression on the place. And there were times when Richard felt both he and Emerald were guests passing through.

The feeling of impermanence haunted him because he knew he was living a lie. He still conducted his business from the suite in the Plaza. As far as Rolf and Caroline and his friends in the City were concerned, he was staying there and he kept up the charade because he had no choice.

He went on like that for nearly two months. Occasionally he'd return to London for a day or so, but it was easy to invent reasons for being away. The takeover talks were demanding much of his attention, and though he could have done a lot of the work long distance he pretended that David was being difficult and needed him on the spot. He lied about quite a few things that summer.

Richard told Emerald he didn't like the fashionable nightspots and preferred to stay in with her. Emerald didn't mind. She was perfectly happy cooking at home for him, or venturing out late to little ethnic restaurants. So long as they had each other, the rest of the world seemed somehow far away and unimportant.

If Emerald had never known David Reuben, they could have gone on like this for a long time, but she had been his girlfriend, and though the affair hadn't been important, he resented being ditched.

She had left David in a particularly heartless way, avoiding his calls and making excuses, and he wasn't having it. If Emerald wanted to call it quits, then she would have to tell him to his face.

So David rang her, and after he had left three messages on her machine, Emerald finally returned his call.

As soon as David heard her voice, he came directly to the point.

'I'd like to know why we're no longer friends,' he said.

She was lost for words. Had David been anyone else, she might have been rude. Or simply told him there was someone else. But the hotelier had been her friend as well as her lover and she owed him more than that.

'There's a lot of explaining to do,' she told him. 'It's hard to know where to start.'

David stopped her right there. 'I'll buy you a drink,' he said, 'and you can tell me about it. How about tomorrow at five? I'll send a car to pick you up.'

Emerald didn't argue. Deep down she felt she had been living in her own private never-never land for too long. She knew Richard was shy of people, but she wasn't and she needed to share what she had.

'I'll meet you in the bar at the Algonquin,' she said.

Emerald arrived before David and to her relief the place was empty. If David was going to be difficult, she'd rather he did so without the benefit of an audience.

She had dressed carefully to meet her old boyfriend. There was no need to make a big deal of the occasion, so she opted for something casual. Ralph Lauren was all the rage that year and she wore his classic navy blazer with a pair of narrow jeans and a silk shirt. As David came into the bar on West 44th, Emerald was glad she had thought herself out.

David was looking decidedly edgy. She knew he was nervous about seeing her and he didn't try to hide it. He was even more florid than usual, and he looked frazzled. If she had been wearing Dior and diamonds, there would have been no way she could have got past his defences.

He came over to where she was sitting and flopped down on one of the generous leather chairs.

'So you decided to come,' he said. 'I wondered whether you would change your mind.'

Emerald put a hand out to soothe him. 'Poor David,' she said, 'I've behaved like a worm. I'm sorry if I hurt you.'

The apology took him off guard. He expected her to justify herself. Maybe even tell a couple of white lies. But she hadn't done that, and he found himself liking her for it.

'I'm a grown man,' he said ruefully, 'you're not the first girl who's turned me down. I daresay I'll live.'

The waiter came over and he ordered drinks for them both. Emerald always drank white wine in the evening and she felt flattered that he remembered.

She looked at him. 'I suppose you want to know why I disappeared from your life?'

David shrugged. 'Not really. Even I could work out you'd met someone else. What I want to know is who is this man who's keeping you away from all your friends. It's got to be serious. Nobody's seen you anywhere for weeks.'

Emerald relaxed and settled back into her chair.

'He's called Richard Hutton,' she told him. 'Actually, you might have met him. He works in your line of business.'

Her companion looked interested. 'What's the name of his company?'

David looked puzzled when she said it was the Weiss Group.

'I know a Richard who works for Weiss. I've been dealing with the guy for the past eight weeks. But he isn't called Hutton. The name doesn't ring a bell at all.'

Emerald fought down a feeling of impatience. 'You must have heard of him,' she said. 'He runs the group for Rolf Weiss.'

David put his drink down and pulled himself together. Emerald might have turned him down, but he still had some feeling for her, and this Hutton guy sounded like he was trying to pull a fast one.

'Tell me a bit more about your friend,' he asked. 'Do you know which division of the company he works in? A lot of guys claim they run the show, when all they're really doing is heading up a department.'

Emerald was adamant. 'Richard's the Managing Director. He told me so himself.'

David held his hand up. 'I believe you,' he said. 'Can you remember if he told you what he's doing in New York?'

She nodded. 'He's trying to take over some hotel group,' she told him. 'I don't know which one, Richard doesn't like to discuss business when he's home.'

The word home jarred on David. From the sound of it, Richard had already moved in on her. He wondered why he would do that and not tell her who he was.

He decided it was time she was put in the picture. 'I think this Richard of yours is taking you for a ride,' he said. 'Nobody called Hutton works for Weiss. If you like I can make a call and verify it.'

She shook her head. 'I'll take your word for it.'

Suddenly Emerald felt out of her depth. She'd been living with a man for two months now who wasn't who she thought he was. Then she thought back to the time she met him. She'd asked him if he was married and he'd denied it. All at once she saw what the problem was. Richard had a wife tucked away in England. Of course he wouldn't want her to know who he was.

Emerald leant closer to David. 'Suppose you tell me a bit more about the man you're dealing with at Weiss.'

David took a deep breath and let it out slowly. 'The man I'm talking to right now is trying to take over three of my properties. So we could be talking about the same character. In fact I'm certain we are. Weiss only has one man who answers directly to him.'

She started to feel faint. 'What's his real name?' she asked.

'Waites. Richard Waites.'

All at once Emerald had a terrible premonition.

'Do you know anything about Richard Waites?' she enquired. 'I mean outside business.'

David didn't hesitate. 'Of course I do,' he told her. 'Richard and I went to school together.'

Emerald swallowed some more of her wine. 'I need to

know where he came from and who his parents are. I've got a feeling he's not English.'

She was shooting in the dark now. Waites was a common enough name. There must be hundreds of Waiteses all over the place. David interrupted her thoughts.

'You're right,' David said. 'Most people assume Richard was born and brought up in the home counties. He has that look about him. Only it's not true at all. He comes from somewhere in the Indian Ocean, Mauritius, I think.'

Emerald had a curious feeling of unreality, as if she were watching a film of her life being played out in front of her and there was nothing she could do to stop it.

'His father was a planter,' she said softly. 'Did he mention he was called Jeremy?'

David confirmed it and all at once the pieces fell into place. She had recognized Richard when he approached her in the 21 Club because she had known his father. The two of them were uncannily alike to look at. The only reason she hadn't connected them before was that Richard and Jeremy were poles apart as people. Compared to his son, Jeremy was nothing, just a small-time ex-pat, easy to brush aside and forget about completely. If it hadn't been for the name, she might never have connected them.

She turned to David again. 'There's one other thing I want to know about Richard Waites,' she said. 'Is he married?'

David thought for a moment. 'I don't think so. If he was he would have told me.'

Emerald decided to walk home. It was still light when she left David and she needed some time to herself to work things out. The streets were full of commuters leaving their offices as she pushed her way across Fifth Avenue and it wasn't until she reached the park that she finally hit her stride.

Emerald liked to walk in the city. While all her friends

had memberships to the gym, she found working out on the Nautilus machines a pointless activity. She could get the same aerobic benefit by pounding the pavements and the view was better. Now she had a clear run back to the apartment, she let her mind go back to Richard.

Emerald thought of her years in Mauritius when she had known his father. Back there Jeremy never took her anywhere either, because of her colour. The idea startled her. It's the 1980s and I'm in New York. Nobody gives a damn about my background. So why should Richard care . . . unless he's like his father.

It was the only explanation Emerald could come up with. Richard was hiding away, pretending to be someone else because he didn't want anyone to know she was his lover. The notion was both laughable and painful as hell. If Emerald had grown up in the West, it wouldn't have bothered her so much. But she was scarred by her girlhood, and she could never forget that the way she looked had condemned her to being one of a lesser species.

I'm good enough to share Richard's bed, she thought bitterly, but he doesn't want to be seen in public with me. The realization was like a body blow, slowing her pace and draining the blood from her cheeks. She had been running away from her past for a long time now, hiding from who she really was, because in America you could be anyone you wanted. Now she was right back where she started. If she went on loving this man, she would be forced to act the poor little native again. She couldn't bear it.

Nothing, not even love, was worth betraying her soul for. When I get back, she decided, I'm going to tell him I've found him out. Then I'm going to tell him goodbye. The thought of it brought tears to her eyes.

Richard was there when Emerald arrived, sitting in the study with its sporting prints and leather-covered armchairs. In front of him on the polished wood table was a half-finished whisky and soda. Emerald wondered how many more of them he would be consuming before the evening was finished.

She walked over to the bar and saw there was a bottle of white wine open and ready for her. She filled a glass and came over to where he was sitting.

'I had a drink with an old friend today,' she said quietly. 'David Reuben. I think you know him.'

The effect of her words was instantaneous. If she had thrown her drink all over him, she couldn't have shocked him more. For a second Richard didn't say anything, filling the silence between them by reaching for one of his flat Turkish cigarettes. When he finally spoke, his voice seemed to come from a long way away.

'So you know all about me,' he said.

Emerald stared at him. 'I know your real name is Richard Waites, and the Hutton character never existed. What I don't understand is why you invented him in the first place.'

'I didn't want you to know who I was.'

Emerald bit her lip. 'That's not all of it, is it? What you really wanted to do was pretend to be the reclusive Richard Hutton so you didn't have to be seen out with me.'

Just for a second Richard wondered if she had lost her mind. 'Why on earth would that bother me?' he asked.

There was a small silence, then Emerald let him have it with both barrels. 'Because I'm Indian,' she said angrily. 'Men like you and your father find it a little shaming to have the world know you're sleeping with a dark-skinned girl.'

Richard started to laugh. It was a mixture of relief and sheer astonishment and he realized he had been behaving like a fool for a very long time.

Here he was losing sleep because he thought Emerald wouldn't talk to him if she knew who his father was and all the time she was worried about something quite different.

He went over to her and took both her hands in his.

'I think you and I have to start telling each other the truth,' he said.

At first Emerald pulled away from him, screwing up her face in indignation, but Richard wasn't having any of it. He and this woman he loved had got their wires inextricably crossed. Unless something was done about it soon, there would be no hope for them at all.

He walked her over to the sofa. Then very firmly he sat Emerald down beside him.

'Before we go on I want to get one thing straight,' he said. 'I don't give a damn about your being Indian. My mother was Indian. If you'd been oriental or Black it wouldn't have mattered either. I love you for you.'

Emerald looked at Richard in wonderment. 'You never told me about your mother,' she said. 'I thought you were an Englishman through and through.'

Richard smiled. 'It's high time we talked about my parents,' he told her. 'Or rather it's time we talked about my father. He's the reason I didn't tell you who I was.'

She started to interrupt, but he wouldn't let her.

'I know all about you and Jeremy,' he said gently. 'Years ago, when I was just leaving school I saw you in a restaurant. You were with Larry Simpson then and Father started boasting about how he had known you first.'

Emerald blushed a dark crimson and he realized he had hit a nerve.

'So how do you think I felt when I saw you again? I knew who you were immediately, but if I'd let on I recognized you, if I'd told you what my name was, you would have been embarrassed. You might never have wanted to talk to me again and I didn't want to risk that. So I invented Richard Hutton, and I was pretty sure I'd get away with it as long as nobody recognized me.'

Emerald's voice seemed to come from a long way away. 'So that's why you hid away?'

Richard nodded.

Emerald moved away from him, looking wretched as she did so. 'Now we're being honest,' she said, 'I suppose I ought to tell you about Jeremy.'

He sighed. 'Not if you don't want to. You just said he was ashamed of your being Indian, so it couldn't have been a very loving relationship.'

Emerald seemed to shrink in front of him, almost as if she wanted to disappear inside herself and Richard felt like a heel for pushing her.

'You couldn't call what I had with your father, loving,' she said finally. 'It was convenient. I needed a roof over my head and a start in the world, and Jeremy needed a diversion. It worked while it lasted.'

Richard remembered the way he had lived as a child. There was never enough to eat and he imagined Emerald's life must have been the same.

So she had sold herself to the first rich protector who crossed her path, he thought. The man could have been an ex-pat with a taste for native girls. Only he wasn't. Her lover had been his father and he felt sad for her.

'It must be difficult for you,' he said, 'knowing who I am.'

'You mean because I once went to bed with Jeremy?' She laughed harshly. 'I was a child when I knew your father,' she told him. 'I've even forgotten how it was with him. Too many other things have happened in the meantime.'

Richard wished he hadn't started it. Only he'd asked for the truth and just because he didn't like the way it sounded, he couldn't tell her he'd changed his mind.

He reached out for her, pulling her close, and suddenly he realized none of it mattered. They'd both made mistakes in their pasts. He'd had his share of women, he was deceiving Caroline now, so how could he judge Emerald?

'We were different people before we met,' he told her.

'Neither of us had ever really loved before. You thought you loved Larry, but I don't think you did. And I never cared for anyone before I knew you. That wipes the slate clean. None of the things we did in the past counts for anything. We start our lives together right now. Right here.'

Emerald looked up at him and he thought he saw tears in her eyes.

'Do you mean that?'

He nodded, but even as he did so, he thought about Caroline. I must tell her everything, he decided. It's the only clean way to end things.

CHAPTER 25

London, 1981

It was the sort of day that made Caroline contemplate murder. Her secretary had failed to book her into Langan's, despite the fact she was a regular customer. She was in trouble with the lawyers over a minor story, and now Rolf Weiss's office had contacted her to say Richard wouldn't be back for another week.

She wondered why he couldn't call her himself. It wasn't the most difficult thing in the world to pick up the phone in New York.

Richard had been away for too long now. His frequent trips abroad had become a fact of her life but this one was different. For when he disappeared to Manhattan two months ago it was as if the city had swallowed him up.

Caroline could never get hold of him when she wanted to, and every time she left a message with his hotel, it took him at least a day to get back to her.

She realized there had to be a woman. No business deal was keeping him out every night of the week.

The knowledge irritated her. She and Richard were virtually engaged. Even his precious Uncle Tim was dropping hints about naming the day. So what was he doing playing around in New York?

Travelling home in the black cab she always took, Caroline decided to have it out with him. She had taken everything lying down today: Langan's, the lawyer calling her names, and now the news that Richard wanted another week with the bimbo he was shacked up with.

There was a limit to her patience, she thought. And it was time Richard knew it.

When she got back to Eaton Square, she poured herself a stiff drink, then she kicked off her shoes and threw herself on Richard's four-poster bed. They had been living together since Christmas, yet she still couldn't get over the novelty of it. If she was too lazy to cook dinner, all she had to do was pick up the phone and one of half a dozen top restaurants would deliver to the door. If she needed to go to Harrods in a hurry, a chauffeur-driven car would take her there.

If she decided to call New York and spend an hour giving Richard a hard time, there was no need to worry about the telephone bill.

She looked at the bedside clock. It was six o'clock London time. That meant it would be midday in New York. She'd just catch him before he went out to lunch.

He answered on the second ring and the minute he realized it was her on the line, his voice took on a cautious note.

'I was just planning to call you,' he told her. 'We have things to talk about.'

Caroline reached across the bed for her pack of cigarettes. So he's making excuses already, she thought. Well, this time he's not getting off the hook without a fight.

'If you're going to tell me about the extra week you want to spend in New York, you can save your breath,' she said.

There was the briefest of pauses.

'So Rolf managed to get hold of you at the office,' Richard said quietly.

Caroline felt the anger building up inside her. 'Exactly what are you playing at?' she demanded. 'I know you're up to something, so there's no point in denying it.'

Richard was back on the line almost before she had finished her tirade. 'You're right, I am up to something,' he said quietly. 'It's the reason I was going to call tonight.'

His answer took the wind out of her sails. She had expected him to lie. To flatter her into believing she was the most important girl in his life. And here he was blurting out a confession she had no intention of listening to.

She climbed down as gracefully as she could. 'I shouldn't have shouted at you,' she apologized, 'but I've had a nightmare of a day. Do you think we can start this conversation again?'

Richard didn't say anything for a minute, then just when she thought there was something wrong with the connection, his voice came back.

'Things have gone a bit too far for that,' he told her. 'Anyway, you deserve to know why I haven't been in touch.'

Caroline cut in on him before he could go on. 'You've met some girl,' she said. 'I recognize all the signs, so you don't have to explain yourself. In fact I'd rather you didn't say anything about it at all. All I'm interested in is when you're coming back and when I'm going to see you again.'

She thought she heard Richard sigh, but she couldn't be certain.

'It's not that simple,' he said. 'This girl isn't just a casual fling.'

Caroline started to get worried. If the stupid sod had gone and fallen for a bimbo, she'd be spending all her time on the end of the long-distance telephone.

She tried to make a joke of it. 'So you're setting up a branch office in New York while the passion lasts. Nice work if you can get it.'

Richard wasn't amused. In fact Caroline realized too late, she'd pushed things too far, for his voice had an edge to it.

'Caroline,' he said. 'I don't want to hurt your feelings, but you have to know the truth. I've fallen in love. Seriously, lastingly in love. When I get back to London, I won't be coming alone. I'm bringing Emerald with me.'

Caroline started to laugh. 'Where on earth are you going to store her?' she enquired. 'I've been living in your flat for the last six months.'

Her voice had taken on a hysterical note, but she couldn't stop herself.

'I hope you're not thinking of throwing me out,' she told him, 'because it's just not on.'

'Darling,' Richard said, more gently now. 'You're bound to be upset and you're not making a lot of sense. Why don't I call you in the morning and we'll talk again.'

He sounded patient, almost patronizing, and it made Caroline see red.

'I'm not a child,' she shouted. 'If you want me out I think I should know about it now, not tomorrow morning.'

There was a moment's hesitation, then Richard said, 'I've been trying to tell you that for the past ten minutes now.'

Every vile name Caroline had ever heard came flooding into her mind. If Richard had been anyone else she would have let them all out of her system. But he wasn't. He was the man she had decided to marry. The rich man she had decided to marry. So she took it easy.

'I get the message,' she said. 'Don't worry, I'll be out of here in a day or so, so there'll be no need to send in the heavies.'

Richard bent over backwards to make amends. She could have all the time in the world to be on her way. Nobody was pushing her. He'd stay out of her hair for as long as she wanted.

But Caroline knew when she was licked. This new girl, whoever she was, had turned Richard's head. When he got her back to England and started introducing her to all his friends, he might feel quite different about her but the first round was definitely not hers. The most sensible thing she could do now was go quietly, and bide her time.

Before she broke the connection, she asked Richard one

more question: 'Do you think I might know who this new girl is? I'll find out anyhow. But I'd like to hear it from you first.'

Richard told her Emerald Shah. 'You might have read about her,' he said. 'She used to live with Larry Simpson.'

CHAPTER 26

Now Caroline knew the identity of her rival, now she was actually in her sights, there was no holding her. Right after she had packed her bags, she made it her business to head for the library at the *London Evening Post*. Hidden somewhere inside the files of yellowing cuttings would be all the information she needed to bury Emerald Shah.

The nerve centre of every national paper is in its archives, for anyone who has ever been exposed to the public glare ends up there eventually. Long-forgotten presidents, movie stars past their sell-by dates and anyone who has had a brush with royalty can be unearthed with a little determined digging. And for those who really know their way round the overstuffed shelves, there are all sorts of secrets just waiting to be winkled out.

Caroline was a past mistress at using the library. In her line of country she needed to be, for the City was notoriously tight-lipped. Many of her best exclusives came to her simply because she knew more about the scandal she was trying to expose than any of her rivals. Her knowledge awed people into telling her things they would rather have kept to themselves.

If journalists spent more time in the archives and less in the pub, she thought, they would find everything they were looking for.

She had been sitting at a big desk in the corner of the library for almost two days now. During that time she had built up a sizeable dossier on the girl who had stolen Richard.

The first thing that registered was she was Indian and from Mauritius. She wondered if she had been some childhood sweetheart.

The cuttings shed no light on that one, so she transferred her attention to the years Emerald spent in Hollywood. There was plenty of detail here. She'd been with Larry Simpson for long enough for the press to accept them as an item. There were endless pictures of them both at premières and industry beanfeasts. In every one the Indian girl looked svelte and expensively cared for.

It was clear that the actor had been enamoured of her, so when he suddenly left her the bulk of his fortune it didn't come as any great surprise. The will being contested was pretty well par for the course too. Nobody expected the Simpson family to take his change of heart lying down.

Caroline had been over every aspect of the ten years of court-room wrangles, but she couldn't find a single fact that led anywhere.

Emerald Shah was the standard devoted camp follower who would have ended up marrying her movie star if he hadn't died on her. She didn't have any weaknesses that Caroline could find. Her drinking was moderate, there was no dependency on drugs, hard or soft, and from all the evidence of the cuttings and the picture libraries there wasn't a smell of a boyfriend.

The only man Emerald had been photographed anywhere near was Shel Johnson, Larry's producer. And he was known to be Larry's best buddy.

An idea that had been lurking at the back of Caroline's mind suddenly took shape. The girlfriend and the best buddy. It was the cliché to end all clichés and it probably wouldn't stand up, but it was worth investigating.

She went through the stack of photographs in front of her again. The three of them seemed to go everywhere together. There was even a set of shots taken in front of the Cedars Hospital after Larry's first heart attack. Caroline studied all their faces searching for clues, but there was nothing. Emerald looked miserable. Larry looked ill. Shel looked protective.

Caroline sighed heavily. Anyone else would have called it a day and gone home. But Caroline wasn't anyone else. She was a dyed-in-the-wool professional and she had an axe to grind.

If she could get a hint of trouble, just a whiff of something that wasn't quite as it should be with Emerald, then she had something to work with. So she got up out of her chair and walked over to the window that separated the librarians from the rest of the office.

When she managed to get some attention, she asked for Shel Johnson's press cuttings. She also decided to go through every picture ever taken of him.

It was far into the night when she finally finished but she had found what she was looking for. Shel and Emerald had taken to having dinner together alone. There were paparazzi pictures of them leaving some of the better-known Hollywood restaurants together. She checked the dates of the appearances and found that they coincided with the period when Larry had been too ill to appear in public.

So, the best friend was stepping in to give comfort and solace. It was all very normal, all very reasonable on the surface. But what went on when the two of them left Chasens or Ma Maison? Caroline knew the library wasn't capable of answering that question. That was something she would have to go and find out for herself.

By the spring of 1983, Richard and Emerald had been living together in London for nearly eighteen months. The arrangement suited them both perfectly.

At least Richard assumed it suited Emerald as well as it did him, for he never bothered to ask how she felt. He would kiss her goodbye every morning and until he came back in the evening he never gave her another thought. His job claimed all his attention and like all busy men, he took his home life for granted.

If he had paid her a little more attention he might have noticed that Emerald was finding it difficult to settle down in London, for she was caught between two life styles.

In New York, she had been a free-wheeling jet-setter, and her slightly shadowy background suited her perfectly for the part. She wasn't rich but she had access to money. She was beautiful, and she had been loved by an international movie star.

Now she was living with Richard her whole persona had changed. In many ways it was almost a move back to her days with Larry, but there was an important difference. International movie stars were not expected to marry their consorts. Living in sin was a perfectly acceptable way to carry on in Beverly Hills where whole families were raised out of wedlock.

In London the atmosphere was different. Emerald was living with a businessman now, not a movie star, and although men like Richard were allowed to sow their wild oats, it was expected that after a decent interval he would marry whichever girl he was sleeping with. The world had expected him to settle down with Caroline, and when he didn't, they waited with the same sort of anticipation for him to make a respectable woman of Emerald.

However, he showed no signs of doing so. There wasn't even an engagement ring, and Emerald found it difficult to get accepted. None of the wives of Richard's business associates ever asked her to lunch. In fact she wasn't invited to anything in her own right. As far as smart English society was concerned, Emerald was a girlfriend in waiting. Until Richard gave her some sort of credibility by making her his wife, she was an outsider – an exotic mistress to be humoured, but nothing more than that.

Emerald might have put up with this state of affairs if

it hadn't been for Caroline. For Richard's friends seemed to delight in bringing up her name.

Every time they went out for dinner, there was always somebody who wanted to talk about the latest controversy in her column. And if it wasn't her career that took their attention, then it was her private life. The journalist was being sighted around town on the arm of a succession of glamorous escorts and there was noisy speculation as to whom she was sleeping with.

Almost overnight, Caroline seemed to be emerging as a glamorous icon and it started to get to Emerald.

If I had been Caroline, she thought, a woman with my own job and my own independence, I would never have put up with this situation. I would have demanded to be married, and Richard would have fallen into line because he would have been scared of losing me.

But what have I got to offer? I have no money of my own. No job. I don't even have any friends in this snobby little city.

She decided to make a few changes in her life. She had no money because Larry's children were still arguing who should have what. If she went on the way she was going, they would probably still be in dispute by the time she was an old lady. Emerald decided to bring the wrangle to an end. There was enough money in Larry's estate for all of them to live comfortably. If she just offered to settle out of court, she was sure they could come to some sort of agreement.

She instructed Steve Brady to make them an offer. Once the whole business with the inheritance was behind her, then she could start thinking seriously about her future.

Now Emerald had a plan, the spectre of Caroline bothered her less. She might well have faded from her life altogether if Emerald hadn't found out that Richard was still in touch with her. The journalist occasionally called him with share tips, and when one paid off spectacularly well, Richard told Emerald where it had come from.

Emerald was less than pleased. 'I didn't know you and Caroline had such a cosy arrangement,' she said coolly. 'Is there anything else I should know about? Anything you haven't told me?'

Richard was mildly alarmed by her reaction. Caroline was so unimportant, so past history, he didn't understand what Emerald was getting so het up about.

'I'm not trying to hide anything,' he said irritably. 'Since we split up, I've only seen the woman once, and that was just for a drink so she could give me back a set of cuff links.'

There was something intimate and domestic about the incident that unsettled Emerald. What was wrong with Caroline sending the cuff links to Richard? They didn't have to have a drink as well.

She asked where they met and when he told her the bar of his club, she hit the roof. She knew London well enough to understand men didn't meet their exes in Bucks.

It took Richard a week to convince Emerald there was nothing in it but the incident had dented her confidence. Something instinctive told her she and Caroline were on a collision course that would end up with their coming face to face. And when they did, she had no doubt that both their lives would alter. She had no idea how right she was.

CHAPTER 27

When Richard had to go abroad on business Tim Waites usually stepped into the breach and kept Emerald company. Often he would take her to the opera or the theatre because he liked talking to her about it afterwards.

Over the months Tim had become very fond of Emerald. She was bright without being pushy, which made her different from all the other women of her generation. With Emerald you could have a discussion. You could even agree to disagree and she didn't try to ram her opinions down your throat.

How different she was from Caroline, the banker thought. She never let me get away with anything.

As he thought of his nephew's two women, Tim realized why Richard had opted for Emerald. No real man wanted the kind of competition Caroline offered. She was exhilarating, he couldn't deny it, but in the end her sheer naked aggression was too uncomfortable to live with.

He considered the evening ahead. Richard had left for Athens earlier on that day and as always Tim and Emerald were dining together. He was disappointed in her choice of restaurant, a noisy, yuppie hang-out, the sort of place where design took precedence over comfort. Tim was tempted to book somewhere civilized like the Ritz or the Connaught and pretend Emerald's favourite was full, but he couldn't go through with it. So at 8.30, Tim found himself pushing his way through a mêlée of designer-clad trendies in an attempt to get to the bar.

Emerald told him she would meet him there for a drink

first. Now he was being trampled underfoot, Tim wished he'd agreed to meet her at the table instead.

He was starting to get thoroughly depressed when he saw her. She was perched on a spindly chrome and leather stool, drinking a spritzer out of a long glass. Any other girl waiting on her own might have appeared anxious, but Emerald looked perfectly at home where she was. It was as if she had been born belonging in places like this and for a moment Tim felt daunted.

It's her beauty, he thought. If I didn't know her I would assume she was some unattainable trophy.

Emerald had spotted him now and quite suddenly the illusion disappeared. She was Emerald again. His Emerald, Richard's Emerald, and Tim hurried towards her.

He saw her spritzer was nearly finished and ordered a bottle of champagne for them both. Then they started to gossip. It had been weeks since they last had dinner together and there was a lot to catch up on.

They didn't stop talking, even when the waiter came and told them their table was ready. And Tim started to forget that he didn't like the place.

Indeed, he might have become converted to the restaurant if he hadn't started to look around him. It was a communications haunt, a place for bright young men on the way up in advertising or broadcasting and it made Tim feel old. He was just wondering if Emerald would be interested in leaving early, when he saw her. She was sitting three tables away from them and from the looks of it she was getting seriously drunk.

He ducked his head in an attempt not to be noticed but he was too late. Caroline had seen him clearly and she was signalling hello.

Tim nodded curtly and hoped that would be an end to it, but his luck was out that night.

'I'll join you for coffee,' she called. 'Can't wait to meet your friend.'

225

Tim groaned. This was all he needed. Caroline half-cut and curious, trying to push herself into his tête-à-tête.

Emerald saw what was going on and raised an eyebrow. 'Who was that?' she asked.

'Richard's ex,' Tim said shortly. 'If we hurry we can finish dinner and get out of here before she gets her head up again.'

But Emerald wouldn't hear of it. She had heard too much about Caroline Fellows to pass up an opportunity like this. Without Richard around, she could actually talk to the woman. She could find out who she was. She might even get to know whether all the gossip about her had been true.

Tim realized he was fighting a losing battle, so he put up little resistance. Half an hour later, when the food had been cleared away, he saw Caroline get to her feet and move away from the party she was dining with.

She was wearing a plain black shift, too tight and too short at the same time. At her ears and round her wrists she was wearing a lot of gold jewellery, and her hair was wild and spiky.

She looks dangerous, Tim decided. I was mad to let Emerald go through with this, but there was no getting out of it. Caroline had already reached them and was settling herself into an empty chair.

The banker made the introductions. 'Emerald,' he said, 'I don't think you've met Caroline Fellows.'

The two women went through the pantomime of greeting. Then Caroline gave Emerald the once-over. Because she was tipsy, she wasn't discreet about it and Emerald felt vaguely annoyed.

'The dress came from Browns,' she said, 'but I got it in the sale, so you can knock off fifty per cent. The diamonds are real and you can put any price you like on them.'

For a moment Tim worried the meeting would deteriorate into a shouting match. But the journalist took it like a trouper.

'I suppose you think I'm a real bitch,' she said.

Emerald shook her head and looked thoughtful. 'I don't think you're a bitch,' she said. 'But I think you're curious. I think you want to know what I've got that you haven't.'

The journalist leaned back and looked at her out of slanted eyes. My God, she's smug, she thought.

'I don't feel that competitive about you,' she said. 'There's no point. Even if you hadn't come along I would have lost Richard.'

Tim did a double take. This was news to him. The way he remembered it, Richard was dotty about Caroline. There was no way she stood the remotest chance of losing him – she'd had him hooked, in bed, at least.

He listened fascinated to what was coming next.

'Richard and I were on the skids,' Caroline said, leaning forward and helping herself to a glass of wine.

She looked so miserable as she said it that Tim almost found himself believing her. Then he realized it was the drink talking.

If Caroline hadn't convinced Tim, she was doing a good job on Emerald, for she was hanging on her every word.

'Did you care about losing him?' she asked.

For a moment Caroline didn't say anything. Then she pulled herself together. 'Of course I cared,' she said. 'Richard was everything I wanted.'

Emerald started to feel embarrassed. It was unfair of her to push Caroline like this. All she needed was one more glass of wine and she'd make a complete fool of herself.

It was an accurate assessment. Without prompting, the redhead started pouring out her troubles. Apparently she had no luck with men at all. There were plenty of them around, but every time she got involved with anyone it always ended in disaster.

'There must be something wrong with me,' she wailed. 'Nobody else seems to have my problems.'

The journalist seemed to have touched a nerve in Emerald's psyche, for suddenly she couldn't do enough for her. Tim was worried now.

Caroline had to be up to something. He had a shrewd idea that the stuff about Richard was pure fantasy, and as for the nonsense about her failure with the opposite sex, he didn't believe a word of that either.

She's not as drunk as she's trying to make out, he decided. This is all a ploy to get Emerald's confidence.

He realized he had to bring this encounter to an end and he signalled the waiter for the bill. As the man arrived, Tim overheard Caroline enquiring as to Richard's whereabouts. The question was put very casually, almost as an after-thought, but the banker wasn't fooled. He'd seen Caroline dig for information before and he hoped Emerald had the sense to be discreet.

It was a vain hope. Emerald was mesmerized by Caroline. If she had been asked for the number of Richard's Swiss bank account, Emerald would have handed it over without a murmur.

To his relief Tim saw the waiter return with his credit card. As he checked the bill and calculated how much tip to leave, he tuned out of the conversation. He regretted it the moment he looked up, for Caroline was moving in for the kill.

'Do you get lonely here in London?' she asked Emerald.

It was the sixty-four-thousand-dollar question. Before Emerald answered, Tim knew Caroline had hit the jack-pot.

'Of course I do,' Emerald said sadly. 'In New York I had half a dozen girlfriends. Over here I'm on my own.'

'I'll help you,' Caroline said softly. 'I think we could be good for each other. After all, look what we've got in common. Why don't we have lunch together one day?' she suggested. 'You never know, it might be fun.'

Emerald thought for a moment. Sitting here in the busy,

noisy restaurant, the idea of spending time with Richard's ex didn't seem so terrifying. She looked at Tim.

'You know us both,' she said. 'Do you think it's a good idea?'

The banker frowned. If he said what was on his mind, she would only think he was putting a damper on things. So he reserved his judgement.

'You're a big girl,' he told her. 'You must make up your own mind about lunch.'

Caroline called early the following morning and told Emerald she'd had a last-minute cancellation for lunch.

'I've got a table booked at Langan's,' she said, 'so if you aren't doing anything I thought we might make use of it.'

Emerald wondered whether to take her up on it. If she'd had more time she could have invented an excuse but Caroline wasn't giving her the chance.

She heard herself agreeing to meet the journalist, then she wondered if she should call Richard in Athens and tell him what was going on. She pulled herself together. I don't have to ask permission every time I go out to lunch, she thought.

When she got to the restaurant, Caroline was already there. She was standing at the mirrored bar in deep conversation with Peter Langan.

Emerald noticed the journalist had cleaned up her act since last night. She was wearing a sharp little suit with power shoulders and a tailored skirt that ended just above her knees. She looked somehow focused now, as if she was in control of herself, and Emerald suspected there would be no more girlish confessions about Richard.

She made her way over to Caroline and the journalist smiled briefly. In one clear moment Emerald sensed how Caroline felt about her. And she wondered why on earth they were having this lunch.

They went over to their table and started to talk about

neutral subjects. The sales had just started in the West End and Caroline was investing a lot of her salary in cut-price designers.

It was the sort of thing Emerald understood. Way back in Mauritius she had imitated the designers Caroline was talking about and now she waxed strong about them. She was so carried away with her memories, that she hardly glanced at her companion. It was only when the redhead didn't reply to something she was saying, that she came back to earth. She saw then her words were falling on deaf ears. Caroline was busy looking over her shoulder trying to get a better view of Michael Caine and his agent.

I'm boring her to tears, Emerald realized.

She started to feel depressed. She had come here today because she needed a friend, and with every moment that passed she realized friendship was the last thing on this woman's mind.

She decided to order something light. If she ate quickly she could be out of this place and away from Caroline, for some instinct told her that she shouldn't be here. That she was putting herself at risk just by sharing the same table as this woman.

When the food arrived, Caroline broached the subject of her law suit. The wrangle with Larry's children seemed to fascinate her and she wanted to know the current state of play.

Emerald's heart sank. This was none of Caroline's business. She didn't have to tell her anything if she didn't feel like it but it was hard to get out of it.

So in the end she told Caroline she was giving up her fight for Larry's inheritance.

'I'm going to settle out of court,' she said. 'It's the only way I'm going to see any money at all.'

For the first time since they'd sat down together, Caroline seemed genuinely interested in what she had to say.

'You're climbing down a bit, aren't you?' she said. 'Won't it weaken your position?'

Emerald thought about it. 'I guess it would if we were still fighting each other,' she told the journalist. 'But that's all over now.'

Caroline sliced into her avocado with surprising viciousness.

'You must be very relieved,' she said.

The conversation turned to Hollywood and Emerald felt herself beginning to relax. She and this former girlfriend of Richard's would never be friends, but right now there was a distinct possibility they might get through lunch without any serious bloodshed.

The illusion was short-lived, for Caroline was only talking about the film business in order to screw some information out of her. She wanted to know all sorts of personal details about the big names. Emerald felt her guard coming up.

'Hollywood was a long time ago,' she said. 'I've forgotten most of the things I knew.'

But Caroline seemed to have an insatiable appetite for gossip and Emerald started to feel nervous. She had a suspicion that if she let anything slip about even the most casual acquaintance, she'd wake up and find it in the paper the next morning.

She tried to deflect Caroline, to change the subject, but it was a bit like trying to stop an avalanche in full flow. Caroline had the bit between her teeth and nothing was going to satisfy her until she had a story. She managed to work her way through twelve major movie stars and any number of studio heads until she got to the name that had been on her mind all day.

'What do you know about Shel Johnson?' she asked Emerald softly, looking like a snake. 'I understand you and he were close at one time.'

Emerald thought she was going to pass out. The noisy,

busy brasserie seemed to be pressing in on her and when she looked down she saw her fists were clenched.

She stared at her interrogator. 'What makes you think I was close to Shel?' she asked.

Caroline leaned forward. 'There were stories about the two of you going around town at one time. I'm pretty sure there was nothing in it, but you know what we journalists are like. We always like to check our facts.'

Emerald should have walked out there and then. This woman had invited her here to trap her. That was clear now, but she couldn't leave. She had to know exactly what Caroline knew.

'Tell me about the rumours you heard,' she said. 'I'm curious.'

Now the journalist really was taking a flyer, but experience told her she was getting very close to what she wanted.

'Everyone was talking about an affair,' she said carefully. 'With Larry sick in bed, his best friend seemed an obvious source of comfort.'

Emerald felt her face go hot. 'That's a dirty lie,' she said. 'Shel Johnson wasn't in the market for comfort. He doesn't know the meaning of the word.'

Caroline smiled. 'But he was in the market for something, wasn't he? You wouldn't be getting this excited if the guy was only interested in being a buddy.'

But Emerald had had enough. She reached under the table for her bag, then she got to her feet as fast as she could.

'I'm not interested in hearing any more of this,' she said, 'so I'm going. Tell them to send on my half of the bill.'

Before the journalist could make another move, Emerald was threading her way through the tables on her way to the main entrance. When she got there she glanced behind her and saw she had been followed.

Caroline was standing just ten feet away from her by

the cheese trolley. She was smiling thoughtfully and staring into space. Anyone who hadn't seen her being snubbed might have thought she had just learned something to her advantage.

CHAPTER 28

Los Angeles, 1983

Hollywood has a way of letting a producer know when he's in trouble. It happens in subtle ways. His name gets left off one or two 'A' list parties. If he was used to having a window table at Spago he suddenly finds he can't get it any more. People in the industry don't ask him what he's working on, and if he tries to tell them, they suddenly find a very good reason for cutting the conversation short.

Shel Johnson had been getting this treatment for longer than he cared to remember, and it made him bad-tempered. If he was honest with himself, he would have admitted that his fall from grace was something to do with the pictures he was turning out, but he had worked in the movie business too long for that kind of candour.

As far as Shel was concerned, every deal he got together was a sure-fire grosser. There was *New York Nights*, a literary novel he optioned and sold to a major studio. He didn't actually read the book, but he'd seen the reviews and they had been enough to convince him he was on to something big. His sales talk managed to convince a name director and a major star to lend their names to the project. The only people he didn't manage to convince was the cinema audience, who stayed away in droves, for the book, which relied on the elegance of its writing, didn't translate to the screen at all.

Shel managed to shift the blame for that failure on the director, whom he criticized as being too arty. He stayed away from culture on his next project.

What he needed to follow *New York Nights* was a flashy,

mass-market success. He thought he had found it in *Jail-bait*, a thinly disguised version of *Lolita* and the perfect vehicle for a sex symbol. In the mid-seventies, when Shel was putting together the package, there were plenty on offer. Goldie Hawn and Tatum O'Neal were both young enough and well-known enough to take the role, as were Cheryl Ladd and Katharine Ross, but Shel decided to go for someone different.

He cast not a screen star, but a darling of the gossip columnists as his leading lady. Apart from being very beautiful, Sylvie Adams had come in for a lot of media attention because she had married two major stars in swift succession. Both her divorces made front-page news and launched her as an overnight celebrity. The public were hot for everything she did so when she signed to do *Jailbait*, the hype astounded even Shel. He sold the property to United Artists for an inflated share of the gross profits and sat back and waited for the money to roll in.

It never happened. Sylvie Adams was effective in every department of her life except for the one that counted with the film-makers. She couldn't act. The performance she gave in *Jailbait* wasn't just wooden, it was embarrassing. The film closed in under two weeks.

After that Shel stopped getting invitations from the studio brass.

He made a succession of low-budget features, which he sold to cable television stations. It was a living, but not the same kind of living he had in the palmy days.

In the early eighties, Shel Johnson was strictly a 'B' list player in the Hollywood game and he looked for a scapegoat for his run of back luck.

There has to be a moment, he thought, when I lost credibility in this town, a point when the skids went under me. He raked back over the past decade, but apart from his own failures, he could find nothing. Then he remembered his old friend Larry Simpson.

He had been involved on Larry's last film, the one he never finished. By the time the star had his heart attack, Shel had handed the entire production over to the studio, but his name was on the credits. The insiders in the business knew Shel had instigated the picture and when it never got made, anyone who wanted to could put the blame at his door. He was, after all, a close buddy of Larry's. Why didn't he talk him into going back on the set?

The more Shel thought about it, the more he was convinced his troubles started with the Simpson picture. If he had been able to get Larry on his own, the story might have ended differently, for when he came out of hospital the first time, the actor wasn't that sick. A few extra weeks' work wouldn't have made any difference to him. But they would have made a helluva lot of difference to the picture. He remembered explaining the situation to that girlfriend of Larry's, but she wasn't having it. She wanted to wrap him up in cotton wool. She seemed convinced that the sight of the studio would send him right back to Cedars Hospital. And nothing Shel could say would move her from that position.

In the end he even tried romancing her. The memory of what he did to Emerald in the privacy of his beach house came back to him. She was one hot piece of ass, he thought. In the end he didn't have to show her what to do, she got there all by herself. But even in bed, he couldn't reach her. She just didn't seem to give a damn that twenty million dollars would go down the drain because she wouldn't let Larry do a few weeks' work.

Every time something disappointed him, Shel would go over this scenario, and each time he did, he would subtly alter the facts to reinforce his theory. Larry's worsening condition was edited from this new version of the story. Emerald's unwillingness to go on with the affair also hit the cutting-room floor. All the producer chose to remember was that Emerald had scuppered his career by keeping

Larry away from a project he had instigated. She was his scapegoat and the knowledge that he could pin the whole thing on her made it easier to sleep at night.

Shel didn't give her another thought until Caroline Fellows came to see him. Then Emerald's life swam into focus again.

Shel Johnson operated from a villa in the grounds of the Beverly Hills Hotel. It was a squat pink construction with louvred doors and a thatched roof. And all around it were the lush tropical gardens that were the grounds of the hotel.

It was an exotic location for an office, but Caroline wasn't impressed. Any number of independent producers operated out of the Beverly Hills because of its popularity with the film colony. For the price of a hotel suite you had a fancy address and unlimited access to the Polo Lounge.

Caroline guessed Shel Johnson was one of the not-so-popular independents who hung around the hotel hoping to waylay any studio executive who would listen to him.

She realized she had guessed right when she arrived at his office. It was 3.30, yet according to his secretary the producer was still at lunch. So he's not all that busy, she thought, taking a seat in the cramped little room.

Because she had time to kill, she made a quick inspection of the suite of offices. There was a room the size of a broom cupboard where the secretary worked. Next to it was a fully equipped bathroom. And the main room where she was sitting the producer did his deals from.

Every surface was covered with scripts. They all looked as if they had been around for some time, for they were dog-eared and used-looking. Caroline wondered if any of them had ever been seriously considered by a studio or if they were simply accessories.

Her reverie was interrupted by the arrival of Shel Johnson. She heard his secretary telling him he had a guest and she braced herself. If the man wanted to be unpleasant, he had every right. She had gate-crashed his office, after all.

She needn't have worried. Shel had been drinking that lunchtime and he was still full of goodwill. When she introduced herself he offered her a cup of coffee and apologized for avoiding her when she had called earlier.

'I was in the middle of a crisis when you called,' he explained, 'so I was a little short of time.'

He handed her a cup of strong black Cona. 'You're from some English newspaper, aren't you? What can I do to help?'

Caroline sat back in her chair and sized him up. It was as she had expected. The man was past his prime, though once, when he kept company with Larry Simpson, she suspected Shel had been important in this town.

It was the way he dressed that gave her the clue. He wore a sombre black silk suit, the sort of thing you would expect to find on the back of a studio head, and his shoes were shiny and obviously hand-made. He spends a lot of money on keeping up appearances, Caroline thought. That means he cares about his fall from grace. I'd better handle him gently.

She spent a lot of time talking about her job on the *London Evening Post*. She exaggerated her importance, pretending she had overall control on which features went in the paper. Shel was as impressed as she'd intended him to be. When she was sure she had his attention she broached the subject she had come to discuss.

'I'm doing a story about the girl who used to live with Larry Simpson,' she said. 'There's a big row going on about the money he left and I thought it might be interesting to get a bit of background material while I'm here.'

Shel looked at his visitor curiously. There was something not quite right about her. The drama over Larry's will had been rumbling on for years now. It was old news. So why does this girl suddenly turn up from the other side of the world and express an interest? She has to have an angle, he decided. And before she left his office, he was going to find out what it was.

'Why are you coming to me for information?' he asked cautiously. 'I'm not exactly an interested party.'

'But you were his best friend,' she pressed. 'So you would have been around when Larry had his heart attack.'

The producer nodded. 'We were seeing each other then. But I don't see where this is leading.'

There was a silence while Caroline finished her coffee and put the empty cup down on the desk. Then she waded in with both feet.

'I told you I was investigating Emerald Shah,' she said. 'If you were close to Larry Simpson, you must have known her as well.'

There was a look about her as she said it. A knowing look that told him she had a shrewd idea of his relationship with Emerald.

For a moment Shel felt uneasy. He had made a point of never talking about the episode, because it made him look like a villain. So how did Caroline know about it?

'Why are you so interested in this matter?' he said.

The journalist started to look uncomfortable. 'I thought I told you that already. My paper's doing a story about the row over the inheritance.'

He didn't bother to disguise his contempt for her obvious lie.

'My dear girl,' he said, 'there is no publication in existence that gives a damn about that affair. It's been dead and buried for over a decade. So why don't you tell me why you really came up here?'

For a moment Caroline was winded. This man might be yesterday's news, but his brain was still in working order.

'I had lunch with Emerald,' she said slowly. 'She lives in London now so she's quite easy to get to. Anyway, when I saw her she told me she was dropping the case against

Larry's children. Apparently she had decided to settle out of court.'

'Sensible girl. That way she doesn't end up giving everything to the lawyers. I would think Larry's children will be pleased as well.'

Caroline took a deep breath. 'Not as pleased as they would be if they got the lot.'

Shel reached into his inside pocket and extracted a thin black cigar. When he had finished lighting it, he turned to the girl sitting in front of him.

'How can the children do that?' he demanded. 'There's not a scrap of evidence against her.'

'I think there is,' she said softly. 'I also think you know exactly what she's done wrong.'

Shel smiled. So that was it. That was her angle. This English journalist had come all the way to Los Angeles to bury Emerald and she wanted to use him to do her dirty work.

'If I can help you, and I'm not making any promises,' Shel said, 'I'd like to know what's going on. You're no great friend of the children. You're not after a story either. Your interest in this whole thing is too personal for that.'

He stared at her out of dark glittering eyes. 'Come on, Caroline,' he said. 'Do us both a favour and level.'

Caroline was no match for him. She realized that now. She also realized that if she held out any longer, he would spin her out of his office at the speed of light, so she told him what he wanted to know.

'I was in love with a man and Emerald took him away from me,' she said miserably. 'I thought if I could get something really bad on her, it would ruin her chances with the children.'

Shel started to laugh. 'So that's it. An everyday story of revenge. Emerald takes your man, you relieve her of her inheritance. It's all a bit rough, isn't it?'

Caroline shrugged. 'Life's rough,' she said. 'I don't

suppose Larry was all that pleased when you started taking his girlfriend to bed.'

It was a shot in the dark, but from the look on the producer's face, she had scored a direct hit.

'Larry knew nothing about it,' he said.

Caroline started to feel better. It was her turn to put the boot in.

'Would you like to tell me your side of the story?' she asked demurely.

'What, so you could write about it in your rag?'

Caroline looked at him as if he were mad. 'I'm after revenge, not the Pulitzer prize. If you tell me what really went on before Larry died, I'll take it straight to Larry's family.'

The producer started to relax. Now the whole thing was out in the open, the way ahead seemed clearer. The affair with Emerald couldn't damage him any more. Larry had been dead too long for that.

And if this girl did what she promised, there could be a bonus in it for him. If he caused Emerald to lose the money that was coming to her, he would have his own back.

The notion suddenly seemed very attractive. He turned to Caroline.

'I could go on talking to you all afternoon,' he said. 'But I'm afraid I'm a bit pushed for time.' He hesitated for a moment. 'If you like we can meet later on and catch up. We can do it over dinner if you're not involved in anything else.'

As of that moment, the journalist was at his disposal.

CHAPTER 29

Dinner with Shel was something of a disappointment. He took Caroline to the Hard Rock Café on Beverly boulevard where the hamburgers were the best she had ever tasted and the background noise was deafening. Rock music from huge speakers was pumped into the room and Caroline couldn't hear herself think, much less understand anything Shel was trying to tell her.

In the end they conversed in monosyllables and concentrated their attention on the focal point of the restaurant, the bar. It was a huge circular affair and something of a gathering place. Every out-of-work actor who wanted to strut his stuff was propped up against it sipping Perrier water. Caroline had never seen so many beautiful young men in one place and she was temporarily distracted. It didn't last for long.

She had come a long way to get the goods on Emerald and a little loud music wasn't going to throw her off. She put her hand on Shel's arm.

'Do you think we could go somewhere else?' she asked. 'I can't seem to concentrate in this place.'

The producer smiled and called for the bill. Then he asked her if she wanted to go to a nightclub.

Caroline nodded enthusiastically. Once the lights were low and they were sitting tucked away at a table for two she'd have no problem getting Shel to unburden himself. She glanced at her watch. It was getting on for eleven. If her luck held, she could be back at her hotel by midnight with everything she came for.

The club was located at the dingy end of Sunset Boulevard, and the guy on the door looked as if he worked as an all-in wrestler in another life.

Shel handed him their entrance money, which struck Caroline as strange. Then Mr Muscles stamped both their hands with the name of the club and they were ushered through.

At first glance it was an ordinary enough disco. There was a dance area, a narrow stage and a long bar at one end. It was pretty dark so she couldn't make out much, except for the video screens behind the bar. They were showing flickering black and white movies. And when she looked closer Caroline realized they were pornographic.

A vague feeling of uneasiness crept over her. She thought she had Shel Johnson neatly summed up as a middle-aged Hollywood producer. Now she wondered if she had been wrong. Before she said anything about the films, she had a good look around her.

What she saw confirmed her worst fears. The place was full of weirdos. Both men and women sported short crew-cuts or shaven heads. Black leather seemed to be the overall uniform and they were wearing tattoos and rings through their noses the way the average Hollywood crowd would be carrying Gucci bags.

'What is this place?' she asked.

Shel looked sly. 'Stop playing the innocent,' he told her. 'I had you down for a girl who's been around.'

He was still wearing the formal silk suit she had seen him in earlier that day, the one that made him look like a studio executive, but now it didn't fool her any more. This man's a pervert, she thought. He might even be dangerous. But the notion didn't frighten her. She'd come too far and laid out too much of her own money to be put off by some sexual eccentricity.

She took a packet of cigarettes out of her bag and lit one. Then she asked Shel if she could have a glass of white wine.

Someone, somewhere had turned on a music machine. She recognized the sound as heavy metal and knew the dancers couldn't be far away. She wasn't disappointed. Up on the stage two go-go girls were giving the sort of exhibition she had seen in Soho strip clubs. It seemed to turn on the crowd who thronged the tiny dance floor boogying as if their lives depended on it.

All around her she detected the unmistakable aroma of sweat and sex. Some of the men had removed their shirts. Another took off his trousers revealing a cock pouch which looked as if it were stuffed with Kleenex. She wondered if her companion was gay, then she glanced in his direction and knew this was her unlucky night. Shel was looking at her as if he wanted to eat her alive and she realized with a sinking heart that whatever she got out of him tonight she'd be paying for.

A tiny piece of her mind detached itself from the turmoil going on around her, and started to figure out what to do next. She had been in tight corners before and she always relied on this cold sanity of hers to come to her rescue.

There was no way that Shel was going to spill the beans in this sordid club. He had just taken her here to warm her up. She imagined that at a suitable hour, he would suggest a nightcap at his place. And then she knew she would have to keep her nerve. She shivered slightly at the prospect of what lay ahead, then she hardened her resolve.

'It's time you took me home,' she told him. 'It's getting late.'

Her companion seemed reluctant to leave, but Caroline had had enough. I don't have to put myself through this, she thought. Either Shel gets on with it, or I'm going home.

She told him as much and the producer got to his feet and took her out of the place. Once they were in the street, Caroline turned to him.

'I know why I'm here tonight,' she said, 'and so do you.

So do you think you could take me somewhere where we won't be interrupted this time?'

Shel got into the car without a word. Then he headed in the direction of his apartment in Westwood. The house he kept in the good days, the mansion in Whitely Heights, had been sold years previously. Now he operated from a two-bedroom walk-up in a down-at-heel co-operative.

When they reached it Caroline wondered what he had brought her to, for the building belonged to the Hollywood of fifty years ago. There was an air of dereliction about the whole structure as if the first good wind would blow the whole thing to the ground.

As she tramped up five floors the journalist tried to visualize how this man lived. When they finally got into the apartment, she was pleasantly surprised. The place was small, far smaller than Shel would be used to, but there was an elegance about the way he had fixed it up that redeemed it. A huge brick fireplace dominated the centre of the main room and Shel had completed the homely, informal look by throwing Mexican rugs over the polished wooden floors.

Caroline settled herself on one of his hessian sofas and got straight down to business.

'You were going to tell me about Emerald,' she said.

Shel poured them both generous measures of vodka over ice.

'What do you want to know exactly? You seem to have most of the story already.'

Caroline prayed for patience. 'I need you to tell me when you had the affair. Was it before or after Larry had his heart attack?'

Shel went over to the fire before he answered her next.

'It was after the attack. That's why I never spoke about it. Neither of us comes out of it very well.'

'But Emerald comes out of it worst,' she told him. 'After all, you weren't in love with Larry.'

The producer smiled. This bitch really did have it in for Emerald. He shuddered to think what she would be telling the children's lawyer.

While she sat and finished her drink, Shel filled Caroline in on the details of his liaison. As he finished his story, he saw Caroline stifling a tiny yawn.

'You can't be tired,' he said, 'it's not even midnight.'

Caroline could see herself getting an argument about staying and she really didn't have the energy to be polite any longer. So she gave it to him straight. 'I'm going,' she said. 'We've covered all the ground we're going to tonight.'

Shel came towards her then and she realized he wasn't going to let her off the hook.

'We haven't even started,' he said, his voice dangerously calm.

Caroline made one last effort to play for time. 'If you want to go in for infantile sex games, you can count me out. I'm not into leather and go-go dancing.'

A look of pure fury contorted Shel's face. She realized she had gone too far.

'I don't give a damn for your preferences,' he told her. 'You got what you wanted out of me. Now it's my turn.'

Before Caroline could get out of the way, he had grabbed her, and a vision of the club they had just left came back to her like a nightmare. The man was a sicko. For all she knew he had a cupboard full of whips and bondage gear.

The notion made her panic and she did everything she could to get away from him. It was a futile effort. He had her trapped, like a butterfly pinned to a board, and there was no way he was letting her go.

He started to kiss her and Caroline's panic turned to hysteria.

Instinctively she lashed out with her nails, raking them across his face, but her resistance only seemed to excite him more for he lifted her up bodily and carried her back to the sofa.

Caroline was wearing a cotton dress that evening. It was a simple girlish construction that buttoned all the way down the front and Shel had it open before she knew it.

He was going to rape her, she knew it now. He would violate her and hurt her and enjoy every moment he made her suffer.

With an effort she closed her eyes. There was nothing she could do to stop Shel doing what he wanted. But she didn't have to join in with the game. She didn't have to watch him while he took his pleasure.

CHAPTER 30

The immigration queue at the airport was one seething mass of humanity. On either side of her, as far as Emerald could see, were tourists struggling with overstuffed baggage and screaming children who didn't seem to belong to anybody.

It's going to be hours, Emerald thought, before I even get near the customs hall. She cursed the authorities who refused to grant her an American passport. That one small document would have cut out all this waiting, all this frustration.

She had been complaining about this particular problem for years now, mostly in the old days to Larry, who brought her in and out of the country every time he had to visit a location, but even he couldn't help her. She was a Mauritian national. Unless she was married to an American she would have to go on being rounded up with all the other foreign cattle every time she entered the States.

She sighed. A passport was not a good enough reason to get married. At least that's what Larry had told her. Then, when he decided she deserved to be his wife, he was too ill to do anything about it.

Emerald felt depressed. If only Larry hadn't left things until the last moment, she thought, she wouldn't be standing here now, for she was only returning to Los Angeles in order to face his family across a courtroom.

Her mind went back three months, to when Steve Brady called her in the middle of the night. The minute she heard his voice on the line, she knew something was up. If he didn't need to speak to her urgently he would have waited for a civilized hour before picking up the phone.

But what Steve had to tell her couldn't wait that long. He had just finished talking to the lawyer representing Larry's children, and the news was bad. The settlement, which had been so close, had gone out of the window. The other side wanted to bring the whole business to court again. Emerald wondered what the hell was going on.

Larry's family had no real case against her. All they could hope to achieve by what they were doing was to waste everyone's time and money. She said as much to Steve. Which is when he sounded the first warning note.

'I've got a feeling the other side is hiding something,' he told her. 'We were so near to agreeing I even had the paper drawn up for signature, when out of the blue everything changed. One minute they were content with getting half of everything. The next, we were back to square one and it was all or nothing. It simply doesn't make sense.'

While her lawyer was talking, Emerald dredged her mind for reasons why she shouldn't get Larry's legacy but she came up with nothing. She had lived with him for years, not just as his mistress, but as his friend. When Larry was troubled he turned to her first and when Larry was seriously ill, it wasn't his children he wanted by his side. He wanted her.

They had no claim on him, except for the claim of shared blood. And if they couldn't make that stand up in court after all these years, what chance did they have now?

'Have you any idea why they're doing this?' Emerald asked Steve.

The lawyer sounded worried. 'They must have something new,' he told her. 'It's the only explanation.'

'When do we have to appear?' Emerald asked.

There was a silence while Steve consulted his notes. Then he said, 'They're talking about some time early in the New Year. So we've got time to prepare for it.'

He'd done the best he could, but without knowing what they were up against, it was whistling in the dark.

Now as she stood in line to enter the United States, Emerald still had no idea of what she would be facing. She realized she was more frightened now than she had been in her entire life.

The sight of Emerald being cross-questioned in Los Angeles woke Richard up. He had been half watching a breakfast show, and suddenly her terrified face was filling his screen.

He saw she wouldn't be drawn about the forthcoming case and he felt relieved. So she listened to me, he thought. She's keeping her mouth shut until she gets into court. Poor baby, she doesn't deserve this trouble. It's not as if she's committed any kind of crime. All she wanted was what was due to her and now she's coming in for more than she expected. He began to feel small. If I had married Emerald the minute we came to London none of this would have happened, he thought.

He wondered what had made him hesitate for so long, but he didn't seriously rack his brains. He knew deep down why Emerald wasn't his wife, and the knowledge made him uncomfortable.

She had been his father's mistress. It was as simple and as complicated as that. It was all a long time ago, and she had been very young at the time, but he couldn't quite forgive her for it.

Now as he watched her being hustled into a limousine outside the air terminal, he realized he had been behaving like a child. She was facing one of the worst times in her life and she was facing it alone because he couldn't live with her past. If I was any kind of man, he thought, I'd be holding her hand instead of getting ready to go into a board meeting with Rolf.

Richard went into the kitchen to make some coffee, but his heart wasn't in it.

The apartment felt empty without Emerald. He thought about the way his life had been since he had brought her to London, and he smiled at the memory. She had fitted in with him so perfectly, it was as if she had always been there. She seemed to know before he did when he wanted to eat, when he needed to rest, when he wanted to go out on the town.

With Caroline, their lives had been a negotiation. She had her own interests and her circle of friends. Richard had had his and they compromised, but it was never quite right, for their two lives never really came together. Richard wondered now if he had been selfish with Emerald. He had never concerned himself with what she did when he wasn't there and he had never seriously wondered what would become of her. He had just gone ahead and assumed they would drift on the way they were going.

She deserves better than that, he decided. He looked at his watch and tried to work out what time it was in Los Angeles. It was nine o'clock, which meant one o'clock in the morning her time.

He considered calling her and waking her up. Then he ditched the idea. You don't propose to a girl by transatlantic telephone. You put the question while standing right next to her, looking into her wide green eyes.

He walked through to the bedroom and picked up the phone. After he had checked the time of the hearing in LA, he got through to the airport and asked if the Weiss jet could be made ready for him. If he hurried he could be at the county court for the start of proceedings.

Standing on her patio at the Bel Air Hotel, Emerald could almost see Larry's old house. It was early in the morning and the gardens that surrounded the hotel were awash with tree ferns, palms and splashy bougainvillaea in full flower. She could almost be in the South of France or Spain, if she kept her eyes away from the estates that dotted the hills and canyons, for only in California could there be such a diversity of building styles.

Emerald always thought that the house she shared with Larry was grandiose until she visited others in the area. Then she knew the Spanish-style ranch house was rather old hat. The vanguards of style in this neck of the woods erected monstrosities that looked like mausoleums.

For a moment Emerald thought about her life in Bel Air, then she cancelled the memory. She had come here to fight for what was rightfully hers, not to get all sloppy about what might have been. With more resolution than she felt she turned her back on the vista and made her way into her suite.

Her breakfast had arrived on one of the big chromium trolleys five-star hotels used for room service. It was built to look like a table, but the crisp linen tablecloth concealed a hidden compartment underneath where the food was carried. As she stood there, the waiter was bringing out muesli, fresh berries and a pot of coffee. On any other morning she would have been ready for it. But now she could muster no appetite at all.

After the night she had spent, Emerald thought she'd never want to eat again. The worry that had been hovering on the edges of her consciousness had finally got through. The children had something on her. Something damaging. Something that could finish her off. Why else would they go to all the expense and trouble to bring this case to court again?

Emerald had hardly slept a wink and now, looking at herself in the morning light, she felt total despair. Her hair was lank, there were black circles under her eyes and she saw the beginnings of an acne spot at the side of her mouth. I look like a criminal before I've even started, she thought. Once the lawyers get to work, what chance do I stand?

She set about repairing the damage. Her years with Larry had taught her how to construct a façade and when she had finished with herself, her mood improved. If you didn't look too closely, her terror was almost undetectable.

Her complexion was matt and flawless, courtesy of Estée Lauder. Her hair gleamed like polished ebony, thanks to Phillip Kingsley and Calvin Klein did the rest. She was wearing one of his tailored suits in pale gaberdine with a narrow skirt and built-up shoulders. Its simplicity made Emerald look younger than she was. Anyone seeing her for the first time wouldn't have thought her capable of stealing anything, let alone a fortune belonging to a movie star.

She made her way through to the lobby where her attorney was waiting for her. The minute she saw his face she knew she had created the right effect.

'You look good enough to eat,' he told her, taking her hand and kissing her on the cheek.

Emerald threw herself down on one of the wide sofas. They had an hour before the car arrived. Just time to go over the programme.

'What time are we scheduled to appear?' she asked the attorney.

'Midday, as originally planned,' Steve replied. 'From what I can see of the other side's witness list, it all looks pretty straightforward.'

Emerald sat up and paid attention. 'Who are they calling?' she asked him.

Steve brought a typed sheet of paper, which he read out loud. The names were all familiar to Emerald. She had been listening to the same group of Larry's former employees give evidence against her for nearly a decade now. They all said the same things. Emerald was too autocratic. She didn't listen to their petty grievances. She didn't care whether they lived or died.

It was all pretty flimsy stuff and she was confident it would be brushed aside the way it had been all the other times. She'd more or less tuned out to what Steve was reading, when he came to a name that stopped her dead. Shel Johnson.

'Why on earth are they calling Shel to the witness stand?' she asked sharply.

The lawyer looked non-committal. 'I wouldn't get flustered about it,' he told her. 'Shel and Larry were close for a long time in a buddy-buddy sort of way. He'll probably testify his chum didn't need any of your tender loving care. He was doing pretty well on his own.' He paused for a moment. 'I don't think there's anything he can say I can't cope with.'

Emerald started to feel sick. Shel wasn't going to tell the world she was a lousy housekeeper, that was for sure. What the producer was going to talk about on the witness stand was infinitely more incriminating.

She flinched at the memory of him forcing her into his bed. I was a fool, she thought. I should never have let him get away with it.

Steve Brady looked at her sharply. 'Is something the matter?' he asked her. 'You look terrible.'

Emerald took a deep breath. In an hour or so she would be facing Shel Johnson across a courtroom. The least she could do was warn her lawyer what he might say.

'I was involved with Shel,' she said softly. 'It was all a long time ago, but I'm pretty sure he'll want to go into it.'

Steve got up from the easy chair where he was sitting and came across to Emerald.

'You're telling me you had an affair with Shel Johnson?'

She nodded dumbly. For a moment neither of them spoke, then Steve pulled himself together.

'So you had lovers before you met Larry,' he said. 'I don't think it's any big deal. He didn't expect you to be a virgin when he met you.'

Emerald started to get a bitter taste in her mouth. 'It wasn't like that,' she told Steve. 'The thing with Shel happened when Larry and I were already together. If the children want to use it against me now, they could tear me to bits.'

Steve sat down heavily.

'Are you going to walk out on me now?' Emerald asked. 'Or do you want to hear my side of the story?'

Steve toyed with the idea of telling her to go to hell. Then he remembered all the years he had spent on this case.

'You'd better tell me all there is to know,' he said. 'Then I'll try to figure out some way of dealing with it.'

Emerald reached over to Steve's pack of cigarettes lying on the table. She'd been trying to kick the habit, but now wasn't the time. She took her time extracting a filter tip and lighting it. Then she inhaled deeply, taking the smoke right down until it hurt. After that she was ready to talk about Shel Johnson.

She started right at the beginning when she and Larry were living together and Shel was the interloper. She was honest about her dislike of the producer, describing how she tried to get rid of him when Larry first became ill.

'But Shel changed,' she told Steve. 'Overnight he turned from being an enemy into a tower of strength. I was so upset about Larry I didn't even notice he was a phoney.'

As the lawyer heard her story, he started to feel angry. Nobody deserved to be manipulated the way Emerald had been. She'd been through hell and had needed a shoulder to cry on.

When Emerald had finished her story, Steve started to ask questions. He needed to establish that the producer had raped Emerald. Then blackmailed his way into the affair. After twenty minutes he was satisfied. 'It's not the strongest case in the world,' he said, 'but we do have some defence. All it needs now is for you to look convincing when you get up in front of the judge.'

CHAPTER 31

Emerald saw Richard the moment she got out of the car. He was standing on the steps leading up to the courtroom and her heart filled with dread.

If this had been any other time she would have run into his arms. But now all she wished was he had stayed at home.

He hurried over and as he came near she saw the joy on his face.

'I've been thinking about you all the time I was flying over the Atlantic,' he told her. 'I couldn't stay away and let you go into this on your own.'

Emerald should have been warm with him, but the prospect of what lay ahead silenced her.

'This is so unexpected,' she stammered. 'I had no idea . . .' Her voice trailed off.

His excitement at being there started to fade away.

'You are glad I came, aren't you?'

She gave him a quick hug and stepped back. 'Of course I am, darling. I'm just overwrought right now.'

She was spared the effort of making any more excuses, for the press corps had spotted them and all at once they were surrounded. Before anyone could ask her anything, Steve Brady had his arm round her and was pushing his way through the crowd.

Finally they reached the comparative peace of the courtroom and Steve led Emerald to the front. The court was in session five minutes later, and right away Emerald knew she was on a losing streak. The judge was around sixty, with a look of almost permanent disdain on his face. It was obvious he didn't have any truck with anyone who wasn't quite respectable. She had seen that look many years ago in Mauritius. It was worn by the colonial ladies and their golf-playing husbands and it said, plain and clear, if you're female, if you're brown, if you come from the servant classes, you don't deserve even our smallest consideration.

The room was filling up now and out of curiosity Emerald looked behind her to see who would be watching her downfall. Larry's entire family seemed to have turned out for this event. She saw aunts and uncles who had only existed for her in photograph albums. She realized then that the children were confident they were going to win. Then she caught sight of their attorney and she knew they had no doubt of it.

Phil Jenson had been taking Emerald apart in courtrooms for years now. She was used to looking at his scruffy suits and worn-out shoes. Today he didn't look scruffy. He was all kitted out in dark blue mohair as if he were going to a wedding. His hair was plastered down with grease and there was a look in his eyes that Emerald recognized as victory.

So Shel really is going to do me down, she thought. She braced herself for the opening addresses.

Phil's speech didn't differ greatly from anything he had said before. He told the court he was setting out to prove she was unfit to inherit Larry's estate. Then he ambled through the list of discontented maids and housekeepers who would testify to this. Shel's name wasn't mentioned at all, and Emerald began to wonder what he was playing at.

She went on wondering for the remainder of the day while the same sad, tired faces she had seen before went on claiming she was hell to work for. Just as she was beginning to lose interest, Phil changed tack. He had

Larry's old butler on the stand when he brought up the subject of Emerald's friendship with Larry's best friend.

'Did Shel Johnson spend much time at the house?' he asked the grey-haired servant.

The old man didn't hesitate, answering the question pat as if he had been rehearsing it all day.

'Mr Johnson only visited when he was coming to collect Miss Shah,' he told the court. 'He didn't seem to be interested in Mr Simpson at all.'

Emerald felt angry. Whatever happened between her and Shel, the producer still managed to spend time with Larry. But the butler would have none of it. Under cross-questioning he insisted that the friendship between the two men had tapered off dramatically when Shel started seeing Emerald.

The anxiety that had been building up all day made her tremble. It was obvious the witness was telling lies and she guessed he was telling them under instruction. Whatever the children's lawyer had in store for her had been a long time in the planning stages.

As the first day of the hearing dragged on, she started to feel dead inside. It was clear to her now she didn't stand a hope in hell against the children. She started to consider the idea of settling once and for all.

Steve Brady would have none of it and told her to forget the idea. Their major strength, their ace in the hole, was Emerald's testimony. Once she got up and told the truth about the affair, the other side wouldn't have a leg to stand on.

Afterwards Emerald wondered why she went along with her lawyer. If she had given in there and then, the world would never have heard what happened between her and Shel Johnson. But she did go along with Steve Brady and because of it she found herself sitting watching helplessly while Shel walked up to take the witness stand.

The years between hadn't changed him much. He still

258

had the lean, fit look of somebody who played tennis every day, and he still insisted on dressing in dark silk suits as if he was a member of the Mafia.

As he turned to the court, Emerald had a clear view of his face. The sheer malevolence she saw there brought back memories she thought she had forgotten. This man liked to hurt. He actually got his kicks from inflicting pain and Emerald knew then she should never have allowed this case to proceed.

Phil Jenson took his time drawing out the producer. He got him to go into detail about his relationship with Larry. Then when Shel was in full flow he shifted the focus on to Emerald.

'If you were close to Larry, what made you go after his girlfriend?' the attorney asked.

Shel considered for a moment. 'I didn't make the running with Emerald,' he said. 'In the beginning I hardly registered her at all. Then she started coming on to me.'

Emerald turned to Steve Brady. 'He's telling lies,' she whispered.

'When you give your side of the story, you can say so. But we have to sit tight till then,' Brady responded.

Emerald found it difficult. Shel's description of the way she behaved had nothing to do with reality. According to him she was a Hollywood housewife, bored and discontented because her lover was ill in bed.

'I'd go up to visit Larry, but Emerald never gave me the chance to be alone with him,' he told the court. 'It was as if she was looking for something to take her mind off of what was going on. Since I was a regular visitor, I guess I qualified.'

Steve Brady was on his feet. 'Move to strike,' he said. 'The witness can't know what was going on in my client's mind.'

The judge turned to the opposing counsel. 'Can the witness justify his assumptions?'

Phil Jenson affirmed that he could.

'Then I'll allow it.'

The feeling of dread which had overtaken Emerald intensified. The man's out to get me, she thought. Shel Johnson can say what he likes today and the court will be right behind him.

She shrank down on to the hard bench, trying to make herself as small and inconspicuous as possible. Then Shel started talking again, and she wished she could have simply disappeared.

The producer got on to the subject of their weekly dates. 'I used to buy Emerald dinner,' he said, 'because in the beginning I felt sorry for her. I was really convinced she cared for Larry and she couldn't stand to see him suffer. Then she told me how she really felt.'

Phil Jenson allowed a silence to elapse before he asked his next question. He had everyone's attention now and he milked the situation for as much drama as he could get away with.

'How did she really feel?' he asked Shel.

The producer started to smile. 'The lady wanted out,' he said. 'Things hadn't been going well with Larry for a long time. If he hadn't got sick she would probably have left him. Only now it looked like her boyfriend might die, she decided to stick around a while longer. They'd been together long enough for her to qualify for a share of whatever he had and she didn't want to blow it.'

'How did you know Miss Shah wanted out?' the attorney persisted.

Shel went on smiling and Emerald started to feel angry.

He's enjoying this, she thought. The cruel bastard's been saving this up for years now.

'I know Emerald wanted out,' the producer told the court, 'because she told me so. She was looking for someone to take Larry's place and she asked me if I wanted the job.'

Everyone in the courtroom started to talk at once. Representatives of half a dozen newspapers started to make for the exits. Steve Brady jumped to his feet demanding a recess. But the judge wasn't interested in postponing things. He called the court to order and instructed the prosecuting counsel to continue examining the witness.

Now Shel knew no one was going to silence him, he let rip. Every detail of the affair he had conducted thirteen years previously was brought out and held up to the light. In essence the story the producer was telling was true. Shel and Emerald did go to bed together while Larry lay dying in his Spanish-style mansion. But it was the way the whole thing was presented that set the seal on Emerald's fate.

As she sat and listened with growing disbelief to Shel's account of things, Emerald hardly recognized herself. The woman he was talking about was a greedy calculating bitch who was interested in sex for its own sake. According to him it was Emerald who instigated the dressing-up rituals, the sado-masochistic sex and all the other sordid deviations.

If the producer had been discussing anyone else but her, she might have been amused. There was something schoolboyish, almost bragging about the tale. The man who stood in the witness box reminded her of the crazies she encountered in Times Square. He had a story to communicate and he didn't mind how garbled it sounded or how preposterous it was – just so long as he got it out of his system.

Surely nobody here can be taking this seriously, she thought.

She turned round in her seat to get a view of what was going on. The moment she saw the faces of everyone present, she wished she'd kept her back to them. If she had been at a public execution, she imagined she would have encountered the same expressions. The people sitting here were hungry for sensation. They didn't care if what they heard was biased, or blatantly untrue. They didn't even care if it was beyond the bounds of belief. All that mattered was they were witness to the spectacle of a former member of the community being completely obliterated.

I don't stand a chance, she thought. I've been tried and condemned before the jury's gone out. She wondered if her testimony would do anything towards changing their minds. While she thought about what she was going to say in her own defence, her eyes searched the crowd for a glimpse of Richard. She located him right at the back of the courtroom. He seemed to be conducting a close conversation with somebody sitting on his left side.

She leaned forward trying to make out who her lover was talking to so earnestly. Then she recognized her. Caroline Fellows, her red hair in a burnished upsweep, was giving her undivided attention to everything Richard had to say. There was a supercilious grin on her face as she replied to some observation of his.

For a moment Emerald felt bewildered. What on earth was Caroline doing here?

Perhaps she's covering the case for her paper, she thought. Then she realized she couldn't be; Caroline wrote a financial column. But Caroline was interested in this case. When they had lunch she had done her best to draw Emerald out about it. And a suspicion started to form.

Soon after Caroline had quizzed her about her financial troubles, she'd come up with Shel's name. At the time Emerald hadn't connected the two. Now, with Shel testifying against her, and Caroline sitting gloating at the back of the courtroom, the whole thing started to make some kind of sense.

It was a wild notion, but what if the journalist had gone to Shel and told him she had nearly solved her problems with Larry's family? What if she had managed to talk him into ruining things for her?

I'm jumping to conclusions, Emerald told herself. No

one would do that to anyone. Not unless they really hated them.

She looked at Caroline making up to the man she loved. Smiling and whispering in his ear as if she were at a cocktail party, and the truth of the situation hit her.

Caroline did hate her. She always had and now there was real trouble in her life, the journalist was there to take every advantage of it.

She started to feel irrationally angry. Her whole world was falling apart and all her enemies were cheering. Her enemies and her friends. For Richard was sitting on the sidelines colluding with all the people who wished her ill.

Emerald focused her attention on Shel again, wondering if it could get any worse.

He was describing one of their intimate encounters and she started to feel sick. If he were allowed to go on this way she would end up as public enemy number one. I have to stop him, Emerald thought. I have to bring this whole sordid business to an end, even if I have to lose everything in the process.

For the first time since the affair blew up, Emerald realized she was on her own. Nobody was going to help her now. Her lawyer was only interested in preserving his reputation.

And Richard? Richard looked as if he were wondering if he should go back to his old girlfriend. Emerald didn't blame him. He was a conventional man, a businessman who set a great deal of store by appearances. She looked at her watch. The court would be breaking any minute now. If she had anything to do with it she wouldn't be coming back here tomorrow.

Emerald made the children an offer they couldn't refuse. She was willing to waive all claims on the house in Bel Air, the apartment in New York and the property in Aspen. They could have the copyright to all Larry's films and the

263

bulk of the cash on deposit in the bank. All she wanted in exchange for walking away was a quarter of a million dollars and settlement of her legal bill.

When Steve Brady looked over her proposal he was staggered.

'You've handed them everything on a plate,' he protested. 'Aren't you going to fight just a little bit? If I pushed I'm sure I could get you more money and maybe the place in New York.'

Emerald was adamant. 'If you push,' she told him, 'we risk landing up in court again, and I want to avoid that at all costs. I've had enough of my private life being turned into a sideshow. What I want right now is an end to this.'

Steve knew Emerald well enough not to argue. Instead he called a meeting with Phil Jenson who nailed the deal down in record time.

By the time the press caught on to the fact that it was all over, Emerald was back in the Bel Air packing her bags.

She had ducked out of the courtroom, avoiding Richard, her attorney and the whole circus that had surrounded the case from the beginning. There was an overwhelming need in her to separate herself now. She needed time alone. Time to think. Time to plan the rest of her life. For she knew it couldn't go on the way it had.

There was no future with Richard now. Or with any man. She had relied too much on being rescued by a father figure. And what good had it done her? Larry had looked after her for a while, but he hadn't protected her. When the chips were down, he knew the only way to ensure her survival was to marry her, and he hadn't done it. He'd relied on some half-baked will to look after her future, a will full of holes, and now the children had shot it down.

She thought about Richard. He had loved her, but in the end how much was that worth? When she needed him, really needed him, he was nowhere to be found. Where were you, she thought, when I got on the plane to face this trial? What were you doing when I was worrying myself sick?

Memories of the men who had loved her and failed her came crowding in, haunting her and making her feel wretched.

Then out of nowhere Emerald thought about Jeremy. He was the one man she hadn't totally trusted and because of it, she had struck out in her own direction. She thought about the dressmaking business she had all those years ago. It was a good business, a growing business, and its success had nothing to do with her sponsor.

I made it work, Emerald remembered, because I put in all the hours that God gave. I plotted and I hustled and I put work out and if I'd stayed on the island instead of running off with Larry I might just have built something I could have been proud of.

As she thought of the one success that she had created on her own, she began to feel stronger. I made it once, she thought, even though I had nothing to my name. Now I've got clothes and jewellery and a quarter of a million dollars in the bank. Who knows what would happen if I attempted the same thing again?

The idea started to grow on her. She could run to a classy establishment now, in the centre of Curepipe. And her years in the company of rich men had given her a gloss, a confidence that would attract the right kind of clients.

I wouldn't have to be a cheap dressmaker now, Emerald thought. I could set up as a couturier like Miss Blanche and make a decent living right from the start.

She was so excited by her new idea, that it was a good five minutes before she realized there was someone at her door. As she rushed to answer it, she wondered whether her attorney had finally caught up with her. But it wasn't Steve Brady outside. It was Richard.

'What happened?' he demanded. 'One minute you were

in conference with Steve. The next, you'd vanished off the face of the earth.'

Emerald looked apologetic and showed him in. 'I decided to call it quits,' she said. 'I couldn't stand to hear any more lies from Shel, so I handed over nearly everything to the children.' She paused. 'When it was done, all I wanted was out. I'm sorry I didn't stay around, but you seemed to have your hands full.'

He had the grace to look embarrassed. 'You're talking about Caroline,' he said. 'I wasn't with her, you know. I didn't even expect to see her there.'

Emerald could have pursued the subject but she couldn't see the point. She had wasted enough emotion on Caroline, and enough on Richard as well. There were other things to think about now.

She walked across to the bar and poured Richard a glass of the wine she was drinking.

Then she said, 'I suppose Shel's little performance must have made you think.'

Richard took the drink out of her hand and swallowed some of it.

'It made me think enough to get hold of Steve Brady afterwards and find out what the hell was going on.' He frowned. 'You were really stitched up in there, weren't you?'

Emerald nodded and said nothing, but Richard went on.

'I still don't understand why you didn't let the court hear your side of the story? You still might have lost, but at least by standing up and being counted, you would have come out of this with some kind of reputation.'

Emerald felt weary. Why was it, she wondered, she always managed to love men who didn't understand her.

For reasons she didn't quite know she started to explain herself to him.

'All my life,' she said, 'I've worried about what people thought of me. It was as if I only had value by looking good. Now I know it's not true.' She hesitated for a moment, wondering whether to tell him everything. 'I've spent my whole life', she told him, 'acting out a part that some man has written for me. With your father I was the compliant mistress, with Larry I was the Indian waif he'd rescued from a life of poverty. Even with you I was busy pretending to be someone I wasn't.'

Richard looked as if she'd just smacked him across the face and for a moment she regretted what she had said, but it was too late to go back now.

'Didn't you ever wonder', she asked him, 'what I did with my life when you weren't there? You used to go out every day to your office, and it never once occurred to you that I might be bored sitting around in a town where I didn't know anyone. At least when I was keeping house for Larry he used to involve me with what he did. We'd talk about his work, and when he was filming he always took me with him.'

Richard took a deep pull on his drink, then he rounded on her.

'I could hardly take you with me to the office,' he said. 'Anyway you never gave me an inkling of what was going on. I thought you were happy with the life we had. I thought you loved me, for Chrissake.'

'I do love you,' Emerald told him, 'I just can't dedicate my whole life to it any more.'

Richard got up and walked over to the window. 'So what are you going to do?' he asked. 'Go out and find another actor to play nursemaid to?'

Emerald felt the beginnings of despair. Richard hadn't been listening to a word she was saying.

'I'm not looking for another man,' she said patiently. 'I no longer want to be a nursemaid, or a mistress or even somebody's wife. What I need right now is to go out and find something I can do on my own. Something I can be good at, so that people can admire me for it.'

She turned to him now, concentrating on what she was

267

saying, willing him to understand how desperately important it was to her.

'When people first meet you,' she said, 'they're not all that concerned with your reputation, are they? They don't care about the girls you've gone to bed with. All they mind about is your ability to succeed at what you do. They measure you by your achievements. Well, I want to be valued by the same system that judges you.'

Richard came back to where she was sitting, reaching out for her hands.

'It's a lovely sentiment,' he said. 'The feminist lobby would be proud of you. But you've forgotten one thing. You have to have something to contribute to the world. Some skill that people will seek you out for.'

Emerald set her jaw. 'I have something,' she told him.

Richard started to smile and she was reminded of an indulgent parent looking at his favourite child.

'What on earth do you do that I don't know about?' he demanded.

The words came out before she could stop them. 'I make dresses,' she told him. 'Give me a copy of *Vogue* and I can run up anything you see on the pages.'

Richard didn't seem impressed. 'I don't see you as a seamstress,' he told her.

Emerald was exasperated. 'What do you see me as?'

He was holding both her hands in his now and she felt the pressure increase.

'I see you as my wife,' Richard told her. 'The talent that you have, the thing that makes you valuable to me, is your capacity to make me happy.'

There was such love in his eyes, such naked need, that Emerald thought her heart would break. If you'd only told me this twenty-four hours ago, she thought, it might have been different. Now it's too late.

She looked away from him. 'I can't do it, Richard,' she said. 'I just told you, it's not what I want any more.'

He wouldn't listen to her. He had just flown across an ocean to ask her to be his wife, and he wasn't prepared to be rejected.

'You're not making any sense,' he told her, 'but then I don't expect you to. After what you've been through you're allowed to be irrational.'

She let him get away with it because it was easier than fighting.

Emerald found it strangely liberating to know she had so much less than before. She had been back in London for three weeks and she still couldn't believe how free she felt. It was as if a suffocating load had been taken away from her and she wondered why she had spent so much of her energy chasing after Larry's fortune.

If he had left me nothing, she thought, I might have gone out and found a job instead of living in limbo for years. Too late she realized that Larry's gifts hadn't been a gift at all. It had been a responsibility, and it had changed her. Now she expected things. She was used to internationally renowned restaurants, and chauffeur-driven cars, and jewellery that needed to be locked in the safe. She was used to being kept.

She started to evaluate herself the way a man would. Her figure was pin thin and if she didn't admit to her age, she could still get away with saying she was twenty-eight. She laughed at herself, remembering a time when she used to pretend she was older than her years in order to be taken seriously by Larry's friends.

Now she realized she had been fooling herself. Nobody looked up to women who looked like her. She was altogether too glossy-looking. Everything about her from her manicure to her coiffure spoke of money and leisure. I'm the kind of woman, she reflected, that keeps whole industries in business. I need to get out of this routine before it takes me over completely.

Since she had been back in London, nothing had changed. Richard still treated her like a cross between a housekeeper and a harlot and she knew that even when he married her it would be the same. But he wasn't going to marry her. Because she wasn't going to be there much longer.

The idea that had come to her in the Bel Air had started to take root. She had been in contact with the Mauritius Export Development Authority and she was convinced she could succeed over there. The new Indian government supported people like her – Mauritian nationals who wanted to set up in business on their own.

Unknown to Richard she sent away for details of houses for rent and found herself a bank in Port Louis. When she was ready, she transferred all the money she had to Mauritius.

She was able to move now, to face the future she had created for herself. All that remained was to say goodbye to Richard. But Emerald couldn't do it, because she loved him. He was wrong for her, and the life he had planned for them no longer made any sense. But she still couldn't say goodbye.

In the end she decided to write him a letter. It was the coward's way out, but at least this way, she wouldn't have to look into his eyes.

CHAPTER 32

Caroline waited two months before making her move. When she did, it didn't look as if she was making a move at all, for she knew that she could ask any man she wanted to lunch and they wouldn't be the least bit suspicious. How could they when a large part of her job was talking business in fashionable restaurants?

She invited Richard to Odins on the pretext that she had some insider gossip. She was always calling him with share tips, so the invitation seemed innocent enough.

The way Caroline looked was another matter altogether. On the morning of their lunch she went to Daniel Galvin and had her hair touched up. Then she went down the road to The Face Place where she invested in a full professional make-up. By the time she arrived at the restaurant off Marylebone High Street, she knew she was pretty enough to win a beauty contest. Or an old boyfriend.

As she went in, she saw that Richard had arrived ahead of her and she was pleased the restaurant had given her the table she had asked for. It was a discreet rendezvous right at the back of the restaurant. Nobody, unless they were very determined, could table-hop her there.

Richard didn't look up as she approached. He seemed to be engrossed in some paperwork he had brought with him and Caroline remembered the gossip about him. Ever since Emerald's sudden defection overseas, Richard had thrown himself into his work. He didn't reply to invitations, and when one of her chums had invited him to dinner (on Caroline's express instructions) he had turned her down flat.

She arranged her features in a purposely bland expression. If Richard had a broken heart, there was no way she wanted to look like a threat.

He was certainly pleased to see her, more than pleased, and after a few minutes Caroline realized why. Richard hadn't had anyone to talk to. The man had suffered the biggest rejection of his life and there was no close friend to share his pain.

A plan started to grow in her mind. She wouldn't try to seduce him, as she originally thought. It was too soon for that kind of thing. Instead she would be a friend to him. She would offer her shoulder to cry on and would listen patiently while he agonized over where he went wrong. And she would bide her time. He would get over Emerald eventually and Caroline would be there waiting.

She organized a bottle of red Bordeaux and told the waiter they would be ready to order lunch when they'd had a drink. Then she did her best to look sympathetic.

'I was very sorry to hear what happened with Emerald,' she told him. 'It must have been devastating.'

Richard hesitated before answering. It clearly hurt even to talk about the affair and Caroline felt a stab of pure jealousy. She pulled herself together. If Richard was going to believe in her act, she couldn't let any of her real feelings intrude.

She stretched a hand out cautiously and ran it lightly across his cheek. It was a motherly, comforting gesture and she could see him relax slightly.

'You don't have to tell me about any of it if it's difficult for you,' she said. 'I've been through it myself and I know how tough it is to let any of it out.'

Her words had the desired effect, for Richard began to unburden himself. In the next hour or so, Caroline learnt that marriage, security and an equal share in his considerable fortune didn't interest Emerald at all. What she wanted was to prove herself on her own.

In the beginning she couldn't quite believe what she was hearing. Emerald, who was used to couture clothes and real jewellery, harboured this insane desire to work as a dressmaker.

'Did she mean it?' Caroline asked. 'Or is it one of those things she has to go through and get out of her system?'

Richard looked morose. 'If I thought it was a whim, I wouldn't be going through all this.' He sighed. 'No, Emerald's deadly serious. She wants to stand up and account for herself. She wants to be valued for what she can achieve, and nobody, not even me, could persuade her otherwise.'

Caroline started to feel more cheerful, though she didn't let it show. It would take years for Emerald to carve out a career for herself. Years buried alive on some Third World island.

Good, she thought. While Emerald's beavering away proving her independence, I'll be here making myself charming for Richard.

She glanced across at him and saw most of his lunch was untouched. He had no appetite. That was a bad sign. He wasn't going to get over this affair as quickly as she'd hoped.

She started to feel restless. She'd been sitting listening to Richard for too long. She had watched every word, every gesture he made, and it had tired her. She needed a few minutes away from this man to breathe deep and let her emotions go.

'Would you excuse me for a second?' she asked. 'I need to go to the loo.'

Richard watched her as she headed down the stairs. She was an elegant creature, rangy and tall and curvaceous. If he had been any other man he would have been happy to settle for her. But he wasn't and his heart was already spoken for.

He thought back to the day he discovered Emerald had left him for good.

He had been working longer than usual that day. A major restaurant chain Rolf had been after had pulled out at the last moment and Richard had been left with the task of getting together a list of alternatives. He had been on the telephone to New York for the best part of two hours when he happened to glance at his watch. It was 7.30 in the evening. Emerald would be waiting on dinner, wondering where on earth he had got to. He always called if he was going to be late.

He buzzed his secretary and told her to put in a call to his home. Then he waited for Emerald to come on the line. She didn't materialize. After ten minutes, he buzzed through to his secretary again.

'Did you try the apartment?' he had asked. 'I don't seem to have spoken to Emerald yet.'

The girl's voice was tart. 'That's because she isn't there. I've been trying the number but there isn't any reply.'

Richard should have known then that something was wrong. Emerald never went anywhere when she knew he was going to turn up any moment. Caroline might have. But not Emerald. It just wasn't the sort of thing she did.

He looked at his watch again and calculated how much longer he was going to be. If he got a move on, he could have Rolf's list completed by eight.

He managed to get to the apartment by 8.30. As soon as he was through the door he knew something was wrong. When Emerald was there she exerted a kind of presence. He didn't have to see her to know she was there. That night he knew she was missing.

For a reason Richard didn't understand, he was seized with a kind of panic. He started walking from room to room calling her name, but there was no answer. There was no trace of her in the kitchen or the bedroom, or even the bathroom where she always left a lipstick or a bottle of perfume she had just been using. It was the bathroom that alerted him. He started opening cupboards and found her bottles and jars had gone. It was then he knew she had left him, for there was nothing of hers there.

He found her note propped up on the bureau in the drawing-room. Emerald had written at length about her reasons for going and her plans to start a new life. It was the painstaking elaborateness of her plans that hurt Richard most. She must have been organizing this move for weeks now and all the time she hadn't said a word.

If only she told me what she really wanted, he fumed. It was at that moment he realized she had told him – and he hadn't taken any notice.

He looked up to find that Caroline had come back to the table.

The sight of her comforted him. She wasn't Emerald. But she was there and she was on his side. It was better than nothing.

Lunch at Odins broke the ice. From that moment on they resumed a friendship of sorts. They were no longer lovers, but they were buddies.

If Richard was at a loose end over the weekend he would call Caroline and see if she was free to take in a movie. If he needed a spare female to take to a dinner party or the races, then the first person he considered was Caroline. He gravitated towards her because she understood him and because she made no demands on him.

Sometimes he wondered why she was prepared to go along with this new relationship they had. It was not as if there was anything in it for her. Then he would feel guilty at judging her so harshly. Caroline is concerned for me, he would console himself. She worries about my state of mind and how I'm coping now that Emerald's gone.

It was a naïve supposition but Caroline didn't give

Richard any cause to doubt it. Whenever they spent time alone together, the first thing she did was draw him out about his lost love. It was almost as if she had never been his girlfriend at all. For what ex-lover could bear to talk about her replacement in such detail?

Because Caroline was being so accommodating, Richard asked her to come down to the country with him for the weekend. Rolf had a considerable spread in Northamptonshire and every so often Richard was asked to put in an appearance. The old Pole liked to use the house to entertain important business contacts and he found it useful to have a little extra help.

Richard didn't mind being called on. Over the years he had developed a fondness for Rolf that went beyond any business relationship. Somehow, Richard identified with him.

They were both of them immigrants. They both had to try harder than the next man, and often when they were wrestling with a problem they discovered their minds ran on similar tracks.

The only area Richard and Rolf differed on was women. Where Rolf bounced from affair to affair with little real emotion, Richard was more serious. When he took someone to bed he liked to feel if not love, then at least commitment. So when Rolf put Richard and Caroline together in a big double suite right at the front of the house, he realized his partner had misread the situation.

As soon as he decently could, he sought out Rolf and explained what was going on.

'Caroline and I aren't sleeping together any more,' he said somewhat lamely.

Rolf roared with laughter. 'Are you mad?' he demanded. 'She's a gorgeous piece of goods. Why on earth are you wasting her?'

It crossed Richard's mind to tell him the full story, but he knew the old man would never understand. To him a woman was a woman. The notion she could be a platonic friend would never cross his mind.

In the end he simply asked for separate rooms and let Rolf think what he liked. Only it didn't work.

His partner had invited half a dozen people to stay for the weekend and the house was full. Either he and Caroline stayed in the same bedroom, or they went back to London.

Richard thought about going back, and said so to Caroline. To his surprise she roared with laughter at the suggestion.

'You can't be serious,' she said. 'You and I were together for over a year. We're used to sleeping in the same bed.'

The idea of lying close to Caroline made Richard feel strangely embarrassed. He hadn't quite acknowledged it yet, but she was starting to have an effect on him.

'Rather a lot has happened since we were together,' he said stiffly. 'Besides it wouldn't be fair on you.'

'Why ever not?' she asked. 'I take it you're not going to insist on conjugal rights.'

It was the way she said it, half mocking, half challenging, that made up his mind.

She's playing with me, he thought. She wants me, but she's going to give me a run for my money. The notion of Caroline treating him like some gauche little boy irritated him beyond measure. She was my mistress, he thought. She lived with me for Chrissake. I don't have to put up with this.

He looked over to where she was standing by her open suitcase, and for the first time in months he noticed she had put on a little weight. Her hips in the tight blue jeans looked somehow fuller, and her breasts were huge.

I'm going to make love with her tonight, he decided. Rolf was right. She's too gorgeous to go to waste.

Before dinner Rolf served drinks in the library. As always there was an interesting mixture of locals and guests from further afield.

It was the strangers that interested Richard.

There were three couples whom Richard might have guessed were in property. The men favoured dark suits and enormous cigars while their wives were overburdened with makeup and jewellery.

One of the women, a rather aggressive little blonde in tight black leather trousers, had managed to get Richard in a corner and was busy telling him how difficult she was finding it to park her yacht in the harbour at Monte Carlo. Richard recalled other similar conversations he had had at the last three drinks parties he had been to, and without meaning to, he stifled a yawn. His companion looked at him sharply.

'I'm boring you,' she said.

Richard was spared having to reply, for Rolf, accompanied by his current girlfriend, an exotic Hungarian, and Caroline, had decided to make an entrance. He had become exceedingly fat in the last few years, not that his girth seemed to interfere with his vitality, for he still lit up the room.

By the time dinner was announced, Rolf had managed to relax the entire group and Richard started to feel more optimistic about the evening.

He found himself seated between the blonde he had met in the library and one of the local hunting fraternity. On the other side of the table Caroline was holding court with two of the property men. From where he was, she seemed to be having a good time. She had taken trouble with herself that night and he wondered how much the gold lamé Valentino she was wearing had set her back. Richard felt slightly intrigued that she should be wearing a dress like that. It was too obvious for her, too showy altogether. He smiled to himself. It would be fun getting her out of it.

He looked over at Rolf. Some of his biggest deals were done over elaborate dinner parties in the country and it didn't take Richard too long to figure out who Rolf was stalking that evening. One of the property men was looking for a buyer for a fast-food chain he owned. The group specialized in American hamburgers and Rolf was itching to get his hands on something like that.

Not that the old Pole was obvious about it. Richard noticed with a certain fascination that Rolf was playing it cool that night. He didn't exactly ignore the man he had in his sights but he didn't make much of an effort with him either. After dinner everyone filed into the conservatory where coffee and liqueurs were being served.

Still Rolf didn't make his move. Instead he raised an eyebrow imperceptibly in Richard's direction. He took the cue. The two men had been working together long enough to know what the other was thinking. Within minutes the younger man was talking earnestly to the restaurant owner. And by midnight some kind of a deal was beginning to take shape.

Richard looked at his watch. If his timing was right, Rolf should be appearing at his elbow any minute now ready to take over. He was within five minutes of being on target. As his partner moved in for the kill, Richard made his excuses and left. It was time he found Caroline and headed in the direction of his room.

It wasn't as simple as he thought. In the old days, when he was at a party with the journalist, all he had to do was touch her arm and she extricated herself from whoever she was talking to. Tonight she wasn't so willing to fall in with his wishes.

She had got herself involved in a backgammon game and she seemed to be winning. When Richard told her he was tired, she turned to him and pulled a face.

'Why don't you turn in ahead of me,' she said. 'This is too exciting to leave.'

Her answer made him impatient. He knew he had no rights to her, but the fact they were sharing a bedroom had been on his mind all evening. For the first time for months he stopped feeling guilty about Emerald. He was a man after all. He couldn't go on mourning her for the rest of his life.

When he left the room, Caroline was still intent on her game. It took her two hours to make it up to their room. Richard knew exactly how long it was, for even though the room was in darkness, he was wide awake. If Caroline suspected this, she didn't let it show. She took great trouble to make as little noise as possible. She even switched on the light in the bathroom and kept the door shut so as not to disturb him.

Richard realized she was beginning to drive him wild. In the next room, Caroline was sliding out of her provocative lamé dress. He started to imagine what she would be wearing underneath it. In his mind he could see her going through the motions of a strip tease and he began to understand what a nervous bridegroom would go through on his wedding night.

At last she seemed to be finished in the bathroom. He raised his head to catch a glimpse of her as she came across the room, but once more she disappointed him. She had turned off all the lights now and was feeling her way towards the bed uncertainly.

He lay very still as she slid in beside him. Then he reached for her. It was at that moment he realized she knew he had been awake all along, for Caroline hadn't bothered to put on a nightdress.

He heard the laughter in her throat as he started to touch her breasts.

'I thought this was strictly platonic,' she protested.

Richard didn't reply. Instead he slid his hand down over the soft curve of her belly until it was resting on her pubis. Then, very gently, he inserted his finger between her legs.

She was ready for him, and her wetness hastened his desire. As he lay waiting for her, he had planned a careful seduction. There would be sweet talk, caresses and a long, soft yielding. Now all that was put to one side. Richard wanted to be inside this woman, to dominate her, and there was no time for niceties.

He reached up and turned on the bedside lamp. Then he threw back the bedclothes so he could see her body. Finally, he did what he had been longing for from the moment he had seen her in her business suit in Odins.

If Richard's encounter with Caroline had happened in London there might have been some hope for him. Any man is allowed a moment of weakness, and the following morning they could have parted friends and put the whole incident down to experience.

But Richard and Caroline were not going their separate ways. The next day they were committed to sharing a bed for at least another night. And that was Richard's undoing.

It had been surprisingly erotic making love to Caroline again. She knew what turned him on and she used her knowledge. Part of Richard knew she was putting on a calculated display and that was the sane part that recognized the difference between love and titillation. But as the weekend progressed, Richard started to lose touch with his sanity.

He hadn't been near a woman since Emerald had left and Caroline seemed to know this too. She traded on his hunger. Halfway through a game of tennis, when she was sure nobody else was looking, she let him discover she wasn't wearing anything under her short pleated skirt. All Richard got was just a glimpse, a hint of her, but it was enough to set his blood racing.

After the game, on the walk back through the gardens, he asked her about it, and she answered his question by taking his hand and putting it between her thighs.

There was something deliciously dangerous about the situation. If anyone had been standing by the house, they could have seen exactly what was going on between them. But Richard's fingers were already probing her entrance and he was incapable of stopping.

In an attempt to preserve some kind of decency, he pushed Caroline down behind a heavy bank of flowering shrubs. There he made love to her with more violence than he thought he was capable of.

She kept up the pressure all weekend. Over the lunch table she would look at him a certain way and within five minutes they were back in the room. There seemed to be no end to Caroline's inventiveness. She seduced him out on the lake in the bottom of a rowing boat. She ravished him in a telephone box in the local village. She made love to him standing up behind the stables at the back of the house. By the time Sunday evening came, he was intoxicated with her.

Even Rolf noticed the change in him. The four of them – Rolf, Rolf's mistress, Magda, Caroline and Richard – were sitting having an early evening drink. The weekend guests had gone and they were all finally able to relax.

'It's good to see you enjoying life again,' Rolf observed. 'You've been on your own for too long.'

Richard looked embarrassed. 'Caroline and I are old friends,' he said. 'We understand each other.'

He noticed Magda looking at him, and the expression on her face was unmistakable.

'I think Caroline is the one who understands,' she said cryptically.

'Just what are you getting at?' Richard hadn't meant to raise his voice, but the woman was being intrusive. Before he could say anything more, Caroline put a possessive hand on his arm.

'Darling,' she purred, 'Magda didn't mean any harm. What she was trying to say was I was chasing you. And she's right, I am. I don't mind admitting it.'

Richard began to feel powerless. He had somehow managed to get himself into a situation from which there was no escape. He hadn't wanted a reunion with Caroline. The last thing he needed was a walk-out with his ex-girlfriend yet that was precisely what he was having. He tried to laugh it off.

'It's been a lovely weekend,' he said, 'but I wouldn't make a big deal about it.'

Rolf smacked his heavy crystal glass down on the table in front of him. 'Why not?' he demanded. 'You and Caroline go back a long way. She suits you. You suit each other.'

Richard was about to say something about Emerald. He felt impelled to speak up for, to defend, her but Rolf beat him to it.

'The last girl,' he said. 'The coloured one. She was a pretty thing, but you couldn't trust her. When I heard what she did to Larry Simpson I wasn't surprised at all.'

Richard's voice was dangerously quiet. 'What are you trying to say?' he asked.

'That you're not the first member of the family she chose to bestow her favours on,' Rolf said flatly.

There was a short, horrified silence. Magda looked confused, Caroline looked intrigued and Richard's expression was pure murder.

His partner was the only one he'd told about Emerald's past and now he wished he hadn't.

He got to his feet abruptly, pulling Caroline after him. 'It's time we were on our way,' he said. 'I've heard quite enough nonsense for one weekend.'

Rolf hurried after him as he strode across the high-vaulted hall to the main door.

'I'm a silly old man,' he said, 'and I went too far. I didn't mean to bring up that business about Emerald.'

Richard regarded his partner, and wondered what to say. It was tempting to call him a fool, but what was the point? If he and Rolf quarrelled now, they could easily end up going their separate ways, and that wasn't going to help anyone, least of all Emerald who was long gone.

He turned to Rolf. 'Why don't we forget the whole conversation?' he said. 'Pretend it never happened.'

He turned and picked up their bags, which were waiting for them in the entrance.

'I'll see you in the office tomorrow,' he said. 'We need to talk some more about the hamburger chain.'

They were halfway to London when Caroline asked about Emerald. She was dying to know which one of his relatives the girl had slept with. But Richard wasn't going to give her the satisfaction of finding out.

'As of this moment,' he told her, 'my former girlfriend's secrets are none of your business.'

'That's not fair,' Caroline protested. 'We might be sleeping together, but we're still friends, aren't we?'

Richard sighed. 'You can't have it all ways, Caroline. You'd better choose what you're going to be – friend or lover.'

It was a calculated risk. After the weekend they had just spent together, there was no way Richard was going to settle for Caroline being his best pal. But he couldn't afford to let her know that. He held his breath and waited for her answer. It wasn't long in coming.

'Do you think you'd like to stay over with me tonight?' she asked. 'It's been a long time since we made love in my bed.'

It wasn't long before they were back in the old routine. Richard's apartment was a whole lot nicer than Caroline's and she re-established herself there.

As the weeks went by, he started to find her things in his closets. There would be a change of underwear, a cocktail dress she didn't have time to go home and get into, a city suit she needed for the office the next day.

It crossed his mind she was moving in on him again, but

he didn't discourage her. They were seeing each other most nights now, and almost every weekend. It was simply too inconvenient to shuttle to and fro between two apartments.

He was on the point of suggesting she made things more permanent, when the reporter in her came to the surface. When Rolf had started uncovering Emerald's secrets, it had sparked her curiosity. Caroline simply had to know what else remained to be uncovered. She started pestering Richard. When he least expected it, she would turn the conversation round to the weekend they spent in the country. 'What was Rolf talking about when he said Emerald couldn't be trusted?' she would ask.

She would look all innocent when she said it, but Richard wasn't fooled. He knew exactly how good she was at ferreting out the truth.

He remembered how she'd conned him into revealing far too much about his childhood in Mauritius and the memory brought a bad taste to his mouth.

He wondered why Caroline was so curious about Emerald. The scandal had broken as far as she was concerned. So why did Caroline continue to pursue her? In the end he decided to have it out with her. They were having dinner in the apartment when he brought the subject into the open.

'What is this fascination you have with my ex-girlfriend?' he asked her. 'You seem obsessed with her. You're not planning to run some kind of story on her, are you?'

Caroline got up from the table, scrunching up her napkin. 'Of course I'm not running a story,' she said crossly. 'The woman's life isn't the stuff financial pages are made of.' She sat down again. 'My interest in Emerald', she continued, 'is strictly personal. You can't blame me for that, can you?'

Richard started to feel impatient. 'I'm not blaming you,' he said. 'I'm worried about you. There's really no need to rake over her past the way you do. She's out of our lives now. She's halfway across the world, for heaven's sake. Can't you just forget she ever existed?'

The redhead pulled a face. 'You haven't forgotten she exists. Every now and then you go off into a kind of trance and I know you're thinking about her.'

What she said was true. Try as he might, Richard couldn't seem to get Emerald out of his mind.

'I just need a bit of time,' he said gruffly. 'Everything passes in the end.' He paused. 'Look,' he told her, 'why don't we cool things down for a while? I don't mean we should stop seeing each other, but we seem to be in too much of a hurry to get back to the way things were.'

Caroline felt a stab of panic. Just when she thought she had Richard in the palm of her hand he was withdrawing from her. And all because of her curiosity.

She did her best to remain calm. 'If you want space,' she said, 'you're welcome to it. But I wouldn't be too casual. I'm not exactly a wallflower you know.'

Richard ignored the threat. Caroline was backing off the way he meant her to, and he felt considerable relief. Her obsession with Emerald had rattled him. She might be thousands of miles away, but he still felt protective towards her. The thought that Caroline wanted to hurt her in some way stirred up feelings he thought were long dead.

I have to resolve this, he thought. I have to find out once and for all whether Emerald's completely lost to me or whether there's a way back to her.

He looked at Caroline pouting and sulking across the table. At least with you out of my hair, he thought, I'll be able to apply my mind to the problem.

CHAPTER 33

Paris, 1984

The bar in the Georges V was filling up. Most of the tables had been taken over by American tourists and their dates. One or two call girls had discreetly edged themselves on to the tall leather stools round the long mirrored counter and right in the centre of the room a noisy group of professional gamblers were debating over which casino they were going to play that night.

Jeremy regarded the sleek hucksters with a certain despair. All the smart hotels in Europe were being taken over by lounge lizards these days. Lounge lizards and undesirables. It's getting as bad as Mauritius, he thought.

He sighed and signalled the bartender for another whisky sour. He needed a decent amount to drink before seeing his son again. It had been three years since the boy had seen fit to contact him.

He thought back to the call he had had from Richard. He had been sitting minding his own business in his office in Port Louis when he came on the line. Jeremy had expected some kind of explanation for his long silence but Richard said nothing. All he had to say was he needed to see him, and when would he next be in Europe?

Jeremy named a date four months hence when he had to see his agent in Paris. He could have brought the meeting forward, but he didn't feel all that inclined. Richard hadn't seemed to need him of late, and it had piqued him. Let him wait till I'm ready, he decided. Then I'll listen to whatever's on his mind.

They had arranged to meet in the Georges V hotel and

here he was at the appointed time nursing his second whisky sour and wondering where on earth he had gone wrong with his only son.

In the early days, after Richard left school, he received letters from him all the time. They were marvellous things as the boy told him all that was going on in his life and that fact made Jeremy feel important.

Then the letters stopped and he kept in touch by phone and the odd visit when he was in Paris. Now he felt a bitter, used-up old man.

Jeremy started to get seriously maudlin by the time Richard walked into the bar. The sight of him put paid to his bad mood, for his son was looking even more like a younger version of himself than he remembered.

He was wearing the same dark city suit that he favoured, and his hair was brushed straight back off his face the way he always had it. So I have been some use after all, Jeremy thought. At least I showed him how to wear himself.

For a while the two men fenced. Richard enquired politely about Christine and Jeremy answered him with equal reserve, knowing full well the boy couldn't give a stuff about his wife.

Then they talked about business and it was the younger man's turn to be defensive.

'I've been up to my ears,' he confessed. 'If I'd had more time I would have been in touch earlier.'

The excuse didn't wash at all. Richard could have used it with an acquaintance he wasn't close to but he realized his father deserved better, for the old man looked petulant.

'So you're too busy for me,' he said. 'I feared it had come to that.'

Richard began to feel small. Why am I lying to him, he thought. Why can't I come straight out with it and tell him the real reason I've been keeping away? He thought about Emerald and wondered how to broach the subject. Of all the girls in the world, he thought, why did I have to fall

288

in love with the one who belonged to my father first?

He turned to Jeremy. 'It wasn't business that kept me away,' he said. 'It was something else.'

The old man looked curious. 'Something else, or someone else?'

'What do you mean?'

Now Jeremy smiled. 'It sounds to me as if you've got yourself involved with some woman.'

Richard felt it was uncanny how well this man knew him. They hadn't spoken in years yet his father knew instinctively what was on his mind.

'There is someone,' he admitted. 'Or rather there was someone. She's gone away now.'

Jeremy signalled for another round of drinks. Then he turned to his son.

'I don't understand,' he said. 'If you were in love why did you have to hide away from me? Why couldn't you tell me about her? Bring her to see me. I don't bite, you know.'

Richard started to feel wretched. He had sought his father out after all this time because he wanted to talk about Emerald, but now it came to it, he couldn't seem to find the words. He forced himself to be calm. There has to be a way to explain her, he thought. He turned to his father.

'I couldn't bring my love to see you,' he said, 'because of who she was.' He paused. 'She was someone you used to know. That's what made it so difficult.'

Jeremy was thoroughly intrigued now. 'Are you trying to tell me, you've fallen for some ex-girlfriend of mine?'

There was no ducking out of it. Richard had gone too far to deny her any more.

'I'm in love with Emerald Shah,' he said, feeling ridiculous. 'I met her in New York over three years ago. We were together till quite recently.'

'You mean until she left you,' Jeremy said pointedly. The

two men regarded each other across the tiny glass table.

'How did you know she left me?' Richard demanded.

The older man sighed. 'Because if you'd left her, you wouldn't be mooning around weeping on my shoulder about it. You want to get her back, don't you? And you think because I once knew her, I might just be able to guide your hand.'

Richard looked at his father in astonishment. 'Is that all you have to say?'

The older man looked weary. 'How did you expect me to react? Fly into a jealous rage? Be your age, Richard. I was a married man keeping a bit on the side. She suited me very well while it lasted, but it was no love match for either of us.' Before his son could say anything more, he leant towards him. 'I've been honest with you. Now I think it's your turn. I'd like to know how you hooked up with Emerald in the first place. I'd like to know the whole story and I think after three years of cutting me dead, you owe me that.'

Richard started to tell Jeremy about the encounter in the 21 Club. At first he was hesitant, expecting any moment to be laughed at or criticized, but his father didn't say a word. He simply listened, and Richard opened up.

He must have gone on for some time, for when he looked up, the bar was almost empty.

'I seem to have overstayed my welcome,' he said.

Jeremy signalled for the bill. Then he turned to his son.

'Stay on and have some dinner with me. We've got a lot to talk about.'

By some mysterious telepathy that exists in all grand hotels, the staff seemed to know the two men's wishes. Almost immediately menus materialized and a table was made ready for them in the conservatory restaurant. As they were ushered through, Jeremy reflected on what his son had been telling him. The boy had behaved like a fool, of course. All that lying about being Richard Hutton was unforgivable and not worthy of him. If he'd just been straight with Emerald, none of this mess would have happened.

He sighed. The mess had happened and Emerald would be a lost cause unless he stepped in and did something. He turned to his son.

'Tell me,' he said. 'Why did Emerald leave you to be a dressmaker in Mauritius? Couldn't you have set her up as a dressmaker in England?'

Richard looked sad. 'I don't think you understand,' he said. 'Emerald didn't want to be set up. She was determined to stand on her own feet.'

The older man thought for a moment. This didn't sound like the girl he knew at all.

'Did Emerald ever tell you how she started in business?' he enquired.

Richard felt uncomfortable. 'You set her up, didn't you? She told me it was her body in exchange for premises and all expenses paid.'

The older man remembered it differently, and he realized Emerald's years with her movie star must have made her tough.

'Did she tell you', Jeremy asked, 'that she suddenly got ambitious? A year after she started, she wanted to expand. The way she was going she could have started an empire.'

Richard was intrigued. 'Why didn't she?'

'Because I wouldn't hear of it. She came to me for a loan for a bigger workroom but I refused because I didn't want her to get above herself.' Jeremy sighed. 'If I'd given her what she wanted, she would have been financially independent of me and I would have lost her. It was selfish, but I couldn't let it happen.'

Richard felt sorry for his father. The only way he could hold a woman was by controlling her. Except it didn't work. Emerald was off like the wind as soon as she found an escape route. He started to get edgy. Jeremy was trying to explain something to him, but for the life of him he couldn't think what it was.

'Why are you telling me about Emerald's ambitions?' he said. 'Knowing she wants to succeed isn't going to bring her back to me.'

His father looked secretive, as if he knew something that put him at an advantage. 'Emerald's drive is exactly what is going to bring her back,' he said. 'But it won't happen overnight. If I'm right about her, she's probably doing fine in Mauritius. She'll be making a nice little living as a fashion designer for the rich families. But it won't be enough. Sooner or later she'll wonder why it doesn't satisfy her and when that happens someone needs to take her by the hand and show her where she's going wrong. I know her well enough to know that.'

Richard was intrigued. 'What happens then?'

'Then Emerald gets the taste of success in her mouth,' Jeremy went on. 'I have an idea that could totally turn her business around. And if it works, your little ex-girlfriend is going to want to get into the big time.'

The younger man leaned back in his chair and lit a cigarette. 'Where do I come into all this?' he asked. 'And how will you bring her back to me?'

Jeremy felt as if an enormous weight had been lifted off his shoulders. For ages he had assumed his son could live his life without him, that he no longer needed to listen to him. Now he realized it simply wasn't so.

'If you just pay attention,' he said, 'I'll explain the whole thing.'

CHAPTER 34

Mauritius, 1985

It was unseasonably hot that day. Standing in the Turf Club on a Saturday afternoon, Emerald felt she was visiting a Turkish bath.

The first race hadn't been called yet, but already several of the well-to-do women were starting to wilt. She looked at them drinking their gin and tonics in the members' bar and tried to work out who had dressed them that day.

She saw at least three silk dresses that had to come from Mrs Henry. The Harel women, all three generations of them, were very obviously still patronizing Miss Blanche. Then she spotted one of her own creations.

It was a tea dress in the palest pink silk with a long flowing skirt. What set it apart from everything else that was on display that day was the way it was made. There was something clean and tailored about its lines. Already the dress was attracting envious glances from some of the younger colonial ladies and Emerald began to relax.

On Monday morning her little boutique in Curepipe would have six new enquiries. The women would want to know how much one of her exclusive designs would cost them and how long it would take to fit and finish.

Out of the six callers three of them would eventually turn up in her showroom as *bona fide* customers. The others would compare her prices with the dressmaker they already had. If she was cheaper they would use the fact to bludgeon the hapless seamstress into reducing her rate.

Emerald didn't lose any sleep over the customers she lost. She had too much new business to occupy her mind.

Since she had set up in a two-storey wooden building in the main shopping area she had been rushed off her feet. Without her having to advertise, people knew exactly who she was. The débâcle over Larry's inheritance had given her a certain notoriety. In New York and London it had made her something of an outcast: to the international set she was just a discarded mistress, a gold-digger who had failed to make the grade. In Mauritius the effect was completely opposite. Here, in this smaller, less sophisticated society, Emerald had glamour. Here, nobody gave a damn whether she had loved Larry Simpson or hated his guts. The fact that she had rubbed shoulders with a Hollywood movie star was all they cared about. She had eaten in expensive restaurants, danced at all the right parties and somewhere along the way she had acquired the kind of style that every woman wanted to emulate.

Her customers made no bones about why they patronized her. Quite simply they wanted to buy what she had. 'Make me a cocktail dress that you would put on for a jet-set party,' they would say, or, 'Design me a suit that would look right in Harry's Bar.'

Emerald did nothing to destroy their illusions. It had been a year since she had run with the international set. Fashions had changed, but she knew better than to tell her customers that.

She brought out the latest issues of *Vogue*, *L'Officiel* and *Oggi* and worked from them. Nobody found her out, for in part, her customers were right: Emerald did know how clothes should look. Any of her rivals could copy something from a magazine but they couldn't imagine how the fabric should hang or even how it should move. For none of them had ever seen real couture clothes in action.

Emerald hadn't just seen them, she had worn them, and instead of being just another high-class dressmaker, she became a consultant and couturier rolled into one.

When she had time to think, she would remember the

days when she was scratching a living making uniforms and curtains. She found it hard to believe she had come as far as she had for in little more than a year she had achieved the independence she had been aiming for.

She could support herself in reasonable style. Her reputation was growing, and if her business wasn't going to make her rich, at least it made her happy. When she was working that was.

In her own time, she was miserable. For Emerald was lonelier than she had ever been. All her own friends, all the girls she had grown up with, were married now. Their lives belonged to their husbands and their children. Although they were pleased to see her, they couldn't relate to her any more. Worse, her Western sophistication made them feel slightly uncomfortable. So they shunned her. It was the same with her family, and it didn't take her long to realize they would have been happier if she had been married to the lowliest plantation worker than living the way she did, for her hard-won independence had turned her into an outcast among her own people.

When Emerald gravitated towards the European community, she found she wasn't accepted there either, for she was still a native girl. Things might have changed since she left. The Indian government gave everybody more freedom and more equality but the one thing that didn't change were people's prejudices. She was good enough to do business with, but she was not worthy to be invited to dinner. Not that she spent all her time alone. She began to find there were other women just like her – career women who didn't fit into the island's tidy little society. As yet there weren't too many of them, but the ones that existed gravitated towards each other. Emerald found herself spending the time she had away from her business with a Chinese girl who supervised staff relations at one of the big beach hotels and a French girl who worked for one of the embassies. They cooked in each other's houses and from time to time they visited the casino together. It wasn't exactly a glamorous life. Emerald would have had a far better time if she'd stayed in London and married Richard. Yet though she missed him sorely, she wasn't tempted to go back. In Mauritius she had regained her self-respect. It was the most precious commodity she had and it made up for all the empty nights and barren weekends.

Weekends like this one when she was forced to go to the races on her own. She had made for the Turf Club bar, because she knew she would be less conspicuous there than anywhere else. Now the first race was being called she was glad of her choice, for the paddock was like a bear garden. All the poor natives on the island seemed to have gathered there this afternoon. They were munching on sticky sweets and babbling away among themselves and she thought back to the days when she was one of them.

I used to be right in the centre of the crowd, she thought, pushing and shoving and waving my betting slip. She shuddered slightly. Then she concentrated her attention on the first race. The brightly-clad jockeys were lining up at the starter's gate and for a moment the crowd fell silent. Then they were off and she was gripped by the excitement she always felt when she had money riding on a horse.

Emerald had put two thousand rupees on the favourite who looked as if he would win by a clear length. Then something happened. One of the other horses bumped into him. It wasn't much of a collision. It hardly knocked him off course but it was enough to make him lose his nerve and he fell behind on the final furlong.

She groaned and tore up her ticket, noticing that the man standing next to her was doing the same.

'I hope you didn't make the same mistake as I did,' she laughed. Then her laugh faded, for as he turned to look at her, she realized who he was.

'Jeremy Waites?' she said, sounding confused.

He had changed a great deal. The dapper English gentleman Emerald had once known had lost his bounce. Where he had walked tall and confident, he now stooped.

Emerald examined him closely, wondering what had happened to cause the change in him. Then she sighed. Nothing had happened. His clothes were as expensive as ever. He still wore his wedding band. Jeremy Waites had simply become old.

He recognized Emerald immediately and extended his hand.

'What a nice surprise,' he said cheerfully. 'I heard you were back on the island.'

Emerald stiffened. 'Is that all you've heard about me?' she asked.

Jeremy regarded his old girlfriend with a certain curiosity. She's still defensive, he thought. I'd better go carefully.

'Are you referring to the court case in California?' he enquired. 'Because if that's so it passed me by. I'm only really concerned with what goes on over here. From what I've heard, you've made quite a success of yourself since you've been back.'

Emerald started to relax. 'You're talking about the dressmaking, or rather the couture business. Do you remember how you once told me I couldn't do it?' she said.

Jeremy made a great show of extracting a cigarette from a slim silver box he carried in his inside pocket. After a moment, he said, 'I didn't say you couldn't do it. I merely told you it would be difficult.'

Hypocrite, Emerald thought. In the days when I knew you, you dismissed me as a poor native girl, a no-hoper destined to sew curtains for the rest of her life. She thought about taking Jeremy up on it, then she thought there wasn't any point. Jeremy was no longer a threat to her.

She decided to go on the offensive. 'What are you doing here today without your wife? I always thought the races were a family occasion.'

Jeremy didn't let her get away with the remark. 'Stop pretending you never knew me,' he said. 'I'm not in the habit of carting my wife around to social events, a fact of which you are well aware.'

He took Emerald's arm and led her away from the balcony towards the bar.

'Do you still drink white wine?' he asked. 'Or do your tastes run to something more exotic nowadays?'

Emerald accepted a glass of chablis as Jeremy asked her if she was going to risk any more money on the second race. She delved in her bag for the racing card she had been given but she couldn't seem to make much sense of it.

The truth of the matter was she had come to the course today to see what the fashionable women were wearing. Racing was a secondary activity. Now she had run into Jeremy the whole emphasis changed, for the old planter was an expert when it came to the horses.

He advised Emerald where to put her money and when she made to go to the tote, he restrained her.

'I have an account with one of the bookies on the course,' he told her. 'If you place your bets through me, you can stay exactly where you are. One of his runners comes up here before each race.'

It was a bit like the old days, with Jeremy looking after her, only there was a subtle difference. Emerald no longer felt anything for him. She was neither frightened of him, nor attracted to him. It lent a piquancy to the situation.

All I want from this man, she thought, is his company, and what's more, he knows it.

It was a good day's racing. Despite the heat and humidity, the horses were running well and Emerald started to get involved with the sport. By the end of the meeting she actually felt she had learnt something. She had also won three thousand rupees.

She bought a bottle of champagne to celebrate her win

and she wondered if Jeremy would attempt to ask her out to dinner.

They would never be lovers again, that was abundantly clear, but they weren't quite friends either. In the end, Emerald forced the issue by looking at her watch.

'I have to be getting along,' she told him. 'I'm late already.'

Emerald wasn't going anywhere in particular, but if Jeremy suspected she was lying, he didn't let on but offered to walk her to the car park instead. When they got to her battered black Peugeot, he helped her in with exaggerated courtesy. Then he waved her goodbye.

'Let's not lose touch this time,' he said. 'Old friends are few and far between.'

A week later Jeremy rang Emerald. The call came at 7.30 when she was just putting away a series of designs she had completed for one of the island's socialites. Normally she would have been excited at the prospect of a lucrative new client but Madame Garnier didn't inspire her. This season, just like the season before, she would be trotting out the same brocade cocktail dresses, the same little gaberdine suits, the same beaded ball gowns.

Madame Garnier wanted a new wardrobe, but she didn't want a new look. Emerald could see in years to come she would be repeating herself ad infinitum. It was with this depressing thought in mind that she picked up the phone.

'You sound a bit low,' Jeremy said. 'Is anything the matter?'

'Nothing I can do anything about,' Emerald said glumly. She heard him chuckle.

'Your trouble is that you give up too easily. Why don't you let me buy you a drink and I'll listen to your problem? I take it it's something to do with your business.'

Emerald was tempted to tell him to go away. She'd had Jeremy involved in her business once before and he hadn't exactly backed her with undying loyalty. Then she glanced around her untidy little workroom. She could sit here fiddling about with Madame Garnier's new spring wardrobe, or she could go somewhere cool and have a drink with Jeremy. There was really no contest.

'I'll see you in half an hour at the Merville Beach,' she told him.

The hotel was a couple of miles away from Emerald's cottage in Grande Baie. There was no harm in meeting Jeremy there for half an hour. Jeremy arrived there before Emerald. When she walked into the little thatched bar by the beach, he was in deep conversation with one of the waiters. They were talking about the new government tax on locally produced liquor and Emerald marvelled at the smallness of the community. In Mauritius you were always running into someone you knew.

She saw Jeremy look up as she approached and despite herself she was glad she had come. Jeremy looked genuinely pleased to see her and she wondered if they might become friends after all.

She began by talking about her business problems. Madame Garnier and all her other clients like her were on Emerald's mind. They worried her because she knew no matter how talented she was, they would stifle her in the end.

'They come to me because they think I've got new ideas,' she told her companion, 'but when it comes down to it, they're not interested in innovation. They want me to make the same clothes for them that Miss Lagane or Mrs Henry has been doing for years and if I want to stay in profit, I've got to go along with it.'

Jeremy seemed fascinated by her problem. 'Haven't you tried reasoning with them?' he asked. 'All those women spend their lives competing with each other. If one of them started setting the style instead of following it, she'd be miles ahead of the game.'

Emerald did her best not to smile. Jeremy was talking about his wife, she knew. She also knew he didn't have the faintest idea of how her mind worked.

'None of the Mauritian ladies want to stick their necks out,' she told him. 'They're worried it would make them look vulgar.'

Jeremy leant forward and poured some more wine into their glasses. Behind him the sun was sinking into the sea making it look like thick dark treacle. It would be dark soon and in spite of all her problems a feeling of contentment stole over Emerald. There was a peace about the tropics that came from knowing that whatever happened the sun would come up hot and bright the next morning. Just for a moment she felt suspended in time for, sitting on the edge of the lagoon, she almost felt as if she had never left this island.

None of it matters, Emerald thought. I fall in love, I lose more money than I could ever spend, I see my entire reputation go up in flames and the world still goes on turning.

'This is not the biggest problem I ever had,' she told Jeremy. 'I'll find a way of working it out.'

But Jeremy wasn't prepared to let it go at that. To Emerald's surprise, he seemed genuinely concerned at her frustration and wanted to see if there was any way round it.

'Have you thought of designing for a different kind of customer?' he asked her. 'You could mass produce a line for the locals, for instance.'

Emerald thought about it for a moment. 'It wouldn't work,' she said. 'My value lies in the fact that I am exclusive. If any girl in the street could wear my dresses, I'd soon lose my regulars.'

They talked around the problem while they finished the wine, but they got no further. Whether she liked it or not, Emerald had found her niche in the world and she had no other choice but to go with it.

She got back to her little beach cottage around ten, made herself supper on a tray and took it out to the patio. She had rented the property at Grande Baie mostly for its view. The wooden deck where she had her dining table and a collection of cane chairs backed on to a lush tropical garden. Banana trees grew freely there and the air was heavy with the scent of the frangipani and hibiscus bushes. But the garden was only part of it. It was the terrain beyond it that really mattered, for through the vegetation it was just possible to see the soft white sand of the shore.

Often when she had finished her evening meal, Emerald would walk on to the beach and watch the night fishermen trawl the shallow waters. If the night was warm she would take a swim in the Indian Ocean.

Tonight she did neither of those things. The conversation with Jeremy had disturbed her. He seemed so insistent that she could do better for herself that she almost started to believe him. She went back over the options he had given her. She could mass produce and work for a totally different kind of market or she could stay with the safe, wealthy clientele she already had.

There has to be a third way to go, she thought. Another option that lets me cater for all kinds of women. She leaned back on the padded wicker sofa and took a sip of her drink. In the background she could hear the faint lapping of the ocean. It was a soothing sound, a night sound and, without meaning to, she let her mind wander. It was then, right at the moment she finally let go, that she found the solution to what was bothering her. Of course I can mass produce, she thought. How silly of me not to think of it before. So long as I don't sell my cheap line in Mauritius, I can do whatever I like.

She sat up till the early hours of the morning planning what she would do. The most obvious thing would be to try her luck in London. It was a tough town, but she had lived there at least, and it had the advantage of being less competitive than New York. If I make a name for myself in England, she thought, I can expand into the States. First, though, I need a line.

Because Emerald had always been fascinated with clothes, she had picked up a rudimentary knowledge of the fashion business. This last year had rounded out her education, for Mauritius as a duty-free zone was beginning to attract a thriving manufacturing industry. One of her friends supervised a factory making hand-framed knitwear, and was convinced that in time the island could come to rival Hong Kong. Already there were signs of it.

There was row upon row of fabric shops all along the crowded streets of Port Louis. Bales of Scottish tweed and rolls of brightly coloured silk spilt out on to the pavements. Everywhere you looked – from the pages of the local rag advertising jobs for machine workers to the white concrete factories going up outside every village – the rag trade was in evidence.

By sticking to a few rich women, Emerald had managed to carve out a living. Now she wanted to do more than that. She wanted to become part of this vibrant new industry that seemed to be taking over the land where she was born.

Emerald spent the next few days leafing through the glossy magazines. If she could steal a bodice from Saint Laurent or a jacket from Chanel, her clients would be convinced she could provide a genuinely international look. Now she needed to do more than merely copy. What Emerald needed to come up with was a clear idea of what women were going to want this season. The couture collections were there to provide clues. They could tell her what length skirts were being worn, what colours to go for, what fabrics were in vogue. Yet in themselves they couldn't tell her what the working girl was going to want in her winter wardrobe.

Only living amongst those girls and knowing their needs

could answer that question. She toyed with the idea of going back to London. She could put up at a cheap hotel and literally walk the streets until she found the elusive idea she was looking for. Maybe the line she was after was already being worn on the King's Road in Chelsea? Maybe the teenagers were experimenting with a revolutionary new concept and all she had to do was visit the discos in Camden?

As things turned out Emerald didn't have to make the trip after all, for the idea she was looking for was hiding between the pages of *House and Garden*. It was a feature on the horsey set who lived in the leafy shires. What interested her about the piece weren't the endless illustrations of jodhpurs and tweeds – Emerald had seen them a hundred times before – what really fascinated her was the fact that all the women in the article went on wearing their riding gear in their day-to-day lives.

Emerald had never seen that before. All the grand ladies she had known in both the US and the UK had changed into twinsets and pearls after the hunt. Something must have happened to the way women wear themselves, she thought, to make them behave like this.

She went back to her international editions of *Vogue*. Now she knew what she was looking for, her task was easier. For what Emerald needed to find was a hint, a suspicion of tweedy tailoring in the Paris collections. She found it almost immediately. The couturiers were starting to cater for the wealthy woman executive. They hadn't put her in tweeds yet, but they were cutting her jackets more aggressively. The shoulders had the same built-up look she had seen on the riding jackets of the hunting women. There was the same waisted look and the lapels no longer looked as if they were built with the express purpose of accommodating an exquisite piece of jewellery.

So women want to look like men, she thought, but they don't want to make it too obvious. Her mind went back once more to the county set. They were wearing their hacking jackets in the drawing-room now. How long, she wondered, will it be before the woman in the high street wants to do the same thing?

Now Emerald had her idea, it threatened to take her over completely. She started drawing lapels and intricate diagrams of sleeves fitting into big square shoulders.

When she was in the middle of supervising a fitting she would forget what she was doing and start making doodles of riding ladies on her notepad.

She went to see tailors, quizzing them on how they cut and fitted their clothes. And when she was sure she understood their technique, she began experimenting on her own tailored jackets. She stayed with the hunting ladies. A hacking jacket for the city seemed an amusing, slightly daring idea. If it caught on, even with a small section of the public, Emerald knew she would have made her mark. She would have to come up with an original idea. She started to talk to her friends in the rag trade. She knew what she was doing was too small-scale to warrant taking on a factory; her kind of operation depended on outworkers, skilful seamstresses who would take her patterns home with them at night and knock up hacking jackets in their spare time.

In a matter of weeks she had organized her workforce. Then she turned her attention to the fabric they would work with. Her contacts among the men's tailors came in handy here. One of them had a supplier in Scotland who provided tweeds in every colour range. For a cut of her profits, the tailor agreed to order tweed for her.

Emerald was loath to go along with it, but she had no other choice. If nobody wanted her jackets she would be stuck with bales and bales of expensive unwanted tweed. This way, with the tailor taking the risk, she was off the hook. She agreed to pay the man his percentage and started writing letters to the London buyers.

All her samples would be ready in a week or so. It was time to go and show them around.

Jeremy sat on the verandah of his large house staring into the sunset. At times like this he would normally take stock of his day, going over the profits he could expect from this year's harvest. This evening, though, his own concern held little interest for him, for all his concentration was focused on Emerald.

She had called him earlier at his office in Port Louis and told him the news that she had found a way of going into the retail business without offending her wealthy clients.

'If I sell my designs overseas,' she had told him, brimming over with excitement, 'nobody here will give a damn.'

Jeremy had been as encouraging as he knew how. He praised Emerald's originality and her sheer nous for seeing an opportunity. She had responded with equal enthusiasm.

'It was you who put the idea into my head in the first place,' she told him. 'If it hadn't been for you I wouldn't have considered mass production.'

She went on to tell him about her plans to take her samples to London. This was the part of the conversation that interested Jeremy most, but he didn't have to push her for details. Emerald was bubbling over with it all. In her excitement she even gave him a list of the stores she had on her itinerary.

'If they like my ideas for this season,' she told him, 'then I can start thinking about taking on a factory the next time round.'

Jeremy did his best to sound casual and uninterested about this latest ambition, but it was a struggle.

'Won't you need backing for a venture like that?' he asked her. 'The banks won't be all that keen to extend your overdraft.'

He had taken the wind out of her sails. Emerald hadn't really considered the full responsibility of what she was taking on. Like many creative people, she thought all you needed was a sure-fire idea and the practical side of things just fell into place. Jeremy had done his best to put her right about that but there was only so much he could achieve over the telephone.

'When you get back from your trip,' he said, 'I'll buy you lunch. I've got a couple of ideas that could make things easier for you.'

He hadn't said any more than that. It would have been easy to offer her a loan there and then, but the last thing he wanted to do was to make her suspicious. When he moved in on Emerald's new business, he wanted it to look as if he was doing her an enormous favour.

CHAPTER 35

London, 1985

Rita Levitt applied more red lipstick to her already over-rouged mouth and thought about the coming weekend. Every year she looked forward to the fabrics fair in Paris because it was an opportunity to demonstrate her importance.

If she nodded in the direction of tweeds, then half the designers would increase their orders and she would be looking at dozens of bulky, hairy suits come next season. If she gave the thumbs up to lace, then every camisole top, every silk blouse would be trimmed with it.

She reached into the top drawer of her desk and extracted her airline ticket. As usual it was first class. Henry's of Knightsbridge liked her to travel in style, because Henry's needed her.

For the past thirty years Rita had been one of the premier fashion buyers in England. Her eye for a fast-selling line of goods had made her invaluable and vitally necessary to any retailer who wanted to stay in profit.

Like most women of her ilk, she had completed her apprenticeship in the North of England, working her way through the system until she knew all the tricks of the trade. Then when she was on top of the job, she moved down to London and took a job in the 'junior mode' department of Henry's of Knightsbridge. She might not have stayed with the store. The salary they were paying her was hardly any inducement to great loyalty but one thing kept her there: every manufacturer in the fashion game fought tooth and claw to persuade a buyer to stock their line. If they couldn't persuade the buyer, they bribed her. At the age of twenty-four, Rita suddenly discovered she could have any treat she wanted simply by asking for it.

If she showed a liking for a particular fur coat, it was bought for her and given as a present at the end of the season. If she said she liked caviar, a mountain of it turned up on her desk at Christmas. At first she was shocked at the corruption of the business. In Manchester she had learnt that a buyer was only as good as her sales figures, and if she bought in the wrong merchandise, she was as good as finished.

Then she discovered that every manufacturer, even the good ones, offered bribes. All she had to do was follow her own taste, order the goods she thought would sell, then make it quite clear she wished to be compensated for her actions.

Rita was never disappointed. The suppliers she favoured were generous in their appreciation of her. Over the years her closets were constantly stocked with the kind of clothes that only a very rich woman could afford.

She got a reputation for what she did, of course. Over the years it became known in the rag trade that Rita only bought from certain houses, but nobody made a fuss about it. All the big stores were full of buyers like Rita. She was one of the things you had to live with if you were going to compete in the marketplace.

When Emerald turned up for her appointment at Henry's she had no idea who Rita Levitt was. As far as she knew, the buyer was just another name on a list, someone who had granted her twenty minutes to look over her hacking jackets.

As she walked into the buying department on the top floor, she did her best not to look nervous. Today would be the first time she had shown her samples and she was anxious to make a good impression. Her intentions were completely lost on the girl who sat outside Rita's office. Emerald had to stand in front of her desk for a full five minutes before she even looked up from her typewriter. When she finally had her attention, Emerald announced herself, expecting to be shown into the buyer's inner sanctum.

Instead the secretary looked at her blankly. 'Do you have an appointment with Miss Levitt?' she asked. 'I can't see your name in the diary.'

Emerald started to feel nervous. Maybe I've got the day wrong, she thought. She reached into her bag and pulled out the list her secretary had typed up in Mauritius. She hadn't made a mistake. She was definitely scheduled to see Rita Levitt of Henry's today.

She told the girl as much, then waited while she rang through to her boss. When she came off the phone, the secretary looked oddly triumphant.

'Miss Levitt says she doesn't remember agreeing to see you, but if you want to wait, she'll try and fit you in.'

Emerald fought down her annoyance. There was no point in having a row. There had probably been some quite genuine mix-up. I'll hang on, she thought. My next appointment isn't until four o'clock and it's not even lunchtime.

There was a sofa and a coffee table at one end of the room and she went over and sat down. While she waited she kept her eye on the office where Rita Levitt was incarcerated. For the next hour a constant stream of store executives came in and out of the door.

At lunchtime, Emerald got a glimpse of Rita herself. She was obviously hurrying out to some glamorous rendezvous for she was all decked out in a red fox coat with a matching hat, but the woman and the outfit didn't go together. Rita was a rather fat woman somewhere in her fifties who wore a vast amount of red lipstick. She was intimidating, there was no doubt about that. In other circumstances, Emerald would have shrunk from getting involved with her, but today was different.

She had been hanging around for nearly two hours now. She knew what she had with her was good. Too good to remain unseen, and the urgency of the situation lent her courage. She got up from the sofa and walked over to the buyer.

'I'm Emerald Shah,' she said, 'and I've been waiting to see you all morning.'

Rita looked up and fixed Emerald with shrewd black eyes.

'I've known designers who have waited longer than a morning to see me,' she said. 'What is it you're trying to push?'

She was wearing a pungent perfume and the cloying smell of it made Emerald feel slightly sick.

'I've come up with a range of jackets,' she told the buyer. 'It's a completely new concept. A casual look for town. I know once you've seen them you'll have to have them.'

Rita looked unimpressed. She had been hearing this kind of spiel for thirty years now. Even if the girl was another Karl Lagerfeld, she'd have to walk into her office with something more exciting than casual jackets.

If her secretary hadn't been sitting by her, she would have turned the girl away, but she couldn't afford the luxury. She might only buy from a favoured few, but she didn't want her staff to know it. She turned to Emerald.

'I'm completely booked up for the rest of the day,' she told her, 'but why don't you refix for the end of next week?'

Emerald was astonished. She only calculated on spending three or four days in London at the most. Now this overweight buyer was asking her to kick her heels for another week.

'I'm not sure I'll still be here,' she said.

Rita shrugged. 'Suit yourself,' she said. 'I'm off to Paris

tomorrow so I can't see you earlier. Maybe I'll catch up with you next season.'

Emerald could see Henry's disappearing over the horizon. She had five other appointments so it would have been easy to kiss goodbye to the store, but something in her rebelled. I need this woman, she thought. I won't let her wriggle off the hook. She buried her pride.

'I'll stay around till next week,' she said. 'What day did you have in mind?'

The buyer sighed heavily. If this girl wanted to make a fool of herself, there was nothing she could do to stop her.

'I'll see you next Thursday morning,' she said briskly. 'Fix a time with Carol here. She keeps my diary.'

She swept out without waiting for a reply.

If somebody had shown even the slightest flicker of interest over the next few days, Emerald might have thought twice about going back to Henry's, but it seemed that nobody who bought for a London store was keen on hacking jackets that season.

A succession of tough middle-aged women made her feel inexperienced and insignificant. Every time she brought out her samples she heard the same excuse: 'It's nice, but it's not quite what I'm looking for.' It seemed to be a stock phrase and there were times when she wondered what on earth the stores *were* looking for. The London streets were full of career girls in tailored suits. All she was offering was the same look translated into an off-duty style. She was convinced that if her jackets ever went on sale, they would be snapped up in minutes. But she was all alone in her belief. The powerful cabal of West End buyers had given her the thumbs-down. As far as they were concerned, she might as well pack her bags and go home to Mauritius. But there was still Rita Levitt of Henry's. She hadn't said no to her. Not yet. The date blazed up at her out of the pages of her diary. Thursday morning, eleven o'clock.

Emerald had underlined it in red and for no reason she suddenly felt optimistic. Rita was her last chance. If she somehow managed to impress the buyer, if she talked her into stocking a rail of her jackets, the whole trip would be salvaged. She started to run through her presentation again, concentrating on the major selling points of her range. When she finally came face to face with Rita Levitt her pitch would be so strong, so irresistible, the buyer wouldn't be able to stop herself placing an order.

When Rita Levitt arrived in her office on the top floor, the first thing to catch her eye was her in-tray. She had been away just a few days and already the damn thing was overflowing. It would take her all day to clear the backlog and she rang through to her secretary to clear her diary.

She knew she had meetings that morning, but they would have to wait. What she had in front of her was infinitely more important.

Carol said she would do her best to take care of the problem. Then twenty minutes later she popped her head round Rita's door and told her she had hit a snag. Her eleven o'clock appointment was uncontactable. She'd tried ringing her hotel, but there was no answer from the room. Emerald Shah had already left and as it was coming up to 10.30, she was probably on her way over.

Rita ran a fraught hand through her stiffly lacquered coiffure. Emerald Shah was that pushy Indian girl who was trying to sell her casual jackets last week. She was about to tell Carol to put her off when she got to the office but she was too late, for coming out of the lift and walking through the double glass doors was Emerald Shah, and she looked as if she meant business. When she had showed up last week, she had been carrying her jackets in canvas holdalls. Now she had somehow managed to get hold of a dress rail and she was pushing it for all she was worth in the direction of Rita's office.

Rita conceded defeat. Whether she liked it or not, she was going to have to see the girl. She just hoped she could get the meeting over with as quickly as possible.

'Good morning, Miss Shah,' she said. 'I take it you're going to try and sell me that rail.'

She saw the girl nod vigorously and for a moment she felt a stab of pity. The poor kid had probably been trailing those jackets all over town. Why did none of them ever learn? Why didn't she approach a *bona fide* manufacturer with her designs, instead of going out on her own? If she'd gone in with somebody who was already on the circuit, she might have stood a chance of getting her goods in the shops.

She sighed. I'm too generous, Rita thought. I haven't got the time to worry about every tinpot little designer who comes into my office.

She motioned Emerald into her inner sanctum.

'You've got exactly ten minutes,' she told her. 'If you haven't got my attention in that time, then I'm afraid it's goodbye.'

She saw the girl tense, then, as if she had been going through this moment time and time again, she started presenting her wares.

The jackets Rita saw surprised her. She had been expecting something in denim or one of the cheaper fabrics, but these garments had a touch of class. Every one of them was made in the softest, most delectable Scottish tweed. There were heather tones she had only seen used in men's tailoring and the browns and oatmeals almost took her breath away. She had been looking for exactly this kind of thing at the fabrics fair last week and there hadn't been a hint of it.

She regarded Emerald with genuine curiosity. 'What made you choose tweed jackets?' she asked. 'There are hardly any around this season.'

Emerald launched into the story of how she discovered

314

the county women in *House and Garden* were wearing their riding clothes to afternoon tea.

'It seemed like a genuine trend to me,' she said. 'Almost an extension of the macho suits all the working girls are wearing now. I thought if I could come up with a soft version of a hacking jacket, then there could be a market for it.'

Rita did her best to stifle her admiration for the girl. Her thinking was spot-on. She could see that Henry's customers would go for this range in a big way.

She sighed. It could never happen, of course. If she took on some unknown designer from Mauritius, her established suppliers would have to make room for the new range, and if it took off, then more than one nose would be put out of joint.

Rita thought about the new mink jacket she was expecting for Christmas. Then she concentrated her mind on the gorgeous supple suede dresses and shirts that were coming in her direction from another of her pets in Margaret Street. I simply can't do it, she thought. Emerald Shah is just going to have to take her goods elsewhere.

She turned to the girl. 'You've got some very nice things,' she said, 'but they're not quite what I'm looking for.'

When Emerald walked out of Rita's office, she was in such a rage that she just put her head down, focused her weight behind the heavy rail of tweed jackets and stormed into the corridor.

The weight of her disappointment blinded her to anything that was going on around her. She didn't see the sober-suited executive who was standing outside the bank of lifts that served the management floor, nor did she notice the fact that he was openly staring at the jackets she was pushing in front of her.

When the lift arrived, Emerald was so intent on getting out of the store that she disregarded her companion completely so that, as the doors opened, the distinguished executive and Emerald's overloaded rail suffered a head-on collision. Emerald was aghast at the havoc she had wreaked. Just because she had suffered at the hands of the store buyer, didn't mean that she could take her feelings out on the rest of the staff.

She reached over and stopped the lift. Then as quickly as she could she did her best to disentangle her victim, who was sprawled across the floor of the lift looking vaguely bemused.

'Are you in the habit of knocking people over with your samples?' he asked her.

Emerald didn't reply immediately. She took hold of the man's arms and hauled him to his feet.

'I'm so sorry,' she apologized. 'I wasn't looking where I was going.'

She expected him to be furious. The rail had hurtled into him with surprising force, and she prepared herself for a barrage of abuse. It didn't come. The man bent down and started picking up her jackets.

'You don't have to do that,' Emerald said apologetically. 'I can manage.'

She was flustered and she knew it, yet her discomfort seemed to amuse him.

'Who did you show these to?' the man asked her.

She explained, then she shut her mouth. There was no point in telling the entire store how she failed to make the grade with her range.

'I bet Rita loved these,' the man said. 'These colours are right up her street.'

The words were out of Emerald's mouth before she could stop them: 'Rita said they weren't what she was looking for.' She scowled and looked down at the floor. 'I guess it just isn't my day.'

Her companion didn't reply at once but took her by the arm and escorted her out of the lift.

'Why don't you and your samples come along the corridor to my office?' he said. 'I'd like to get a closer look at what my senior staff are turning down these days.'

Emerald was in turmoil. She had heard that department stores were riddled with politics. I've put my foot in it this time, she thought. When Rita hears one of her colleagues is trying to help me, I'll never get through her door again.

The grey-suited man saw her hesitate. 'What's bothering you now?' he asked.

'I don't want to make a nuisance of myself,' Emerald said dumbly. 'I'm perfectly willing to take no for an answer.'

'Well, I'm not,' replied her companion. 'I like the look of what you've got and I want to know more about it.'

She was about to protest further, when they arrived at the door to a suite of offices. The name written outside said simply: Gerald Hopkins, MANAGING DIRECTOR.

Emerald fought down panic. The situation was getting out of hand.

'Your boss isn't going to be interested in a few tweed hacking jackets,' she said. 'He's got more important things to think about.'

For a moment the older man looked confused, then realization dawned.

'I am the boss,' he said extending a hand. 'I'm surprised you didn't recognize me.'

Emerald felt embarrassed. 'You'll have to excuse me,' she muttered. 'I haven't been in the trade all that long.'

He ushered her through the door of his office suite.

'I'm getting tired of listening to you apologize,' he said. 'If you took that attitude with Rita, no wonder she sent you packing.'

'I wasn't like that with your buyer at all,' Emerald protested, angry now. 'I made a proper presentation, a hard selling pitch. If you'd seen it you would have known I meant business.'

Gerald Hopkins regarded the dark-haired woman in

317

front of him and wondered whether he would have given her the time of day if she hadn't been such a stunner. Then he smiled to himself. The world was full of injustice. Rita had turned down a saleable range because she wanted to protect her regulars and the perks that came with them. Now he was going to reverse her decision because a pretty girl had caught his eye in a lift. The rag trade was a wicked business.

When the boss of a big department store gives the nod to a new range, a chain reaction sets in: the manufacturer hotfoots it back to base, where production is started instantly. When the garments are ready, they are piled on to a plane and, providing everything goes to plan, they arrive at the store in time for the agreed deadline.

The three dozen jackets Emerald was called on to produce reached Henry's several days ahead of schedule, for she had left nothing to chance. She had pushed her outworkers until they screamed at her to let up. She'd seen each one of her crates as they were loaded into the hold of the aircraft. Because this was her one big chance, she accompanied the goods personally.

As Emerald's jackets came out of their Cellophane wrappers, she was there to see there was no damage to the consignment.

After that the system took over. The jackets went to the floor manager, who like all floor managers was well aware of the politics behind the delivery and made sure she put the jackets in a prominent position.

When they started to move, she contacted the marketing department. They also knew about Gerald Hopkins' involvement and decided to give Emerald's jackets their own window display.

If the merchandise had been no good, several people would have lost their jobs, but Emerald had guessed the public's mood with uncanny accuracy. Every woman walking down the main shopping street paused outside Henry's plate-glass windows. As the jackets caught their eyes, they assessed them, coveted them and quite a number of window shoppers made a decision to buy.

By the end of the weekend, the store had sold over half of Emerald's range and Henry's knew they were on to a winner.

They weren't the only London store to know it. Selfridges had been alerted by the window display and were monitoring sales. That afternoon Emerald had a call from the Oxford Street store's fashion buyer. They had turned her down when she did the rounds a few weeks previously. Now all that was forgotten. Selfridges wanted to stock her jackets. Their only question was how soon could she deliver?

Emerald did a quick calculation. If she got back fast, she could have the jackets on the plane by the end of October. The buyer seemed satisfied with her answer and Emerald put in a call to the airport.

Before she left, she paid a visit to Rita Levitt at Henry's. Ever since the managing director had smiled upon Emerald, Rita had given her no trouble at all. If anything she was too friendly these days.

As soon as she put in an appearance, Emerald was whisked through to Rita's inner sanctum where she was plied with tea and biscuits.

'What can I do for you?' crooned the fashion doyenne. Emerald was not taken in by the woman. She was all sweetness and light today, but if the jackets stopped selling next week she knew she wouldn't get through her door again.

'What you can do,' said Emerald briskly, 'is to tell me whether you want another consignment. I'm going back to Mauritius to make up an order for Selfridges, so if you want I can set the wheels in motion for you as well.'

Emerald knew she was pushing her luck. The jackets had only been on sale a week, but she had an instinct about

Rita. The woman was running scared now. She couldn't afford to be caught on the hop if stock sold out.

Emerald was right. The buyer came through with her offer.

'I can't commit for nine dozen, as we originally said,' she told Emerald. 'The sales don't justify it. But can we compromise on seven or eight dozen with an option for another two in the next month?'

It was better than Emerald had hoped for. Henry's and Selfridges between them would run her off her feet. She started to wonder if the Scottish supplier could come through with enough tweed. It was as if Rita could read her mind.

'While you're in London you should check everything,' she advised. 'Buttons, fabric, sewing silks. You can't afford to be caught short when you're thousands of miles away.' Rita paused for a moment. 'By the way,' she asked, 'have you done the rounds of the other stores?'

Emerald's head started to spin. All she had hoped for was a moderate success with Henry's. The Selfridges order had been a bonus. Now suddenly she was faced with the prospect of a major operation.

'I don't think I can cope with any more business,' she replied. 'I've only got so many workers back in Mauritius.'

The older woman gave a look of impatience. This kid was all fire when it came to hustling a deal but she didn't show any imagination when it came to backing it up.

'Look,' she said as patiently as she could, 'I don't think you realize what you've got on your hands here. Most manufacturers would sell their sisters to have your kind of success. Those damned jackets of yours have hit some kind of buying nerve with the public. By the end of next week every fashion follower in this town is going to want some version of your line.'

Emerald started to feel desperate. 'What do you think I should do?' she asked.

The buyer wondered whether to tell her the facts of life. This little designer had landed her in a whole lot of trouble with her management. She didn't exactly owe her anything. Still, she decided to help her.

'The first thing you've got to do is stop worrying about getting workers,' Rita said. 'The only reason any of them do a day's work is for the money. If you have a problem attracting people, raise your rates a bit. I don't think you'll have any difficulties after that.'

Emerald felt as if a weight had been taken off her shoulders. I've been thinking too small, she thought. I keep imagining everyone's doing me a favour when they do a job for me.

She turned to the fashion buyer. 'I misjudged you, Rita,' she admitted. 'I didn't think you cared about what happened to me.'

Rita gave her an old-fashioned look. 'I don't,' she told her. 'You're not my kid sister or anything. The person I'm thinking of right now is me. If you stay in business, my department stands to make a bit of money.'

That season, Henry's did very well out of Emerald. The stores that came in later also turned a healthy profit on her range. By January, the London streets were full of women wearing waisted tweed jackets in an assortment of rich colours. This fact did not go unnoticed by Thelma Lewis who ran the fashion page for the *London Evening Post*. Her reputation was based on keeping up with the latest trends in the city and this latest craze was too good to miss. It had all the elements of a really good story. Most of the new jackets were the product of a totally new designer, one she'd never heard of before.

A couple of the cheap manufacturers had come in with their own versions at the end of the season but the garment everyone wanted, the article that was coveted, bore the 'Emerald' label.

Who on earth is Emerald, Thelma wondered. Has one of the big boys got hold of a bright new designer, or is Emerald a one-off?

She decided to investigate. She started ringing round the buyers who stocked the range but they were cagey about the label. All of them had plans to buy Emerald's next collection so none of them wanted the whole world beating a path to her door.

In the end Thelma rang Gerald Hopkins. She knew Henry's had had the jacket at the very beginning. Anyway Gerald owed her a favour.

To her relief he was surprisingly forthcoming. It turned out the Managing Director had in some way been responsible for finding the new line. And now it was a rip-roaring success, he wanted to take full credit for it.

So he told her that Emerald was a real-live girl, an Indian designer living out in Mauritius.

'Has she done anything before?' Thelma asked.

Gerald Hopkins wasn't sure. 'I'll tell you what,' he said, 'why don't you give Emerald a ring in her office? I think I've got the number.'

The journalist waited while he searched around for it and asked whether Henry's were still selling the line.

'If you do the piece in the next week,' Hopkins told her, 'the answer is yes. After that we start our sale.'

Thelma squinted at the schedule pinned up on the wall opposite her. If she switched things around she would be able to feature the jackets the day after next.

'I'm going with the feature on Wednesday,' she told him. 'It's a good enough story to make the centre spread, so if you send me over some of the range, I'll make sure Henry's gets a credit.'

After she'd put the phone down on Hopkins, she checked the time in Mauritius. The island was five hours behind England. If she tried Emerald now, she'd just get her as she arrived at work. She started dialling the number jotted down on her pad.

Caroline was strolling past the features desk when she saw the half-finished fashion proof. None of the text was on the page yet. So all there was were white space and pictures. It was one of the pictures that caught her eye. It was a face she knew. A face she would remember all her days. Emerald's face.

What on earth is she doing on the fashion spread, Caroline wondered. She walked through to the end of the open-plan office searching for Thelma. If anyone could answer the question, she could.

Thelma Lewis was one of the new breed of fashion editors. Fresh out of one of the trendy polytechnics, she had got to Fleet Street on the strength of her street cred. Unlike her predecessors, she knew nothing about the nuances of *haute couture*. All Thelma knew was what the kids in the suburbs were crying out for, and it stood her in good stead. When she ran an offer or a promotion, the response was overwhelming and was clear proof that the readership was right behind her. Which is why she took no shit from the likes of Caroline.

As soon as she saw the financial columnist come into view, she did her best to look busy, burying herself in a pile of glossy eight by tens. The pictures were all part of the hacking jacket feature and Caroline descended on them with a whoop of glee.

'Tell me,' she asked Thelma. 'Why are you using these shots alongside Emerald Shah's picture?'

The fashion editor looked at Caroline suspiciously. 'What's it to do with you?'

The redhead was not going to be fobbed off. The bolshy little girl was still her junior in the general scheme of things and if she wouldn't answer her question, then she would go and find someone who would.

Thelma seemed to realize this, for she raised her head from the set of photos.

'You're not going to give me any peace until I tell you the whole story, are you?'

Caroline smiled. 'What do you think?'

Thelma sighed. She'd heard Caroline could be very tiresome when crossed. She imagined she'd better humour her.

'Emerald Shah is the name behind the latest tweed jacket craze,' she said. 'She started the whole thing off last autumn when she designed a range for Henry's. Are you satisfied now?'

Caroline pursed her lips together. 'Not quite. I'd like to know the size of her operation. Where she works from. And how serious she is. You never know, there might be something there for me to write about in my column.'

The fashion editor started to relax. So Caroline wasn't looking for trouble after all. She was just looking to fill a bit of white space on her page. She turned to her.

'I don't think I'd waste my time if I were you. Emerald's outfit is strictly junior league. She works out of Mauritius and she hasn't even got a factory.'

'So why is she wasting her time taking on the big manufacturers?' Caroline asked.

Thelma shrugged. 'Maybe she was bored. When I talked to her she told me her main business is making expensive one-offs for society ladies. The hacking jacket idea was a way of using up some of her creative energy. My guess is now she's proved her point and got a little success into the bargain, she'll go back to what she was doing all along.'

Caroline was satisfied with what she heard. So Emerald wasn't thinking of taking London by storm after all. She was going to stay in the Indian Ocean where she belonged and leave everyone in peace.

As she walked back to her office, she rehearsed what she was going to say to Richard that evening. She would show him the fashion piece, there was no point in hiding it, and she would fill him in about Emerald's new business.

She doubted if he knew what his ex was up to these days, so she could tell the story any way she wanted.

At least this fashion feature will bring the whole Emerald thing out in the open again, she thought.

For a moment she curbed her reporter's instincts. Do I want to dig into her life, she wondered. Sure, I'd love to know more about her, but I'm risking a hell of a lot if I get on the wrong side of Richard again.

It hadn't taken her long to worm her way back into his life, but she never got near to moving in again. It was as if there was an invisible barrier between them now. She could get so close, but no closer and she put this whole show of reluctance down to Emerald.

She haunts Richard, she thought. He can't get the woman out of his mind. Now she's starting to make her mark in the rag trade, he won't have to.

Caroline couldn't quite believe Emerald was as small-time as Thelma said she was. After the success she's had, she'd be a fool to go back to dressmaking, Caroline thought. Now she's tasted blood she'll probably set her sights on becoming a proper manufacturer.

She tried to imagine what would happen if Emerald decided to take the rag trade by storm. She would have to find herself a factory and a proper PR. There would be a London office, of course, and possibly one in New York.

The thought of Emerald at the helm of an international manufacturing business was unbearable to Caroline. Before, she could dismiss her as an armpiece, a rich man's accessory. Now she couldn't do that any more. Emerald as a career girl was a daunting prospect. Richard would find her irresistible, and that would put Caroline right out of the running.

She took a deep breath as she reached her desk, then slowly counting to ten, she made herself sit down and get a grip on reality. The woman she was so frightened of had a tiny business on a small island. She had no capital and no prospect of capital. Without the necessary backing, there was no way she could think of manufacturing.

Emerald got a lucky break, thought Caroline. She hit the jackpot with a trendy idea, but it will take more than ideas for her to be a force in the land.

CHAPTER 36

Mauritius, 1986

Emerald arrived at La Plage in Grande Baie on the dot of one. Jeremy said he would meet her in the bar a few minutes before the hour, but she didn't want to be the first to arrive.

She was acutely aware that a few years ago, she wouldn't have been allowed past the reception area of the luxury hotel on the beach and the memory made her self-conscious. For all around her there were reminders that on this island her race belonged to the servant classes.

The place oppressed her to such an extent that she hesitated before crossing the square marble atrium to the tiny bar directly above the restaurant. There she saw Jeremy looking rather nervously at a tall rum drink with far too much fruit floating in it and the sight restored her confidence. If the staff of La Plage could bamboozle Jeremy into behaving like a tourist, then there was still hope for her.

She hurried over to where he was perched uncomfortably on a bar stool shaped like a coconut, her heels ringing out across the vast empty hall.

The noise made him look up and she could see the relief clearly visible on his face.

'This place gives me the creeps,' he whispered. 'If you'd been any longer I would have been forced to take a walk in the grounds.'

Close to, the rum concoction that Jeremy was trying to drink looked even more ridiculous and Emerald started to laugh.

'What on earth made you decide to have lunch here? There are tons of other restaurants we could have gone to.'

Jeremy pulled a face. 'I didn't want to go anywhere where I was known. This island is such a village that everything we talked about would have been common knowledge by sundown.'

Emerald stiffened. What she had suspected had been true. Jeremy wanted to get involved in her new manufacturing business.

Right from the very first moment, when all she had was a dozen samples, he had been dropping hints about how he could be useful to her. Now that the season was at an end and she had made her success, he was all ready to move in for the kill.

It crossed Emerald's mind to come right out with it and tell him she wasn't interested in going into partnership. Then she looked around her at the hushed expensive surroundings and she decided against being blunt. This man had gone to considerable trouble for her. It seemed silly to hurt him unnecessarily.

'Why don't we make our way down to the restaurant,' she said brightly. 'It looks a damn sight more comfortable than this place.'

Jeremy was on his feet almost before she finished speaking and together they made their way down the curving white stone staircase into the dining area.

La Plage had probably the most attractive setting on the island for it catered exclusively to the very rich. There was a surcharge on everything from the Perrier to the vintage champagne. The ratio of waiters to diners was roughly three to one, but what struck the visitor immediately was the emptiness and the privacy of the place.

The tycoons who paid through the nose to come here weren't looking to be disturbed by other holidaymakers. Nobody who wasn't actually staying could buy a drink at the beach bar or take a dip in the sea that lapped on the exclusive white sand. The result was a view from the restaurant unspoilt by trippers.

Jeremy started lunch the way he always did in these sort of places. He made a thorough inspection of both the menu and the wine list, then summoned the head waiter and spent the next ten minutes in earnest discussion.

The whole performance made Emerald feel slightly sick. It was over ninety degrees outside where they were sitting. She could feel the hot clammy air making her silk business suit stick to her skin. What she most longed for was a glass of cold water and a plate of fruit, but she knew she wasn't going to get away with it.

Her heart sank as she saw Jeremy order palm hearts, followed by first a fish course, then the roast of the day.

The complicated order seemed to set something in motion. All at once half a dozen smiling girls, barely out of their teens, besieged their table. In rapid succession there was wine, mineral water, French rolls and a selection of crudités. Emerald, who had been in grander places than this, felt overwhelmed, almost intimidated by the sheer intensity of the service.

'Imagine staying here for a week,' she said to Jeremy. 'You'd find yourself forgetting what it was like to pour yourself a drink.'

Jeremy laughed. 'The whole purpose of this lunch is to encourage you to embrace this life style. People with money want to live like this.'

Emerald kept her face as impassive as she knew how. 'You're going to turn me into a rich woman. Is that what you're saying?'

Jeremy didn't expect her to be so direct but now she had got to the nub of their meeting, there seemed little point in backing away from it.

He signalled one of three hovering waiters to pour out their wine, then he leant back in his chair.

'You've done very well for yourself these past few months,' he said. 'I know I half pushed you into mass production, but once you'd started there was no holding you. You had an original idea, you didn't let anyone talk you out of it, and you sold it so convincingly that half the stores in London carried your goods.'

'You seem to know a lot about what I've been doing,' Emerald said cautiously.

Jeremy looked embarrassed. 'I have friends over in England I do business with,' he said shortly. 'They kept me in touch.'

Before Emerald could enquire who these associates were, Jeremy was up and running.

'Now you've made your first killing,' he told her, 'you'll want to follow it up with a proper collection next season. To do that, you're going to need a proper organization behind you. Factories, offices, staff, accountants –'

Emerald interrupted him. 'Is that what you're offering me?' she asked. 'Because if you are, I don't want it.'

Jeremy looked genuinely confused. 'What do you mean, you don't want it?' he demanded. 'Of course you want it. Even in my day you were doing your best to talk me into backing you.'

Emerald prayed for patience. 'Your day', she told him, 'was a very long time ago. I was a little girl then and I thought the only way to succeed in the world was by getting help from somebody like you.' She paused, catching her breath. 'I learnt the hard way that simply isn't true. I may not have any money of my own,' she continued, 'but I'm perfectly capable of building a business. If you must know, I've already made a start.'

Jeremy started to feel disorientated. He hadn't expected the conversation to go this way at all.

'Before you tell me about your plans,' he said gently, 'at least listen to what I have to offer you.'

Emerald wasn't interested. The decadent, over-indulgent

restaurant had made her nervous. All she wanted to do now was finish her lunch and get out.

'I don't want to hear what you can do for me,' she said firmly. 'I'd only be tempted and I don't want that.'

She paused and looked at Jeremy intently. 'I don't mean to sound rude,' she said, 'but I have to make this thing work on my own. If I took your offer now, I'd be selling out and I've already done that too many times in my life.'

Jeremy felt irritated. He had worked everything out so perfectly. He'd won Emerald's attention, set her on the right path, and now when everything was coming to fruition, she was behaving like a nervous horse at a fence.

He wondered what to do next. In the old days, when she was his mistress, he would have shouted at her. If he tried that now, she'd walk out, and then where would he be? In the end he settled for gentle persuasion.

'I'm not going to force you to take my money,' he said smiling. 'What I am going to suggest is that you don't dismiss it altogether. You might just need a little help one day and if you do, you know where to come.'

Emerald looked relieved. 'It's very sweet of you to be so patient,' she said. 'A lot of other businessmen would have put a line through my name and moved on to someone more reasonable.'

Jeremy signalled the waiter to clear away the dishes, then he turned to her.

'I'm not like other businessmen,' he said seriously, 'because our relationship didn't start out that way. I actually care about you, Emerald. I want you to succeed and if I have to take a back seat while you struggle for a while, then I'm happy with that.'

All of a sudden Emerald grinned. It was a wide happy expression which travelled all the way up to her eyes, giving them a dangerous green glitter.

'I wouldn't count on my struggling,' she said. 'You haven't even begun to see me in action.'

When Jeremy got back to his office in Port Louis's main square, he put in a call to London. There were no gremlins in the telephone system that day, for within minutes he was connected to the Weiss Group switchboard. Seconds after that his son was on the line.

'Did Emerald show up today?' Richard asked. Jeremy noted the urgency in his voice and dreaded what he was going to tell him.

'Of course she did,' he said, playing for time. 'She had no reason not to.'

'So she doesn't suspect you're up to anything?'

'Give me some credit for knowing her, will you?' Jeremy snapped. 'I've been a friend and an adviser but I haven't been heavy with her. It's the one thing that will frighten her off.'

There was a silence. Then his son said, 'There's something else that will panic her and that's if she finds out I'm involved.'

'But she doesn't know you're involved,' Jeremy said. 'How can she? She never brings up your name.'

He realized Richard was thinking that one over, for there was another awkward silence.

Finally he said, 'Doesn't she ever talk about her personal life? It seems odd after all the time you've known her.'

The older man sighed. 'Not really. Even when she was my girlfriend, Emerald didn't confide in me. Anyway, we're not interested in that sort of conversation. What we need her to discuss is business. We worked that one out in Paris.'

To his relief, Richard took the point, for the next question he asked was about her designs.

'How did the first line do?' he wanted to know.

Jeremy told him in detail what had happened. 'She made

332

such an impression that the buyers are clamouring for whatever she produces next season.'

There was tension in Richard's next statement. 'So she's going to need a backer. She won't be able to meet the demand without one.'

Jeremy's heart sank. 'I sounded her out about that, but she didn't seem to be interested.'

'What do you mean she wasn't interested? I thought you said she was ambitious?' Richard was baffled.

The older man prayed for patience. 'She is ambitious. But she doesn't want to sell out to a partner. She'd rather struggle on with what money she can raise from the banks.'

'So you were wrong all along,' Richard spat. 'I might have known I couldn't trust you. You were talking pie in the sky when you said you could convince her she needed you. It was such a half-baked plan. You pretending to be her backer and me putting up the money so I could have some sort of hold on her. It was doomed to failure and I was a fool not to see it.'

Jeremy waited until his son had got the whole thing out of his system. Then he subtly changed tack.

'It's not completely over yet,' he said cautiously. 'Emerald may want to go it alone, but there's going to come a moment when she'll need a swift injection of cash. I don't think she'll ever take on a full partner, but she could be forced to sell a minority interest. Would you be interested in that?'

He listened to the faint crackle of static while thousands of miles away Richard did his best to come to grips with the new situation. Suddenly he sounded less sure of himself.

'It's not the best solution,' he said, 'but I can live with it. Even if I have a small investment in her outfit, I'm still connected to her.'

Jeremy smiled. This boy of his might be an international wheeler-dealer, but when it came to women he was strictly junior league.

'Are you quite sure she's worth all this trouble? Wouldn't it be simpler to find yourself someone else?'

'There already is someone else,' Richard said sharply, 'and she won't do at all. Look,' he continued. 'We went through this whole thing in Paris. You know exactly how I feel and exactly what I want. So do something for me, will you? Go out and negotiate a slice of Emerald's business for me. I'll do the rest after that.'

CHAPTER 37

He was the kind of man Emerald's mother dreamt she would marry: a Hindu with his own business and a high enough caste to bring honour on the family.

He was handsome too, if you liked the tall, lean, half-starved look. But Emerald wasn't looking for a husband: she was looking for a factory. So when she went to see Ashwin Awasthi she was all business.

She had heard that the modern plant outside Floreal was going broke a couple of weeks ago. The French designer who had used it had gone out of business and now Awasthi was destined to go the same way unless somebody stepped in fast.

Emerald started to sound him out about his machinery. He could have all the spare capacity in the world, but if he didn't have the right facilities then they were both wasting their time.

At first the factory manager wouldn't be drawn and Emerald got the impression he resented her cross-questioning him. It was as if she had no right to be putting him on the spot like this. She began to get irritated.

'Look,' she said finally, 'I've been looking at factories for nearly a month now and nobody so far can provide what I need. If your machinery can't make separates, just tell me and I'll get out of your hair.'

A look of pure panic passed across the finely chiselled face and Emerald knew only too well what was going through the man's mind. He didn't like having to deal with her, but there was no way he could afford to lose her business.

He got up from behind his desk and motioned for her to step on to the factory floor. All around her, shining expensive sewing machines stood idle, shackled to wooden benches. There must have been thousands of dollars' worth of equipment there and Emerald suddenly felt sorry for the pompous little man who owned it.

'What were you making for the French designer?' she asked in an attempt to be friendly.

Awasthi scowled. 'We made suits and coats.'

A feeling of relief washed over Emerald. If this plant produced suits and coats, there would be no difficulty making the range of separates she had designed for her first season.

'I think we might be able to help each other,' she said cautiously. 'Why don't we go back into your office and start discussing the possibility?'

As she started to lay out her terms, Emerald noticed a certain stiffness in the man's manner.

He should have been grateful to her for rescuing him from bankruptcy, yet he was treating her as if she was a lesser form of life. If she hadn't needed him so much, she would have told him what he could do with his factory. Instead she did her best to understand him.

This man's probably never done business with a woman in his life before. It must be purgatory, hammering out a deal.

Nevertheless they had to agree terms, so she took a deep breath and went on with her proposal. She was prepared to pay the rent, the staff's wages and the maintenance of the building for the next month. In return for that she wanted seventy per cent of the profits.

Awasthi started to haggle with her, as she knew he would. Seventy per cent was too much. He couldn't afford to eat on what she was taking. Did she want to divest him of everything he had?

It was nonsense, of course. Seventy per cent was high, but it wasn't impossible. If Emerald had been a man she might have told him to take it or leave it but she was a woman and she had to work with this chauvinist. So she made a concession. She'd take sixty per cent, she told him. But no less.

He accepted her offer with breathtaking speed and Emerald realized she could have probably got away with sixty-five per cent if she hadn't been so worried about his ego.

She sighed as they closed the deal. Okay, she thought, so I'm making slightly less than I should be. At least this way I'm going to keep out of trouble.

The factory was working to full capacity within a few weeks. Emerald's range of separates, like the hacking jackets that preceded them, answered a very real need among the working girls that bought them.

They all wanted to look as if they had more clothes than they actually possessed, and the cleverly co-ordinated jackets, skirts and loose-fitting trousers made them look affluent. If she wanted to, a girl on a budget could put on a different look every day. As Emerald's customers discovered the possibilities of the range, the orders came rolling in.

For the first time since she started this new venture, Emerald started to relax. The bank loan, which terrified her, looked like it would be paid back in record time. Now Awasthi was overseeing things for her at the factory, she had the chance to give some attention to her couture business.

Then one day, one of her regulars cancelled at the last moment and Emerald decided to drive over to Floreal. She hadn't been there for over ten days and she needed to satisfy herself Ashwin Awasthi was doing everything he promised.

She realized he wasn't when she checked a run of shirts. Her pattern specified three buttons on the cuff. So why were there only two?

Before she went up to the office, she took a look at the jackets that were coming off the production line. Now she really was alarmed. She had expressly specified velvet on the lapels yet these garments were faced with tweed.

That manager and his promises, she thought. He's probably watching television instead of talking to the machinists.

She hurried up to the office as fast as she could and when she got there she found the factory manager deep in a pile of paperwork.

'Is anything wrong?' he asked, looking up. 'You seem flustered.'

He might have been speaking to one of his juniors and Emerald felt her hackles rise. She was carrying the offending jacket and without saying anything, she threw it down on the desk in front of him.

'What's the meaning of this?' she demanded. 'The jacket I designed looked nothing like this.'

Awasthi remained calm. The woman was having a hysterical tantrum like all women. When she'd calmed herself, he'd talk some sense into her. He stayed silent for a good five minutes. Then when he suspected the girl might physically attack him, he said his piece.

'I changed the designs of a few of your things because the workers were having problems with them.'

Emerald felt like screaming. 'What sort of problems?'

Awasthi smiled and looked pleased with himself. 'Technical problems. Take this jacket. Velvet is difficult to work with. It's fiddly, so I changed it to tweed so the production would go faster.'

'I suppose it's quicker to sew on two buttons rather than three,' Emerald said shortly.

The factory manager nodded. 'Clever girl,' he said. 'Saving time in this game is the same as saving money. Now things are faster we'll make even bigger profits.'

Emerald walked around the desk until she was facing him. Then she drew up a chair and sat down.

'You're wrong about making more money,' she said quietly. 'If we go on the way we're going, we'll make no money at all because we'll be out of business.'

The man cocked his head to one side and Emerald was reminded of an intelligent monkey.

'I don't quite understand what you're saying.'

She sighed heavily. 'Then I'll spell it out. My customers in London have ordered this line as I designed it. If they had wanted different lapels or cuffs with fewer buttons, they would have said so. But they didn't. They expect to get exactly what's on my blueprint.' She paused. 'When they get your version of my designs, they are quite within their rights to send them back.'

Awasthi tried to laugh it off. 'They won't do that,' he told her. 'They probably won't even notice the difference.'

She felt the last vestiges of her patience beginning to snap. 'I didn't hire you to second-guess my clients,' she said. 'And I certainly didn't hire you to improve on my designs, so unless everything goes back to normal, I'm going to have to look for another factory.'

Emerald got up and walked towards the door. 'I'll be back tomorrow morning,' she said, 'to find out what you've decided.'

The next day everything was back in place. Her jackets looked like her jackets again, and when she checked her shirts, trousers and her fitted knee-length skirts, every detail was as she had designed them.

She looked into the office. 'I'm glad we managed to resolve our little difference,' she told her manager. 'I'll be here more often from now on.'

If her remark needled him, he didn't show it. In fact every time she went to the factory he put on an exaggerated show of courtesy. Every garment was displayed for her approval. He fell over himself making her coffee and lighting her cigarettes. If she didn't suspect otherwise, Emerald would have thought she had the ideal partner in Awasthi. But she did know otherwise.

Awasthi was a Hindu. His whole life was dominated by his pride, his sense of honour. For a woman to challenge him the way she had was bound to incense him. She waited to see how he would retaliate.

Nothing happened. The clothes kept coming off the production line the way she'd designed them. The manager went on being respectful and she wondered if she hadn't judged him too harshly. Her partner was nothing if not realistic. Without her he knew he simply couldn't survive. So he decided to do the sensible thing and put his masculinity on hold.

It was difficult to believe, but she had to cling to something.

She would have gone on believing everything was going her way if she hadn't gone window shopping in Grande Baie.

One of Emerald's nieces was getting confirmed and Emerald decided she didn't have the time or the energy to make a new dress for herself. The boutiques on the resort coast boasted the best of the local designers, and if she was lucky she could just find something to fit her off the peg.

In the third shop she came to, she found a selection of her designs. There were two jackets that had been specially commissioned for Selfridges, three skirts and several pairs of trousers. At first Emerald couldn't believe it. There was no way that any of this consignment could have found its way into the shops over here.

Everything she made was packed up the moment it came off the production line and sent out to the airport.

There were special security men to make sure nothing

was tampered with, and now she started to wonder if they had been sloppy.

Before Emerald went back to her office, she decided to check the rest of the shops along the front. When she'd finished, she was glad she'd done a double check for she found her designs in four more boutiques. Nearly everything she had created for the English market was for sale at a fraction of the price right here on the island.

Emerald's first feeling was one of despair. The main reason she had gone into manufacturing was to keep her dressmaking business exclusive. If any of her clients saw the 'Emerald' label in one of the tourist dress shops, they would be tempted to ditch her. She couldn't afford that to happen. Not yet. Not until she had paid off her bank loan and she was starting to make real money. There would be a time, she knew, when she would have to fold up her couture business, but she would be the one who decided when it would be.

She didn't want to be forced into it by somebody stealing her designs.

She decided not to go back to her office. She slipped into her car instead and drove to the international airport in the south. If her crates had been opened over the last few weeks, she needed to know about it. The best way to find out was to have a quiet word with Jay Patel, the security chief.

She and Patel had come from the same village and had both attended the same primary school. They shared the deep bond of childhood and Emerald knew Patel would help her. If somebody had robbed her, he was bound to find out who it was quicker than if she went through the official channels.

After half an hour of sitting in the security chief's smoke-filled office, she was no wiser. Jay Patel, true to form, had checked back over the last eight weeks and not one of her cartons had been opened. They had arrived at his depot as tightly wrapped as when they left Floreal. Not one piece of tape, not one layer of cardboard had been touched between then and the moment they left on the plane to England. Emerald looked at the tall, balding man in desperation.

'I suspected I might have a problem,' she told him. 'Now I know for certain I have got one.'

Patel lit one of his pungent French cigarettes, blowing several smoke rings in the process.

'Do you want to tell me about it?' he asked. Emerald went through the whole story, starting with the moment she found the clothes she'd designed for Selfridges on sale in Grande Baie.

'I thought straightaway someone was stealing from me. Now I know they're not. I don't know what could have happened.'

The security chief looked at her appraisingly. He'd been handsome when he was a boy and even though he'd put on weight and lost most of his hair, he still believed in himself.

'There's more than one way to steal somebody's designs,' he told her finally. 'Have you ever heard of pirating?'

Emerald shook her head. 'What's that? It sounds very romantic.'

'It's not,' the big man replied. 'It's a tacky little crime, committed by tacky little people. People with an axe to grind. Do you know anyone like that working for you?'

Emerald thought about Ashwin Awasthi and her heart sank. Surely he can't be working against me, she thought.

'There is someone in my office who could be bearing a grudge,' she said cautiously. 'But tell me what pirating is and I'll have a better idea.'

The security chief laid it out for her as well as he could.

'A pirate', Patel explained, 'is somebody who doesn't actually break into factories or steal from packing cases. It's a white-collar crime and the person you're looking for

342

is usually in management because he would need access to the designs you're manufacturing.'

Emerald thought about Awasthi again.

'You're talking about the blueprints the machinists work from?' she said, understanding at last.

Patel nodded. 'When everyone has left the factory, the pirate makes a copy of the blueprints he wants, then puts them in his briefcase and walks off with them. His next port of call is usually a friend's factory somewhere else on the island. He's got the designs and it's a simple matter to have them made up. All he has to do is hawk them around the local shops and split the profits with his friend. It's a relatively easy operation if you have the right contacts.'

Emerald sighed. It had to be her factory manager and in her heart she wasn't too surprised. A man like Ashwin Awasthi was too proud, too set in his traditions, to take what he took from her and not retaliate.

'How do I find out for certain who my pirate is?' she asked her friend.

Patel grinned. 'You don't do any snooping around on your own account,' he told her. 'You need to protect your reputation — particularly as you're just starting out. No, what you do is leave Uncle Jay to make a few calls. I know most of the proprietors of those boutiques. If I talk to them in confidence they'll tell me which factory they're buying your designs from. When I know that, I can pay them a visit.' He winked and for a second Emerald caught a glimpse of another Jay Patel. This was a man who could strike terror into the hearts of the guilty. She knew the security chief would have no trouble at all in nailing the pirate once he reached the root of the crime.

Emerald was worried, though. Awasthi might be a rogue and was almost certainly stealing from her, but her line was still being made in his factory. Until she could make other arrangements, she didn't want to rock the boat.

343

She turned to her friend. 'I want you to promise me something,' she said. 'When you find the man who's stealing from me, would you leave him alone? If he's who I think he is, he could make my life very difficult if I made a fuss.'

Patel looked at her in disbelief. 'You're not going to let him get away with it, are you?'

Emerald felt suddenly weary. Being in business on her own was more complicated than she had first thought.

'I might have to let him run for a bit,' she replied. 'But in the end I'll catch up with him. And when I do, he'll be sorry he ever took me on.'

Two days later Jay Patel called her at home and confirmed that Ashwin Awasthi was pirating her designs. Emerald thanked her old schoolfriend for his help.

'I thought it was him all along,' she said. 'He's the only person I know who has a reason for resenting me.'

Patel sounded worried. 'Are you sure you don't want me to do something about him?' he asked. 'He should be stopped, you know.'

'I know,' replied Emerald, 'and he will be. But I have to do it my way.'

She had already formulated a plan. She was going to find another factory to manufacture her designs, but she was going to have to be careful. If Awasthi knew she was looking around, he could throw a tantrum and pull the plug on her. She couldn't afford that. She was in the middle of her second season, and the buyers were hooked.

When Jeremy came into her mind, Emerald had no idea what put him there, for in her heart she had made a vow she wasn't going to go to him for help. There were too many conditions attached to a deal made with him. But when it came down to it, what alternative did she have?

All her friends in Mauritius either worked in the rag trade or knew people who did. If she went to any of them, the entire island would know she wanted out from her factory in Floreal.

With Jeremy on her side it would be different. He wasn't interested in gossip. He was interested in being effective and doing business. Emerald wondered if she dared approach him again. She had nothing to offer him. She still wasn't prepared to hand over any part of Emerald Designs. As long as she could get by on her bank loan, she didn't see any point in giving up her independence. Yet, he had wanted her to succeed. He had even said so when they last met.

I wonder if he really meant it, Emerald thought.

She decided there was only one way to find out. She would have to ask him.

She debated whether to invite Jeremy over to her beach cottage for cocktails. The garden was in full bloom and she felt like showing off her new status on the island. Then she realized she was being silly, so she decided to be straight about it.

She made an appointment with Jeremy's secretary to visit him in his office in Port Louis and at 9.30 the next morning, Emerald arrived at the white concrete skyscraper in her best business suit.

The porter in the front lobby seemed to be expecting her. He checked her name off against a list when she announced herself, then took her to the elevator and told her she would be met at the sixth floor.

Emerald was impressed. When she had first known Jeremy, he had operated from a warehouse on the waterfront. This was a step up in the world and it gave her confidence. If she was going to go to this man for help she needed to be sure he knew what he was doing.

Jeremy's office left her in no doubt of that. It was vast, the size of a small bowling alley. There was a thick pile carpet that tickled her ankles and a large boardroom table made of polished mahogany.

Jeremy didn't invite her to sit there, however. He guided her over to the far end of the room where there was a sofa, a coffee table and what looked suspiciously like a bar.

'Do you do a lot of entertaining here?' Emerald asked.

Jeremy pulled a face. 'If you call drinking with sugar traders entertaining,' he replied wearily. 'Since the increase in our export quotas, I find I spend a lot of time sweet-talking and massaging egos.'

He stopped short. 'You didn't come here to find out how I make a living,' he said. 'You've got your work cut out running your own business.'

Emerald stiffened. He knows something, she thought. She did her best to look unconcerned. 'What have you heard on the grapevine?' she asked.

There was the slightest pause, while Jeremy marshalled his thoughts. 'I'm told you're doing very well,' he said slowly. 'Far too well for someone so new to the business. They also say you have staff problems.'

Emerald swallowed hard. So Jeremy did listen to gossip, after all. For some obscure reason she was disappointed.

'As you seem to know all about me,' she said, tartly, 'perhaps you'll tell me what I'm doing wrong.'

She sounded defensive and she knew it but Jeremy seemed to take it all in his stride.

'As far as I can see, the only mistake you made was going into business with Ashwin Awasthi. He's got a stinking track record. If you'd consulted me in the first place I would have steered you away from him.'

'How could I consult you?' Emerald burst out. 'I thought I made it clear I didn't want a partner.'

For a moment she thought she had ruffled Jeremy's smooth surface. But only for a moment. Years of negotiation had taught him to cover his feelings and when he next spoke his voice was dangerously neutral.

'I don't need to own a stake in you to hand out advice,' he said. 'That comes free. It always has done.'

Emerald hesitated. 'So if I needed help now, you'd come through for me?'

Jeremy didn't say anything. He waited while his secretary poured coffee and offered croissants. When she had gone, he returned to the subject of Emerald's difficulties.

'The only way I can help you,' he told her, 'is to move you away from Ashwin Awasthi and that means finding another factory.'

Emerald felt depressed. 'I knew it was hopeless,' she said, 'I knew it before I came to see you.'

Jeremy put his coffee cup down on the table in front of him. 'Would you still say that if I told you I knew of a place?'

She was all attention now. If she had been more of a businesswoman, she might have hidden her excitement but Emerald wasn't cut out to play executive games. She was a designer with a flair for knowing what women wanted. She played right into Jeremy's hands.

She demanded to know all about the factory on offer: where it was, how much capacity it had.

Jeremy was more than accommodating. He rang through to his secretary who returned with a sheet of paper that had all the details neatly typed in order. It was almost as if he had anticipated her request and had prepared the ground in advance.

It didn't bother Emerald. Her immediate worries were too urgent for her to harbour suspicions about old friends. Besides, Jeremy didn't want anything for his help.

He took her out to see the new plant in the south later that day. It fulfilled all Emerald's requirements. In many ways it was a better proposition than the plant she used now. 'How fast could I move here?' she asked.

Discovering that she could start straight away, she made her deal there and then.

He didn't know it yet, but Ashwin Awasthi was in for a big surprise.

Over the months that followed, Emerald came to rely on Jeremy. Now she knew his advice came with no strings attached, she sought his opinion all the time. There was something reassuring about him. She wasn't quite sure whether it was his experience of running a large company that made her feel safe or that he was one of the oldest friends she had on the island. Whatever it was, she trusted him.

If she had a problem with one of her staff, she would call and tell him about it; if she was unhappy with the job her accountant was doing, she would consult him right away. Little by little, almost before she knew it, Jeremy had become an integral part of her business. There was no aspect of it he didn't know and understand better than she did.

Emerald began to wonder whether she had been too hasty about turning him down as a partner, for the day-to-day mechanics of the production line had begun to irk her. She never encountered another Ashwin Awasthi, but there were too many men amongst her workers with his attitudes. Men who had been brought up in traditional Indian families where women had the status of servants. Emerald couldn't reason with men like that. They simply didn't listen to her. Often she would have to send in one of her senior staff to deal with them.

It wasn't the best solution. Tempers became frayed, communications frequently broke down, but it was the best she could do and she often wondered if she wasn't wasting her energy on petty trifling matters. Her strength, she knew, was as a designer, and the backbreaking detail of running a manufacturing business seemed increasingly to be a waste of her time.

Emerald kept her feelings to herself until her fourth

season. It was then that she came to a turning point. The London stores she supplied had given her the ultimate vote of confidence. They wanted her to make up orders for their provincial branches. This effectively quadrupled her business and brought her a new headache.

She needed a bigger bank loan. It was a simple equation when she looked at it: to produce four times the amount of stock she needed four times the amount of money for a period of thirty days. After that the stores settled their accounts and she was solvent again.

Emerald explained the whole thing to the credit manager of the Consolidated Hong Kong Bank where she had her overdraft, yet she didn't seem to make much of an impression.

Jonny Chang might not have had the traditional Indian upbringing, but as far as his attitudes about women were concerned he could just as well have done. He simply didn't believe Emerald was capable of handling the overdraft she was demanding.

'It's a big responsibility,' he told her. 'Supposing your clients don't pay up on time, then where will you be?'

She assured him that after two years of dealing with them she could vouch for the reliability of the English stores, but Chang wasn't convinced.

'There's always a first time,' he said. 'And the money you're asking for is just too much to take a chance on.'

Emerald sat and haggled with the credit manager for over an hour but it was no good. Chang didn't believe in her.

After that she made an appointment with his superior and put her case to him. She got the same reception — except the senior man was more outspoken.

'You're a woman in business,' he told her with badly disguised contempt. 'I'd be risking my job if I trusted you.'

Emerald didn't run to Jeremy, not immediately. She had too much pride to admit defeat after only one setback. There had to be a bank manager on Mauritius who would go for the opportunity she was offering.

She couldn't find one. She trawled round all twelve banks on the island but none wanted to gamble on a woman.

If Jeremy had gone to any one of them with this proposition, Emerald thought, they would have accepted him without question. She told him so when she saw him. He was immediately sympathetic.

'You should have let me go in your place,' he told her.

'How could you?' she asked. 'You're not a director of Emerald Designs.'

He looked at her steadily. 'That's easily rectified,' he said. 'I told you a long time ago you needed a business partner.'

Emerald made a face. 'And you're willing to step into the breach.'

Jeremy looked wary. 'Only if you want me to,' he said. 'If the idea of me looking over your shoulder makes you nervous, then forget it.'

Emerald realized she was being silly. This man had been guiding her hand for well over a year now. She didn't pay him anything for it and he had no shareholding in her company, yet increasingly she leant on him.

'If we were to go into business together,' she said cautiously, 'I suppose you'd want me to make it worth your while.'

'No,' Jeremy told her. 'I would make it worth your while. You just told me you were having a problem raising money. I can provide that money.'

For a moment neither of them said anything, then Emerald broke the silence. 'How much would you want of my company in return?' she asked.

'I think twenty-five per cent would be fair.'

It was less than the banks were asking for, and Emerald knew now that Jeremy wasn't trying to cheat her.

She held out her hand. 'Let's do it,' she said. 'It's the best offer I've had all week.'

CHAPTER 38

London, 1988

The advert was like every other he had seen in *Vogue* magazine. It showed an angular model girl power-dressed in padded shoulders and a short tight skirt. On her ears and pinned to her lapel were the great lumps of glitter all the girls seemed to be wearing nowadays. But it wasn't what she wore, or even how she looked that interested Richard. The discreet line of type at the bottom of the page was all he wanted to know about. It said simply: 'Emerald Designs. London and New York.'

So she had finally made it to the Big Apple. His money had helped her, of course. She would never have had the leeway without it. The sheer investment in time and materials would have been too much for her.

It wasn't just his capital that had put her on the map, though. If she had been less talented, or less determined, he might have lost every penny. His father made him aware of that right from the start, but then Jeremy put him in touch with a lot of things.

For the past two years he had followed the progress of Emerald's life in Mauritius. He knew who her friends were and where she lived. He was in touch with every aspect of her business. He even knew the minutiae of her daily routine: what time she got up, where she had lunch. Sometimes when Jeremy was with her, he even knew what she had to eat.

Richard couldn't know Emerald first-hand any more, that privilege had been taken away from him. He could merely observe her from the sidelines and it consoled him when he felt lonely, and he did feel lonely. Increasingly lonely as the affair with Caroline wound to an end.

What brought it to a head was her wanting to move in on him. Richard was resisting. He knew they couldn't go on like this. Either he committed himself or they called it quits and he wondered why he was dithering. It wasn't like him to behave like this. If his mistress had been a subsidiary of his that was foundering, he would have stepped in and taken action.

The notion amused him. What if Caroline were a business problem, he thought. How would I handle it? He started analysing it the way he always did, heading a piece of paper with her name and dividing it into sections. At the top of one column he wrote down, 'Reasons to continue'. At the top of the other, 'Reasons to terminate'.

He thought about the first heading. She was beautiful and accomplished. He could take her everywhere from the races to the opera and she was the perfect companion. His friends liked her – well, most of them at any rate. Tim didn't have much time for her and it wouldn't occur to him to introduce her to his father, but then there were other reasons why he wouldn't do that.

With an effort he concentrated on the piece of paper in front of him. What else did Caroline have going for her? He laughed at himself for leaving such an obvious accomplishment last. She was very sexy. When it came to pleasing him in bed, this girlfriend of his had no equal. But she doesn't stir my heart, he thought absently.

He moved on to his second category. Reasons to terminate. For a moment he could think of nothing. She didn't have any bad habits he could think of. Apart from her wanting to move in, there was nothing they disagreed about.

There has to be something wrong with me, Richard thought. He took a hard look at himself in an attempt to discover what it was. When the answer finally came, it was so obvious he wondered why he hadn't thought of it before he started this silly game.

He didn't love Caroline, and because he didn't love her, it was wrong to go on pretending.

He looked back over the last four years and wondered how he could have deluded himself for so long.

I put up with second best, he admitted to himself, because I didn't have the courage to go after what I really wanted. I was too frightened of failing to try and find Emerald again. I've resorted to behaving like a schoolboy. I bought a stake in her company so I felt I owned a part of her. I got my father to spy on her and send me progress reports.

He sighed, realizing he had wasted his time. All I needed to do, he thought, was to get on a plane to Mauritius and ask her to come back to me. Win or lose it's what I have to do now. Because if I don't, I'll never be happy again.

The Weiss Hotel on Park Avenue was famous not for its decoration, which looked a little like the inside of a Viennese chocolate box, nor for its cuisine, which regularly won prizes in *Gourmet* magazine. What this swish joint on the Upper East Side had that everyone came back for was simply the most stunning view of the park.

The architect who designed it had made sure that every window in every room looked out on a vista of tall trees and rolling turf. It was easy to imagine you weren't in the city at all, but somewhere upstate where life was quieter and more genteel.

The quiet life was the furthest thing from Emerald's mind as she went through the last details of the show she was staging in under an hour.

All the clothes were there, pressed and ready on the rails. The accessories that went with every outfit were sitting in large cardboard boxes and the makeup artistes, the hairdressers, model girls and assistants were all in the process of preparing themselves for the final deadline.

Emerald suddenly felt superfluous. She had worked herself to a standstill for six months for this moment. Now it had come and the show had been prepared, there was nothing left for her to do. Her only role was to stand by on the sidelines and watch all the people she had paid to go to work for her.

She felt oddly frustrated. The show could be a riproaring success or a damp squib and there wasn't a damn thing she could do about it.

For the tenth time that afternoon, she checked her appearance. She was standing in front of the mirror the model girls used and the view she got of herself was brutally honest. I look hard, she thought, checking her flawlessly applied makeup. In a few years that hardness will translate into something matronly. The realization made her shiver.

How did it happen, she wondered. When was the moment I stopped being a girl and turned into this? When she showed herself in public today, she wanted the world to believe she was powerful and successful, and she'd designed herself an elegant, formal little suit that shouted success.

I've certainly achieved that, Emerald reflected. If I was doing business with me, I'd be scared out of my mind.

She glanced at her watch. It was seven o'clock already. All the buyers should be here by now, sipping the vintage Bollinger and wondering what kind of clothes they'll be seeing.

I should be out there, Emerald thought. She grabbed hold of her quilted leather bag and hurried through the doorway into the main ballroom.

The buzz in the air communicated immediately. Emerald had experienced it on first nights and film premières in Hollywood. Everyone there was expecting something new, something dazzling, and she latched on to their excitement and started to breathe it in. It was as intoxicating as the champagne in her glass and she discovered she wasn't frightened any more. The buyers from Bloomingdales, who had put the fear of God into her, no longer affected her. She found herself flitting between the groups of stern-faced, powerful women who between them controlled the purses of the city's biggest stores.

Jeremy would be proud of me, she thought. When I tell him how I handled this party, he'll feel sorry he wasn't here to see me in action.

For a moment she missed her partner. Building Emerald Designs had been lonely for her and she often wondered how she would have fared without him there in the background. She laughed at herself. If the feminist lobby knew what I was thinking, she told herself, I'd be drummed out of the sisterhood.

She saw her guests assembling on the tiny gilded chairs positioned around the catwalk. She had a vision of her models struggling into the clothes. It propelled her backstage. She knew she couldn't do anything to help her show right now, but she needed to be there behind the scenes.

Her staff were waiting for her. They had set up a chair in the wings so that she would see the mannequins as they came out on to the ramp.

As she sat down, somebody in the back clicked on the music tape, and the strains of Vivaldi's *The Four Seasons* flooded into the room. Then Emerald caught sight of the first girl.

She was wearing one of the city suits Emerald had designed for the autumn. It had a casual unstructured jacket, and as the girl walked past her and out into the room she could sense the audience's reaction. It was a mixture of surprise and something else.

They're intrigued, Emerald realized. They had to be. Nobody in New York has seen a jacket like that from any other designer. She held her breath as five more girls walked on to the catwalk in her suits. They were all permutations of the same theme and she wondered how the tough businesswomen would finally judge her. She could get their attention, she knew that, but could she make them buy?

She pushed her worries to the back of her mind as the show went on.

Along with the suits, Emerald had completed a range of separates, some formal dresses and a cocktail collection. As her models paraded each look, she listened as hard as she could for another signal. But this audience had seen it all before, and they weren't giving away any secrets.

She sighed. There were fifteen minutes to go before it was all over. Fifteen minutes before Emerald had to step out there and take her bow. I'll know then if I've won or not, she thought.

The show seemed to drag on for ever. Occasionally there was a polite rustle of interest when one of her newer ideas came on. But that was all. Then came the grand finale.

Without ceremony, two of her models grabbed hold of her and pulled her on to the catwalk. She wasn't fully aware of the moment when the audience started applauding. They could have started at the end of the show or waited until she made her appearance. When she walked right out into the middle of the ballroom, all she could hear was the thundering of dozens of pairs of hands. Then she heard her name being called and she realized they liked her after all. Her first show in this town looked like it was an unqualified success and she felt dizzy with relief.

When Emerald had left America last, it had been with her tail between her legs. She had been branded a failure then.

The world has a short memory. Now she was returning in triumph and nobody in the room could even remember the girl she once was.

She walked right up to the end of the catwalk and sank

to her knees in a deep bow. All around her, her models strutted and posed in the glitter that was the high spot of her collection. As she rose on her feet, Emerald let her eyes take in the audience. Everyone was there, and Emerald peered into the crowd trying to recognize who was who.

All of a sudden her gaze stopped. For three rows back, looking for all the world as if he owned the place, Richard was sitting nursing a glass of champagne. He couldn't have known Emerald had seen him, for he seemed fascinated by the antics on the catwalk, but she was taking no chances. As soon as she could, she turned on her heel and hotfooted it back to the changing-room.

Almost immediately she found herself at the centre of an hysterical crowd of model girls and drunken sales staff. Normally they would have absorbed all her attention, but the sight of Richard had rattled her. Emerald had managed to put him out of her mind for four years, to pretend he didn't exist. Now she was fighting a losing battle. For somewhere outside he was waiting for her.

She wondered what she was going to do about it. There was a back way out of the hotel. When she had finished with her staff, she could quietly disappear into the night and she and Richard need never meet.

Then she realized he wasn't here by chance. Men like Richard didn't go to fashion shows. He came expressly to see me, she thought. If I avoid him now, I'll never know why.

She decided to go out in front and find him. Without pausing to check herself in the mirror, she started to push her way through the mêlée.

The room, when she got to it, was in total disarray. Half-empty champagne glasses littered every surface. A number of people appeared to have dropped their canapés on the floor and there was a sad, end-of-party feeling about the place.

He must have gone, Emerald thought. Nobody with any

sense would have hung around here any longer than they had to.

She felt a hand on her arm, and before she'd even turned round she knew it was him.

'Congratulations,' said a familiar voice. 'The new collection's going to make a fortune.'

He hadn't changed at all and Emerald was startled at the effect he still had on her. For some part of her, a part she'd lost touch with, wanted to run into his arms. She stifled the impulse.

'What brings you here?' she said, keeping her voice light, doing her damnedest to look as if she didn't care.

She didn't fool Richard for a second. 'You brought me here,' he said softly. 'But you know that.'

There were a thousand things Emerald wanted to ask him, but before she did, there was one thing she had to know.

'Why did you take so long?' she asked. 'I'd almost given up on you.'

Richard smiled, and there was a sadness in his eyes she hadn't seen before.

'I didn't know you were waiting,' he told her.

Emerald felt herself starting to blush. Until that very moment, she hadn't known she was waiting either.

She suddenly felt helpless, as if she had been overtaken by a force stronger than her will and she couldn't think what to do next. Richard must have sensed this, for he took her gently by the arm and steered her into a corner.

'You look as if you need a strong drink,' he said. 'What can I get you?'

Emerald grinned, recovering some of her composure. 'It's not a drink I need, it's a square meal. With all the excitement I haven't eaten all day.'

Richard asked where she wanted to go and Emerald thought for a moment. If they went somewhere quiet she knew she would be lost. She was more vulnerable to this man than ever and she didn't want to be backed into a corner.

At least that's what her head told her. Her heart was communicating an entirely different message. But she refused to listen.

'Why don't we grab a steak at Smith and Wollensky?' she said.

Richard looked at her, thinking she had temporarily lost her sanity, but he didn't veto the suggestion. If Emerald wanted to eat salt beef in the middle of Times Square, he would have gone along with it.

When they got to the steakhouse, there was a line of people standing waiting to get in. It was a good twenty minutes before they even got a sight of the bell captain and even then they had to wait for a table.

Standing by the bar, jostled by Irishmen on every side, Emerald began to have second thoughts about the place. It had started to remind her of a locker-room in an all-male club and she longed for the comfort of the Pierre or the Côté Basque.

She looked at Richard nervously. 'Maybe we should try somewhere quieter,' she said.

But Richard was starting to enjoy the atmosphere. There was something masculine about the dark wood dining-room. In a difficult situation, it gave him a certain comfort.

'The table will be ready any minute,' he assured Emerald. 'It's too late to change our minds.'

He was right. Five minutes later a tan-jacketed waiter, built like a quarterback, came to show them through.

As she walked behind Richard, Emerald realized she wasn't hungry any more. She had lived on champagne all day long and now, when she really needed a meal, she was past it.

She glanced at the tables on either side of her, seeing plates full of lamb chops the size of fists. There's no way I'm going to get anything down me, she thought.

As soon as they sat down, the waiter went into his spiel. 'Who gets the sirloin?' he boomed. 'Which one of you guys will get lucky with the split lobster?'

Richard ordered for them both and Emerald felt grateful.

Richard went on making things easy for her. Instead of talking about why he was there, he steered the conversation round to her business. He seemed fascinated with everything Emerald had achieved and he wanted to know how she'd done it.

With a certain hesitation she told him about Jeremy. 'I ran into him at the races,' she said. 'He was the last person I expected to see, but he was so nice to me, I couldn't really ignore him. Then a week or so later, he rang and asked me for a drink.' She paused before going on. 'I should have turned him down. I wasn't all that interested in going over old times. But I had a problem with my business and nobody to talk to about it.'

'So you went to him for advice,' Richard said.

Emerald nodded. 'Jeremy was unexpectedly helpful. He actually put the idea in my head to go for the export market. I don't think I would ever have got there on my own.'

Richard observed Emerald as she spoke. She was looking very beautiful that night. Better than he remembered and he knew that her new sophistication was everything to do with her success.

He wondered whether to tell her that the whole thing with his father had been the idea they had concocted between them in Paris. All he'd wanted to do was get back to her through her business, only he'd got in deeper than he'd anticipated. Emerald was starting to depend on Jeremy, she actually needed him, and Richard didn't have the heart to disillusion her.

She'll have to know the whole story one day, he thought. But not yet. Not until we're a couple again and none of it matters any more.

He turned his attention back to Emerald, doing his best to concentrate on what she was saying, but it was hopeless. The noise in the restaurant wasn't just intrusive, it was deafening.

With a certain relief Richard saw their dinner was arriving. There was something basic about the food which at another time Richard might have relished. Tonight it made him feel slightly queasy.

He glanced at Emerald and saw she was having the same problem. I've got to get her out of here, he thought.

'Come on,' he said rising from his seat. 'We're leaving.'

Before Emerald could ask why, Richard was standing beside her, pulling her to her feet.

'But what are we going to do about dinner?' she asked.

Richard grinned. 'Don't worry about dinner,' he told her, 'I've decided to feed us back in my suite. The service isn't much, but the food's a damn sight more appetizing.'

Years ago, when Emerald had first met Richard, she had eaten dinner with him in a New York restaurant and gone back to his hotel suite afterwards. Now she was doing so all over again and she wondered what the hell was going on.

It wasn't that she didn't want him. To deny that would be to deny herself. But there was something casual about the way he assumed she wanted to be alone with him that bothered her.

He thinks he can behave as if nothing has happened in five years, she thought. That he can just click his fingers and I'll come running like some geisha girl.

They were back at the Weiss Hotel on Park Avenue and Richard was escorting her into the elevator that serviced the private apartments. Emerald stopped at the entrance and looked at him coldly.

'You haven't asked me if I wanted to come up to your room,' she said.

For a moment Richard looked confused. Then he realized what she was getting at.

'I wasn't planning a seduction,' he told her. 'I just thought after Smith and Wollensky, you might appreciate dining in private.'

With a great show of reluctance she let him show her into the elevator, then as they made their way up, she kept her mouth firmly shut. If Richard wanted to make the running, he was welcome. Emerald was in no mood to put herself out for anyone after her tough day.

The apartment at the top of the building was a revelation and was unlike any hotel room Emerald had ever seen before.

The nearest thing she could compare it with was a ritzy duplex a television actress friend of hers had on the Upper East Side. The whole area was open-plan, with a circular staircase connecting the two levels.

'You look like you're doing pretty well these days,' she observed.

Richard smiled and walked over to a lacquered cabinet, which concealed a bar.

'Things improved when Rolf officially retired at the end of last year.'

He changed the subject. 'Would you like a glass of champagne?'

He's spoiling me, Emerald thought. He's lured me into his parlour like a spider and now he's moving in for the kill.

All of a sudden it didn't really seem to matter. Richard wasn't some pick-up, for heaven's sake. What could she lose by letting him make a fuss of her?

She accepted the champagne, then she let him talk her into dinner.

'The kitchen downstairs could conjure up something elaborate for us,' he told her, 'or I could cook you an omelette.'

In all the time she had known him, Richard had never cooked for her. Not even once. 'I never knew you could handle yourself in the kitchen,' she said, smiling.

'I'm a hotelier,' he told her. 'I worked my way up through the system. If you like, I'll demonstrate how I wait on tables as well.'

She let him take over completely. While she sipped at the crisp, sparkling wine, Richard went to work on the dining table in the corner of the vast room. There was a certain grace about the way he did it. Most men wouldn't have had a clue about dressing a table, but Richard knew every move from folding the linen napkins to the order of silver. It was as if he was creating a work of art and she saw the satisfaction it gave him.

I lived with this man for over two years of my life, Emerald thought, yet I never knew this about him.

Almost before she knew it, Richard was putting things on the table. There was hot garlic bread, an exquisite green salad and the omelettes themselves.

There was a certain knack to cooking them that Emerald had never quite mastered. It was something to do with browning them on the outside while leaving the centres meltingly moist. Richard had the technique off pat, and even though she didn't think she could eat a thing, Emerald found herself finishing everything and wiping the plate with what remained of the bread.

He watched her like an indulgent parent. 'Don't eat everything on the table,' he admonished. 'You won't have any room for dessert.'

She looked at him. 'You mean there's more?'

He disappeared back into the kitchen and when he returned he was carrying a concoction of meringue, ice-cream and hot black cherries.

'I can't pretend I did this all myself,' he said. 'The hotel generally leaves one in the freezing compartment for me. All I have to do when I get back is heat it up.'

A feeling of utter contentment started to seep through Emerald, beginning in her toes and working right up to the roots of her hair. Sitting in Richard's suite at the top of the Weiss was like being cocooned in the nearest thing to her mother's womb. Everything she could possibly want was to hand. She didn't even have to reach out for anything.

'Do you always live like this?' she asked him.

He looked thoughtful. 'What do you mean?'

'Are all the places where you stay as well run? I don't remember anywhere like this when we were together.'

She wished she hadn't said it, for when she saw his face she realized she had made him sad.

'When we were together,' he told her, 'I didn't need this standard of service in my apartments. I had you to look after me.'

'It couldn't have been that difficult finding someone else to do what I did.'

Richard didn't answer her immediately. He walked over to the bar where he located a very old French brandy and poured some out for each of them. Then he motioned her to join him by the vast granite fireplace.

'Do you want me to be honest with you,' he said handing her a glass, 'or are you in the mood to be flattered?'

Emerald sighed. 'Give it to me straight.'

Richard looked into the fire and she had the feeling he was going over and discarding whole paragraphs of conversation. Finally he said: 'It was very easy finding someone to take your place. I have a certain influence, I'm not that bad-looking. There was a queue of candidates a week after you walked out on me.' He took a sip of his drink. 'There was only one problem. I wasn't interested in any of them. I'm still not.'

Emerald looked at him from under her eyelashes. 'I can't believe you've lived like a hermit.'

He shrugged. 'Of course I haven't. There's a girl around I've known for a long time. When there's nothing better to do we go through the motions.'

There was something a bit too studied about the way he

365

said it. Nobody was that offhand about their mistress. He was concealing something from her.

'Have I met this girl of yours?' she asked him outright. Richard looked uncomfortable. 'Actually you have. It's Caroline.'

Emerald wanted to hit him. The whole evening from beginning to end had been a setup. Richard hadn't come flying across continents to beg her to come back to him. All he had done was re-establish contact with one of his old faithfuls.

He probably has a string of us in different parts of the world, she thought. Now he knows I'll be spending time in Manhattan, he's got me earmarked for this part of his territory.

She snapped down her drink on one of the polished surfaces and made to leave. 'It's time I was on my way,' she said.

'Don't go,' Richard pleaded. 'We haven't settled anything.'

Now Emerald was really cross. 'What on earth have we got to settle? I'm not interested in becoming another one of your girlfriends, if that's what you're after.'

Richard looked pained. 'It's Caroline, isn't it?' he said. 'You're upset about her.'

Emerald was on her feet now and marching towards the door. 'What's there to be upset about?' she demanded. 'If you want to sleep with her, it's nothing to do with me. You and I ceased to be an item a long time ago.'

It was pointless arguing with her. She had a funny set expression on her face Richard had noticed earlier when she got into the elevator. He cursed his bad judgement for mentioning Caroline. He might have known it would have had this effect on her, but he wanted to be honest.

He went after her, reaching out for her elbow and swinging her round to face him. 'I need to explain things,' he said. 'At least hear me out.'

Emerald struggled to get out of the hold he had on her but Richard was strong and in the end she stopped trying.

'I don't want to hear your excuses,' she said curtly. 'I'd be happier if you'd just let me get out of this place in one piece.'

If she hadn't looked at him then, if she hadn't seen the desolation on his face and been moved by it, she might have been all right. As it was, something in him cried out to her and the feeling was so strong, she was incapable of walking away from it.

'What is it that you want?' she snapped.

Richard didn't say anything, but pulled her close. As she came within the orbit of his familiar warmth, she felt herself weaken.

'This isn't going to solve anything,' Emerald told him. But he didn't seem to hear a word she said.

He kissed her, and in that moment she stopped arguing.

The touch of him seemed to have turned her into a totally different woman. A woman without logic or pride or any kind of control.

Emerald felt herself reaching for him, burying her fingers in the nape of his neck where the hair grew thickly. When they were together she had always done this as a prelude to making love. It was a signal between them, an intimate secret ritual and he recognized it and responded.

They were standing in the hallway and Richard scooped Emerald up and carried her back into the room, gently depositing her on the long leather ottoman in front of the fire. Then he started taking off her clothes. There was nothing urgent about the way he did it. It was as if he knew instinctively what was best for both of them and Emerald let him take the lead.

He had caressed her a hundred times before, yet every time he touched her nipples, her belly, the tender skin inside her thighs, she shuddered the way she had done the very first time.

Then something changed. She stopped him leading the way. There was a subtlety about the way she did it. Richard almost didn't realize she had taken over until it was too late.

They were lying side by side on the sofa and Emerald rolled over until she was sitting astride him. She could feel his penis hard against her stomach and she took it confidently in both her hands and guided it inside her.

She had never been in so much control before, for she had always wanted her lover's pleasure. Now she needed to satisfy herself first. It was as if she was oblivious to any feelings but her own and Richard didn't stop what she was doing. It was curiously exciting to see her like this and he wondered where she lost her meekness. Something has happened to her, he thought. Or someone. And the thought of a rival made up his mind. If it takes me all night, he vowed, she will finish up as mine again.

It was like a duel between two evenly matched gladiators. What drove them on was not lust, or even pleasure, but the need to preserve their own separate identities.

Nobody won. Nobody could win, for what neither of them predicted was the final moment of their union.

After it happened they looked at each other with a kind of wonder.

'Do you think we've been very silly?' Emerald asked.

Richard nodded. 'We were out of our minds,' he told her. 'You and I shouldn't be allowed to spend four days apart, let alone four years.'

Emerald looked around her. They were still surrounded by dirty dishes and the embers of the dying fire. There was something familiar and domestic about the scene and she felt a longing to straighten everything up the way she always did in the past when they were together.

'Do you want to go back to where we were?' she asked him.

Richard looked at her seriously. 'You're asking if I want

you to move back in with me?' He hesitated for a moment. 'Darling,' he said, 'I think it's a terrible idea. I would no more have you as my permanent mistress than fly to the moon.'

He saw the dismay on her face and he drew her into his arms. 'I'm not turning you down,' he said softly. 'I'm asking you to be my wife. It's the only way I can see us being together.'

Emerald pulled away from him. Then she got up and went over to the table where she started to stack the dishes. Richard looked enquiring.

'Have you listened to a word I've been saying?' he demanded. 'Or has it all gone in one ear and out the other?'

She smiled. 'Of course I've been listening to you,' she told him. 'I think getting married is a wonderful idea. I just don't know how you're going to explain it to Caroline.'

Richard had a very simple plan. He wanted Emerald to fly back with him to London where they would be married by special licence. When their future together was finally settled he told her all the other elements of their lives would fall into place. Emerald wasn't convinced.

'Where will we live?' she wanted to know. 'In Mauritius where I have my business, or London where you have yours?'

Her question took Richard by surprise. He'd never seriously considered that he would have to compromise. He was the main breadwinner, after all, the man with the important international career.

'Surely you can move to London?' he said. 'After all, you only manufacture overseas. You can design anywhere you want.'

In essence he was right. It wouldn't be difficult handing over the responsibility of the factory to Jeremy but Emerald didn't want to be a complete pushover. If they were going to make a fresh start, Richard had to know she wasn't going to behave like an accessory.

'Manufacturing isn't my only interest,' she told him. 'I have a dressmaking business that needs me two days a week. What am I meant to do about that?'

'You're going to have to close it down,' Richard told her firmly. 'We both need to make some sacrifices.'

If she hadn't loved him, she could have quite cheerfully strangled him.

'What sacrifice are you going to make?' she wanted to know.

It was a tactless question for it brought them back to the subject of Caroline. They had been quarrelling about her for days now. Richard didn't want to have things out with the journalist and as far as he was concerned their relationship wasn't that serious. If he just got married and told her about it afterwards, he was convinced she would understand.

Emerald didn't think it was right. She had every reason to dislike Caroline, but there was no way she wanted her treated like dirty laundry.

In the end they called a truce. Richard would do the decent thing and let Caroline down lightly, and while he was organizing his life, Emerald would fly back to Mauritius and rearrange hers.

As she boarded the flight on Sunday night, she realized she was going to have her work cut out. The whole structure of her business was going to need reorganizing and getting rid of her couture interest was going to be difficult. There were clients who had been around for a long time now. Women who depended on her. How was she going to explain to them that it was no longer convenient to design their wardrobes?

Emerald strapped herself into her seat while she wrestled with the problem. It makes sense, she thought, to do what I'm doing. Even if Richard wasn't in the picture, I'd still have to ditch the dressmaking. Now I've launched the American collection, I need to concentrate on the mass market and I need to spread my base. There's no way I can keep in touch with everything from a beach house in Mauritius.

She saw the stewardess approach with a tray of cold champagne. Normally she avoided alcohol on long flights, but she was so preoccupied with her problems that she took a glass to help her think.

I'm going to need Jeremy, she thought. If I have to move away, he's the only one I trust to keep an eye on things.

Then she wondered how she was going to explain everything to him. He knew nothing about her and Richard. She'd made a point of never mentioning his name. Now she regretted it.

It's so out of the blue, she thought. One moment I behaved as if he didn't have a son. The next, I calmly announce I'm going to marry him.

She finished her drink and signalled for a refill. The prospect of telling Jeremy about her love life was starting to worry her.

Where do I start, she asked herself. Do I go right back to that first meeting in New York and level with him, or do I pretend I ran into Richard a few days ago and it was love at first sight? Neither solution pleased her. Jeremy was never going to believe the love-at-first-sight story. And the truth? The truth simply made her look vulnerable.

She had invested a lot of time building a professional relationship with Jeremy. She liked what they had now, for there was respect on both sides.

If I tell him I'm Richard's girlfriend, she thought, he'll never look at me the same way again.

In London, Richard had his own problems. He had a date with Caroline that evening and he wasn't looking forward to it one little bit.

This is the second time I've had to tell her it's over, he thought morosely. By rights she should slaughter me.

What made everything worse was that Caroline was cooking dinner that night. He had wanted to take her somewhere expensive, but she wouldn't hear of it.

'I want you all to myself tonight,' she told him when he called her at her office.

There was no way he could talk her out of it and at 7.30 he knew his mistress, armed with an electric whisk and a basketful of groceries, was going to descend on him like an avenging angel.

The prospect of it made him splash a little too much whisky into his glass. He wondered how he let himself in for it but he knew the answer to that one already. He had let Emerald talk him into behaving like a gentleman.

It occurred to him to telephone Caroline and call the evening off but just as he was making his way over to the phone, the doorbell went. He looked at his watch. It had just gone seven. The woman was early.

He did his best to look pleased to see her, but it was an effort, for she so obviously had gone out of her way to please him. From the look of her, she had spent all afternoon in the hairdressers and she seemed to be wearing far too much makeup for a cosy evening at home.

'Steady on,' he said. 'I haven't been away for six months.'

Caroline's enthusiasm couldn't be damped. She was determined to put on a production and nothing, not even a reluctant lover, was going to stand in her way.

Without even stopping for a drink, she whirled through to the kitchen where she proceeded to set everything in motion for a gourmet feast. Stock was put on to boil, vegetables were arranged in neat rows on the chopping board and an array of casserole dishes and saucepans Richard had never seen before started to appear in front of his eyes.

She must have brought these in when I wasn't looking, he thought. His heart sank. He had done his best to be casual about this liaison, he hadn't wanted Caroline to assume she was a permanent part of his life, but she had had other ideas. Only now, when he was going to call it quits, did Richard realize how badly he had underestimated her.

He started to feel shabby. I can't have her dancing attendance on me tonight, he thought. It would be too cruel.

He took hold of her arm and started to lead her out of the kitchen.

'Dinner can wait for a moment,' he told her. 'There are a couple of things I need to talk to you about, and I can do without you chopping onions.'

She didn't argue, but went over to the drinks cabinet and got herself a glass of wine.

Richard noticed how surely she did it. It was almost as if she owned the place already and the irritation he felt with her attitude gave him the courage he needed.

'We seem to be misunderstanding each other at the moment,' he told her without preamble. 'You're behaving as if there's something serious going on between us. Things aren't that way at all.'

Caroline reacted as if Richard had smacked her.

He wondered if he was being too hard, for when she spoke her voice came to him in a whisper. 'What are you trying to tell me?' she asked.

He set his face. 'I'm saying,' he went on, 'that there's no future for us. There never has been.'

When he looked at her again, he saw that she was crying.

'Are you turning me out? Is that what you're doing?'

He cursed his stupidity in drinking too much whisky.

Now he really needed a slug, he was terrified it would send him into oblivion. He made do with a cigarette instead.

'It's not the end of the world,' he said as kindly as he could. 'You'll soon find someone else.'

But Caroline had no intention of making things easy for him. The tears coursed down her cheeks like a minor flood, smudging and blurring the heavy makeup she had put on earlier. She didn't cry quietly either. Great sobs emanated from her.

If Richard hadn't felt like such a heel, he might have let Caroline run herself down but he couldn't stand by and let her do it. They had been friends as well as lovers. He owed her some kind of solace. So he went over to where she was sitting and put his arms round her.

'I didn't know you cared about me that way,' he said. 'I'm so very sorry.'

But Caroline wasn't interested in his sympathy. She pushed him away and the small act of rejection seemed to give her courage, for she got out of her chair and announced she was going to the bedroom to tidy herself up.

Richard wondered whether the worst was over, and if she would bother to cook the meal she had brought. He rather hoped she would throw the whole thing into the garbage and demand to be taken to the Ritz.

Twenty minutes later, Caroline came back. The chignon the hairdresser had given her had been taken down. Now Caroline's hair was crinkly and back to normal. To Richard's relief she'd scraped off most of the makeup as well and she looked almost human.

He couldn't think of anything to say, so he went and fetched the bottle of white wine and offered her another drink. She refused it.

'In my condition, I don't think I should.'

Richard did a double take. 'What condition?' he asked her.

Caroline paused for a moment, allowing an ominous silence to settle between them. Then, when she had his full attention, she made her announcement.

'I'm pregnant,' she said quietly. 'I thought you would have guessed by now.'

Suddenly it all made sense. The new hairdo, the home-cooked dinner, the hysterical tears over the end of what was a better-than-nothing affair. He must have been blind not to have seen all the clues.

'How long have you known?' Richard asked her.

Caroline made a face. 'I was almost sure before you went away, but I got the results of the test yesterday.'

'What are you going to do about it?'

Caroline looked very calm, almost serene and Richard

felt uneasy. She was settling back on to his sofa like a broody earth mother and he knew her answer even before she opened her mouth.

'I'm going to have the baby,' she said firmly. 'I thought about it all last night and I've decided that's what I want.'

Richard felt trapped by the oldest trick in the book. Move in on a man and when he shows no signs of settling down, get pregnant and force his hand.

'What made you do this?' he demanded of Caroline. 'You know I wasn't committed. I never have been.'

She looked stricken and somehow pathetic. 'But I was committed,' she insisted. 'I truly believed that if we gave it time, you'd realize you wanted me all along.'

Richard thought he was going to explode. 'We've given it years,' he told her snappily. 'We even lived together once and it still didn't work.'

Caroline started to cry all over again, only this time he wasn't moved to comfort her.

'How are you going to look after this baby?' Richard asked. 'It's not like taking on a dog or a cat, you know. What you're taking on is a full-time responsibility. Have you thought about how it's going to affect your work?'

The question didn't rattle her. 'My work isn't a problem,' she said. 'I'll take maternity leave like every other woman executive who's had a baby. Afterwards, I'll hire a nanny. A lot of working girls do that sort of thing nowadays. I'm not exactly breaking new ground.'

But she is breaking new ground, Richard thought. She's simply not the type to go all maternal. The Caroline I know is interested in the City and queening it at cocktail parties. In that order.

He made one last attempt to talk her out of it.

'I don't think you're being quite rational,' he said. 'When you're in your right mind again, you could regret this.'

Caroline looked stubborn. 'Not as much as I'll regret killing it,' she shot out.

The reality of what she was saying hit him. Caroline was going to have his child, the baby they had made together. It wasn't a wanted child or a planned child, and if he'd been in his right mind, Richard would have walked away from the whole thing. But somehow he didn't have the heart. He had been unwanted himself. For years while he was growing up, his father had denied him and he still couldn't quite forgive him for it. He was an adult now, yet there were times when he looked at Jeremy and blamed him for keeping his distance.

Will my son look at me like that in years to come, he wondered. When I'm married to Emerald, will Caroline's illegitimate boy hide his face in shame when my name is mentioned? I can't do it, he thought. I can't put a child of mine through that kind of suffering.

He looked at the sharp-featured girl sitting opposite him and he was overcome with sadness, for she wasn't Emerald. She wasn't the woman he wanted.

'Can I ask you something?' Richard said. 'Did you ever love me, or was I just convenient?'

Caroline looked at him in puzzlement. 'Of course I loved you,' she said. 'I still do.'

Her reply finally made up his mind. He would never love her, he had known that for a long time now, yet he owed her something. He couldn't turn his back on her.

'I know it's a little late in the day,' Richard said, 'but would you consider marrying me?' The wan, suffering expression Caroline had been wearing for the last hour disappeared completely, and in its place she produced a smile so radiant, it was like the sun coming out.

'Do you really mean it?' she asked. 'Or are you just saying it because it's the "done" thing?'

Richard was tempted to tell her the truth. Then he realized he couldn't, that would be no way to start a life together. The least he could do was to pretend that he cared.

He crossed the room and took Caroline in his arms. And this time she didn't turn him away.

CHAPTER 40

Mauritius

What surprised Emerald about Jeremy was his lack of surprise. She had expected him to be all ears when she told him about her wedding plans. After all, they had come out of the blue and she was getting married to his only son, but all her partner did was look quizzical and offer his congratulations. He didn't seem remotely interested in finding out how Emerald had met Richard or even how this new turn of events came about, and she felt hurt.

It wasn't as if she and Jeremy were casual acquaintances. They went back a very long way. They had been lovers in another life. The memory of that provided her with an explanation for his behaviour, perhaps. It was possible that Jeremy was jealous.

If Emerald had had more time, she might have taken him to one side and explained herself, but Richard was expecting her in London in just over two weeks and her hands were full.

She decided to close down her dressmaking operation first. She knew it wouldn't be easy, but she wanted to get it out of the way so she could concentrate on her export business.

As soon as she got into her showroom in Curepipe she set a chain of events in motion. She prepared a formal letter to all her clients telling them she was going back to Europe and that from next month she would cease trading. She assured everybody she wrote to that all outstanding orders would be honoured.

Then she turned this promise into a reality by issuing a

detailed set of instructions to the women in charge of her workroom. She had decided to cut all the new patterns herself. It would take her a week if she worked all night but it was the only option she had. The clients had started her off in business. Without them she would still be struggling to keep her head above water. The least she could do was to make sure they didn't suffer because she was going abroad.

It all took her longer than she had thought. Every one of her long-standing customers came to see her to find out what was going on. By the end of the week she began to realize that Jeremy's indifference to her news had been a blessing in disguise. She had told her story so many times that in the end it began to bore her.

'It's not as if I'm doing anything that special,' she told her friends. 'I'm just getting married. Hundreds of women do it every day.'

She didn't know it at the time, but those words were to come back and haunt her.

The day Emerald got rid of the lease of her workroom and paid off all her seamstresses she heaved a sigh of relief. It had been hell winding up, but now it was behind her. She set her shoulders and prepared herself for her next task. There was exactly one week left to turn her manufacturing interests over to Jeremy.

Because he was in such a funny mood with her she decided against taking him out to a restaurant. She needed to show him, to reassure him really, that she was fond of him. So she asked him to have lunch with her at the beach cottage. That day she decided not to go into her office and when the second post arrived, she was still in her jeans. If she had been sensible she would have delayed opening her mail until after she was dressed but one of the letters bore a London postmark and her curiosity got the better of her. As soon as she opened the envelope she knew something was wrong, for the first lines of Richard's letter were full of apologies and regrets. She wondered what on earth he was getting at. Then she read the letter right through to the end and she knew exactly what he was trying to tell her.

The wedding was off. At first, the full meaning of the letter didn't get through to Emerald. It was almost as if Richard was talking about something that was nothing to do with her. There had been a problem in London. Something to do with Caroline expecting a baby and it had changed everything.

I hope one day you will find it in your heart to forgive me, he had written, *but I can't deny this child. And I can't deny Caroline. For both their sakes I'm going to take responsibility for the situation.*

Emerald's knees felt strangely wobbly, as if she had been walking for a long time. She sat down abruptly on the cane chair in her hallway and tried to make sense of what Richard had written. He hadn't said he was going to marry Caroline exactly, but he was going to take responsibility for her, whatever that meant. And this 'responsibility' seemed to rule out their wedding plans.

Emerald felt curiously light-headed. Her brain seemed to be made of cotton wool. Try as she might, she simply couldn't make head or tail of what was going on. Just over a week ago, she and Richard were making plans to spend the rest of their lives together. Now Caroline was having a baby and it was all over between them.

She seemed to have lost all sense of time, for when Jeremy arrived for lunch she was still in her jeans drinking a Coke direct from the can.

He was surprised to see her like this and said so.

'I thought we were going to do some serious business today,' he said. 'Have you changed your plans?'

Emerald did her best to come to, but her mind seemed to have gone blank.

'It's so hot today,' she said vaguely. 'I can't seem to concentrate on anything.'

Jeremy looked at Emerald with confusion. This wasn't like her at all. Whenever they had business to discuss she always dressed to the nines. It was part of her ritual. The heat never bothered her normally, it couldn't – she was born and bred here.

'Is something the matter?' he asked her gently. His enquiry seemed to act as a trigger, for quite suddenly Emerald seemed to collapse. One moment she was standing on her terrace looking out over the ocean. The next she had crumpled up into a heap.

Jeremy hurried over to where she was lying and helped her into a chair. Then he stood over her and demanded to know what was going on.

Emerald didn't answer him but pointed at Richard's letter which was lying beside the drinks on her low coffee table.

Jeremy had no idea what to expect, and under normal circumstances he would never have helped himself to Emerald's private correspondence, but she seemed so devastated that he went over and picked it up.

It took him less than two minutes to realize what had happened. His son was being blackmailed by a woman in England. He marvelled at Richard's naïvety. It was clear that Caroline, whoever she was, had her hooks well and truly into him and was using the baby to force him into marriage with her.

Jeremy's heart went out to Emerald. She didn't deserve this, not when she had put herself on the line so completely. Hell, he thought, she even closed down her business so she could be with him.

He walked over and held out his arms. 'You need to cry,' he said. 'And when you've finished, we'll sit down and talk.'

Emerald went to him then, seeking out his strength, and Jeremy didn't fail her. He simply stood there and held her tight while she opened up and let all the pain spill out of her.

When it was over, he led her to the table and poured her out a stiff drink.

'It's not finished with Richard if you don't want it to be,' Jeremy said. 'You could stand up to this other girl and force her to back down. I know for a fact she isn't what he wants.'

Emerald passed a weary hand across her eyes. 'How can you be so certain?'

There was a moment's hesitation, then Jeremy told her all the things his son had confessed to him in the strictest confidence. He went right back to the meeting he had had with Richard in Paris when he had first heard Emerald was in his life.

'From the moment he met you,' he told her, 'he knew there would never be anyone else for him, and when you left him, he never recovered.'

He had Emerald's full attention now. 'You mean you knew about the affair all the time?' she said, quizzically.

Jeremy nodded. 'But I couldn't let on because it would have got in the way of Richard's plan.'

Emerald was in full command of her faculties now and was curious. 'I think it's time you told me about Richard's plan,' she said. 'I need to know what's been going on.'

Jeremy wondered whether it was quite ethical. After all, it was Richard's money that had bought twenty-five per cent of Emerald Designs. Didn't that give him the right to explain it to her himself?

He laughed at his own stupidity. After what his son had done to this girl, he didn't have any rights with her any more. All that mattered now was that Emerald knew what had been going on under her nose.

It took him half an hour to explain the ins and outs of

it, and as he was telling the story he was aware he didn't come out of it very well.

He expected Emerald to protest at the way he had connived with his son, yet she seemed to take the whole thing in her stride.

'So let me get this straight,' she said when he had finished. 'You're not my partner at all. Richard's the one I should be answering to.'

Jeremy nodded, and Emerald sat and thought about it for a while.

Then she said, 'Why on earth did he want to buy into me? I'm not the best investment in the world. Nobody in the fashion business is.'

Jeremy smiled. 'I don't think Richard was thinking of you as a serious investment. All he wanted to do was keep tabs on you and buying a partnership seemed to be the best way at the time.'

'Does Richard think he can buy everything and everyone he sets his sights on?' Emerald asked. She said it with such fury that for a moment Jeremy was shocked.

'It wasn't quite like that,' he told her softly. 'Richard loved you. He would have done anything to find his way back to you.'

'Even use his father as a go-between?'

Jeremy sighed. 'It was a clumsy plan. I know that now. But it worked. You would have been married if things hadn't gone wrong.'

He saw her think about that one too. It was as if she were reviewing the whole of her past. She softened slightly and started to look tearful all over again, then she pulled herself together.

'Richard's out of my life now,' Emerald said. 'I still can't quite get used to it, but it's a fact and I'm going to have to face it.'

He looked at her. 'So you're not going to fight Caroline?'

'What's the point? You never win with women like that.

Whatever I do, Caroline will always out-manoeuvre me and in a way she's welcome. I've never had to fight for a man in my life, and I'm not going to start now.'

She looked vulnerable when she said it, very female, and Jeremy decided his son had been a bloody fool to let her go.

For a moment he thought about his own position. He might not have been a true partner, but to all intents and purposes he had behaved like one and he had enjoyed being in business with her. Now all the cards were on the table, he didn't think that would be going on for much longer.

'I imagine you'll want to buy yourself out of your arrangement with Richard,' he said.

Emerald nodded. 'It wouldn't be right to have any more contact with him the way things are.'

Jeremy started to feel sad. 'I'll miss you,' he said. 'It's been fun getting the company on its feet.'

'More fun than running a sugar plantation?'

He took a sip out of the glass of wine sitting in front of him. 'Much more fun. The other business is purely a matter of routine.'

Emerald allowed herself to smile for the first time that afternoon.

'Then why don't you stay on and help me?' she said. 'I've needed you more than you'll ever know these past few years.'

Jeremy looked doubtful. 'It wouldn't be quite honourable –' he started to say, but Emerald interrupted him.

'I don't expect you to work for nothing,' she told him. 'Those days are over. From now on I want everything between us to be honest and above board.'

Jeremy should have declined. He was a busy man with hundreds of claims on his time. Then he looked at Emerald and saw how animated she was. She had had the worst rejection of her life, but she hadn't let it get to her. Instead, she was busy making plans for her future.

If I turn her down now, he thought, it could just destroy her and I don't want that on my conscience. Not after what Richard's done to her.

He held out his hand towards her. 'You've just hired yourself a director,' he said.

CHAPTER 41

London

Getting married suited Caroline. It gave her a glow which her friends put down to being in love and her enemies decided was greedy anticipation, for she made no secret of the fact that landing Richard was everything she had always wanted. Her work had been fine at the time. It had paid the rent and given her a fair amount of kudos, but a successful career had never been her ultimate ambition.

In a way it had been a means to an end, for it had given Caroline access to the kind of man who could keep her in luxury for the rest of her life. Any number of those men had slipped through her fingers over the years but one had finally stuck. Richard Waites. Now there was no doubt that she had landed him, she began to make the most of the situation.

Her job had to go, of course. As soon as the large solitaire engagement ring was on her finger, she handed in her notice. It had been fun, she told her City editor, but she had more important things to do now.

The first of these was to find somewhere suitable to live. And that didn't mean Richard's apartment. The address was right, she couldn't fault that, but it was a place for a wealthy bachelor, not a man with responsibilities. She made her feelings clear soon after she had finished registering with every estate agent in the Knightsbridge area.

'If we're going to bring up a family,' she told him, 'we're going to need the right kind of atmosphere.' Roughly translated this meant that Caroline had set her heart on a six-bedroomed house with a library, a wine cellar and the kind of dining-room where she could entertain in style.

Richard tried to reason with her, but she wouldn't be budged. How could she be expected to live, she protested, in a place that had so many ghosts? A place she had been turfed out of to make room for Emerald Shah? No marriage could stand the strain of it.

In the end Richard was forced to agree, though after Caroline had taken him round to inspect a few properties, he started to have second thoughts. His fiancée seemed to be hellbent on spending millions. Just furnishing one of these places could empty his bank account and he started to wonder about the future Caroline was planning for them both.

Yet even as he felt the first creeping doubts, he was ashamed of himself. If Emerald had wanted to live in a mansion he wouldn't even have queried it. So how could he deny Caroline, the mother of his child, anything?

Richard's reservations did not go unnoticed. Caroline had taken to watching him like a hawk. She knew exactly how reluctant her bridegroom was, and there were times when she suspected he might try to duck out of the whole thing. Her suspicions were confirmed when one of her gossipy friends told her about Emerald. Richard and she had been seen together in New York quite recently and this one piece of information convinced her. She dropped her plans for a lavish engagement party immediately and concentrated on the main event. She was going to have a big white wedding with all the trimmings. She had set her heart on it, and she brought it forward before Richard could start having second thoughts.

She also pushed her parents to one side. Now she was near to getting what she wanted, she didn't want anything to ruin her chances. She told Richard that they were both too elderly and too frail to concern themselves with something as taxing as a reception for five hundred at the Ritz. Then, without waiting to listen to how he felt about a party of that size, she set about making it happen.

Right at the beginning of the planning stages, Caroline would consult Richard about some of her choices. Should they have vintage champagne all evening, or just at the start? What did he feel about having two dance bands? Did he think it was an inspired idea to fly a chef in specially from Maxims?

To all these queries Richard had one reply.

What on earth made her want to have their wedding reception at the Ritz? He was the Managing Director of the Weiss Group of hotels. Wouldn't it be more appropriate to have the party catered for by his own staff?

When Richard started to question what she was doing, Caroline went off the deep end. The Weiss hotels, she told him, were for the bourgeoisie. If he wanted to save money and go down market, it was his prerogative, but he should think about the effect it would have on their friends and the people they wanted to impress. Everyone was expecting a society wedding and what he was suggesting they do was put on a glorified business party.

In the end Richard gave into Caroline. If she hadn't been pregnant it might have been different, but Caroline got so damned upset when she couldn't get her own way that he began to have severe worries about the baby.

When Shel Johnson stayed at the Connaught Hotel he made a point of reserving a place in the restaurant well before he arrived. It was one of his private nightmares that he would go down to the elegant old-fashioned dining-room with its antique mirrors and fancy screens and the maître d'hôtel would tell him they were booked solid for the next fortnight.

They had a way of looking at you in the Connaught that unsettled him. In Los Angeles he had a reputation. They still put out the red carpet for him in restaurants. In this joint it was a different story.

There were times when he wondered why he put up with their snotty attitude but he didn't wonder very seriously. There was a cachet about staying in the hotel on Carlos Place that more than made up for any slights he had to endure. Tonight, as he dined with the BBC's Head of Drama, he knew that cachet would mean money in the bank.

He glanced around the tiny room he occupied at the top of the building. That was an investment too. Nobody he entertained downstairs had to know he stayed in a broom cupboard. What counted in his business was show, front, image, and for the purposes of this trip, Shel Johnson had more front than Selfridges.

At 7.30 on the dot, the producer made his way down to the lobby. His plan was to buy the drama head a drink in the clubby-looking bar. Then when he was suitably softened up, he would take him through to the over-booked, over-rated restaurant where he would impress the hell out of him.

The evening went exactly as Shel envisaged. The BBC man had the half-starved look that all servants of the corporation seemed to wear. He had the power to commit a million dollars to the producer's budget, but his expense account didn't stretch to dining in anything grander than a bistro.

When Shel told him about supper in the restaurant, the man was overjoyed.

By the time the maître d'hôtel was escorting them across the dark red carpet to the table he had reserved, Shel knew the deal was as good as done.

It was a tedious evening because neither man had much in common with the other. Shel lived in a world of film gossip and his guest occupied an altogether higher plane. After an hour of intellectual conversation about the latest fringe productions, Shel started to feel restless. Necessity made him play the charming host, but he was on overdrive.

As unobtrusively as he could, he signalled the waiter for the bill. If he had to listen to this garbage all night, at least they could go someplace where they had music. Music and girls. Annabel's was just across the square. If they started making tracks now, they'd be there at just the right time.

At the precise moment that Shel was making his way across the lobby of the Connaught, Caroline came spilling through the revolving door that led into the hotel. She and her companions had just come from Covent Garden and they were all in high spirits and looking forward to dinner.

Shel recognized her immediately. He had only been looking at a picture of her in the *Mail* that morning. He searched his mind to remember what it was about. Then he had it. She was going to marry Richard Waites, the guy she and Emerald had been fighting over when she first came to see him.

He had to hand it to this girl: she was as stubborn as all hell. She'd set her mind to destroying Emerald and nothing was going to get in her way.

As she approached he raised his hand in a salute. 'Hi, gorgeous,' he said. 'Still fighting off the opposition?'

For a moment, Caroline didn't appear to recognize Shel. Then everything seemed to click into place, for the redhead stopped dead in her tracks.

'Shel Johnson,' she said, 'what are you doing here?' Her voice seemed to be coming from a long way away and he wondered if she was feeling quite well.

He hurried across to where she stood and as he approached her he noticed there was something different about Caroline. When he had known her, there had been something desperate about the girl, as if she was making an enormous effort to please the whole time. Now she didn't appear to give a damn and he noticed a smugness in her face he hadn't seen before. Getting engaged to Richard Waites clearly suited her.

'I saw the story about you in the paper,' he said. 'Congratulations are in order, I guess.'

Caroline nodded and allowed herself to be kissed on both cheeks, then Richard came over and asked to be introduced.

Shel realized she hadn't expected this to happen, for Caroline looked embarrassed and mumbled something about an old friend she hadn't seen in ages. She seemed to be in an awful hurry to get to the restaurant and Shel started to feel piqued. He was an important Hollywood producer with a room at the fanciest hotel in town. Caroline couldn't get away with brushing him off like a nobody.

He held his hand out to Richard. 'The name's Shel Johnson,' he said. 'I'm a film producer. This lady and I once had important business together.'

Shel realized he had the man's attention, for Richard looked curious. It was almost as if he was telling him something he didn't know.

'I had no idea Caroline was interested in films,' he said pleasantly. 'Tell me about it.'

If Caroline had introduced Shel properly in the first place, he might not have gone on with the conversation, but she hadn't. She'd tried to treat him as if he didn't exist and he wasn't going to let her get away with it.

'The business I had with Caroline was nothing to do with the movie industry,' Shel explained. 'She wanted . . .'

He didn't get to finish the sentence, for Caroline started to tug at Richard's arm. 'Darling,' she said impatiently, 'I'm absolutely starving. We're not going to stand around in the lobby all night, are we?'

Normally Richard would have paid attention to her but there was something about the situation that intrigued him. He had no idea Caroline even knew this man, let alone had dealings with him. He turned to his fiancée.

'Give me two minutes, darling, will you? There are a couple of things I want to clear up.'

He took hold of Shel's arm. 'Weren't you the man who gave evidence against Emerald Shah in the Larry Simpson case?'

The producer looked at him. 'That was me.'

Richard relaxed his grip slightly. He paused and thought for a moment. Then he said, 'What business did you have with Caroline?'

He had no idea why he was pressing this stranger but some sixth sense told him to keep going. There was something important buried here and he needed to get to the bottom of it.

He could see Shel Johnson was getting shifty. He leaned closer to catch what he was saying.

'The business I had with Caroline,' he said softly, 'was to do with Emerald.'

Before he went on, the producer glanced over his shoulder. Caroline was standing near enough to hear what was going on and she looked scared to death.

He started to grin. She hasn't told him, Shel thought. This man she's going to marry doesn't know Caroline talked me into testifying. He wondered whether to sell her down the river completely, then he thought, no, she only needs teaching a small lesson.

He looked Richard in the eye. 'Let's just say that I didn't know Emerald was still tussling with Larry's children, until Caroline came and told me about it. She was very informative about your ex-girlfriend.'

Caroline had joined them now, and she was anxious to bring the encounter to an end.

'You're exaggerating the whole thing,' she said briskly. 'I might have mentioned Emerald in passing, but we had lots of other things to talk about as well.'

'Sure we had,' Shel said. 'I wanted to know if you were free for dinner.'

For a moment none of them said anything. Then Richard turned to the producer.

'Was she free?' he asked.

The old Hollywood dealer started to laugh. 'She certainly was,' he said. 'For dinner and everything else as well.'

Everyone in Richard's party realized there was something up, for their host hardly addressed a word to his fiancée. In a group that size it should not have been noticeable but it was, because of Caroline. She kept trying to attract Richard's attention, almost as if she was trying to find out if he still cared for her. She would say something about the house they had just bought behind Harrods or she would raise the subject of their wedding. Each reference to their future plans was met with a stony silence. Tim Waites, who was hosting the evening, did his best to draw attention away from the two of them. He talked about the opera they had just seen, purposely keeping the conversation general while he tried to work out what could possibly have gone wrong. His nephew was on the verge of getting married to a girl he had known for years. A girl nobody liked, he had to admit that, but nevertheless a girl who was a known quantity.

There was no way at this stage in the game Richard could possibly have found anything wrong with her. Or could he? There was something impatient about him tonight. Something restless Tim hadn't seen before.

The boy's behaving, Tim reflected, as if he wants to be anywhere but this hotel. He thought back to the beginning of the evening. Richard hadn't been in this mood then. He had been vaguely irritated when Caroline complained that Mozart bored her, but he hadn't snapped at her the way he might have done now.

Tim did a quick appraisal of the redhead. She was looking particularly appealing that night, in a long black Jean Muir that emphasized her sleekness. She had gained a few pounds, which knowing her condition didn't surprise him, but she didn't look bloated. She's probably one of those women, he thought, who won't even start to show until the sixth month.

He wondered how children would suit her. The City, with its sudden dramas and changes of direction, seemed the ideal place for someone of Caroline's makeup. Bringing up a family needed more patience.

Tim pulled himself out of his reverie. It's not my problem, he thought. None of it is. If Caroline turns out to be a terrible mother, and they decide to fight like cats and dogs before their wedding day, it's nothing to do with me. I did my duty by this boy years ago. What he does with his life now is outside my responsibility.

Somehow they all got through the evening, though when Richard stood up and said he needed to get home early, the party seemed visibly relieved. His obvious animosity towards Caroline had cast a gloom over them all. With both of them out of the way, the guests stood a chance of seeing the evening out on a happier note.

Neither of them said a word on the way home. The presence of the chauffeur kept Richard silent and Caroline, who suspected the game was up, wasn't going to commit herself to anything she didn't have to.

As soon as they got to the apartment, Caroline headed straight for the bedroom.

'I really have to put my head down,' she said stifling a yawn. 'I'm absolutely finished.'

But Richard wasn't letting her get away with anything.

'You are absolutely finished,' he agreed grimly, 'but I think it's high time we sat and talked about why.'

Caroline made an attempt to look startled, but it didn't come off. Shel had already sown the seeds of her destruction and she was stuck with playing the whole thing out to the end.

Wearily she gathered her long skirts around her and made her way into the main room. There was a fire still burning in the grate, but that night it gave her no comfort. There was only one way now of lifting her mood and she took it. She went straight to the drinks tray and poured herself three measures of Armagnac, which she carried over with her to the sofa.

Richard, she saw, had stationed himself over by the fire and was standing up. She made one last attempt to smooth things over.

'Come and sit over here,' she said patting the cushions beside her. 'At least we can be friends, can't we?'

But Richard was no longer interested. What he wanted to do now was to find out exactly what Caroline had been up to with Shel Johnson. He didn't waste time with small talk but got straight to the point.

'It was you, wasn't it, who pushed Shel into giving evidence against Emerald?'

Caroline started to shake her head, but Richard wasn't convinced.

'Look,' he said. 'You went to see Shel in Los Angeles. You can't deny it because he told me it happened. He also told me, in front of you, that you were there to talk about Emerald and the children.'

Caroline took a big swig of her drink and wondered what to say next. If she could have dreamed up a story, she would have done so, but she had been racking her brains all evening and nothing seemed to come. Caroline, who had been telling tales all her life both for pleasure and for profit, had finally run dry. All she had left now was the truth.

'I found out on the grapevine,' she said in a small, timorous voice, 'that Shel and your precious Emerald had had an affair. To be honest, I was shocked. Here was this woman demanding the lion's share in Larry Simpson's fortune and all the time she had been cheating on him with his best friend.'

Richard looked at her over the rim of his brandy glass. 'So you decided to set the record straight?'

Caroline's confidence started to come back. Maybe she could talk her way out of this situation after all.

'Of course I wanted to set things straight,' she said. 'What Emerald was doing was dishonest. I'd met Larry's children a few years before then and I thought they deserved better.'

She paused, checking to see if any of this was registering with Richard, but his face was without expression.

She ploughed on. 'Anyway, I went and sounded out Shel and he felt the same way as I did. So we concocted a plan.'

There was the briefest silence. Then Richard said, sighing, 'So I was right the first time. You did talk Shel into giving evidence but it wasn't just the children deserving the money that made you do it. There was a bit of jealousy too, wasn't there? You couldn't bear the fact that Emerald had everything you wanted, including me. You had to knock it out of her hands.'

Something happened to Caroline's face as Richard spoke. Some hardness he hadn't seen before came to the surface, making her look curiously middle-aged.

If I'd married her, he thought, that's what I would have woken up with every morning. A tough bitch with ice in her veins. When she spoke again, he realized he was right.

'You're such a gallant knight,' Caroline said sarcastically, 'with such high ideals. And such limited vision.' She picked her glass up and tipped the rest of the brandy down her throat. 'You probably don't realize this, but I've done you a bigger favour than you know. The woman's a slut. A cheating slut. All I did was put you and the rest of the world in touch with the fact.'

Richard watched her get up and walk unsteadily towards the drinks cabinet. She was about to refill her glass for the fourth time that evening, when he went over and stopped her.

'Don't you think you've had enough to drink tonight?' he said quietly.

Caroline turned on him. 'What are you worried about?' she asked. 'Hearing the truth about your Indian tart? I wouldn't think anything I could say about her would come as a surprise.'

Richard hit her then, lightly and expertly across the face, and for a moment it quietened her.

'Your remarks about Emerald don't worry me,' he said. 'I stopped listening to your lies about her a long time ago. My concern is for the baby. I don't think all that brandy is a good idea.'

Caroline didn't reply immediately but splashed more alcohol into her glass and swallowed as much of it as she could.

'I wouldn't lose any sleep over my pregnancy,' she said. 'It doesn't exist. I made the whole thing up.'

She had said it to hurt him and she had succeeded.

Richard looked as if his whole world had fallen apart at the seams.

'But you convinced me about the baby,' he protested. 'You even look pregnant.'

She was tempted to laugh. Men were so easy to dupe.

'What do you know about pregnant women?' she asked. 'You've never even been married. Look,' she went on, 'all I did over the past few weeks was put on a little weight. Your imagination did the rest.'

A feeling of despair washed over Richard. From the first moment he met her, all Caroline had ever done was lie to him and he had believed everything like some amateur sucker.

'You must have thought I was a real idiot,' he faltered.

There was something about the way he said it that made Caroline realize she had gone too far. The baby she had invented had been her one big advantage. Her ace. They were even getting married to give it a name. Now she realized her chances of a white wedding were disappearing.

'Richard,' she said softly, 'just because I'm not pregnant now, doesn't mean I can't be. We could conceive a child tonight if you wanted it.'

He started to back away from her. 'You're not staying here tonight,' he told her.

But the drink had made Caroline bold, and she wasn't taking no for an answer. With a deftness born of practice, she reached behind her and unzipped her dress. She wasn't wearing a bra that night and Richard could see her nipples were already hard with desire.

The sight left him curiously unmoved. He had seen tarts in high-class brothels behave like this. You could say anything you liked to them and they still stripped for action.

It crossed Richard's mind to take advantage of the situation. Caroline was leaning back on the sofa and spreading her legs now, but he forced himself to look away.

'Get dressed,' he said roughly. 'That tired old routine isn't going to work this time.'

He heard her laugh. 'Of course it's going to work,' Caroline said. 'If it wasn't, you might allow yourself to look at me. I'm not forcing you to do anything you don't want.'

Richard was angry now, angry with himself for his weakness, angry with Caroline for exploiting it. It was this emotion that saved him, for when he allowed himself another glance at her, all he could feel was disgust.

He walked over to the other side of the room and put his glass down, then he took off his jacket and threw it across to her.

'Cover yourself,' he said coldly. 'You're starting to look ridiculous.'

The remark seemed to sober her up, for she did as she was told. Then she said, 'What are we going to do about the wedding? Everything's planned for the day after tomorrow.'

Richard shrugged. 'Then it will have to be unplanned. There's no way I'm going through with it now.'

For the first time that evening, she realized she had lost. There was no story she could tell, no trick she could pull to reverse the situation. She cursed inwardly. One drink, she thought, just one too many brandies and I throw away everything I've worked for.

She felt her eyes fill with tears. It's not fair, she thought. It wasn't meant to happen like this.

'What will people say?' she asked weakly. 'They were expecting a big wedding.'

It was a silly argument, but it was all Caroline had left and when Richard didn't answer her, she thought she had got through to him. Then he told her what he was planning and she realized she had been deluding herself.

'There will be a big wedding,' he told her, 'but it won't happen in two days' time, and it probably won't happen here.

'The girl I'm going to marry lives in Mauritius and she'll have her own ideas about where she wants to tie the knot.'

CHAPTER 42

Mauritius

Richard had been flying first class all his adult life. He was used to being woken up with hot towels and orange juice. This morning he didn't need the attention. He didn't need anything apart from being left alone, for he was going home.

Through the window he could see the dark red ball of the sun begin its climb over the Indian Ocean. By the time they were on the ground it would be high in the sky, bleaching the landscape with its tropical brightness.

He tried to visualize the terrain surrounding the airport and he wondered whether the sight of Mauritian soil would overwhelm him with nostalgia. He laughed at his naïvety. I'm putting down on an island in the sun, he thought. There's no cause to get things out of proportion.

In the seat in front of him a well-to-do matron and her paunchy husband were busy adjusting an expensive camcorder.

Over the past few years Mauritius had become a playground for the rich and Richard wondered whether the whole island had been adapted to please the tourists. He had a vision of the plantation where he had grown up suddenly transformed into Disneyworld. He shuddered. Everything changes, he thought. Even the things you once took for granted aren't as they appear.

He thought about Caroline. She was the biggest illusion of them all. Pretending she loved him, that she was having his child, when all the time she was just trying to trap him.

The thought depressed Richard, casting a shadow over

his homecoming. He was so distracted he almost missed the announcement on the Tannoy. They were coming in to land. In ten minutes they would finally touch down at Plaisance.

As if somebody had waved a wand, Caroline disappeared from his mind. As Richard saw the runway come up to meet him, she finally ceased to exist. She belonged neither to his past nor his present now.

When he rose to leave the plane, he felt he was walking taller than he had been in a long time.

His father had suggested meeting him at the airport, but Richard had declined the offer. He needed to be alone at this moment and when he got through customs and out on to the concourse he was glad of his decision, for all his fears had been unfounded. There was no Disneyworld. Mauritius was exactly as he remembered it.

I've been away too long, he thought. How could I have ever doubted it would be like this?

Richard was expecting an air-conditioned car to pick him up, but it was late. In a way, he was grateful for the delay, for it allowed him to take the island into himself, to absorb all the bustle and the energy erupting around him, to smell the smells and tune into the sounds, to become part of it all over again.

As he stood there in the heat and humidity, a change came over him. Suddenly he was no longer Richard, the international hotel chief. Instead he was Ravi, a little half-caste boy in a pair of battered jeans with only his dreams to protect him against an uncaring world. But what dreams they were, he thought. What sterling ambitions.

I was going to take the West by storm and make my fortune, he thought. And while I was doing that, I was going to turn into an English gentleman.

He smiled at the memory of himself and the fact that he had achieved all the things he had set out to do. Yet there was a sadness in him too. A melancholy that refused to leave him. He realized too late that he had discarded too much of himself.

Where is the Indian in me now, he wondered. What happened to my roots? Then Richard realized that nothing had happened to his roots. They were still there buried inside him. Without them he could never have got as far as he had. Without my birthright, he thought, I would have been my father's son. An elegant failure.

He looked around him at the chattering natives, trading, arguing, hustling, and a sense of his own identity started to grow. He was like none of the men on the concourse, yet he was like all of them, for he carried their genes and in the end he carried their destiny.

All at once he was glad he had come here. He hadn't just returned to the island. He had returned to himself.

He wondered if Emerald had felt the same sense of belonging when she finally returned. He couldn't wait to find out. Then he thought about a conversation he had had with his father a month ago, and realized he might not get the chance.

Jeremy had called him when Emerald received his letter. Apparently he had been with her at the time and, not surprisingly, she had taken it badly.

He couldn't blame her. They had both been stringing each other along for too many years for it to end like that. Yet the way she turned her back on him had hurt. She didn't reply to his letter but communicated with him through her lawyers and through Jeremy. Her message was simple. She wanted to buy back his shareholding in her company.

'She wants nothing to do with you,' Richard's father had told him. 'She doesn't even want to remember she once knew you.'

Richard took the message with a pinch of salt. Emerald was angry with him. It was only natural. Once she had calmed down, she might see matters in a better light.

If things had been different he might have told her he was coming to the island but in her present mood it was better to surprise her.

'I need to get her off guard,' he told his father. 'That way I'll have a better chance of explaining myself.'

Jeremy wasn't all that encouraging. 'Emerald isn't a little girl,' he said. 'She's not going to respond to tricks like that. Anyway I don't think she's all that interested in what went wrong with Caroline. You can talk about it all you like but the fact remains that you let her down, and she doesn't trust you any more.'

Richard fought down a feeling of quiet despair. They were both against him. Emerald and his father. He wondered what it would take to earn their forgiveness.

The hire car finally arrived twenty minutes later. It didn't bother him. He was already adjusting to the chaos of Mauritius and he greeted the driver with a tolerant smile.

'I'm booked in at the Palm,' he told him. 'How long will it take us to get there?'

The man went into a long description of the new highway traversing the island. And at the end of it, Richard was still no closer to knowing what time he would be standing under a cool shower, but it didn't matter. He wasn't on a business trip. There was no urgent meeting waiting for him when he arrived. All he had to do was unpack, think about having lunch and wait for his father to arrive at drinks time.

He got in the car and gave himself up to the scenery. Driving through the island was a sentimental journey, for all the signposts of his childhood were there. The strange twisted volcanic mountains still loomed out of nowhere. The flame trees in full blossom still straggled by the road and he wondered if everything else was the same.

They were driving along the stretch of road that led to the capital, Port Louis. On a whim, Richard instructed the driver to take him through the town.

The detour would add twenty minutes to the journey, but he was curious to see the place again. He wasn't disappointed. There was no duplicating Port Louis. The town still had the dilapidated, corrupt feeling he remembered from the sixties.

When they reached the main square with the statues of old colonial governors, Richard told the driver to take the scenic route. He wasn't interested in looking at concrete office blocks. What he wanted to see were the tiny winding streets at the back of the town. Nothing had changed. The Chinese emporia seemed to be selling the same bales of silk as they always had. The kiosks he remembered on every street corner were doing a brisk trade in chapatti and Pepsi Cola and the two-storey wooden buildings that bulged over the street still looked as if they might collapse in a heap of rubble any minute.

I'm home, Richard thought. I'm back where I started. Nothing is different, except for me.

Although he felt nostalgia at being there, he knew he could never stay. He had grown out of this place the moment he had left it. He would always want to visit it, he wouldn't neglect that obligation to his past, but he couldn't settle here. In his heart he knew Emerald couldn't either, for they had both changed since their early days. Only my father belongs here, Richard thought wryly. And he was born in the English counties.

He arrived at his hotel an hour before lunch, expecting a bustle of holidaymakers in the foyer. They'd be wanting drinks before they settled down to the cold buffet, he imagined. But he was wrong. The entrance to the Palm was almost deserted as he walked through to reception. And the few people he saw didn't look like tourists at all. The women were all in silk dresses and their escorts were sporting lightweight tropical suits.

He was relieved at the formality of the place. He had worked too hard all his life to feel at ease in resorts. At least here nobody expected him to put on a flowered shirt and start drinking rum punches.

Jeremy had booked Richard into a two-storey villa in the grounds of the hotel. As soon as he made his way through the lush tropical garden that surrounded these rooms, he realized the standard of luxury here was comparable with Puerta Vallarta or Cap d'Antibes. He sent a silent vote of thanks to his father for considering his needs. At the Palm he could live as he always lived – privately and with the elegance that comes of being used to spending a lot of money.

He spent most of the day walking along the shore. He had long forgotten the stillness of the Indian Ocean and it brought him a tranquillity he hadn't known for years. In a way he felt suspended in time somewhere between his past and his future. Until he saw Emerald and settled their lives once and for all, he could see no way forward. He could make no plans. So he didn't try.

When his father eventually found him, Richard was sitting on his private verandah staring into the dark red sunset.

The sun was already starting to make him look swarthy and Jeremy was surprised at the change in him. He had expected an immaculate international businessman, not a beachcomber in faded jeans. He wondered what Richard was up to.

'I take it you're in Mauritius to have a meeting with Emerald over the shareholding?' he said cautiously.

The younger man nodded. Her lawyer had made a formal approach to buy him out just over three weeks ago but nothing could go ahead until the two of them agreed terms.

If it had been anyone else's business but Emerald's, the whole transaction would have been completed by now, but it wasn't and Richard was still dragging his feet.

He poured out two glasses of chilled wine from the bottle in front of him then turned to his father.

'I thought I might try and get hold of Emerald tomorrow,' he said. 'Why don't you fill me in on her movements?'

Jeremy looked uncertain. 'What exactly did you have in mind?'

'I haven't really decided,' Richard admitted. 'Maybe I'll just turn up wherever she is and take it from there.'

Jeremy started to get impatient. First he wasn't allowed to let Emerald know Richard was coming to Mauritius. Now he was planning to make some kind of dramatic entrance. The whole thing was most unbusinesslike.

He took a sip of his wine. 'Wouldn't it be easier if you let me organize this get-together. Emerald's not going to refuse to see you, you know. She's far too anxious to get her shares back for that.'

Richard considered the possibility. Knowing his father, the meeting would be in a hotel suite and the three of them would sit around a polished table and try to pretend that all they cared about was the transaction in front of them. Emerald would be hiding behind her makeup, and Richard and his father would be doing their level best to act like strangers.

All of a sudden he couldn't bear the idea. If getting back her shares was that important to Emerald then she could have them. Gratis. Richard had only bought them as a way of finding her again and now he'd finally blown it there seemed no point in hanging on to them.

He regarded his father. 'I don't see any point in going through this agony any longer,' he said. 'I've decided to let Emerald have her twenty-five per cent back free of charge. Tell her it's a goodbye present from me. She'll understand.'

Jeremy looked startled. 'You mean you're not going to try and contact her?'

The younger man fought down bitterness. 'What's the point? You told me yourself Emerald wasn't interested in hearing me plead my case. All she wants from me now is her business back and that's exactly what she's got.'

He rose from his chair and walked into his room to change for dinner.

'I'll be on the Air Mauritius flight out of here tomorrow morning,' he said. 'If I were you, I wouldn't even bother to tell Emerald I've been here.'

In the tropics there are sometimes nights when every star in the sky is clearly visible. In this kind of brightness the fishermen come out, trailing their nets in the shallows by the beach, hunting for unwary stragglers.

When he was tiny, Richard's mother would take him to see the fishermen. Now, as he walked by the shore, he thought of her.

He wondered whether Jeremy would have acknowledged her existence if she'd lived, or whether he would have gone on sending money and turning a blind eye. He had asked his father that question over dinner but Jeremy had side-stepped it.

What he didn't avoid talking about was Neeta herself, and Richard was surprised at how fond the old planter was of his memories.

He had no idea how the conversation got on to Emerald. He had done his best to avoid any mention of her name all evening but Jeremy seemed determined to force the issue. He wasn't impressed with the way his son had thrown away his shareholding and he was very vocal about it.

'Emerald's going to be big over the next few years,' he had said. 'You've probably kissed goodbye to a fortune.'

Richard did his best to suppress a smile. 'I already have several fortunes of my own,' he assured his father. 'I'm not going to miss anything Emerald could have earned me.'

It didn't stop the old man from rambling on about her success. As he listened, Richard realized just how tenacious she had been. It hadn't been easy for her in the beginning, yet she hadn't let it discourage her. She'd gone on fighting until she had her company running the way she wanted it. And he felt a surge of admiration for her.

In her own way, Emerald had exactly the same get-up-and-go that Richard had in the early days. Just for a second he recalled the natives he had seen at the airport that day. They were all of them the same, he realized. Emerald, the natives, even himself. They were traders, people struggling to make a future for themselves against appalling odds.

He looked at his father, sentimental now. All his life he had wanted to emulate this man and only today had he realized he had been wrong. He loved Jeremy and he owed him for everything he had done but he didn't want to be him any more. All he wanted now was to be himself. The man he had discovered when he came back home to the island.

The two men parted around eleven and when Richard finally got back to his room, he decided it was too early to go to bed, so he changed back into his jeans and went down to the beach.

The shoreline was usually alive at this time of night. But the beach at the Palm was deserted. Richard realized his money had somehow separated him from the mainstream of life, for the exclusive hotel that protected his privacy also prevented the rest of humanity from walking past his door.

He stood and looked out over the smooth dark sea for a long time. After a while he realized he was no longer alone. Someone else, some other presence, was standing just behind him, beyond his range of vision. He had no idea how he knew she was there, or even why he knew, but he recognized her even before he turned and saw her face.

'Emerald,' he said softly. 'So you came after all.'

He saw she wasn't wearing any makeup that night and her hair was loosely bound in a braid behind her back.

'Of course I came,' she said gently. 'What did you think I would do?'

She sounded so sure of herself that Richard realized she had known he was there all along.

'Who told you I was at the Palm?' he asked.

Emerald hesitated for a moment, as if debating whether to level with him. Then she said, 'Your father told me two weeks ago, when he made the booking. I know he shouldn't have done, but he couldn't help himself. He was so anxious to get us together again.'

There was something unreal about her unexpected appearance on the beach and now there was this new revelation about his father. Richard wondered what on earth was going on.

'He never gave me any idea he wanted us to be together,' he said, shaking his head. 'In fact, he made it more than clear I didn't stand a chance with you.'

Emerald laughed at him then. A low husky sound as familiar as her green eyes.

'Your father,' she said, 'has a certain respect for my honour. He thought I should give you a hard time before taking you back. So he made out that all I wanted was my shareholding back and nothing else. It was only when you took him at his word, that he realized he'd gone too far.'

She paused, remembering the way Jeremy had got her out of bed that night, leaning on her doorbell and not taking no for an answer until in the end she had been forced to put on a dressing-gown and find out what the hell was going on.

'I don't think you have any idea how worried he was that you were going to flounce off the island and never come back.'

The reality of what nearly happened suddenly came home to Richard.

'But I nearly did,' he said. 'I'm booked to fly out on the first plane tomorrow.'

Emerald looked at him. 'I know,' she said. 'Your father told me all about it half an hour ago. I wouldn't have let you get very far. Once I knew you'd called things off with Caroline, you didn't stand a chance.'

She looked very serious as she said it and Richard realized he had been a fool to doubt her. This woman loved him, not for his money or what he had achieved in the world, but because she felt she belonged to him.

He remembered that twice in his life now he had nearly lost her and it was at that moment he decided she wouldn't get away again.

'Would it mess up all your plans if I made you my wife in the next week or so?' he asked.

Emerald didn't say anything. Instead, she came closer to him and there was no mistaking the message in her eyes. Very gently, as if she was a young girl he had just met, Richard started to kiss her. And she responded with the tenderness she had always shown.

Living Doll
Trudi Pacter

A fiery, tantalizing novel from the golden pen of the Queen of Glitz.

Vanessa Grenville is beautiful, wealthy and slightly hopeless; Liz Enfield is sexy, working-class and ambitious, with her eyes fixed firmly on the top. Modelling brings the pair together and they seem inseparable in the heady days of the '60s when friendships blossomed on photographic shoots and wild parties filled the nights. Then Vanessa leaves London for New York and falls in love, while Liz marries David Dearing, heir apparent to a newspaper empire.

Years later their fates touch when Vanessa's daughter, Freddie, comes to stay with Liz in England. Liz is now all '80s woman: face-lifted, power-dressed and immensely energetic. And she's not sure whether her life has room for Freddie – a Freddie whose appealing insecurity is dangerously attractive to David . . .

ISBN 0 586 21187 X

☐	PREY Ken Goddard	0-586-21861-0	£4.99
☐	BLACK EAGLES Larry Collins	0-00-647643-0	£4.99
☐	FAR CRY Michael Stewart	0-00-647265-6	£4.99
☐	ALL BEING WELL Rosamond Stern	0-00-654485-1	£4.99
☐	LABELS Harold Carlton	0-00-647316-4	£4.99
☐	NEW DAWN Elizabeth James	0-586-21767-3	£4.99

All these books are available from your local bookseller or can be ordered direct from the publishers.
To order direct just tick the titles you want and fill in the form below:

Name: _____

Address: _____

_____

Postcode: _____

Send to: HarperCollins Mail Order, Dept 8, HarperCollins *Publishers*, Westerhill Road, Bishopbriggs, Glasgow G64 2QT.
Please enclose a cheque or postal order or your authority to debit your Visa/Access account –

Credit card no: _____

Expiry date: _____

Signature: _____

– to the value of the cover price plus:
UK & BFPO: Add £1.00 for the first and 25p for each additional book ordered.

Overseas orders including Eire, please add £2.95 service charge.

Books will be sent by surface mail but quotes for airmail despatches will be given on request.

24 HOUR TELEPHONE ORDERING SERVICE FOR ACCESS/VISA CARDHOLDERS –
TEL: GLASGOW 041-772 2281 or LONDON 081-307 4052